What the Bride Wore

JADE LEE

sourcebooks
casablanca

Published by Sourcebooks Casablanca, an imprint of
Sourcebooks, Inc.

P.O. Box 4410, Naperville, Illinois 60567-4410
(630) 961-3900
Fax: (630) 961-2168
www.sourcebooks.com

Printed and bound in the United States of America
10 9 8 7 6 5 4 3 2

Thank you to Deb, Dom, Susie,
and everyone at Sourcebooks.
I feel like I've been welcomed home.

One

FIRE, ALCOHOL, AND YOU. COULD YOU DO ANYTHING more stupid?

Grant Benton, future Lord Crowle, glared at the dog. It really hadn't been Dandy, the very ugly collie, who'd spoken. No, the irritating voice of his madness merely pretended to be speaking via the family dog. It didn't matter. Grant did as he always did: he ignored the voice and the idea that he was insane.

"Who goes first?" asked Harry, the future Earl of Boudon. "Coin toss?"

Grant nodded as the young man pulled a guinea out of the pile of coins on a nearby rock. It was the stakes of the bet, and Grant could feel his hands itch at the idea that soon this small mound would be his. Unlike these toffs, he needed the money. Meanwhile, the boy expertly flipped the coin into the air. Grant called… and won. Then he gestured graciously at the young Harry. "I shall allow you the first attempt," he said softly.

Yes, do let's burn the guests to a cinder. I'm sure your sister will be very pleased.

It was for his sister that he was doing this mad escapade. She'd just gotten married this morning, to a man more than twice her age. She did it for the money. Thanks to their idiotic father and grandfather, the earldom was nearly broke. Gambles like this were the only way Grant could pay for the festivities.

The bet was simple: who could blow the longest and greatest plume of fire. The prize was enough money to pay for half his sister's wedding, which had just occurred some ten hours before. The judges were all young bucks—friends of Harry—who had added their coins to the pot. And as the mound of guineas grew, Grant felt his luck settle thick and hard about his shoulders.

That's gas. You have a rather noxious belch.

Harry stepped into the cleared area beside the Crowle family barn. It was a big building next to an open pasture. The main purpose in coming here was for safety. He had a couple buckets of water handy and would make sure there would be no lasting damage to the rather handsome Harry.

You can't control fire.

Calculated risk then. Plus, destiny and luck.

Farts and bad breath.

Grant shot a glare at the confused dog, who whimpered in anxiety. "It's perfectly safe," he said, patting Dandy's head. Then he took a discreet sip of brandy from his flask. He wasn't quite as drunk as he pretended, but he was certainly more topped than ever before when doing a fire-breathing stunt. But bloody hell, he kept seeing his sister's face when she said, "I do." She was terrified of her future, and damn it, it shouldn't have happened.

He swallowed another hefty slug, feeling the brandy burn like fire in his belly. Damned father. Irresponsible ass. And where was the idiot on this day when his only daughter sold herself for money? Gone with the Earl of Willington on some fool errand. Gambling, most likely. Especially since his father had promised him quite clearly that he'd get all the money sorted right and tight.

Sure he will. And a fairy is about to drop a fistful of magic beans in his pocket too.

Grant snorted, for once in agreement with his madness. But then he sobered. With his father off doing whatever ridiculous thing, Grant was the one left to find a way to pay for the festivities.

"Come on now," cried Grant, egging on the suddenly nervous Harry. Good on him, Grant thought. The boy had a brain. "Tell you what," he offered. "You don't need to do it at all, you know. Just forfeit the purse to me, and you won't need to set fire to your handsome mug."

Nice try, but your luck doesn't run that way. Thought you'd learned that by now.

Grant didn't respond, even in the privacy of his own thoughts, because he could see the future earl was considering the possibility. Harry was hesitating despite the derisive sneers of his friends. Meanwhile, Grant waved negligently with his fake bottle of brandy. In truth, it held a tiny bit of brandy mixed with a fat load of lantern oil.

"I'll still do it," he offered. "And you can judge if the show is good enough for the purse." That was the safest bet all around. He knew what he was doing.

He'd spent more than a month training with a gypsy to learn the trick.

Here's the thing: if you pick stupid young men to be your marks, you can't really expect them to be smart, can you?

Just as his madness predicted, Harry gave in to the pressure from his friends. They egged the boy on, and in the way of all privileged bucks—especially the drunk ones—Harry thought he could do something just because he was talented and rich.

"I'll do it!" Harry said as he puffed up his chest. "Seen it at a fair just last week. Spent a time talking to the gypsy about it."

Of course he had. That was the exact same gypsy who had taught Grant. And the man who had suggested Harry as the mark.

"Then do it!" bellowed his friends.

The dog—the real dog—released a long-suffering sigh. Rather disconcerting that. Meanwhile, one of Harry's friends lit a torch, but Grant nabbed it. Last thing he needed was two burnt, rich lordlings. He marked the direction of the breeze and made sure to stand well upwind from the soon-to-be-without-eyebrows Harry.

"Ready?" Grant asked.

Harry nodded, his eyes huge as he filled his mouth with brandy. Then while Grant held the torch out, Harry leaned forward and tried to mist out his mouthful of brandy.

It didn't work. Or rather, it worked very badly. The mouthful of brandy came out more as a huge watery glob. The splat hit the torch then *boom!* Fireball! The heat flattened Grant's face, pressing on it like a hot blanket, but he had been prepared. He'd wet his face and slicked back his hair. Harry hadn't done either. And as the man stumbled forward, trying to extend his short glob of brandy, the fire had crackled into his hair. The boy reared back, but too late.

Then Grant was there, a drenched towel in his free hand. With a flick of his wrist, it wrapped halfway around Harry's face. Another roll of his elbow and wrist, and the man's entire face was turbaned.

"Gahck!" Harry exclaimed, his hands pressing drunkenly about his head.

"Hold still. Make sure everything's out."

Harry quieted, while Grant spared a glance to his friends. Every young buck was standing there with eyes wide in horror.

"It's cold," came Harry's muffled voice.

Grant judged it time for the unveiling. "Stand still. Let me get this off you." And so he did, taking his time for the maximum effect. After all, the towel had been sopping wet, straight from the bucket. Certainly it had doused the fire, but it had also shed water onto Harry's coat, waistcoat, and cravat—all of which were now drooping and wet. Then he unveiled Harry's poor face.

Red and ragged. His cheeks, nose, and mouth were red from the heat, and his hair had been burned to a jagged mess. But what was more ridiculous were his eyebrows: all gone except for two dark smudges on the farthest sides of his face. He looked like a lumpy potato with two tufts of greenery pushing out beside his eyes. He blinked as he emerged, looking to his friends for reassurance in the way of all young bucks.

And his friends collapsed in laughter.

"Are you all idiots and fools?" A loud voice interrupted. His brother. Bloody hell.

Exactly what I was saying. You, farts, and your brother. All explosive.

Grant spun around to face Will, but he still held the wet towel in one hand and the torch in the other. A bit hard to appear innocent in that position. Still, he tried.

"Will! What are you doing here?"

"Are you trying to burn yourselves alive?"

Grant grimaced. His brother was four years younger than Grant's twenty-six years, but ten times more of a killjoy. Once the boy had worshipped him, but time and bad parenting had changed that. Three years ago, Will had been forced to return home from school because of a lack of money for tuition.

Grant, who had been older, also left his education, but for London where their father introduced him to gambling, wenching, and all sorts of fun ways to lose money. Will, on the other hand, had returned home to become what he was: the best damn steward in England. The man actually loved the land he tended and showed all the signs of becoming as sour a Yorkshire man as it was possible to be.

"Why would you do this?" Will demanded, grabbing the torch and tossing it into the waiting bucket of water. "Diane is trying to impress her new husband's family, not burn them alive. What if you set fire to the hay? The woods are not that far away! Or the house! Try to behave like a decent gentleman for one bloody day!"

Tick... tick... tick... It was his madness's way of

indicating that Grant was moments away from doing something foolish. Sadly, his madness was correct.

Grant felt his hackles rise. He never took well to being scolded in the first place, but to have this dressing down in front of Harry and his friends was beyond ridiculous. Especially since there had been no risk, and Grant knew exactly what he was doing. He was paying for their sister's wedding!

"Will, it's perfectly safe—"

"The hell it is! Now get out of here—all of you. And go find father. He's been missing for hours, and I don't like it."

Grant struggled to hold on to his temper. With him and Father in London most of the time, Will had gotten used to giving orders. He'd forgotten that he was the *second* son, and not the bloody heir.

"I will do as I please," he said softly, "on the lands that *I* will inherit."

His madness got louder. *Tick! Tick! Tick!*

"As a drunken fool trying to burn everything to the ground? By all means then, kill us all."

Grant clenched his hands tight. He would not punch his brother. The God's truth was that both of them were half drunk and spoiling for a fight. It had killed them to watch Diane sacrifice herself in marriage. But neither of them had the wherewithal to offer her another option. They couldn't frank a Season for her. They couldn't even tell her to go find a man she loved because the only man she'd fancied had been the third son of a nearby squire. A sweet enough boy to be sure, but nowhere near her station, even as an impoverished daughter of an earl.

So Grant and Will had watched in twisting agony as she had said, "I do," and now, they were both dealing with their failures in the only way they knew how. Will became pompous and angry before stomping off to brood in his beloved woods. Grant was drinking and gambling. But at least he did it with a good purpose in mind: that nice pile of coins that Harry was inching toward.

"Hold on there!" Grant cried as Harry started to pick up his purse. "We're not done with the bet yet!"

It was Will who stomped forward. "You bloody well are!"

They couldn't be. Because if Grant didn't breathe fire—for whatever reason—then Harry would be declared the winner. Grant would lose the winnings plus his stake in the pot, something he could *not* afford to lose. He had to win this bet! But first he had to get rid of his interfering, sour pot of a brother.

"Go on, Will. Go glare at the creek like you always do. I'll stay here and see to things."

"See to things?" his brother snorted. "By being a drunken ass?"

I'm pretending! Grant wanted to scream. Well, he was mostly pretending. But that didn't matter. "I am entertaining our guests," he ground out. Then, before his brother could say anything else, Grant held up his hand. "I swear upon my honor that I will not blow fire out here."

That produced a hoot of delight as Harry gleefully held aloft the pot of coins. "I win! I win!"

"Go Will," Grant practically hissed at his brother. "Just go."

Will hovered for a moment, clearly not trusting his older brother. But in the end, he grunted and stomped away. Grant watched him retreat for a bit, knowing with a silent curse that the man would hover. He would be out of sight, but he'd keep a wary eye out just in case Grant went back on his word. Well, the devil with that! He grabbed Harry's wrist, stopping the man from dividing coins with his friends. "We are not done yet," he said in a low voice.

Harry frowned. "But you promised. Swore on your honor. You can't go back on that."

Around him, all his friends nodded dumbly in agreement.

Grant all but rolled his eyes. "I swore I wouldn't breathe fire *out here*. Didn't say anything about somewhere else." He looked hastily around, trying to think of the safest place. It had to be an open area away from people, but still out of sight of his brother in the woods. "The barn," he quickly said. "I can do it inside the barn."

"*Inside* the barn?" echoed Harry. "Isn't that rather dangerous?"

It would be if he hadn't been trained. If he hadn't practiced until his face and mouth were raw and blistered. But the threshing was done. There was enough open space, not much straw on the floor, and he would be careful where he blew. In some ways, it would be safer inside because there was no wind.

"I can do it," he said. "Follow me in there, or forfeit the coins if you're too afraid."

"Ha!" the boy chortled. "You won't do any better than I did. I had a good pop there, didn't I?"

His friends all agreed that indeed, Harry blew a rather good ball of flame. Grant actually smiled. They hadn't seen anything yet.

"Then let's get inside." He made an elaborate gesture toward the front of the barn. If Will were watching, he'd see them amble toward the house. Then they'd duck at the last moment to the front of the barn and slip inside.

It went exactly as planned. They slipped inside the dairy parlor where six cows remained. There had once been twenty here, but most had been sold to pay their father's debts. The last one had gone for the wedding, but this bet would go a long way to buying it back. There were horses here too. Their guests' animals, stored temporarily—about a dozen, stalled quietly without even a whinny to bother the cows.

Meanwhile, they climbed to the threshing floor. As expected, there was barely an inch of straw on the floor. Most of the hay was in the loft above. Grant lit a lantern. Fortunately, he knew where candles were kept. It wasn't as safe as the torch, but it would serve well enough. He had practiced with both.

The boys arranged themselves with a variety of jeers, cheers, and drunken giggles. No one had come bellowing after them to ruin the fun, so they were getting a little bolder in their ribald comments. The only one who seemed worried was Dandy, as the dog dropped onto his haunches and stared mournfully at Grant.

"It'll be all right, old boy," Grant said. So long as he kept his hands steady and his wits about him. He debated taking another swig from his flask—if only to

face when Will found out he'd burn
. It was manageable if it was just t
couldn't lose the cattle. They couldn
led inside, coughing and gasping as
e cows. But the horses were nearest. H
sest stall and slapped the thing to get
as dumb as a cow, he decided, becaus
ed, but then ran.
oing, one stall after another. Then h
ws. He didn't so much find them as fal
. Thankfully, the dog had started to d
rking and biting to get the stupid thing
h Dandy's help, Grant cursed and kicked
ntil every one of the dumb creatures ran
the flames.
six? Had he gotten them all? What about
Were there more? Grant couldn't tell.
breathe, and he sure as hell couldn't see.
t like it was crackling, and he stumbled
erything was ablaze. Where was the door?
straw in the hayloft, all the wood, every-
blaze and falling down around him. He
ection and rushed forward, but he couldn't
e tripped again and dropped to his knees.
crawl. Which way?
ng grabbed his wrist. He blinked, sweat and
eyes. Dandy? It was the dog, tugging him
hat way? Must be.
e dog. *When all else fails, trust the dog. He's*
er than you.
With Dandy leading the way, Grant crawled
barn. He was safe. The cows were safe.

steady the thumping of his heart—but realized what he was about to do would require attention. So he chose the prudent course and tucked the real flask away. Then he made a show of picking up his fake flask. That was what he needed now: a jolly good show.

"It's harder, you know, with candles," he said loudly. "I might just blow them out." True enough. "So if I do just as good a show as Harry there, I get the win because this is harder."

"No, no!" hooted Harry's friends. "We're judging the beauty of the fire, old boy. Not Harry's fault your brother soaked the torch."

Grant grimaced. It was a delicate line handling a drunken bet. Push too hard, and the "judges" would declare Harry the winner just because they could.

"Fine. Length and beauty of the stream," he said. "Longer fire, prettier fire."

He gathered a fistful of candles in his hand. He'd likely burn his hand from hot wax, but he counted it a necessary sacrifice. And with every blister, he'd damn his interfering brother for the pain.

Harry stepped forward and lit the four candles Grant clutched in his fist. Good long wicks, thank God, so the flames rose high. *Time to burn!* he thought somewhat gleefully, despite Dandy's whimper of anxiety.

Grant gestured for Harry to back away. The last thing he'd need was an amateur getting in his way. Then he took a big mouthful of lantern oil. Hideous taste, but he was used to it by now. Then he took a lungful of air, held the candles aloft at the right distance, and misted the oil.

Perfect! The oil fluted just right. The candle flames

touched the mist and the flume of fire appeared. Glorious! He'd never done better!

Ka-boom! whispered his madness.

No ka-boom. A steady plume of flame that kept growing and growing. And growing. What the hell?

Dust. Bloody hell, the *dust!* This was a threshing floor. The problem wasn't the few bits of wheat left on the threshing floor. Well, that wasn't the problem at *first*. First, it was the damned dust in the air. So fine that he hadn't even noticed it. After all, it was a barn. That's what barns smelled like. But it was in the air, and it was flammable.

He watched in slowly dawning horror as his plume of fire grew, sparking and firing randomly in an expanding cone that fell steadily to the floor. Oil would have extinguished in the air before chest level because he'd aimed upward. But not when the dust motes caught fire and *kept* catching fire. All the way down to the floor where a thin layer of straw sparked immediately.

He gasped and started stomping it out. Then he reached for the bucket of water that he always kept nearby. The bloody bucket of water that was still *outside* with the torch in it.

He stomped on the flames, but it was too late. Hot wax splattered on his hands as he jerked the candles out, but it was a useless act. The fire spread lightning fast. He was still uselessly stomping on the nearest bits when the whole floor burst into flame.

The boys screamed. Harry managed to strip off his jacket and beat at the flames near Grant, but the fire was too big and was rapidly growing too hot.

"Out! Out!" G

Grimly, Harry face. Then they bo then that he heard downstairs. The ca cattle! It would ruin horses scream, and l horseflesh down thei

He had to get the had to herd the anim slamming a smaller s aiming for the main c roar of the flame—lou

It took all his streng shoved them wide, the it gave the fire more life a screaming inferno.

Where were the cow to run out. They had t would have to be hei couldn't see! The flames everywhere, and the smc breath burned.

He stepped forward an he hadn't a clue. Yes, he c The *herding* dog!

He whistled twice—twc could manage in the thicker time to get the cows to pa wink with Grant stumbling roaring flame.

He wasn't thinking about

of his brother's
down the barn
barn. But they

So he stumb
tried to find th
ran to the clo
moving. Not
the thing rear

He kept g
found the co
on top of on
the work, ba
moving. Wit
and shoved u
out through

Was that
the horses?
He couldn't
His skin fel
forward. Ev

All that
thing was
picked a dir
make it. H
He had to

Somethi
soot in his
forward. T

Trust th
much smar

He did
out of the

The barn collapsed behind him.

I stand corrected, his madness drawled. *Lots of luck here tonight. And all of it bad.*

Two

WAKEY, WAKEY! YOUR LUCK ISN'T DONE WITH YOU YET.

Unwilling to listen to his inner madness, Grant focused on the externals. He heard the sound of buzzing and felt a heavy hand shaking him awake. He murmured, tasted something hideous in his mouth, and cracked an eye to find someplace to spit. What he saw, however, made no sense whatsoever.

He was in the woods? Couldn't be. He hadn't slept outdoors since he'd been a child. A very young child. A gentleman slept indoors and on a bed. And with a willing woman curled around him.

Could be your understanding of yourself—as a gentleman or otherwise—is rather flawed.

Grant blinked, but the vision remained the same. He was in the woods and not even in a clearing. The buzzing came from some dratted insect—a bee, he now saw—among the leaves and dirt. He tried to shift, just to see better, but the ache in his muscles had him groaning aloud. What the hell had he slept on?

"You might as well face it. It's not going away," the voice said. A man's voice, deep and clearly aggravated.

He recognized it, though it took a moment for his brain to come up with a name. Robert Percy, Lord Redhill, and once his good friend at school.

Then before Grant could process more, the man squatted in front of him and held out a flask. Grant moved for it out of reflex, his hand gripping the thing and bringing it to his mouth, even as his brain tried to talk him out of it. More alcohol was not what he needed just then. A bath and a strong coffee, yes. Brandy—

"Gah!" It was water. He choked on the taste then spit it out. But a second later, he realized he needed it more than he hated it. So he took another swig then emptied the flask. "Thanks," he rasped.

"I didn't do it out of charity. I need you clearheaded."

Grant sighed. That didn't sound good. In fact, that sounded very, very bad. With a groan, he slowly, carefully, rolled to a sitting position, while letting fly with his most colorful curses. God in heaven, he hurt. Everything hurt. And even worse, his memory was returning.

Oh yes! Let's review your lucky evening, shall we?

The bet, the barn, the fire.

He'd rescued the cattle. He remembered that. But the barn. Hell, the barn was gone. He remembered it collapsing. He remembered dropping to the ground and seeing the disaster fill his vision.

There had been shouts. People had come to help. But he hadn't the voice to direct them. He'd tried, but—

Then his brother had appeared. Will had run up and bellowed orders. Guests and servants alike had helped with buckets of water. But there was nothing to do to save the barn. Their efforts had been to simply contain the disaster. The last thing anyone wanted was for the fire to leap to the woods or the house.

Grant had helped as best he could, but he hadn't the breath and… He looked at his hands. He hadn't even noticed, given the general agony of his body, but now he saw the burned patches, blisters, and oozing spots all over his arms. And he was covered in soot.

"How did I get out here?" he rasped.

Robert shrugged. "Don't know. Probably just crawled here after the worst of the fire was contained."

Grant grimaced. Obviously, the fire hadn't hit the woods. Thank God. "The house?"

"Fine. Everything's fine, except for the barn, of course."

Damned lucky, wouldn't you say? His madness's voice was thick with irony.

"You got the animals out, even the cows. Though the tack is gone. And that dog has seen better days."

He blinked, suddenly alarmed. "Dandy? Dandy's hurt?"

"Singed. Not so pretty anymore, though how could you tell? But all the ladies are pampering him, feeding him treats, and calling him a hero, so I guess he's come out ahead." Robert's head tilted as his expression hardened. "Your family is worried sick. They have a search party looking for you."

Grant blinked, startled. Then his groggy brain adjusted, and he shook his head. "Mother is worried. Will…" His voice broke. Now he remembered the last of it. The reason why he'd crawled out here, hoping to die. His brother. His little brother Will, who had once worshipped him, had found him after the worst of the fire had died.

Grant had been half sitting, half lying against a tree, watching the last of the barn fade to ashes. Will had come over, had looked him up and down, and spit. A hard, dark, greasy glob of spittle had landed in the dirt near Grant's hand. That was it. No words, no questions, just that black glob landing with a splat.

Grant had looked up at him, trying to find the words. There weren't any, even if he had the voice to say them. He'd created a disaster, and the shame was crippling. Or so he thought, until his brother simply turned and walked away—the cut direct from his own brother.

That's when true shame hit. When self-disgust overwhelmed him, and he wished with all his heart to die. Right there, right then.

But he didn't. And he hadn't the strength to find his own horse and leave. So he'd simply crawled away as deep into the woods as he could manage before he collapsed right here. His last conscious thought was for God to take him in his sleep. A fervent prayer to die and put an end to the miserable folly that was his life.

Sorry, lad, but God isn't that merciful.

No surprise there. If God were in the habit of listening to any of the Crowles, their lives would be vastly different.

"My brother isn't worried," he finally managed. "It's probably just Mama."

"And she's not important?"

Grant cursed. "Of course she is!" He thought night and day of little else but what poverty his mother survived. He sent everything he could back to her and Will, but it wasn't enough. It was never enough.

Robert grimaced and shifted until he sat on a convenient rock. "Well, I've sent a message back that I've found you. That you're safe. I needed to talk to you before you face that lot."

Grant shook his head. He knew from the look on his friend's face that it was serious. That it was terrible, in fact, and he wasn't ready. But Robert didn't give him the luxury of hiding. Instead, he said words that struck terror into his heart.

"Our fathers had a right good time of it yesterday."

Grant bit back a groan. Drinking buddies with titles. That's what their fathers were. Drinking buddies with grand ideas and the belief that everything they touched was gold. How many afternoons had he spent cleaning up after his father had enjoyed a "right good time?" And he knew that Robert was just the same. Though there was more money to back his title, Robert had easily spent just as much time quietly managing his father's disasters. That was, in fact, one of the things that had drawn them together as boys: the solid belief that their fathers were idiots.

"No," he murmured. He couldn't face it. "Not yet."

Remember that luck you said was surrounding you last night? It's come home to roost, said his madness. *Listen to it.*

Meanwhile, Robert waited a bare thirty seconds. Grant took the time to listen to the buzz of the bee, feel the whisper of a breeze across his chilled body, even absorb the ache in his muscles. All were miserable sensations, but they effectively blocked the disaster to come. For thirty seconds. Then Richard spoke.

"They bought a mill."

Grant snapped his head up, but then immediately regretted it. "A—they—what?"

"A mill. A couple hours ride from here. A factory that makes cloth. They bought it."

"The devil they did! With what money?"

"Your father sold every inch of your land to Lord Lawton. You know that Welsh nabob just back from the Orient? Buried in money, that one. Gave your father a good price for the land."

"That's Crowle land!"

Not anymore, it isn't.

Grant shook his head, heedless of the pain it caused. "No, no, no, no!" The one word grew louder and more painful with every utterance. And still it echoed in his head. No, he couldn't possibly have burned down the barn. No, his father couldn't possibly have sold all their land. It was the one thing sheltering the animals that *fed* his mother over the winter. No, he wasn't covered in soot, disowned by his brother, and *still* had to manage his father. And no, he wasn't allowed to kill his bloody idiot of a sire and just be done with the disasters! "No!"

Robert waited out his bellow. They both knew from long experience that one had to get through the fury first before facing what came next. For Grant, it faded out all too fast. He hadn't the strength to spend in anger, and he didn't have the tears to shed in self-pity. All he had was a looming, overwhelming sense of shame.

His father, his grandfather, and yes, even Grant—all were useless, pathetic disasters of men. The only one worth anything was his prig of a brother Will.

Oh lucky day. At last you understand.

"Are you done?" inserted Robert.

No, he'd never be done. Not until his father was in the grave. "Yes. Have the papers been signed?"

"The mill purchase, yes. The land sale, no."

Grant sighed. "Well, that's something. At least I can stop that."

"So you have enough cash on hand to pay for his half of the mill?"

Grant winced. No. They didn't have enough to pay for the wedding they'd just celebrated. Or the tack from all those expensive horses. Saddles were deuced expensive! Not to mention rebuilding a barn that was now nothing but charred stumps.

"We can't afford the mill, Robert. We haven't got that kind of money."

Robert didn't answer at first. He just sat there and looked hard and cold at his one-time friend. Grant noticed it and winced. He knew that expression, and he knew he didn't want to hear what was coming next.

In all their time as boys at school, in all the years of friendship that they'd shared, over ale and girls and paternal disasters, there had been only one thing they disagreed on. One particular thought that separated the two boys from being of one mind.

Robert believed that a real man worked. The man found a secret pleasure in laboring day and night, in coming home exhausted and sweaty. In turning down the invitations from friends in order to study ledgers and tallies. In truth, Robert probably lived to make money like the lowest, crassest bootblack. It was his greatest failing as an aristocrat and was the one thing that would keep Robert from the highest levels of society. This focus on money was just too plebeian, and everyone with breeding could sense it.

Grant, on the other hand, believed a gentleman had certain standards to uphold. The peasants needed to see something better in their leaders. And that sweat was the most ungentlemanly affect, unless it appeared in the boxing ring or during a horse race. And even then, of course, it needed to be washed away immediately.

Grant believed in standards. Robert believed in money. That was the core of their difference, and the source of hours of endless debate at school. But they weren't at school now. And Robert had that look on his face. The one that said Grant was in the soup, and there was no avoiding it.

You're a worm on a hook, my boy. Best get it over with quick.

"Just say it," Grant finally spit out. Because suddenly, Robert's greatest failing was going to be Grant's salvation. If anyone could figure out a way for the Crowles to come out of this disaster, it would be Robert. His moneymaking mind would have the answer, even if Grant would hate every second of it.

"Sell the land. Fix the mill."

Grant reared forward. "We can't sell it! It's the only support we have!"

"And it needs more repairs. It needs investment that you can't do. Lawton can. You're always talking about the obligation of the titled. Well, your people have been suffering, and you haven't the wherewithal to help them."

"Will works hard. He's been trying—"

"He's only one man, and he needs capital."

Grant looked at the trees. "And how does Mama survive through the winter?" Will would work. He was a damn good steward. Grant could survive on his own just on gambling. Always had. It was just his parents who were the problem: his father's gambling and his mother's life as a titled woman. At least she pinched every penny she could. Had to, given the excesses of her husband. But there were certain standards to be maintained, or so he'd always been told.

Meanwhile, Robert leaned closer. "I've been to the mill. For once our fathers weren't completely hoodwinked. There's something there. Something that can be built on."

Grant looked up. "Can you turn it around?"

"No, I can't."

What little hope he'd been feeling was crushed flat, and Grant slumped backward. "Well then, how do we sell it to some bigger fools?"

"We don't sell it. You run it."

Grant choked on a laugh. "I don't know a bloody thing about mills."

"So learn. You're smart. You've got this amazing focus. I've never seen you fail when you set your mind to it." Then he folded his arms. "You knew how to breathe fire, didn't you? You learned how."

Grant looked away. "I might have spent some time with a gypsy or two."

"A month, I'd wager. Learning the skill." Robert grimaced. "Why do you feel the need to hide hard work? A man shouldn't be ashamed of honest labor."

This was an old argument between them, and Grant

answered automatically. "Because a gentleman doesn't *labor*. He *thinks*. That's the benefit of an education."

"And maybe he should think *and* work. Like at a mill making cloth." Then he flashed a rueful smile. "You've always had an eye for clothing. Assuming you don't burn it off."

Grant snorted. "I've got an eye for pretty girls too. Doesn't mean I know how to make one."

Robert's eyebrows shot up, and Grant had to remember his words to understand his friend's expression. When he did, he grunted in disgust.

"Well, yes, so I know how to *make* a girl. Doesn't mean I can *manage* one. Or profit from it."

"Well, I can't either. I haven't the time, and my life is in London."

"So we'll make our fathers do it. They're the ones who bought it."

Sure, that will work.

Robert unknowingly echoed the mad voice. "And where will that get us?" His voice took on the dull, exhausted note that so often lingered in Grant's. They both hid it, of course. There were some gentlemanly pretenses even Robert maintained. A casual insouciance was one of them. But here, alone in the woods, and faced with a shared parental disaster, even Robert let his facade slip. "Our fathers would destroy what little value is there."

"Then they'd turn it into a drinking parlor and start getting more ideas."

Robert agreed with a sharp laugh, but then the man quickly sobered. "Here's the truth, Grant. You're facing ruin. Not just you, but your whole family."

"I know!" He spoke sharply, hoping to forestall the coming lecture, but his friend was relentless as he outlined the facts.

"Your lands and your people are destroyed without a huge infusion of cash, which you don't have. You'll have to replace the barn at a minimum, and—"

"Yes, I know!"

This time it worked. Robert paused long enough to exhale a long breath. "You do have half share in a mill and a buyer for the land. So that takes care of your responsibilities to your people—"

"And what about my mother?"

"Save a bit from the land sale for her. Put everything else into the mill. And then, make the best damn cloth in the land."

Grant took a breath, but it didn't help. He already felt the noose tightening around his neck. Or the hook in his mouth, to use his madness's imagery. "You want me to sell the land and work in a factory." He thought about it a moment, but then shook his head. "I can't. The value is in the land. And it's been in our family since Henry II."

"Your people can't eat history. Lawton can do more for them in one month than you have in ten years. You know it's true."

It was. Their finances had been a disaster since the day his grandfather took the reins. And yet, the very idea of selling the land where he'd grown up, where generations of Crowles had lived and thrived, was physically nauseating. To leave the open space to work in a mill offended every titled cell in his body. And yet, what choice did he have? That's what

Robert was so clearly telling him. There were no other options.

"How can I work a mill? I know nothing about it."

And when has that ever stopped you?

Meanwhile, Robert leaned against a tree. "How much did you know of fire-breathing six weeks ago?"

Grant sighed, already seeing where this conversation was going. "Nothing. Not a damned thing."

"So what happened in the barn?"

"Threshing dust. I didn't think about the dust."

"But otherwise, you could have won the bet?"

Grant felt his lips curve in a faint smile. "Easily. And I planned to use the same bet at a few other country parties. At least until the news got out that I could do it."

"Hmmm. So you learned. You listened to those who knew how to do it. You practiced and focused. And in a month's time, you had a marketable skill."

"Breathing fire is a party trick, Robert."

"One that would have brought in coin for a while at least."

"I burned down the barn."

"Well, your luck has always been uncertain." The man abruptly leaned forward, his eyes gleaming with intensity. "So now do something that doesn't require luck."

"Factory work?" Grant spit out the words. He couldn't breathe for the shame in the idea. He was going to be an earl, damn it. There were only a handful in the world, and he would be one. While toiling in a mill? In his head, generations of Crowles screamed their horror, while his madness bellowed back a sharp, *shut up!* "I can't," he whispered. "I can't do it."

"You can. You can apply that clever mind and that amazing focus to doing something better than a sideshow trick. Something that makes real money."

Grant waited while the noise in his head subsided. It never happened, but he slowly shifted the noise into a mental tally of possibilities, even though his stomach roiled in horror. "How much real money?" he asked quietly.

Robert shrugged. "I don't know. Possibly a very great deal."

"Enough to buy back the Crowle land, you think?"

Robert didn't answer. He didn't need to because Grant had already seen his path. The only path open that would keep at least a shred of honor to him and his family.

And the fish is caught! crowed his madness.

"All right," he rasped, the words choking him on the way out. "All right. I'll do it."

"You'll run the mill? You'll turn it around?"

"I will. But I have some conditions."

Robert didn't speak, his only expression was a raised eyebrow.

"I'll become a bloody laborer, Robert. I'll sell the land—every inch that isn't tied up in the entail. I'll give up everything, and by God, I'll make that damned mill the most profitable place in the world. And then, when I'm done, you're going to buy it off me."

Robert reared back. "What? Why would you sell it?"

"Because I'm going to buy back my land. Because after I give my soul to that mill, I'm going to buy every acre back from Lawton, and then I'm going to make damn sure father signs a new entail. We're never going to sell that land again."

Robert huffed out a breath. "You think you can do it? Think you can convince Lawton to sell you the land back?"

Grant snorted. "He'll sign. I'll see to it." Then he pinned his friend with a hard stare. "You'll buy me out? When the time comes?"

Robert nodded. "I'd be a fool not to. You'll have made the place into a gold mine."

Then they both sobered. There was one more obstacle. Robert was the one who voiced it. "What are you going to do about your father? None of this works if he accrues more debt."

Grant released a low, dark laugh. "You think I'm going to shame myself alone? He bought the damned place. He's bloody well going to work right by my side until it's done."

"You think you can keep him there? Working with you?"

"I'll chain him to a loom, if I have to."

Robert nodded. "So you've decided."

Grant closed his eyes and took a deep breath—his last as a titled gentleman. "One more thing."

Robert had pushed to his feet, but he stopped at Grant's words. "What?"

"My name is Mr. Grant. If I'm going to be a bloody peasant, I might as well have a peasant name."

His friend snorted. "You think too much about your name."

"You never understood the grandeur of being an earl," he shot back.

"It's not grand if it's broke. It's just a lie, and a dangerous one at that."

Grant slowly moved to his feet, feeling an ache throughout his body. But it was nothing compared to the pain in his soul.

With Robert's help, he found an inn and bathed. He got his clothes and his gear, and met with Lord Lawton. Turned out the Welsh nabob wasn't a fool, and he bargained like a fishwife for what he wanted.

The agreement they signed had the following provisions:

1. Will remained as steward at a very healthy salary.

2. Grant had five years to buy back every inch of the land. After that, Lawton was free to dispose of the land however he wanted.

3. The sale would be at a fair price.

Five minutes after the document was signed, Grant forgot about that third provision. He was too occupied with forcing his father to help with the disaster the man had created.

Three months later, he forgot to lock up his father's horse. The man grabbed it and rode off, never to be seen again.

A year later, Grant learned that his father had died of a fever. Grant had already missed the funeral and wouldn't have known about the death if there hadn't been legal papers to sign regarding the shift in title. Grant was now an earl, finally able to do with his heritage as he saw fit. What he chose to do—after the papers were signed—was to take a bath. A good long soak in tepid water. Then he roused himself and spent the rest of the evening working numbers in his ledger.

Robert would be proud, his madness mused when Grant finally closed his eyes to sleep. But all Grant felt was a sick humiliation.

Then four more years ticked by.

Three

Five years later

AFTER FIVE YEARS OF LONG, HARD LABOR, GRANT WAS finally going to have his moment.

Oh lord, are we back to this again? I thought you'd learned.

Grant ignored his madness's voice. Instead, he leaned back in his chair and imagined his coming moment. It was crystal clear in his head because it was the one vision that had kept him going these last five years. And now, it was here. A great day built on nights spent hunched over books and days sweating over broken machinery at his textile mill. He'd gone without food as he poured money into the new dying process. Many nights he'd slept on a cot in his office, and for a time, he'd just lived there because it was cheaper. He'd sweated and bled for today, and now, it was here. His Great Day when everything paid off.

My God, you've become a bloody bore. And, in case you haven't noticed, you can't have your glorified Moment, if you don't sell your cloth.

Grant grimaced, knowing his madness was right.

Mr. Knopp, purchaser for A Lady's Favor dress shop, had been scheduled to arrive ten minutes ago. Grant was waiting for him in an inn parlor on the outskirts of London. He'd placed bolts of fabric on five chairs set strategically about the room. And in the forefront of his mind was a number, the exact number of pounds he needed before he had his Great Moment. That money would come from Mr. Knopp today. Grant intended to take every penny the man had by selling the idiot all his merchandise for triple the cost to make it. But he couldn't do that unless the man showed up!

Five years ago, Grant would have called for a drink and set about killing time in the only way he'd known how: numbing himself insensate. But he wasn't Grant Benton, the dissolute Lord Crowle today. He was the patient and cunning Mr. Grant who would enjoy his Great Day as soon as Mr. Knopp showed.

Fortunately for his sanity, a moment later he heard a soft knock at the door. Grant put aside his papers—he was always studying papers and their neat columns of numbers—then straightened his jacket and put on a congenial smile.

"Enter," he called.

The door opened, and a woman stepped in. She was tall with soft skin and black clothing. The dress was out of date and somewhat shabby, but her smile was warm, though very tiny, like a bud of new growth on a dark stick of tree. Meanwhile, he stifled a sigh as he pushed reluctantly to his feet.

"I'm sorry, ma'am, but you've got the wrong parlor."

No, she doesn't! Bring her in! Take off her dress! Grant didn't even wince as his madness suggested all sorts of filthy things. Sometime in the last five years, his madness had shifted from the grumbling, annoying voice of conscience to the grumbling, annoying voice of temptation. As Grant learned how to spend every day and night in toil, his madness pushed for debauchery. At first he'd found the change disconcerting. Now, he just pushed it to the back of his mind. He'd gotten better at that too over the last five years.

Meanwhile, the woman didn't so much as blink. "Are you Mr. Grant?" she asked.

He nodded. "I am, but—"

"You're waiting for Mr. Knopp, I presume?" she said as she untied her bonnet with quick movements. "That's me. Well, not the mister part, obviously. I'm Irene Knopp. Mr. Knopp was my late husband."

A widow! Make her merry!

Grant stared at her, his mind struggling with the woman in front of him. Mr. I. Knopp was a woman? A *woman*! And a widow still in mourning, given her black clothing. He stifled a curse and tried to find a way out. There wasn't one. The deadline was today, and he needed her money to have his Great Moment. His conscience would give him hell for taking advantage of a widow, but what choice did he have?

Take advantage of her! In at least four different positions!

Mrs. Knopp gave him another small smile. "Please, sir, I find myself somewhat fatigued. Do you mind if I sit down for a moment? Might we order tea?"

"Uh, of course," he said. That's what one said when a widow said she was tired and wanted tea. He rang the bell and made the order, while she set her coat aside. Her hair was a glossy black, the exact color of a foal he'd once coveted as a boy. And though her clothing was shabby, he noted a grace in her movements as she stripped off her gloves and settled on the couch. Lord, she looked so tragic. How could he put his family's need before hers?

Then she turned to him and smiled. It was a brief flash full of tragedy and quiet perseverance. At that moment, he had a revelation: it was all a lie. The widow's weeds, the tragic air, even the way she perched like a delicate, frightened bird on the edge of the couch—all of it was a carefully constructed lie.

He sat in his own chair, relishing the coming moments. He didn't care if she was a thief, charlatan, or just a smart salesgirl. Whatever her true nature was made no difference. She was about to make his last five years worthwhile.

Get her drunk first.

He felt his lips curve. Drinking wouldn't be the most subtle ploy, but it often worked anyway. "Instead of tea, I could order wine. More bracing, I think. They have an excellent brandy here too or—"

"Oh heavens!" she said with a flash of white teeth. "Tea is fine for me. But please, feel free to order some for yourself."

Step number one: ineffective. On to step two: establishing a friendship.

Kiss her senseless!

"I don't mean to offend," he said. "Your attire suggests you're still in mourning. That must mean your loss was recent. Please allow me to express my deepest sympathy."

She nodded, holding his gaze for perhaps a moment too long. "Thank you," she said, before dropping her eyes. "In truth, it's been some time since Nate's death, but I still feel it."

There was true emotion in her eyes, so the loss must be real. He felt a twinge of sympathy, but immediately quashed it. Outside, though, his expression was tender concern as he leaned forward.

"So was he the purchaser? Are you taking over his job?"

Her expression shifted to stern, as if she were preparing to do battle, which he supposed, she was. "I think that the best purchaser for women's clothing is a woman, don't you agree? A man couldn't possibly understand things as well."

He nodded slowly. "Naturally, you have advantages. But in the world of business, there are some drawbacks to your gender."

"Spoken like a gentleman," she said, obviously not meaning a word. Then they both fell silent as the tea tray arrived. She reached for it immediately.

"Shall I pour?" she asked, as if she were a matron in a society parlor.

"Of course. Just add a little lemon for me." He hadn't allowed himself sugar or milk for the last five years. In fact, the lemon would be a treat.

Boring! Get on with the naked part!

She nodded and poured, her hands steady, her every movement graceful. There wasn't anything special in what she did. Thousands of women throughout England did the same thing every day. And yet the sight stopped his breath. His belly tightened, and his chest squeezed painfully. And, worst of all, his cock reared like a thing coming alive for the first time in five years.

Finally!

What the hell? She was just serving him tea!

He narrowed his eyes, trying to judge the situation dispassionately. He noted each item individually, like marks on a tally sheet. First, she was lovely, but she didn't dress to emphasize that. If anything, her attire was modest and old. Second, she moved with the inborn class of a lady, and yet everything about her told him she was of the working class. He'd known this already, so what had changed in the last second?

It was the way she served tea, he realized. As if she were born to something better, but had fallen on hard times. Terrible times that he couldn't fix.

And there was his answer. His mother had served tea like this, and his sister too. With an innate dignity and a silent grief. Not for a man, but for a dream that was lost. A possibility that would never come to fruition. That was how the women in his family served tea. And now, Mrs. Knopp too. It roused his protective instincts. It reminded him that women should be cherished. And damn, it made him long for a better way.

Of course, none of that explained his thickening cock. He had no interest in bedding anyone. And if he did, it certainly wouldn't be this tragic figure before him, especially since it was probably a well-constructed lie! And yet, nothing he said had the tiniest impact on his imbecilic organ.

Don't question it. Use it! Repeatedly. And in a thrusting motion!

"Mr. Grant? Is something amiss?"

He swallowed then reached for his teacup. "Nothing at all," he said. He took an obligatory sip then held the cup and saucer in his lap to hide his embarrassment. "Perhaps we should get to business. You are purchasing fabric for A Lady's Favor dress shop, and I have the best wools in England."

"My goodness, that's quite a statement."

"It's true nonetheless." Then he leaned forward, deciding that he might as well use his discomfort to his advantage. If he was attracted to the woman, then he should let it show and flirt. "In fact, I have the most gorgeous bolt just for you. It's a little heavier—meant for late fall—but the color would be spectacular on you."

"On me? But I assure you, I have no need—"

"You're coming out of mourning soon. You must be." He set aside his tea and crossed to the nearest pile of fabric. Sorting through them, he lifted then discarded his choices. He knew what he was looking for. So where was it? "Oh yes! I set it aside for a different customer," he lied. In truth, he'd meant to bring it out later as a temptation. After the primary order was made, he would bring it out as a last temptation to increase her order. But now that she was here, he knew that it had been made just for her.

He lifted it up, feeling the exquisite softness and seeing the design. He had been the one to first draw this pattern, not that he'd tell her that. But when he turned and held the fabric up to her face, he knew he'd done it all just for her.

"This is it," he said softly.

He angled her toward the mirror and let her see.
The fabric was a dark rose, light enough to be joyous,
but still not a full pastel. It brought out the color in
her skin. But what made the piece truly stunning was
the intricate pattern embroidered on top. Nothing so
girlish as flowers. This was a design in abstract. He'd
been looking at a candle flame, and the pattern had
come to him. Yellows, oranges, and red burned on the
area that would be the bodice. There were matching
flames for the skirt. The end result would make her
appear to be wreathed in candlelight.

"Touch it," he said. "It's a special wool that we
make mixing in the fur from a thousand rabbits."

"Rabbits!"

"Angora rabbits, in fact. Go ahead. Feel it against
your skin." He didn't wait until she complied. Instead,
he brushed it across her cheek.

She gasped, as he knew she would. The first feel
of angora wool was always the best. Wool from sheep
was one thing—and his factory had some of the
best—but nothing could compare to his angora blend.

"Imagine yourself walking into a ballroom wearing
this. The chandeliers are above you, but the crowd parts
seeing only you. Like a living flame among them."

"Mr. Grant, I am not a woman who likes flattery."

"Every woman likes flattery, Mrs. Knopp," he
countered. "But in this, I only speak the truth. I'll
show you. But first cover your eyes."

"Mr. Grant!"

"Shh!" He gently set his hand over her eyes. She
closed them, of course, and he told himself the caress
across her brow was only in the service of his sale. Still,

he couldn't help but note how soft her skin felt or that there was heat in her face. When was the last time she blushed? he wondered. Not lately, he'd wager.

Meanwhile, he draped the fabric about her, covering her ugly black dress with ease.

"Shall I look?"

"Not yet," he said. He quickly crossed to the window and pulled the curtains shut. Then he lit two candelabra, setting them on either side of her. Just as he'd thought, the dress picked up the dance of the flames. When she moved, she would draw every eye in the room.

He smiled, proud of his creation. But more, he was awed by her beauty. "Now," he said. "Open your eyes and see."

He watched as her impossibly long lashes lifted, and she looked into the mirror. She blinked then she frowned, but not in disappointment. She seemed more startled than anything. As if she had forgotten what she looked like in anything but black.

"Your skin is flawless," he said as he stepped behind her. "A gown made from this will bring out the color of your lips and the blush across your… cheeks." The hesitation was deliberate as his gaze dropped lower to where the soft curve of her breasts might show.

"The design is so pretty," she murmured, touching the precise stitches. "It's like…"

"Fire?"

"Yes, but more delicate." She met his gaze in the mirror. "It's beautiful."

"It was made for you," he said, meaning every word. *Dance with her,* his madness prompted. And for once, he obeyed, touching her elegant fingers with his own.

"I can see you at a ball, Mrs. Knopp. The men have been watching you, but someone has claimed the waltz. He bows before you and takes your hand."

"Really, I don't think—"

"It's harmless, Mrs. Knopp. Let yourself pretend, if only for a moment." He didn't give her the chance to object. Lifting her hand to his lips, he kissed her flesh before bowing. Once he had been counted a good dancer, and he drew on that memory now. She was wrapped in fabric, so he did what he could, draping the tail end over his shoulder. Then he began to hum.

"That's a pretty tune."

"Really? Trust me, I'm accounted a much better dancer than a musician. And now, if you will, Mrs. Knopp?"

He resumed humming and then swept her into a waltz. There was very little room, but he had danced on crowded floors before. In truth, it made it all the more thrilling as he spun her around and around.

Her mouth opened on a gasp, but he was focused on her eyes. They sparkled. It was the candle flames reflected, but it was also the way her skin crinkled at the corners. Her cheeks flushed, and her mouth curved. She had not spent much time dancing. Neither had he, in truth, and none at all for the last five years.

So while he hummed his tune, he let himself go as well. He whirled them both around, and he gloried in the feel of a flesh and blood woman in his arms. One who meshed with his steps, even though there were layers upon layers of clothing between them.

One who delighted in the play and smiled as if it were Christmas morning.

They danced for as long as he could manage, but eventually, their steps slowed. In time, they came to a stop, breathless, and still he could not look away from her eyes.

Kiss her!

He swallowed, the desire nearly overwhelming. But he had a task here, and so he forced his words to something equally lustful, just not as inappropriate.

"You must make a dress from this fabric," he said. "I designed it for you. I didn't know it at the time, but I do now. It was meant for you."

Her eyes widened, and she looked at the embroidery. "You made this design?"

Damnation, he hadn't meant to confess that. As a rule, ladies preferred women artists for their clothing. He stepped back, but he was held in place by the fabric he'd tossed over his shoulder. "O-of course not," he stammered. "We have ladies who—"

"Poppycock," she interrupted. "It was you." She grabbed his arm. "I think it's a wonderful design."

"I—" Now *his* face was heating. And when was the last time *he'd* blushed? "Thank you, Mrs. Knopp. You are very kind."

"And you are very talented."

He all but rolled his eyes. "Pray don't say that. I cannot let it be known—"

"That a man has created such a beautiful thing? I shall make a bargain with you. If you do not tell the other factories that Mr. Knopp is a woman, then I shall not share that the Wakefield Design Factory is run by a man."

He felt his lips quirk in a smile. "Oh, you can tell everyone a man *runs* the place. You just cannot share that I take a hand in the more artistic aspects of the work."

"And you do all the artistic designs?" she asked as she gently lifted the fabric off his shoulders.

"Of course not," he said immediately. "I have some talented women who do the work for me. I only dabble every now and then. And really, it is the ladies—"

"If you continue to lie, I shall become cross and refuse to buy a single yard."

He bit his lip and stepped back. "Did you not begin our conversation by saying that a woman knows a woman's fashions best?"

She grimaced. "I did, I suppose. So perhaps we should agree that gender means absolutely nothing if one is clever or talented. And I believe, Mr. Grant, that you are both."

"And you, Mrs. Knopp, are full of surprises."

She smiled as she began folding the bolt of fabric. Her hands lingered on the exquisite material, stroking the soft angora. He watched her closely, seeing the wistful expression, and he knew a moment of alarm. She did not intend to buy! She had the look of a woman putting a treat away.

"But you must buy it," he said. "It was made for you!"

"No, Mr. Grant. It was made for a woman who goes to balls and dances with handsome young men."

"Surely you attend parties. And you will not always be in black. How long before your mourning ends?"

"I—" She smiled, but it was a sad smile. "Soon, I suppose. But—"

He abruptly stepped forward, pressing it into her arms. "A gift then. Make it into the most beautiful gown, and dance in it."

"A gift!" she gasped. "I can't!"

Neither could he, if he were honest with himself. After all, his family's future depended on the money he needed today. But the urge to see her in this gown was overwhelming. And so he did something he rarely did: he dispensed with games and became brutally honest.

"I need a sale today, Mrs. Knopp. Five hundred pounds."

"Five hundred! Surely you do not expect that to come from my dress shop!"

"Surely, I do, Mrs. Knopp. You are the most exciting new dressmaker in London. Thanks to the new Lady Redhill, you are flooded with orders and cannot possibly have purchased all you need for the coming season."

"You sell wools, Mr. Grant. Not ballroom silks."

"Angora wool, Mrs. Knopp. For the older ladies or the ones not so plump in the pocket. For wraps against the cold and for dresses when the autumn leaves have fallen."

She smiled, but shook her head. "Five hundred is too much."

"For all this," he said in an expansive gesture. "It is a bargain, and you know it."

She blinked, looking about the room. "You would give me all of it?"

He nodded. "I would. For five hundred pounds cash. Today."

"Today! I don't carry that much money. Anyone who does is daft!"

True enough. "Banker's check then. Surely you have that."

She bit her lip, looking at the piles of bolts. Five hundred pounds was a bargain for all this. In truth, his conscience would be pricking him on the morrow for selling everything he had at such a low price. But he needed the money today, and she was his only hope.

"Are they damaged in any way?"

He stiffened. "Absolutely not!"

She looked about her slowly. Her good sense was telling her to say no. After all, five hundred pounds was a fortune. But the way she stroked the angora told a different story. She was tempted.

So he crossed to her side, stepping as close as they had been during their waltz. And he looked at her, saw the desire in her eyes, and remembered the feel of her body swaying in his.

Seduce her, his madness whispered.

He refused to do that. And yet her gaze shot to his and held. In it, he saw thoughts upon thoughts. Calculations, most likely—the rolling scroll of numbers in the brain that made one's head ache. He knew the feeling well. And he knew if he let it continue, good sense would prevail, and he would be lost.

So he distracted her. He touched her cheek as a man might stroke his lover. He hadn't intended it to be so intimate, but once his fingers met her cheek, his touch became a caress. His gaze slid to her lips. Her mouth was parted, an unconscious invitation. How he wanted to kiss her. How he wanted something a great deal more from her.

But he couldn't. Not now. Probably not ever. So with a silent curse, he pulled back on his lust. Eventually, all he managed to do was moderate his words to a hoarse rasp.

"It is a good bargain," he said. "For us both."

You're a fool, his madness said.

"Yes," she whispered. For a moment, he thought she was agreeing to something else entirely. But then she elaborated—because she was a smart businesswoman—making her wishes very clear.

"Yes, Mr. Grant, I will buy everything you have for five hundred pounds."

Idiot! You're worth more than that!

"Sold."

❧

Grant's madness was strangely silent as he sauntered into Mr. Rigby's office. It made him nervous, but nothing could suppress the simmering excitement in his blood. Meanwhile, he was startled to see that Lord Lawton was already in the solicitor's office. He was reading the newspaper as he sat across from Rigby's huge desk. Both aristocrat and solicitor rose to their feet as Grant entered. In truth, Grant was somewhat surprised to see Lawton there. Certainly the man had been invited to this meeting, but aristocrats, as a rule, did not arrive at appointments on time. In fact, Grant had once thought himself punctual if he reported within an hour of the agreed upon moment.

He greeted each man cordially, but then quickly

got down to business. He couldn't suppress a grin as he handed the solicitor a neat stack of papers that included Mrs. Knopp's banker's check right at the top.

"It's all there," he practically crowed. "Took me until this morning, Lawton, but I finally did it."

"You've enough to buy back your lands?" Lawton asked, surprise clear in his voice. Mr. Rigby wasted no time in sitting down to inspect every sheet. As he worked, Lawton peered over the man's arm. "Amazing. And here I thought I'd been summoned to endure begging for an extension."

Grant stiffened at the insult, though God knew there'd been reason to doubt. That was exactly what the old Grant would have done. Five years ago. Before he'd turned over a new leaf. Before he'd learnt what it meant to work in a factory, day in and day out, until his hands bled and his mind screamed.

"I wouldn't insult you like that," he said stiffly.

Lawton shrugged as he straightened up. "Wouldn't be an insult. Besides, I would have just said no. Got plans for that land."

Grant leaned back in his chair. "Of course, you do. You're selling it back to me. Every last rock, leaf, and drop."

Lawton looked over to where the solicitor was making a neat column of figures. The man was tabulating. Grant barely minded. Solicitors had to make their money somehow, and he would personally damn any man who wasn't excruciatingly correct with his accounts. So, he didn't begrudge the man the time he took. Well, he didn't begrudge it much. Not until the man started going through it again. For a third time.

"It's all there," Grant said. "A statement from my bank and my solicitor detailing the amount I have at my disposal. Add in Mrs... er, Mr. Knopp's check, and it's more than adequate."

"Of course, my lord," the solicitor answered without more than a cursory glance upward. "But if you will forgive me a moment, I really must check a few things."

Grant had no choice but to agree. So he waited in a pretense of patience as Lawton tried to make small talk.

"Have to say, I was surprised to get your note. Haven't heard a whisper from you in five years. Your brother said he hadn't heard either."

Grant just nodded. His brother Will was steward of the Crowley land. Always had been, practically from when the boy'd been in leading strings. Best damn steward in England, and it had hurt to watch the man work for Lawton these last five years. Grant couldn't wait to tell his little brother that they could finally work together, just as it ought to be. Crowles running Crowle land, making the most of their heritage as had been for centuries. Assuming one ignored the rather ignoble last five years. Fortunately, that was all at an end now.

And on that thought, the solicitor finally stopped tabulating. The total was at the bottom of the page. Exactly right, he noted with pleasure. And exactly the amount needed to buy back the land.

"I'm so sorry, Lord Crowle," Mr. Rigby said. "But there is not enough. Not enough by far."

Grant bolted upright in his seat. "The devil you say!

That is absolutely everything I need! In fact, it's 335 pounds more than our agreed upon total!"

Far from appearing alarmed, Mr. Rigby barely blinked as he pushed forward a document. It was the same damned document that he'd signed five years ago. The one that gave all the Crowle family's land—every inch that wasn't entailed—to Lord Lawton on the condition that Grant had five years to buy it back. That five years ended today, and here he was ready to buy it all back.

"You are correct, my lord," the bastard solicitor was saying. "The amount you've brought is approximately 335 pounds more than what the land was worth five years ago."

"That's what I said!"

"Yes, my lord. But if you would look here." The bastard leaned over his desk to point at a particular clause. "It says you have five years to buy back the land *at a fair price*."

"This is a damned fine price, and you know it!"

Mr. Rigby pursed his lips and looked at Lord Lawton. Grant followed the gesture, turning to his nemesis. Lawton looked almost apologetic, but there was no compromise in his words. If anything, there was an undercurrent of anger in his voice. "Perhaps you were unaware of the improvements I've made to the land."

Grant swallowed, his breath abruptly caught in a tight throat. Five years ago, he hadn't understood much about improvements and what they did to profitability and value. He hadn't bothered to think that far ahead. But he was now, and he couldn't stop the fear that churned inside.

"Yes," continued Lawton. "I've made significant improvements to the crofters' homes and their livestock."

"I knew you would. That's what the extra 335 pounds are for."

"And I built a canal."

Grant blinked. A canal. Bloody hell, Will's idea for a canal. Lawton had gone and done it. "That was my brother's idea," he murmured. And it was the first improvement Grant had intended to make once he gained control.

"Perhaps it was," Lawton said with a grin. No question now. There really was an undercurrent of malice there. "Do I need to explain what that means to the value of the land? Doubled, Crowley, at the very least. If not tripled."

Grant's mind churned, trying to grasp at straws. "Is it done? Did you get everything connected like it should be?"

Lawton grimaced. "It will be done within the month. If it were complete, the price would be double."

"So it's not complete yet! The land hasn't gone up as much as it could. If you would just give me a little more time—"

"*No.*" Lawton's one word echoed in the room and Grant's skull. And if it didn't, the way he slammed his hand down on the desk did. Grant had a moment to wince, to realize he'd just begged for an extension, when he'd started this meeting by decrying that possibility. My, how little he'd changed. Meanwhile, Lawton continued speaking, every word heavy and cold. "You and your brother have led me on a merry dance, haven't you? Getting me to cover all the improvements before you stole it out from under me."

Grant looked up, his mind trying to wring sense from Lawton's words. "Stole it? How? Damn it, I want to *buy* it!"

Lawton shook his head. "You know, your brother is worth ten of you. I might forgive him. I'm bloody well going to have to, aren't I? But I'll be damned if I let the likes of you steal it all away now."

Grant shoved to his feet, his hands clenched in a fury. This was his Great Moment! How had it suddenly gone wrong? And what the hell did all this have to do with his brother? Yes, Will was ten times the man he was. But that's what this whole five years had been about: proving that Grant was a man too. That he deserved the title. That... "I have the money," he whispered. "The mill will turn more profit—"

"You don't have the money," Lawton said coldly. "And I won't be selling a single rock, bush, or drop to you ever. Good-bye, Crowle. And if you cause a scene at the wedding, I will beat you senseless." With that, the man grabbed his hat, nodded at his solicitor, and strode from the room.

It was a quick exit, perfunctory and final. It took awhile for Grant to process what had happened. He would not be getting back his family's land. After five years of blood and sweat, it was all over. He'd failed. He'd shamed his name, failed his ancestors, and now, he had no way to redeem himself in his mother's or his brother's eyes. After everything, he'd proved himself useless. Again.

The disappointment of that crushed him completely.

In truth, it was a shock to realize some fifteen minutes later that he was still alive.

It wasn't until he stumbled back to his tiny inn room that his madness chose to reassert itself. Two words formed a question with no answer.

What wedding?

Four

WHAT LINGERED MOST IN IRENE'S MIND WAS THE WAY he'd smelled: clean. Not with the perfume of the aristocracy. He smelled of the same harsh, lye soap she'd used as a child at school. That, plus a fresh mint leaf, as if he'd chewed, probably right before she'd arrived. It had been just a hint on his breath, but it had made her lean toward him when he spoke. And once she'd leaned in, the rest had happened as if by magic. The talk, the dance, the kiss.

Well, she hadn't kissed him, had she? Not in truth, but in her fantasies? Oh yes. In fact, they'd kissed a million times in the barely twenty-four hours since she'd first met the sweet-smelling Mr. Grant. Which was wonderful and terrible all at once.

Wonderful, because really, what woman didn't dream of kisses? It was a sign that she was coming back to life as a grown woman, not a widow. Terrible, of course, because Nate had been the one to teach her about kisses, and she should not be thinking of another man's mouth on hers. There was no moral or legal law against it, of course. Nate had died three years ago.

And yet, she felt as though she were betraying the man she still loved with all her heart.

"Lady Irene! I deeply apologize. We're having a bit of a problem, and I was delayed."

Irene turned around, her mind stumbling at the use of her correct title. Few people knew her as the daughter of an earl. To nearly everyone, she was simply Mrs. Knopp, the widow of a sailor and daughter-in-law to a wealthy shipping family. "Father Michael," she said with a smile, holding her hand out to the young priest. "No apology necessary. I was just enjoying the delightful architecture here at St. Clement," she lied. Then she winced, thinking that of all places, a church was not the place to lie.

"Why yes, it is stunning," Father Michael said as he settled into a subject he extolled by rote. "We're an old Roman church, rebuilt after the Great Fire by Sir Christopher Wren. There are quite a few distinctive features." He put on a rather pained smile. "Did you wish a tour? I could fetch Father Alfred. He knows the most about—"

"That won't be necessary," she said to save them both. "You mentioned a difficulty? Nothing terrible, I hope."

The man shook his head, but at that very moment a crash came from the back of the church, near the vestry. Then they heard a small child wail.

"Oh goodness," breathed Irene. Clearly some disaster had just occurred. "I believe you should go check on that."

"Er, yes. I'm terribly sorry." But he hesitated, looking painfully back at her. "I do not wish to delay our conversation, Lady Irene—"

Of course, he didn't. She was here on a charitable mission, and he didn't want to lose that. "Please, Father Michael, the boy sounds quite desperate." Then she touched his arm. "We can go talk in there together. I quite enjoy children." She winced again at uttering a second lie in as many minutes. Truthfully, children pained her a great deal, as she likely would never have any of her own. But she kept that from her expression. "His wails are growing quite loud."

"He is hungry, my lady," the father answered.

"Then by all means, let us convene in the kitchen."

He walked quickly, his dark robes flapping as he moved. They passed through a door to the side of the altar and then back into the offices of the church. It was dark and cramped back here, and now, she heard another voice—a young girl's—but there was no lessening in the child's wail.

Then she saw them. The boy was thin and sporting a swelling bruise on his face. He was held in the arms of a girl of approximately eight years. About them lay the scattered remains of a pile of books. Clearly, one had hit the little boy.

"I'm sorry, Father," the girl said, her eyes welling with tears. "He grabbed for the cup, and it all tumbled."

Only now did Irene see a heavy stein had rolled under a table.

"No matter," said Father Michael as he knelt to pick up the boy. At least that is what she thought. In truth, he picked up both children—boy and girl—holding them together in his arms. The novelty of it startled the little one into temporary silence. "Where is your mother?"

Just what Irene was thinking. The answer came when the girl waved her arms to a bench. There, slumped like a sack of old rags, was a young woman with sunken cheeks and a frightful pallor. For a moment, Irene feared the woman was dead, but when she looked, she saw the slight movement of her chest. The woman was asleep and clearly exhausted, since she'd apparently dozed through her son's book disaster.

"Come along, shall we?" said Father Michael as he began walking down the hallway. "Let's let Mama sleep a bit." He smiled at the boy who was still perilously close to wailing again. "I promised you some broth."

He started walking faster, bouncing his arms as he went to keep the boy quiet. Irene spared a last glance at the paper-thin woman then rushed to follow. They made it to the kitchen where a tiny woman with gray hair stirred a watery stew. "There's not much left," she said by way of greeting. "And it's mostly water." Then she took one look at the boy and grabbed a hard piece of bread and shoved it into his hand. The child went to work on it immediately.

Meanwhile, Father Michael set the children down, putting the boy into a rickety high chair.

"Lady Irene, I'm sorry—" Father Michael began.

"Please don't bother about me. I can happily wait," she interrupted as she watched the woman ladle what little there was into a bowl for the girl. "Is there nothing else?" Then she mentally chastised herself. Hadn't the woman just said there wasn't anything more?

Meanwhile, the woman glanced significantly to the larder—a small closet, but it should have been filled with foodstuff. To Irene's shock, it was nearly bare.

But that made no sense! This was a large church, one of the oldest in London. Certainly she knew it served a poor segment of the population—it was dedicated to the patron saint of sailors, after all—but they needed more than just water to feed the children.

As if reading her mind, Father Michael gave her a wan smile as he gently tied a rope around the boy's waist to keep him in the chair. "We're a poor parish, my lady, despite our grand architecture. The diocese is talking about closing our doors."

"Closing them!" she gasped. "But why?"

He shrugged and looked pointedly at the empty shelves. "Not enough money, congregation too poor. We're a significant drain on the church coffers."

"But that's what the church is for, isn't it? To aid the poor."

He nodded. "But there are a great many poor, my lady. A great many."

She looked down at the children. She had come here specifically to donate some of her newfound wealth to the church. After all, her in-laws had more than enough money. She worked to give herself something to do, not because she needed the funds. It had only made sense to give a portion of her earnings to a church that catered to sailors and their families. She had no idea that it was on the verge of closing.

Father Michael said nothing, too busy pushing a spoonful of broth into the boy's mouth. The child didn't want to stop gnawing on the bread, so it was a laborious task. And next to the boy, the little girl slurped from her bowl as if she hadn't eaten in a week.

"Their mother…" Irene said, unable to voice the question.

"Sad case that, but all too typical. Her husband died of a fever on his last voyage."

Irene nodded, a wave of misery washing over her. That was exactly how Nate had died, and she had refused to leave her bed for a month after getting the news. She couldn't imagine what would have happened if she'd had children to care for.

"What about his family? Hers?"

Father Michael shrugged. "Gone. Fever one side, drunken disaster on the other." He sighed. "She's on her own except for us, and she's worked to the bone to keep them above water. You see how exhausted she is. Sadly…" He didn't have to complete the sentence, as the rest was obvious. Sadly, they hadn't the money to support this woman or her little family. Not to mention however many other families like her were slowly dying of starvation.

With a snort of disgust, Irene fished into her reticule and pulled out all her coins. She'd meant to donate most anyway. Passing them to the older woman's hand, she said, "Let us start there. Get a chicken and some bread that doesn't have to be softened to eat. No one could survive on that thin paste. Not them, nor you."

The older woman's eyes widened, but the money disappeared fast enough. She bobbed a curtsey and gibbered a quick, "Thank you, my lady. Most gracious. I'll go right now."

Irene waved her off watching as the woman set the stove to rights, then grabbed her hat and rushed off. Meanwhile, Irene's gaze turned to the children.

"We are deeply grateful to you, my lady," said Father Michael in his rich tones. He had a beautiful voice, she realized. Quiet and soothing—most perfect for a man of the cloth. She was so intent on listening to his voice that she nearly missed the meaning behind his next words. "I only wish that we had a way to get past more than the next meal."

"What?" she said. Then she frowned. "No, no, don't answer. I can see your problem, of course." As a child, she'd also had to live from hand to mouth, constantly wondering where she'd find her next meal. Her father had been a gambler and a wastrel, and there were times she and her mother had been in very dire straights. "I came here looking for an apprentice. A boy who knows numbers and can help me lift and carry." She shook her head. This boy was too young, and if the mother was ill, the girl was needed to care for her brother.

Meanwhile, Father Michael was clearly thinking hard. "I might know of someone, though most boys who are presentable in an elevated household are already apprenticed."

"I can read," said the little girl. "Mama taught me."

Irene smiled. "Well, aren't you a clever girl. How old are you?"

"Ten years, my lady," she said in a clear voice. "I know my numbers too and have a good memory. Mama teaches me all sorts of things, but she's been too tired lately."

Irene glanced at Father Michael. "What has the mother been doing?"

"Looking for work, mostly. But no one wants to hire a woman with two children in tow."

"Of course not." Irene sat down, pleased at the solidness of the heavy worktable. At least that was as it ought to be, but everything else showed desperate need. Very odd, given the age and standing of this church.

She focused on the little girl. "What's your name?"

"Carol Owen, my lady. And my brother is Gavin, after my father."

"Lovely names. Tell me a bit about your life, will you Carol? What did you do yesterday?"

The girl started talking. Her eyes were huge, and she kept looking to Father Michael for her answers. He didn't do anything but give her an encouraging nod. And as she spoke, Irene's heart broke into a thousand little pieces. The girl and her family were indeed in terrible straits. And when Irene's rude interrogation ended, Father Michael set a gentle hand on the child's head.

"The need is real, Lady Irene."

Irene sighed. "Is the church really in danger of being closed?"

Father Michael nodded grimly. "I'm afraid so."

She winced. "I cannot help you more, Father Michael. I am but one woman and…" And she'd just spent all her money buying Mr. Grant's goods.

"Lady Irene—"

"Stop calling me that. Everyone knows me as Mrs. Knopp. I should prefer to keep it that way."

"Er, of course, my—er, Mrs. Knopp. Is there not—"

She held up her hand, effectively silencing the man as she studied Carol. "I am not a grand patroness, Father Michael. You have just received my last coin but…" She bit her lip. She could do small things, could she not? In a small way. "I have need of a smart girl with a good memory." It was her third lie of the day, but it was one she hoped God would not damn her for. She had no real need for a too thin, too young girl, even if she was the cleverest child on the planet. She'd come here looking for a strong boy. But who was she to discount a child merely because of her sex? She knew better than most that a smart girl could do the work of ten dumb boys.

Meanwhile, Father Michael was eyeing her with a frown on his face. In time, it grew irritating enough that she exhaled a long breath. "What is your worry, Father Michael?"

"The family needs steady income, my—Mrs. Knopp. Steady pay, not a grand gesture today and—"

"And disappear tomorrow. Yes, I am all too aware of that particular nightmare." Her father had been a master of the grand gesture. Wild extravagance today, only to have nothing more for weeks, if not months. She had learned young not to trust grand gestures. So she crouched before Carol. "I have need of a secretary. You could be that, child, provided you know your sums, can read tolerably well, and have an excellent memory. Those are things you have promised me Carol. Were you lying?"

Carol mutely shook her head.

"Good. I shall have Father Michael test you though. And you will have to stay home to help your mother until she is better. Then you may come to my address, and we shall see if you will fit my needs." She straightened, her heart twisting at the sight of the children before her. "I cannot keep your church open, Father," she said softly. "But perhaps I can help Carol."

And with that, she left quickly. The very first thing she had to do was visit the dress shop. It was possible—just possible—that they already had the funds available to pay her for her last purchases. If that were the case, then she had the money to pay Carol's salary for a month at least. If they didn't... She grimaced. Well, she could always ask her father-in-law for a loan, although that thought soured her stomach to the point of pain. Still, she was very hopeful. The dress shop was doing well. She ought to have some funds waiting.

Her hope lasted until she walked into the back room of the shop. One look around at the tight faces of her friends told her that something was amiss. Something very bad indeed.

Five

"No one has paid?"

Irene slowed her steps as she walked into the workroom of A Lady's Favor dress shop. Her best friend Helaine was there—back from her honeymoon—and she was obviously going over the books with her fellow owner Wendy, the seamstress. Helaine was hunched over the desk while Wendy spoke from behind her table deeper in the room. The worry in her voice did nothing to interrupt the steady pace of her needle as she stitched a seam.

"A few have paid," Wendy said as she adjusted the fabric on her lap. "Francine has, God bless her. And our clients from before you got married."

"But the aristocrats haven't?" pressed Helaine. "None of the *ton* have paid their bill?"

Wendy grimaced. "It's one excuse after another with them. My man does that. The Lady does that. Come after quarter day."

"Quarter day. Of course." Helaine rubbed at her chin. "I expected some problems. God knows I've juggled my share of debt collectors before. But I never thought they would *all* ignore us."

Irene snorted, then belatedly realized she'd been eavesdropping. She stepped into the room as Wendy and Helaine turned to greet her. "I'm sorry," she said quickly. "I didn't mean to overhear."

"No, no," said Helaine with a distracted wave of her hand. "You've as much a right as anyone to hear. Especially since…" Her voice trailed off on a sigh, and Irene picked up the rest of the thought.

"Especially since you haven't the money to pay me right now." She shrugged, the faith inside her shrinking despite her love for her best friend. Of course, the aristocrats would duck their bills. That's what aristocrats did.

"It's just so maddening!" fumed Helaine. "They're wearing the gowns. We deserve to be paid!"

"Which is exactly what my father-in-law says every time he has to deal with a peer." She held her hands tightly together and forced her exterior to remain casual. "Well, not about the gowns, of course. But he'd much rather deal with the craftiest captain than any nobleman in England."

Helaine grimaced. "Well, that's a sorry state of affairs for our country. So what does he do?"

"He's got his own brand of collection agents. Rough men. Ugly ways of demanding payment. He doesn't talk much about it, but sometimes I overhear."

"I'm not sure I can do that." Helaine lifted up a list of debtors. "These are ladies of the *ton*. Lady Brandleton is in her sixties!"

Beside her, Wendy snorted. "Well, we'll have to do something. And do it quick."

Irene quickly scanned the neatly tabulated column of funds owed and funds available. The shop's bookkeeper Anthony had a way of summarizing everything down to simple numbers. And what she saw told her that the shop was in trouble if they didn't get paid. Immediately.

Then Helaine snapped her fingers. "I am going to throw a ball."

She spoke as if that were the answer to their prayers, which—obviously—it was anything but. Irene frowned. Wendy was so confused, she stopped her needle in the middle of a stitch. Neither spoke. Meanwhile, Helaine looked up at their sudden silence.

"You don't understand. I'm the newly married Lady Redhill, co-owner of a dress shop, and daughter of the Thief of the Ton."

"Yes dear, we know—" said Wendy, but Helaine waved her to silence.

"If I throw a ball—in a week's time, I think— then everyone will want to attend. I've only been back a day, and already we're flooded with cards." She pointed to the list of ladies who owed the shop. "Why, I believe Lady Edith has called on us twice."

Irene nodded, understanding starting to flicker. "Everyone will want to attend."

"Exactly. It will be the talk of the town."

Wendy blew out a slow whistle. "You're going to restrict the guest list, aren't you?"

"Nonsense! There will be no restrictions. Only a butler at the doorway with a certain list in his hands." She lifted the list of unpaid bills. "Anyone on this list won't be allowed to attend. That's all."

Irene nodded. "But can you put a ball together that fast? You've only just returned."

Wendy added her concern. "And can you get the word out that fast? A threat does no good if no one knows about it."

Helaine's eyes took on a martial gleam. "I can, and I will. You'll see." Then she pinned Irene with a dark glare. "And you're coming to the ball too." She shot Wendy a glare. "Both of you."

Irene and Wendy started sputtering their objections. Irene didn't even have a ballgown. The last time she'd attended anything had been before her marriage to Nate. But Helaine refused to hear one word. She simply folded her arms across her chest and waited until her friends grew silent.

"Then it's settled. You're coming. And not dressed in black," she added with an extra glare at Irene.

"Helaine—"

Her friend ignored her, raising her voice to the upper stairs where her mother's rooms were. "Mama!" she called. "Mama, I need your help. We're going to throw a ball."

The squeal of delight ended any objection. Helaine's mother had suffered a great deal in her life. No one would take a treat away from her. Even if the treat was a ball.

"Well," said Irene as she turned to Wendy. "I guess I need a gown."

"Guess we all do, though heaven only knows how I'll get them sewed in time."

Irene set down her reticule and rolled up her sleeves. "Well, come on then. Tell me what I can do to help."

And so it was done. Irene was going to a ball.

Grant found Lord Redhill at his club. Grant wasn't a member of White's anymore. At one time he had been, though only briefly. He'd lasted about five weeks before he'd lost a bet on a pair of rats—or was it a cricket match between actual crickets?—and he'd had to let the membership lapse. No money to pay his tab, and so he'd been asked not to return. The only reason they let him in now was because he sent his card in to Robert who gestured him inside.

Robert ordered him a drink—a tepid tea—then leaned back to smile warmly. "I was just going over your last report. Amazing job you've done. Never would have thought you could turn that mill around. Not this well at least, but you've done it. I'm impressed, Grant. And I'd never thought I'd say that to you."

Grant acknowledged the statement with a shrug. He could be proud of himself too. He had been all set to be proud of himself. Until he'd found out his brother had built a damned canal that had doubled the price of the land he needed to buy back. Now he was scrambling to do the one thing he'd thought he'd never have to do: marry for money.

Maybe the widow has money, suggested his madness. *She's certainly got assets!*

"The mill's making solid money," he said, ignoring the lecherous giggles of his madness. "And the new manager seems to be holding up."

"So have you found me so I can sign the papers?" Robert leaned forward. "I have to say, I don't like you selling your share right now. Doesn't make good business sense."

Grant flashed a rather sick smile. "It doesn't, Robert. Which is why I'm not going to do it. I needed the cash to buy the land back."

"Problem?" Robert asked, his eyebrows raised.

Grant swallowed then slowly explained the details to Robert.

"Tough luck," his friend murmured. "Damn tough luck."

"It's the only luck I seem to have."

Ah quit your whining, interrupted his madness. *Good lord, you've gone boring.*

You'd rather I burned down a barn again? He shot back at his madness. Then he took a deep breath, realizing his insanity was getting the better of him. He was here with his friend, and for the first time in a very long time, he had no urgent need to read a mill tally of numbers. So he drank his tea and... he simply drank his tea.

Robert did the same, and so they remained for a good minute or two. Which was long enough for Grant to notice something close to earth-shattering. Robert was relaxed. Usually an intimidating man, Robert seemed downright casual today. He smiled easily, he wasn't sitting ramrod straight or silently fuming, and he'd just chuckled at a joke spoken at a nearby table. Robert Percy, Lord Redhill, had chuckled.

"Good God, man," Grant said with a bit of awe in his voice. "You've found it."

"What?"

"Marital bliss."

Robert's eyes actually sparkled. A slow, lazy smile appeared, and he took a happy sip of his tepid tea.

"Yes, it appears I have," he said. "In fact, I highly recommend it."

Grant stared at his friend. The man had all the luck. Sound business sense and now a happy marriage. Sadly, Grant doubted he would be so lucky in his choice of a woman, but he didn't say that. Instead, he set down his teacup with a click. "Actually, that's what I wanted to talk to you about."

Robert's eyebrows rose in surprise. "Found a woman, have you?" At least he didn't sound doubtful. More... pensive.

A widow!

"It's not like you think," Grant said with a sigh. "Lawton's put my family land into his eldest's dowry. Her name's Josephine or Megan. Don't know which."

Robert blinked. "Josephine, I think. Megan's the younger one." He leaned forward. "He refused to sell so he could make his daughter an heiress?"

Grant nodded. "I mean to marry her, but that means courting—balls and the like. So can you invite them to your ball? And me as well?"

His friend reared back. "Ball? What ball? We just got back in town yesterday."

"It's all the talk. Seems no one's allowed to attend unless they've paid their shot to your wife's dress shop. Damned clever, if you ask me."

"A ball?" Robert huffed. "I was hoping to ease her into the social whirl."

"You mean ease *you* in," Grant countered.

Robert didn't answer except to glower at his tea. Grant chuckled, pleased to see a flash of the old Robert. The one who always knew everything about business, but absolutely nothing about society. Thank God marital bliss didn't change everything. Meanwhile, he waved to the waiter. "I think Lord Redhill is about to ask for something stronger than tea."

Robert grimaced. "A brandy. What about you, Grant?"

Yes. The finest brandy Robert can afford. It's been so very long!

Grant shook his head. He hadn't touched a drop for five years. He wasn't about to change that while he still had a campaign to run, so to speak. "So will you talk to your lady wife? Put the Lawtons on your guest list?"

"And you as well, yes."

The widow's prettier.

Meanwhile, Robert curled his lip at Grant. "You have to dress the part, you know. You can't show up at my wife's first ball looking all shaggy-eared and haggard. And I won't even dignify whatever that is at your neck. Not a cravat, that's for sure. You show up like that, and Helaine will wonder what kind of friends I have."

Grant chuckled. "Too late for that. She's married you."

"There's reason to stay in a wife's good graces," Robert retorted. "So if you want your name on the guest list, you'll get a haircut and something that isn't Yorkshire wool to wear."

Grant stiffened at the insult, mild though it was. "This is the best damn wool—"

"Yes, yes. Finest in all the land. It's all I wear since you took over. But you can't dance in it. Not while it's still hot outside and not while it hangs on you like a sad sack. You've lost weight, my friend. Been working yourself to the bone, I know, but you need to loosen the purse strings. Get yourself a decent outfit for a ball."

Pretty widows like pretty gents.

Grant snorted, knowing it was true. "Well, since I don't need to save my pennies to buy back the land, it appears I must use it to dress the dandy."

"You never lacked for style before."

"I'll dress to dazzle. Promise." Once, that would have made him smile in delight. Once, he'd taken great pride in his clothing. But that had been years ago. Meanwhile, Robert grunted an acknowledgment, his mind obviously somewhere else.

"Good man. Now I've got some questions about the mill. I'm still half owner, you know, and you've made rather free with the changes."

"They made good sense and are paying off handsomely."

Robert waved for paper and pen. "Very well then, *Mr. Grant,*" he said, emphasizing the name Grant used to manage the mill. "Prove to me that you're not the biggest idiot alive."

"With pleasure," he said. Then he grabbed the pen and began to sketch on the paper. The numbers would come later. First he had to draw the cloth-making process with pictures and arrows and all manner of designs. Thankfully, Robert listened with serious attention, and eventually, he nodded with approval. It was quite a heady moment for Grant, more potent than any brandy had ever been. More potent than winning a pony at rats or crickets.

Too bad he would have to give up his newfound sense. In order to win a dowry, he'd have to go back to the frivolous ne'er do well he'd always been. The man the ladies adored, even though he had no substance to his life. But that was what happened to a man forced to court his fortune rather than earn it. He just hoped this Josephine wasn't a total disaster. But how wonderful could she be? After five seasons and no husband?

It didn't matter. He'd sworn to get the Crowle land back, and she was the means. She could have a harelip and the breath of a goat. He'd still kiss her on the day they said, "I do."

And it would all begin at Redhill's ball.

Fun again. Huzzah! crowed his madness. *But sleep with the widow first then court the girl.*

Six

GRANT DID HIS BEST NOT TO TUG AT HIS NEWLY TIED cravat. Once they had felt as natural as breathing, but it had been five years since he'd worn one arranged so elegantly. These days he often went without the thing all together.

He looked at himself in the mirror, for once seeing the changes the last five years had wrought. His baby face was lean now, almost haggard. The muscles that had once filled out his clothing were still there, but no fat softened his body. He'd lost inches everywhere, except for his height, which was above average for a man. The whole effect could be considered dashing for a scarecrow. Provided he remembered how to flirt with a wallflower—how to find that twinkle in his eyes the girls had once swooned over.

Was it even there anymore? Wasn't that a product of a bland insouciance about life? The idea that because he was titled, things would always work out? That the creditors would not come banging on his door to drag him to debtor's prison?

Of course, that had never been him completely. If

he were honest—and he'd tried for five years to be brutally honest with himself—the specter of the end had always haunted him. Juggling debts—and controlling his father—had been an exhausting process, especially as he'd maintained the air of a Titled Tom about Town. Winning had been about survival, not fun. And losing had always cut deeper because he had to pretend it meant nothing.

Oh, stubble it! You think too much. After five years, we're finally attending a party! Smile, you damned fool!

Grant frowned, wondering for perhaps the thousandth time if he were completely insane.

Of course, you are. Now go enjoy yourself!

That was it then. He was mad. Not surprising really. Only a madman or a fool would believe that five years of hard labor wouldn't change him. That he could pick up his old life as if he were putting on a favorite shirt or tying an intricate cravat. But it wasn't easy. Perhaps it wasn't even possible. After all, he'd been out of the game for five years. Could he charm a girl who'd gone five seasons without a proper offer? All he knew about her was that her name was Josephine, and she was generally considered too outspoken to make a proper bride.

That's good. Proper brides are boring!

He flashed on the delightful Mrs. Knopp. Now there was a woman! Five years ago, he wouldn't have bothered. Her general demeanor was rather dour, especially in her severe black. But now, he had some understanding of the strength it took to continue after something devastating. She'd lost a husband. He'd lost his entire lifestyle. That she'd had the fortitude to not only survive, but to work as a buyer, impressed him. She was smart too, which was fun. But what really set his heart to pounding was the way she'd relaxed into his arms as they were dancing.

Imagine what other things you could coax her to do!

He tried to resist his madness's suggestions, but some thoughts would not be denied. Her body was too stiff, but once she'd started enjoying their dance, he'd felt the suppleness that came with delight. Her body had molded to his, her eyes had widened in surprise, and her lips had gone soft and moist. After years of hard things—the bed, the factory, the ledgers—her softness against him had felt like a miracle. That it hadn't come easily to her either made the sensation all the sweeter.

You should have kissed her!

Yes, he ruefully admitted, he should have. Now that he was about to sell himself into an unwanted marriage, he wished he'd indulged himself one last time with a woman of his own choosing. He could have peeled Irene's severe black off her body. He'd bet a pony she had a body that would glow. Skin that would flush rosy pink, legs that were long and strong to grip a man, and a sweet wetness that would taste like ambrosia.

He closed his eyes, imagining the moment when he penetrated her. He'd watch her eyes widen, her lips part on a gasp, and then he would stroke her slowly. He'd build the passion with a steady thrust and grind that never failed to delight both man and woman.

There's still time to do it! Tonight, before you set to seducing the heiress.

He couldn't do that, he told his madness. He had to focus on charming Miss Josephine, the too wild heiress.

He stepped into the ballroom a half hour later. He'd walked to save money, using the time to calm his racing heart. But what had really happened was that his mind began spinning with a million possibilities and possible outcomes. So much so that when he was announced at the top of the stairs, "Lord Crowle," spoken in booming accents, the shock of unreality had him swaying slightly on his feet.

It all looked the same. The ballroom, the people, the slightly bored stares as they turned to inspect him. It felt exactly the same, as if it were still five years ago. And yet, damn, it wasn't the same! Or rather, he had changed, while the rest of the *ton* hadn't.

He descended slowly into the ballroom proper, trying to orient himself to this old landscape. With his merchant's eye, he noted the cut of fabrics, the new styles, even the details of cloth and stitching. He'd never have seen that before. But with his old eyes—the bored aristocrat's eyes—he saw the women inspect him, the men raise their eyebrows in greeting, and the elegant spread of food that would feed him this night. Fortunately, no one was shocked to see him again. He'd spent the last week visiting his old chums, such as they were, to garner invites to all the balls this season. He couldn't very well charm an heiress if he wasn't invited to the balls. And then he looked for Miss Josephine.

There!

His body suddenly jerked to a stop. He saw her. Not Lawton's daughter, but Mrs. Knopp. Except it wasn't the woman as he'd seen her before—all widows weeds and canny intelligence. No, this time she'd discarded the black. She wore *his gown*. The fabric he had designed with the flames building up from the skirt. It was stunning, especially as the seamstress had stitched gold threads throughout, giving a thousand tiny sparks to the fabric. And it brought Irene to life. Suddenly, she appeared to him as a woman mysterious, passionate, and on the verge of flaring to life.

Her black hair was pulled back into an elegant chignon, one that emphasized the length and whiteness of her neck. And between her breasts hung a single stone: a ruby, and not that large. It dangled on her white flesh, and he wondered what sound she would make if he tongued her flesh all about the stone without even touching it. Then he mentally chastised his madness for such thoughts, even though the voice had not been the one to think it.

He took two steps toward her before his mind engaged. She was not the person he was here to see. He wondered briefly how she had managed to get an invitation to the ball. At least that question was easily answered, once his brain disengaged from his lust. This was, after all, Lady Redhill's ball. And Lady Redhill was co-owner of A Lady's Favor dress shop. As Mrs. Knopp was their purchaser, it made sense that the woman would be invited to the ball.

A fortunate thing, he decided, as he worked through the crowd to her. It took longer than it should have, but a number of people hadn't seen him in five years. They all wanted to stop and ask him where he'd been. He brushed them off with the same thing he'd told everyone else: oh, here and there. Nowhere of account, doing no good at all!

They invariably laughed at that, and he swallowed the shame that he'd been working as a common laborer these last years. Robert was the rare peer who thought well of him for his sweat. Meanwhile, he finally made it to stand next to the intrepid Irene.

"Good evening, Mrs. Knopp," he said as he bowed over her hand. "Let me be the first to express how lovely you look out of black."

She smiled warmly. "Mr. Grant! Good evening!" She blushed prettily, the color tinging the flesh around her ruby. "And as for being the first," she continued, "I'm afraid you are sadly out on that. Every one of my friends has said the same thing a dozen times." She looked at her gown, her skin flushing rosier. "This cloth and the design are beyond beautiful. I feel... well, both odd and wonderful, if that makes any sense. Part of me is appalled, but the other—"

"Feels like it's a new beginning. Uncomfortable, and yet wonderful, all the same." He looked about, feeling the truth in his words.

"That's very poetic, Mr. Grant. Shall I guess? Is this perhaps your first ball?"

"Not my first, but the first in a long time. It feels like putting on an old jacket..."

"One that really doesn't fit well anymore," she finished for him.

He smiled, feeling a connection with her. "Would you like a glass of lemonade?" he asked. "We could toast to new clothing."

"I should like that very much." But when he turned to get it for her, she touched his arm. "Would it be awkward if I walked with you? I'm afraid I feel rather at loose ends here standing all alone."

"But where are your friends? It's abominable that they have left you."

She shrugged. "Well, Helaine is busy as hostess, of course. And to be honest, I have ducked away from my mother-in-law. She is so thrilled to be here that I had to escape just to breathe. That's her on the left."

Grant looked to where she gestured and saw two older women in gowns of the latest fashion. The mother-in-law in question was a rather large person, one who might have been called stately, if it weren't for her huge eyes, bursting grin, and the way she craned her neck this way and that in order to see everything. She was sitting close to a woman of the same ilk—obviously new money—and they watched everything with gleaming eyes.

"All that unbridled enthusiasm wearing upon you?" he asked.

"Exhausting. She has spoken of nothing else since she heard of the ball. I fear that the actual evening will be sadly disappointing."

"I shouldn't worry there. She seems to have found a friend."

"Mrs. Schmitz? Oh, I prevailed upon Helaine to let Mama bring her best friend. They'll be disdained completely by the *ton* as horribly bourgeois, but at least this way, they might not notice."

"And you get to escape to enjoy the party in peace?"

She smiled, and he noticed how much younger her face appeared. Her pale cheeks filled out, the hard cut to her chin softened, and her eyes sparkled. How very odd. They really did seem to twinkle as if she were a girl at her first ball—heady excitement and suppressed anxiety all in one.

"You really have had a hard time, haven't you?" he asked softly.

She blinked, obviously startled. So was he, truth be told. So to cover, he held out his arm.

"I believe we were about to walk to the lemonade."

"Um, yes, of course." She set her hand on his arm, and he smiled to feel the warmth of her hand there. Her fingers were long, her touch barely there, but he knew the strength in her hands. She was a woman who worked, carrying bolts of fabric and boxes of buttons, and he found that appealing, even as the aristocratic side of him was appalled by his own thoughts. He should not be attracted to a common laborer. And yet he was.

To cover his conflicting emotions, he began walking, skillfully moving them through the crowd while he avoided anyone he'd once known. He hadn't missed that she'd called him Mr. Grant. She didn't know he was an earl, and he was loathe to change that. The ruse wouldn't last, but he wanted to remain in a guise that gave him comfort. After all, Mr. Grant was a hardworking, responsible man. Lord Crowle was decidedly not.

She was the first to break the silence, her words tentative. "If I may be so bold, are you a particular friend of our hosts?"

He nodded. "Lord Redhill and I attended school together." She jerked slightly in surprise, so he quickly voiced a partial truth. "We have been unlikely friends for a long time. He knew I was in town and so invited me to attend."

"How fortunate for me then. I am short on acquaintances tonight, so I am grateful for your presence."

He smiled, wishing he could say the same. Everywhere he turned, there seemed to be someone he wished to avoid, simply to keep his identity secret for a moment longer. "How long have you known Lady Redhill?"

"Same as you and her husband, I suppose. We went to school together. Then when the dress shop began to prosper, she came to me and offered me the position. I was a widow by then, and time was an endless, slow tick of the clock."

"You began to work?"

"My mother-in-law was horrified, but I cannot express how wonderful it is to have something to fill my days. In truth, I'm considered terribly vulgar because I enjoy my job and do it out of desire, not necessity."

He turned to look at her, surprise widening his eyes. He couldn't imagine a woman—any woman—choosing to work. Every female—and male for that matter—applied himself to his job out of necessity. If it hadn't been for the disaster five years ago, he might still be practicing circus tricks to win bets.

The very thought made him shudder in horror now, and wasn't that a revelation? Sometime in the last five years, he'd found a disgust of his former gentlemanly life.

Good Lord, stop thinking about yourself! You've found the girl. Now seduce her!

He opened his mouth to say something. What—he

wasn't exactly sure. But in that moment of confusion, another woman intruded. She came as an announcement, spoken in the booming voice of the major domo.

"Lord and Lady Lawton and the misses Josephine and Megan Powel."

Grant's gaze jerked sideways to the top of the stairs. His heiress was here. He straightened his shoulders and gathered his wits. He needed to start his seduction before the news of Josephine's dowry made the general rounds.

Meanwhile, Mrs. Knopp withdrew her touch from his arm. "Mr. Grant?"

He blinked, abruptly jerking his attention back to her. "I'm sorry?"

"You suddenly looked very… fierce."

"Really?" he said as he tried to smooth his expression. Once it had been easy to assume a bland exterior, but he found it difficult now. "I just saw someone I need to speak with."

"An unhappy client?"

"Never." Then he shrugged. "Someone who needs my attention, that's all." And he needed to get away from the intriguing Irene Knopp. She distracted him too easily, and he shouldn't be seen with her while courting a different woman. And yet, he was loathe to abandon her.

It was folly really—just the merchant part of him clinging to a life that had become familiar. But he wasn't a mill manager anymore. He was Lord Crowle, and he needed to pursue that future, not cling to a past that had been a five-year aberration. Still, he couldn't leave her flat. That would be ungentlemanly. So he lifted Irene's dance card.

"May I beg the favor of a dance?"

She flushed as she showed him her card. It was extremely thin of names. Just two: Lord Redhill, and his brother, Baronet Murray.

Excellent, you can be the hero. Take a waltz. Take two!

Grant hesitated, then hastily scribbled "Mr. Grant" beside two country-dances. He couldn't let her be a wallflower on her first ball out of mourning, but he couldn't very well claim the waltzes either. Not if he were to catch Miss Josephine.

Better hope she forgives you when she finds out you're Lord Crowle.

He grimaced, horrified at that thought. But there was no changing it now. So he focused on the next step. He grabbed lemonade for her then escorted her back to her mother-in-law. A quick bow later, and he was off to catch an heiress.

It took him a while to make it to Miss Josephine's side. First he had to wait until Lord Lawton had been pulled into a discussion with some friends. Lawton's dismissal of him two weeks ago still rang in his ears. Then he had to wait even longer for her mother to be distracted before he approached the surprisingly lovely girl.

And as he waited, that strange sense of destiny gathered around him again. It was yet another bizarre happenstance, especially as he hadn't felt it in years. But it was there—just as it had been on the night he'd burned down the barn. Back then he'd thought it was luck, not even considering the idea that it might be *bad* luck. This evening, he was not so blithe. That his madness remained stubbornly silent caused his belly to tighten. It was imperative that he dazzle the girl. And when they were wed, he would finally be able to hold his head up before his family and his ancestors. He would finally feel worthy of his title.

The moment arrived. He had a friend ready to perform the introduction. He and Mr. Scott Klein stepped forward and bowed over her hand, Scott speaking just as he ought.

"Forgive me, Miss Josephine, but my dear friend has been pestering me for a week now to gain an introduction to you. Miss Josephine, may I introduce you to Grant Benton, Lord Crowle."

The woman cried out in surprise, the sound a little more loud than proper. Then she laughed. "Lord Crowle! But there was no need for a formal introduction. We are, after all, about to be related."

Grant frowned, his insides freezing. "I'm sorry?" he managed.

She sobered, a frown of confusion on her face as she brought up her left hand to cover his. There, clear as day on the fourth finger of her gloved hand, was an engagement ring. Why hadn't he seen that before? True, it was rather small, but somewhere in his fuddled brain, he recognized it.

"No, I'm sorry," she countered. "I thought you knew. But then Will said you've been gone for five years, and he had no way to contact you."

Will? As in his *brother* Will? His mouth was dry, his throat tight, but he still managed to speak. "I don't understand."

She grinned, happiness shining through her eyes. "I'm engaged, Lord Crowle. I'm to marry Will, your brother."

Will? As in Will, the second Crowle son, was to marry the heiress? His younger brother would gain all the profitable Crowle land? That was excellent. At least a Crowle would have the land. But... but Grant was the heir. And without that land, he would have nothing but a crumbling castle to support his title.

"I can see this comes as a surprise," drawled a male voice behind him.

Grant spun around to face Lord Lawton. Finally the pieces fell into place. Lawton had called him a feckless Crowle. Lawton had said the land would never go to him. And Lawton had said he would beat Grant senseless if he caused a scene at the *wedding*.

Oh, drawled his madness. *That wedding! The one where your brother gets everything, and you get nothing.*

"Papa, be nice," admonished the blushing bride. "We are to be related, after all."

"Don't distress yourself, Miss Powel," Grant pressed through numb lips. "Your father and I understand each other very well. I couldn't be happier." At least he hadn't choked on the lie. After all, he'd been lying for five years now, pretending to be something other than the unlucky, doomed Lord Crowle. "I came to offer my felicitations. Welcome to the family."

Then he endured a few more awkward moments of gushing happiness from the bride before he escaped. He walked blindly through the ballroom crowd, not stopping for anyone or anything. But a few moments later, he realized he had indeed been heading somewhere.

He'd been heading for a footman. Robert, after all, had an excellent bar.

Seven

IRENE WATCHED MR. GRANT LEAVE THE BALLROOM with a sickening disappointment. She knew from experience years ago with her father that once a man went into the card room, he would not emerge for the rest of the ball. Time disappeared for a man while gambling. And the free-flowing liquor did nothing to help them keep promises, no matter how heartfelt they were when uttered. She might as well scratch his name off her dance card because he would not remember to claim them.

She didn't. She thought about it, but then hope whispered traitorous words into her heart. Perhaps Mr. Grant was different. Perhaps it was only aristocrats who were gamblers and fools.

Fortunately, a new arrival distracted her completely from her own dark thoughts. At the top of the stairs, Penny Shoemaker and her new fiancé Samuel entered with Wendy stepping in behind. Penny looked lovely, of course, and Samuel had managed to keep his cravat on straight. Well, he did for a moment, but as he descended the stairs, a self-conscious tug had it out of place. But that was nothing compared to the sensation of seeing Wendy fully revealed before she too descended the staircase.

My God, she was stunning. Her honey brown hair was pulled up in a topknot, her elfin face lifted in a quiet challenge that made her look regal, and her dress—sweet heaven that dress!I It was the most amazing creation she'd ever seen. An emerald green silk so shimmery rich, Wendy appeared a living gem. There was little decoration on it. It had likely been sewn quickly and only for this party. But it didn't need adornment. The color was beautiful, and the body it sheathed was beyond amazing. Irene felt a little flash of guilt that she hadn't realized how beautiful Wendy was. The little seamstress had always appeared hunched, always working, her brow furrowed in lines of strain.

At this particular moment, Wendy could have been a duchess. And Irene wasn't the only person to notice. All around her people turned their heads—men and women alike—and every mouth whispered, who is she? What is her name?

While Lord Redhill greeted Samuel, Helaine went directly to Wendy. There was no disguising the warmth with which the two women embraced. Irene saw the first flash of uncertainty cross Wendy's face. The girl bit her lip, and she squeezed tight enough to crinkle Helaine's dress.

Without even thinking about it, Irene crossed the ballroom floor. These were her best friends in the world: Helaine, Penny, and Wendy. And she was welcomed into their circle with enthusiastic grins.

"I cannot believe how beautiful you look," breathed Penny as she stared at Wendy.

"Not just me," Wendy said as she tugged awkwardly at her bodice.

"Don't fuss," Helaine said with a laugh, but her slap was sharp on Wendy's hand. "It messes with the line."

Then they all laughed because Wendy had said—and done—exactly that to every client at one time or another. Meanwhile, Wendy looked about her uneasily. "I shouldn't be here. I am not one of you."

"You are my dearest friend," returned Helaine. "You will always be the first person on my guest list, and if you do not belong here, then everyone else should leave."

"But—"

"No more, Wendy! You are here. There are men lining up to meet you. And I shall make it my mission in life to introduce you to the best and most eligible bachelors of the land."

"Indeed," agreed Helaine's husband from the side. "Cinderella has arrived. So who will be your Prince Charming?"

"No—" whispered Wendy, and Irene saw panic growing in her expression. So she stepped forward, reaching out between Penny and Helaine to touch Wendy's hand.

"Stay with me, Wendy. We shall be wallflowers together, you and I."

"I doubt she'll lack for partners," drawled Samuel, his eyes narrowing on the men who were angling for an introduction.

"Shhhh!" hissed Penny. "She's nervous enough. But don't you worry. We shan't leave your side."

"But—" began Samuel, his expression adamant. "Just look at the men." That was the logical side of the Bow Street Runner coming out, insistent on the facts rather than the emotional subtleties.

Penny rolled her eyes as she pulled Samuel to the side. Meanwhile, Irene took hold of Wendy's gloved hand, startled to find that the girl was trembling. "It will be all right. I will introduce you, and everything will be fine."

Wendy didn't answer. Instead, she closed her eyes a moment, took a deep breath, and squared her shoulders.

"Good girl," whispered Lord Redhill in approval. "Lady Irene will keep you safe." Then he touched his wife's arm. "Come along Helaine. We have more guests to greet."

Helaine left reluctantly. With Penny and Samuel still deep in discussion in a corner, Irene was left as Wendy's sole guide through the crowd. She headed steadily to her mother-in-law and Mrs. Schmitz. The two women would be thrilled to keep an eye on Wendy.

"Where did you find that silk?" Irene asked as they walked. "I didn't buy it, but I sure would like to get—"

"Don't know," Wendy interrupted. "It was a gift."

"Goodness! From whom?"

"I..." Wendy blushed. "I..."

She didn't want to say. Irene watched as fear, confusion, excitement, and perhaps a little lust, filtered across the seamstress's face. All of that emotion clogged the mind and colored her skin pink.

"It's all right," Irene said. She remembered being just as confused when Nate had started courting her years ago. "You needn't talk now, if you don't want to. Just know that I can be a discreet ear if you need one."

"Thank you," Wendy breathed, gratitude in her eyes. Then they arrived at their spot on the floor, and the men started crowding around. Fortunately, Samuel and Penny joined them a moment later, and as fortune would have it, Samuel was known to most of the hovering men. Which meant they could finally gain a proper introduction to Wendy. En masse, they stepped forward with cries of greeting to Samuel.

"Morrison, dear man!"

"Good to see you, Samuel!"

"Wonder if I could prevail upon you, ole chap—"

"Introduce me to your lovely companions."

So it began. Samuel, with his ears red and his cravat decidedly askew, was pressed into service to introduce more than two-dozen gentlemen to the ladies at large. He did his duty exceptionally well, using everyone's correct titles, including Irene's as Lady Irene. And then, by way of a nod of approval or a disapproving tightening of his lips, he let everyone know his opinion of the gentleman in question.

The most diligent chaperone could do no better. And very soon, everyone's dance card was filled. Even Irene's mother-in-law and Mrs. Schmitz were prevailed upon for a couple of the more sedate country-dances. Which meant that as first balls went, this was absolutely beyond her wildest dreams.

Irene danced. She laughed. She even flirted, while beside her Wendy seemed flushed and happy as well.

Then came the country-dance with Mr. Grant's name upon it. She looked around hopefully, but as she'd expected, he was nowhere in sight.

She tried to suppress her disappointment, but she couldn't. It buried her in a wave of sadness well out of proportion to what had occurred. A gentleman had forgotten their dance. That was nothing unusual and certainly not a hanging offense. She was grateful for the respite in any event. Didn't her feet hurt? She grabbed a cup of lemonade from one of Wendy's admirers and drank it down.

That's when she saw him. He all but stumbled out of the card room, his eyes hooded, his gaze dangerous. That was the word that flitted through her mind: dangerous. And he was headed straight for her.

She watched his progress across the ballroom. She noted that his hair was wild, as if he had been running his hand through it over and over, without even being aware. His cravat had the uneven look of a man who had tugged at it then tried to right it afterwards. But what she saw the most was the way his body moved. As Mr. Grant, he had been charming, seductive, and even a little bit fun. He had coaxed her into dancing with him, tempted her into buying his wares, and charmed her into thinking him a friend.

This man who crossed the ballroom wasn't Mr. Grant. No, he was a man with a dark madness inside. She knew the symptoms and had seen them in her father often enough. And like a fool, she could not look away.

He was stopped multiple times as he wended his way across the ballroom. She saw him grimace more than once at the interruption, though his eyes remained locked on hers. The thrust of his chin, the force of his step, and the dark need in his eyes—all created a cage around her body and her mind. It was ridiculous. She was a strong, mature woman, but she was helpless as he stalked steadily, carefully, inevitably across the room.

"Lady Irene, I believe this is our dance," came a man's voice from her side.

Irene blinked, brought back to herself almost painfully. "What?" she said as she turned to a young man at her side. Mr. Palmer.

"Our dance, I believe," he said.

"Oh yes. Of course." She dredged up a smile and willed herself not to look back at Mr. Grant. She almost succeeded. But as she took up position for the dance, he finally made it to the point directly across from her. Then he stood there, like a dark force, and he watched her dance. She tried to ignore him. After all, it wasn't her fault he'd missed his chance to partner her. But every time she turned, every shift in position, had her eyes inevitably drawn to his.

This was ridiculous, and it made her angry. At herself and at him. By the end of the dance, she had worked herself up so much that she snubbed him as she walked by. He held out his hand, he gestured to her, but she blithely walked by. It was unfair to him. He was clearly trying to apologize. But she did not like his hold on her, and so she stepped right past him and gave her most brilliant smile to her next partner.

That strategy worked for a time. After all, her dance card was filled. But she had forgotten about his second slot on her card. And worse, it was the dance before the midnight buffet. He would expect to take her to supper, most likely. She had not promised her hand to anyone else, and so she would be stuck.

She was still deciding what to do when he stepped up to claim her hand for his dance. She turned, her heart pounding in her chest so much she wondered if she would be able to hear his voice. Apparently she could, especially as she watched his mouth shape each phrase.

"I am a cad," he said. "You have every right to be angry."

She lifted her chin, but her eyes remained locked on the shape of his lips. They were somewhat full, she realized. Not thin or tight as with so many men, and she decided she liked it. "I'm not angry," she lied. Then when his eyebrows rose, she huffed out a sigh. "Very well, I admit it. I prefer a man who keeps appointments."

"But I did keep it," he said. "I was just tardy. Much as you were some days ago."

She frowned then abruptly flushed. She had been so absorbed in the ball, so strangely caught up in the life she'd never had as a feted debutante, that she'd forgotten how a man could be delayed. People made mistakes. And only a shrew would be angry that he had missed a dance.

"I—I beg your pardon," she stammered.

He caught her hand. "No, it is I who am behaving badly. *Again*. We are at a ball, and I should not have made reference to…" His voice trailed away, and he appeared acutely uncomfortable.

"To an association outside of a party? But Mr.

Grant, I am not ashamed of my job. Anyone can know of it."

Of course, almost no one did. They thought of her as Lady Irene, school friend of the new Lady Redhill. And if they really pressed, they thought of her as chaperone to Miss Wendy Drew, the stunningly beautiful woman who was stepping onto the dance floor with her latest partner.

"The set is forming. Shall we?" Mr. Grant asked.

She placed her fingertips to his. "Of course."

He took much more of her hand that she expected. His hand was large and powerful, and her long fingers felt engulfed by his strength. After spending the evening dancing with dandies who used their hands simply to hold their horses' reins or lift a drink, she appreciated a man who labored. Who seemed as if he could hold her up with just one hand should she stumble.

She liked that in a man, and she felt her anger melt as they formed the pattern of the dance. They moved easily enough. She had recalled the motions after the first hour of dancing, but he seemed to dance as though it was second nature—very odd in a fabric salesman. Even more unnerving was the way he watched her through the entire pattern, completely ignoring whomever danced opposite him.

"You are amazingly athletic," she said as the dance pulled them together. "You must have practiced this."

"I danced with my mother," he said simply, his gaze canting away for the first time since he'd left the card room.

"Not this," she countered. "This cannot be done with just two."

He flashed her a smile. "Most perceptive. But there was also my brother and sister." His voice broke slightly on the word "brother," but it may simply have been because the air was dry. At least her mouth felt incredibly dry.

They moved apart again, and her hand felt weirdly empty until she was brought back to him. Ridiculous, and yet, the impression was so strong. In the end, the next step was inevitable. As the dance came to its end, he smiled.

"Please, will you join me for the supper buffet? Allow me to apologize for being tardy on the dance floor?"

"Of course, I will," she said with a gracious smile. Because of all things, she had been taught to be gracious when a man offered to apologize. After all, it happened so rarely.

They gathered up Wendy and her partner. Her mother-in-law waved her ahead, obviously wishing to discuss something in detail with Mrs. Schmidt. So the four spent a happy mealtime discussing everything inconsequential from the weather to the musicians. Soon Mr. Grant had them laughing at a silly story. He was speaking of a carriage race that had happened many years back. It was the kind of story that was hysterically funny, unless one thought about the dangers to horse and driver, not to mention any hapless stranger on the road. She laughed along with everyone else, but the note cut at her mood.

He caught her eye then, and not wanting to spread her ill humor, she smiled. But he must have seen her hesitation. He must have understood that something was amiss because he frowned back at her. Or rather, he frowned, not at her, but at himself as he clearly began thinking hard.

But then the meal was over, the musicians were tuning their instruments again, and Wendy was laughing into the eyes of her gentleman. For her part, Irene was feeling her joy return. Just seeing Wendy so happy erased any uncomfortable moments. The woman was usually so tense, always stitching or mysteriously absent. Every one had noted the dark circles under her eyes. And yet right here, she was smiling, her eyes sparkling, and the lines of care that usually pinched her brows beautifully gone.

Disaster struck in an instant. It was so fast that Irene didn't even see it happen. A man appeared. A gentleman she didn't know, but that meant very little. She scarcely knew any of the men in society. But he slipped in beside Wendy and took her hand. She turned, laughing because of something Mr. Grant had said, and then suddenly her body went rigid.

Beside her, the gentleman's expression turned to glee. "I knew it," he crowed. "I would know you if you wore sackcloth."

Wendy stood there, her mouth slowly gaping open while the blood drained from her face. For a woman who always had a tart answer ready, something was clearly wrong. Without even knowing what was going on, Irene stepped forward and firmly disengaged the man from Wendy's side.

"I'm terribly sorry, sir, but I'm afraid we haven't been introduced."

"Oh, my name isn't important. It's Miss Drew's that is so very interesting."

"Miss Drew *is* her name, and it is completely unexceptional," Irene snapped. "Good evening."

With that, she walked away, pulling Wendy along. The girl moved woodenly, all her earlier animation gone. Behind them, Mr. Grant had taken up a position to block the impertinent man's approach. Irene felt reassured with him there, so solid behind them.

"I shouldn't have come," whispered Wendy. "I knew it was wrong."

"Of course, it wasn't wrong," Irene said. "But there is clearly something at fault here. Who was that man?"

Wendy shook her head. "I don't even remember. That's the horrible part. I don't remember."

Irene aimed them straight to the ladies' retiring room. Sadly, as it was just after supper, there were a host of women, and all were gossiping. Irene wanted to change course, but they'd already stepped inside. So with a significant look at Wendy—one that said their discussion wasn't over yet—both ladies set about fixing their hair. And they listened to the gossip with a rather distracted air.

It was nothing they hadn't expected. After all, this was Helaine's first ball as Lady Redhill. This was also her first time in society after her true identity was revealed. She was not actually Mrs. Mortimer, dress designer extraordinaire at A Lady's Favor dress salon. She was Lady Helaine, the daughter of the *Thief of the Ton*. And the biddies—young and old—were ready to crucify her for that fact.

Or so it seemed by the murmured talk in the retiring room. Irene absolutely hated that these women could come to Helaine's ball, eat from her table, and enjoy her hospitality, while simultaneously damning the woman for being common. It was ridiculous, and she burned to give them all a piece of her mind.

Sadly, she knew that any amount of argument added fuel to the flame. Besides, Helaine could defend herself, especially with the powerful Lord Redhill as her husband. Wendy was the one who needed her attention right now. The girl was still pale and shaking.

"Come along, Wendy," she said, pitching her voice to a clutch of shrews. "The air is foul in here. Poisoned by people who know nothing of life because they have never done anything of worth."

Wendy gasped at her words, though there was a gleam of delight in her eyes. Irene was a little startled herself. After all, if things had gone how she'd wished so many years ago, she would have been one of those girls. Titled, pampered, and firmly settled in the belief that such things made her a woman able to judge other people. What a shock it was—albeit a small one—to discover how wrong her entire childhood education had been.

In any event, they were out of the room now. She had perhaps twenty seconds of privacy in which to grill the quiet Wendy. Irene seized it with both hands.

"Out with it, my girl. What is going on?"

Wendy shook her head. "I cannot say. Not here." She looked around. "I can leave, can't I? I've stayed long enough that it won't reflect badly on Helaine?"

Irene grimaced. Trust Wendy to be worried about Helaine when clearly she was the one feeling threatened. "Yes, of course you can leave now. It's perfectly acceptable—"

"I'll go then. Thank you, Irene. Thank you for helping."

"But Wendy—"

"I'll tell you everything later. Maybe tomorrow. But I must go now." And with that, she rushed for the door. Not so fast as to draw attention, but quickly enough that Irene would have to run to catch up. And that, of course, *would* draw attention. She gathered her skirts, planning on making an attempt, when Mr. Grant appeared at her elbow.

"Let her go," he said softly.

"What? But she's—"

"Safest out of here. Come along. I had a discussion with the rude Mr. Marris. If you would care to walk with me…"

She nodded, her eyes narrowing as she watched Wendy top the staircase on her way out the door. "I should see that she gets home safely."

Mr. Grant saw the direction of her gaze. "I'll see that she gets into a hackney. She likely walked here."

Irene nodded, knowing it was true. "And I'll tell mama that she's taken ill and that I'm seeing her home."

"Excellent. I'll call for your wrap and meet you at the door."

"Done." Then just before they separated, she grabbed his arm. "You promise to tell me everything you've learned?"

He flashed her a grin. "Of course." Just for a moment, she saw the darkness in him again, the predator that drove him. It sparked a shiver of excitement down her spine—part fear, part attraction, and wholly inappropriate. It was what she felt when entering a difficult negotiation. It was the life that roused her from her bed every morning and filled her days with excitement. And here it was with him, except they were likely going to negotiate something a great deal more important than simple money.

"Very well," she said, a smile tugging at her lips. "I'll meet you at the door."

Eight

IT WAS A STRUGGLE TO KEEP THE GORGEOUS SEAMSTRESS from fleeing, but Grant managed to delay her. She was twitching in her anxiety, but apparently felt better once her cloak was about her shoulders, the hood covering nearly her entire face.

"You don't want to be seen," he said in a low voice. "I understand. But rushing away will draw more attention than a leisurely stroll away from a ball."

She nodded, showing that she'd heard him, and to his relief, her anxiety eased. Then Grant was pleased to see Irene join them. He took a moment to help her with her own cloak, settling the heavy black fabric about her shoulders.

More black. Blech.

For once Grant agreed with his madness. It was a crime to cover her beauty with such dreariness, but this wasn't the time to discuss her attire. Then with a lady on each arm, he headed toward the street.

"Shall I call a hackney?" he asked.

Irene hesitated, her gaze on the seamstress who

adamantly shook her head. "I don't want the expense," she said. "It's a short walk to the shop."

Beside him, Irene gasped. "Surely you're not going to work now!"

Miss Drew stuck out her chin. "We've got orders coming in. More'n I can handle. And if the nobs won't pay their shot, then I've got to finish the orders for those that will."

"Wendy," Irene said with a sigh. "You're upset and frightened. If you could tell us—"

"I need payment, that's all. We all do!"

"But—" Irene began.

Grant forestalled an argument by walking faster. The ladies followed suit. They were headed toward the dress shop, which probably represented a place of safety for the seamstress. Meanwhile, Wendy was getting herself under control, speaking as much to herself as to the others.

"Helaine's plan has worked. Most have paid. We've got money now or will have soon. Then everything will be all right."

Grant nodded and made sure to keep his voice gentle. "To pay off Demon Damon?" he asked. "Is that why you're working for him?"

Both ladies stiffened at his words, but it was Wendy's reaction that was the most telltale. While Irene just gasped, "What?" Wendy pulled back and looked around guiltily.

Then she opened her mouth—likely to deny it—but Grant didn't give her the chance. "I spoke with Mr. Marris, that man who said he knew you."

She nodded. "Is that his name? He's sat at my table, but I don't ask their names so they won't ask mine."

"Your table?" Grant pushed. "Cards or dice?"

"Cards. *Vingt-et-un* most of the time, but sometimes, Damon has me sit at the hazard table. Taking bets mostly, but usually just…"

"Distracting?"

She swallowed and nodded. "And making sure they keep drinking."

That made sense. A smart girl like Wendy, especially with her body, would be a potent attraction at a gambling den.

Meanwhile, Irene was struggling with this new information. "Why would you do that, Wendy? Doesn't the shop earn enough?"

"It earns plenty!" she shot back. "Even without the nobs paying, I have enough. It's just…" She sighed. "Bernard." She said the name like it was a heavy weight.

"Your brother?" Irene asked.

Grant all but groaned. That was a losing game for sure—a sister paying a brother's debts. He made a mental note to visit this Bernard and explain that a man's responsibilities were to protect his sibling, not expose her to huge risks.

Then he turned those words to his life and flinched. After all, he'd failed to protect either his sister or younger brother. Meanwhile, Wendy was spilling a secret she'd obviously been keeping much too long.

"Bernard got in the wrong at the gambling house. They were going to kill him, and I didn't have enough—not by far—so…"

It seemed she didn't want to continue, so Grant picked up the tale, his guesses easy because he knew how a man like Damon thought. In truth, he'd nearly fallen afoul of the man years ago and only luck had kept him safe.

"So Damon smiled sweetly at you and offered you both a deal. You could work off your brother's debt as a dealer."

"Bernard works too! He mans the door and watches for trouble. He's big, you see. Much bigger than I am, and he can throw a man across a room if need be."

"And how much longer before you clear his debt?"

"By dealing cards alone?" the woman scoffed. "Years."

Irene spoke up, proving that she understood the situation completely. "But if you get the money from the dress shop—everything owed—then how long will it take?"

A martial light entered Wendy's eyes. "As soon as we're paid, I'll pay off the Demon."

Grant nodded. That was good. Unless…"How sure are you that Bernard hasn't been racking up more debt? How sure—"

"Because I told him I'd skin him alive if he did it again," said Wendy. "No more gambling. If he so much as touches dice or cards, I'll cut off his hands."

She looked like she'd do it too, and Grant smiled in approval. Sadly, such threats didn't always work on gamblers. "If you give me his address, I can have a word with him. If you like, I can make sure—"

"I've got Bernard under control," she interrupted, her voice steady. "And the Demon."

"*No one* controls the Demon. Don't fool yourself."

She sighed, crossing her arms tight to her chest. "You don't think Mr. Marris will talk, do you? It won't harm Helaine, will it?"

Grant was silent, his gaze catching Irene's. Anything was possible with the *ton*. Any rumor could destroy or enhance a reputation. It was all in the telling and the fickle whims of the *ton*. And he could see the same understanding in her eyes.

Meanwhile, Irene pulled Wendy into a quick hug. "It shouldn't be a problem. We'll keep an ear out for news, and in the meantime, just do our jobs. After all, Helaine and the shop are already notorious. A salacious rumor about the seamstress might bring in more business."

It could, thought Grant grimly. Or it could tip the scales and make the *ton* flee the shop like rats from a sinking ship. Either way, there was little they could do about it now.

"I spoke harshly with Mr. Marris. No need to worry about him for the moment. But you must end things with the Demon. Right away."

Wendy swallowed as they finally made it to the front of the shop. "I know. I will."

"I could go with you when—"

"Other gents make him tetchy," she interrupted. "I can handle him myself."

"But—"

"Thank you, sir. But no."

He had no choice but to agree. She did not want him there, and he could not force her, though a shared look with Irene told him she was likewise worried.

"Perhaps I—" began Irene.

This time he was the one who jolted, his words snapping out before he could think how it sounded. "Absolutely not! The Demon would not hesitate to reel you in as well. One woman on his hook is enough." Irene opened her mouth—mostly in shock at his sharp words—but he didn't allow her to speak as he pressed his card into Wendy's hand. "Let me come along. Let me speak to Bernard. Let me help in some way, but do not—"

"I will not be bringing in any of the other women," Wendy said firmly. "I don't like the way he looks at them. And the way he talks is even worse—very sweet and sly. I don't like it."

Well, at least she understood that much. "Contact me. I will go with you."

She nodded slowly and under his steady gaze, she tucked his card into her glove. It wasn't an agreement, but she was at least thinking about it. Though, truth be told, he wasn't entirely sure what he could do to help. If Demon Damon wanted to cause trouble, the bastard had any number of armed brutes around to do it. And one man or one woman could do little but surrender. Still, he was willing to try. And hopefully, she was willing to let him.

Meanwhile, she opened the shop door.

"Wouldn't you prefer to go home?" pressed Irene.

Wendy visibly shuddered. "No," she said. "I have work to do here. There's Penny's brother and Tabitha upstairs. I'll be safe."

By implication, she meant safer here than at home. He did not like the sound of that. But she was a stubborn woman, and one glance at Irene told him she understood that as well. So together, they gave in to Wendy's wishes. He went inside the shop first to make sure everything was as it should be. And how bizarre that he was doing the same prowl here—in a dress shop—that he'd done for nearly five years at the mill.

Everything was fine. The workroom was empty. Upstairs in the living quarters, the child—presumably Penny's brother—was asleep, as was the girl Tabitha with a pile of half-stitched fabric on her lap. Wendy gathered up the soon-to-be dress with a grimace.

"I'll just finish this," she said as they all went back to the workroom.

There was nothing left to say except good-bye. And while Irene was giving her friend an earnest hug, Grant took the time to look about the workroom. He had enough experience now to read the chaos of a business in a quick assessing glance. What he saw impressed him. There were receipts and orders, compiled on a desk, and clear stations throughout the room. Everyone appeared to have their area and their tasks, all nicely organized, if not exactly neat. It was the sign of a thriving business, and he was inordinately pleased. Especially since he saw fabric from his own mill already in process for numerous items.

Then it was time to go. He and Irene stepped outside, and Grant started looking for a hackney. "I'm afraid there aren't many cabs in this area of London right now."

"No, no," she said. "I'd rather walk anyway. Though it is rather far."

He held back his laugh. There was nothing that far away in fashionable London. She told him her address, and they headed toward a very expensive neighborhood.

"That's not far at all, Mrs. Knopp," he said. Her name sounded awkward on his tongue, especially since he'd been calling her "Irene" in his thoughts since their first dance nearly two weeks ago.

"Please, you must call me Irene. And I shall be glad of your escort, Mr. Grant."

So she hadn't heard his real title yet, and right then, he was faced with a decision. Did he tell her the truth? He really didn't want to. He had no wish to expose that he was "that feckless Crowle," and so he simply shrugged.

"Please, just call me Grant. It's how all my friends refer to me."

"Grant?" she asked. "But isn't that rather rude?"

"Not if I specifically request you to."

She gave him a curious look, but didn't press. In the meantime, they began walking, her hand on his arm. It was a lovely night, the summer heat giving way to autumn crispness. The cooler temperatures were welcome, especially in the city, and Grant found himself feeling again the rhythms of a city he'd left five years ago.

"I'd forgotten how nice London can be in the evening."

She smiled. "The city does have its charms. Do you get here often? Or do you spend most of your time in Yorkshire?"

"Yorkshire," he answered firmly. "But that's changing. I've just hired a new manager, and I need to let him have his head for a bit."

Her eyes widened in surprise. "You *own* the mill?"

He smiled. "Partially. Lord Redhill and I bought it—"

"Oh my God!" she gasped. "You're Lord Crowle! Grant Jonathan Benton, Earl of Crowle!"

He blanched, caught flat-footed. All he could manage was a strangled, "Uh—"

"Good lord, I'm such a fool!" she continued. "I should have realized earlier, what with you coming to the party and all. And everyone stopping you." She shook her head at her own stupidity. "And you've been missing for five years. Five years! You were running the mill. Of course!"

He gaped at her, impressed. How could she know all that? She must have seen his expression. She must have because she tilted back on her heels and crossed her arms.

"You didn't think I'd do business with you without a thorough investigation, did you? I don't just meet anyone in a London inn. And I certainly don't buy goods without learning everything I can about the factory."

Finally, he was able to gather his wits enough to speak. "You are an unusually perceptive woman."

She snorted. "An unusually perceptive woman would have figured this out before meeting you in the inn."

"I assure you. You are the only purchaser to know my real identity." Then he took a deep breath. "I apologize for deceiving you. It's usually easier to do business without a title muddying the waters." Especially a title as murky as his own.

She waved that away and resumed walking. "No, no, I understand why you did it. I don't advertise that I'm a woman. I can't hide that as easily."

He didn't have an answer, and so they walked quietly for a time. Their steps were easy, the night pleasant. And before long, he began to relax again. He was unaccountably reassured that she understood his choices, and better yet, she hadn't heard of his reputation.

In a world of setbacks, that was like a breath of clean air. Suddenly, his step was lighter, the air was sweeter, and he believed that good things waited around the corner. He felt his luck gathering again. He knew better than to trust it, but it was a sweet sensation nonetheless.

"Actually," she said, interrupting his thoughts. "There is something I need to confess as well."

He turned, seeing the chagrin on her face. It was rather adorable, really. Her white skin flushed rosy, and her lips plumped as she bit the lower one. Her chin was down slightly, so she was forced to look up in coy embarrassment. On another woman, he would have found the expression too manipulative. But he had spent time with her now. Such games were not her usual method of operating, so for her to look so gamin now became endearing.

"You have me breathless with anticipation."

She flashed him a rueful look and then opened her mouth to speak. But the words never came out as from somewhere behind Grant, a man's growl roared out. It was an angry sound, harsh and guttural in the evening air.

Grant moved by instinct, shifting to face the sound, while simultaneously shoving Irene behind him. That quick reaction was the only thing that saved her life. But somewhere between the attack and the defense came something else: the hot flash of pain.

Bloody hell, he'd been cut.

Nine

IT ALL HAPPENED SO FAST, BUT EVEN AS IT WAS GOING
on, Irene's mind grappled with each and every second,
repeating it over and over in her head, and all with
exclamation points.

Someone had growled!

That someone had a knife!

He was attacking!

Grant and the man were fighting!

Grant was *bleeding*!

She didn't know what mobilized her into action.
Heaven knew she stood there in shock for long
enough. Perhaps it was the sight of blood that finally
pushed her out of her frozen state. Or maybe enough
time passed for her to gather her wits. Either way, she
would not stand idly by as the two men fought.

The first thing she did was scream—loud and long.
But they weren't in her neighborhood yet. They'd
been walking along a street of shops, all of which were
closed for the evening.

Meanwhile, she tried to figure out what to do. The
men were grappling, rolling on the ground as they fought

one another. If they would only slow down a little, she could kick their attacker. Or grab him. Something!

But they didn't stop, and so she just waded in. She couldn't allow Grant to risk his life while she stood by and screamed. So she stepped closer, feeling the impact on her leg as they fell against her.

It was a heavy impact. Probably because Grant had been rolling so that he would end up on top. But she'd stopped that plan, so it was up to her to fix it. She leaned down, grabbing the attacker. She saw now that he was a smallish man, grizzled and wiry. Her fingers tore through his thin clothing as she took hold.

She hauled upward, trying to lift him off Grant, but his shirt gave way. He fell out of her hands, and she saw him swipe at her legs. Her skirt caught the weapon and his hand, but not for long. While she cried out in alarm, Grant was able to maneuver into a better position.

But it was too late. Their attacker rolled to his feet and ran before she could do more than reach out her hand to stop him. With a curse, Grant was on his feet and three steps down the street after the man. But then he stopped and spun back.

"Are you all right?"

"I'm fine." She was looking down at the long tear in her skirt. Her beautiful gown made from the material he'd given her. She hadn't been touched. No blood. No pain. And yet, she couldn't stop staring at the gaping hole.

A breath later, Grant was at her side. His hands were gentle as he stroked her arm and ran his hands down her shoulders before efficiently checking her legs. "Are you sure?" he asked, his voice thick. "Is there any pain?"

"I'm fine," she repeated, feeling his hands, large and reassuring on her body. There was nothing sexual in his touch. Just a calm that helped bolster her scattered thoughts. Then she remembered the blood. His blood!

"But you're hurt! I saw the blood!"

He frowned then looked down. There was a dark streak across his shirt—blood—and the patch was growing. He cursed, the word explosive as he held out his torn jacket. The blade had split it neatly from mid-torso out toward the buttons. "I just bought this!"

She might have laughed if her hands weren't already touching the wet fabric of his equally torn shirt. He hissed in pain.

"Sorry," she murmured. "We need to get you a doctor. My home is a few more blocks—"

He shook his head. "My rooms. An inn. Half a block that way."

She nodded, coming to a swift decision. "Lead on," she said as she tried to support him to stand. He couldn't quite reach his full height, but stooped alarmingly due to his injured rib.

"But..." He winced as they started to walk. "Your reputation—"

"No one will know. I told Mama I might stay the night with Wendy. Your inn is closer, and we can send for the constable and doctor from there." Besides, much as she loved her in-laws, Mama adored the drama of anything unusual. Irene didn't feel strong enough to face the woman while still shaking from the encounter.

"I should see you home, but I'm afraid this burns dreadfully." Then he shot her a rather piercing look. "Are you sure you're all right?"

"I'm fine. But…" Her gaze darted about the dark street as she pressed him to walk more quickly. "I want to be inside."

He speeded up. "It's safe," he said, his tone bracing. "The man fled. I doubt he'll be back."

She guessed that he was reassuring himself as much as her. "No need to be gallant, my lord—"

"Grant," he pushed out, his tone curt. "If you start 'my lording' me, I swear I shall collapse right here."

She searched his face, momentarily alarmed. He looked at her, then flashed a rueful smile.

"A jest, Irene. I'm in no danger of losing consciousness, I swear. But when I shed blood in defense of a lady, I do like her to call me by my Christian name. Call it a foible."

"I agree. I'm afraid I shall struggle to remember you as Lord Crowle in any case. You shall always be Mr. Grant in my mind."

He seemed to think about that a moment, then shrugged. "A rose by any other name…" he drawled, clearly referring to the Shakespearian line.

"Well," she teased, "I shall not say you have always smelled sweet, but yes."

He chuckled, and then hissed in pain. "Don't make me laugh," he ground out, but without rancor.

"But you have never smelled bad either," she continued. He had a spicy, masculine scent. Clean, but something uniquely his. Given that she spent much of her time around the docks and with laborers, his scent was beyond pleasant. She might even say, intriguing.

"Damned by faint praise," he muttered.

"Vanity, Grant," she admonished. "I have never enjoyed the scent of blood. I would be grateful if you would stop releasing all that stuff onto my hands."

"Of course, Sweet Irene. Anything for you."

She didn't answer. Truthfully, she was alarmed by the stickiness of his clothes where she supported him. He was walking steadily, but every once in a while, he would flinch, she would grip him tighter, and wetness would alarm her all over again.

Fortunately, they made it to the inn after a dozen more steps. Within moments, Irene had roused the innkeeper who sent for the night watch and a surgeon. Irene would have sent for a doctor, but Grant would have none of that.

"A doctor is for old ladies with a cough. I require stitching, and that, my dear, needs a surgeon."

She didn't argue. With the innkeeper at her side, they quickly divested Grant of his jacket and blood-soaked shirt. She tried not to look at the honey blond hair on his chest or the chiseled cut to his torso. He was injured, and she was a degenerate looking at him so hungrily. But she had only seen her husband half naked like this on a bed. Nate had been a large man, broad like his father. His skin had been weathered by the sun, and the muscles had bulged like living rocks.

Grant was constructed in lanky angles. His muscles stretched across his body. They did not look like rocks so much as ropes of corded strength, tightening as needed. It was mesmerizing to watch as he disrobed.

And when she began to wipe away the blood with a wet cloth, she watched him flex against the pain.

She was hurting him, and yet her mouth was dry at the sight of his body. She felt her nipples tighten and her belly grow liquid. She did not want to be aroused. He was lying there bleeding, for God's sake! And yet, he was a beautiful man.

"It's not that bad," the innkeeper said. "The surgeon will stitch it up all right and tight."

Grant opened his eyes and wiggled his eyebrows. "Then I'll have a dashing scar. All the best gentlemen do, you know."

"I think you have plenty of those already," she said tartly. She hadn't intended to sound stern, but she felt so breathless around him. Especially as her eyes traced the thin white scars mostly along his forearms. But there were others too, set randomly about his chest and belly. "Machinery?" she asked.

He shrugged. "Stupidity, mostly. I was an idiot before I became a manager."

She might have said something. The pain that haunted his eyes at those words meant something. But there wasn't time to ask as both surgeon and constable arrived.

The next hour wasn't pleasant, but it had to be done. She explained the incident to the constable. Sadly, that went rather quick with the following summary from the man: "Sounds like a footpad. Glad nothing was stolen, though of course, the knife cut is upsetting."

That was it, beyond more sadness regarding Grant's wound. Then the man tipped his hat and left, while the surgeon got down to business. She tried to distract Grant, but there was little she could do. In the end, he just gripped her hand while she winced at every push and pull of the needle.

"You are being very brave, you know," she said, her voice strained.

"It takes little courage to lie in a bed," he quipped, though the words came out as breathless gasps.

"I assure you, I am impressed by your strength. Would you like a piece of leather to bite down on?"

"I'd rather you promise to kiss me when it's all said and done. A reward for my bravery."

"Done," she said.

"You promise? A kiss?"

She smiled. Trust the man to be making jokes between hisses of pain. "Yes, Lord Crowle, I will kiss you."

"Maybe more than one?"

"My, you are feeling strong, aren't you?"

He nodded in absolutely seriousness. "Very."

"Then I shall promise you two kisses." When he opened his mouth to ask for something more, she pressed her finger to his lips. "Do not ask for more, or I shall change my mind about the first two."

He obediently nodded and pressed his lips closed. But his eyes stayed open and steady, looking at her the whole time. Eventually, it was done. It probably hadn't taken that long. When she finally dared look, there were only a few stitches, but she felt as if she had run a footrace that lasted weeks. Any marks on his beautiful skin were wrong.

She reached out, wishing she could smooth away the wound with a caress. She couldn't. In fact, the idea was silly, and she only interfered with the surgeon as he bandaged the area with brusque motions.

"That will keep you, my lord," the man said. "I shall leave you some laudanum—"

"No, thank you," Grant said, his voice strong.

"But it may help you to sleep. The pain—"

"Is not so bad that I shall need that. Take the bottle away."

The man nodded and returned the vial to his bag. Meanwhile, Grant grabbed his purse to pull out a few meager coins to press in the surgeon's hand.

"My lord!" the man said stiffly, curling his lip at the few coins. "I'm afraid that the cost is somewhat higher—"

"On the contrary," Grant drawled. "I know exactly how much getting a few stitches costs, my man. I refuse to pay triple just because you learned I've got a title."

The surgeon started to protest, but even he could see it was useless. He grabbed the few coins with a sniff. "If it starts to go rancid—"

"I can drain it myself."

"You'll do no such thing!" Irene cried. "I shall be sure to call the good surgeon back."

Grant subsided with a shrug. "I'm afraid if it goes rancid, there is little either he or I can do. But let us pray that it doesn't get to that."

A glance at the surgeon saw that he agreed, though his expression sobered. "There are poultices and the like, my lady. Some things can be done. Call me if his condition worsens."

Irene opened her mouth, about to protest that she wasn't his wife, but a quick squeeze from Grant's hand distracted her enough that the words never left her lips. And then the surgeon was bowing before he left, shutting the door quietly behind him, which left her and Grant alone.

"He thought I was your lady wife," she said, embarrassment burning in her cheeks. Normally, she would simply laugh at the silliness, but a part of her took the idea a great deal more seriously. Enough that she couldn't look at him as she said it. After all, she was a proper lady, but she was here unescorted in his bedroom. And he was half naked.

"I told him you were."

She jolted in surprise. "But... why?"

He shrugged. "Because only a wife can stand by my bed and hold my hand. I'm sorry. That was selfish of me, but it's the truth. I... I wanted you here, and that was the easiest way to do it."

"You don't care if you ruin me in the eyes of the London *ton*?" Her voice was calm, thank heaven, but inside she was twisting. She liked that he wanted her here. She'd wanted to remain by his side. But the lie wasn't proper. Her being here wasn't proper. And what Grant had just done was highly improper.

"He wasn't of the *ton*. He was a surgeon, and..." He snapped his mouth shut.

No need to think twice about what he'd been about to say. "And no one believes we're married anyway. They think..." She swallowed, the idea hitting her sideways. They already thought her his mistress.

"Absolutely not!" he said, starting to sit up. But a lance of pain contorted his face, and he dropped back with a grunt. "Irene, no one will think any the worse of you for tonight. I swear it!"

She flashed him a quiet smile. She was being ridiculous. The rules were different for her than when she'd been an unwed girl. She was a widow now. She could do as she pleased, and few people would question her. A surgeon, an innkeeper, and a constable knew she was here. They were nothing in her life. After tonight, she'd likely never see them again. In truth, she didn't really have a reputation. The *ton* knew nothing of her. Her in-laws thought she was with Wendy. She could spend the night in Grant's arms and return home tomorrow completely secure. Nothing in her life would change.

It was a heady, seductive thought. "I should depart immediately," she said, though she didn't move.

"You could, but I never thought you one to shirk your debt."

"What debt?" she asked, though she knew very well what he meant.

"Two kisses. You promised."

"That was before you ruined me. What if Mama finds out that we pretended to be husband and wife all alone in an inn?"

"Immaterial. A promise has been made. It must be kept." Then when she arched a skeptical brow, he placed a hand on his chest and mock groaned. "I am a wounded man, you know. I could die on the morrow."

She knew he was teasing. That in truth, he would probably heal quickly. But the specter of infection lingered over all wounds. And once a cut went foul, there was little anyone could do.

"Grant," she whispered, worry in the word.

His expression immediately sobered. "I was only

teasing." Then he huffed loudly. "Keep your kisses if it makes you look so tragic."

"Terribly tragic!" she shot back. But then she leaned over, bracing her arm on the far side of his head. Their faces were a foot apart. "You're horribly ugly, you know. I shall have to do this with my eyes closed."

"It's the only respectable way anyway. Imagine trying to keep them open. You'd be cross-eyed and staring at my ear."

"Well, your ear isn't that hideous. I suppose I could look at it if I had to."

"Don't risk it," he said in a terribly serious voice. "You never know what imperfection might appear, then you would come away with a sudden horror of ears. And those, my dear, you can't avoid no matter what you do. Everyone has them."

"Very true," she said as she lowered closer to his lips. "I suppose I shall just have to close my eyes then."

He reached up, his fingers slowly winding behind her neck, massaging gently before slipping into her hair. She'd kept the style simple, pinning up the sides, while the rest curled lazily down her back. Her locks were rather short anyway, and so she thought the look acceptable.

Apparently, he found it very acceptable because his hand slipped upward to cup the back of her head. He didn't pull her down, but he coaxed her with his fingertips. And his lips teased her with his nearness. But what really caught her were his eyes. Dark brown with flecks of gold. They called to her. It wasn't the gold. That was more an accent, a lightness that made the dark brown all the richer. She sunk into the fine mink of those eyes, felt them surround her and hold her safe. How odd to feel as if his eyes held her safe, but they did.

Then she touched her lips to his. Her eyes drifted closed. Not on purpose. Truth be told, she could stare into his eyes for years. But she wanted to experience his mouth without distraction. She wanted to enjoy the touch of his lips, the heat of his breath mixing with hers, and most of all, the thrust of his tongue against hers.

His lips were soft. That was a bit of a surprise as everything else about him was cut so lean. But the feel was exquisite—like the finest velvet—as he moved against her mouth. She thought at first that he was murmuring something, but the shift of his mouth was not so coarse as to form words. No, it felt more like a silent song in his kiss. A high tremble counterpoint to the darker, harder beat of his mouth.

She stilled against him, her breath suspended to feel more. But she could not hold herself apart for long. The temptation to join him was too strong. So she did. She brushed her lips against his. She tilted her head and opened her mouth, needing to feel his heat mix with her own.

His tongue dashed out—a strong, bold melody against her mouth. She matched it as she pressed harder against him, uninterested in the lighter notes now. She wanted the heavy beat of his thrusting tongue. He thrust, she played, and suddenly, this song was not enough.

She was a widow. She knew the orchestral dance of bodies. His mouth, her mouth, they were simply the prelude. The dance of one instrument. She pulled back, her eyes opening as she searched his. "How much does it hurt?" she rasped.

He blinked, a frown pulling his face tight. "No pain," he whispered. Then his eyes blazed darker, his meaning scandalous. "Just fullness, Irene."

She swallowed. "And I am so empty."

She knew what she was asking, knew that what she wanted was immoral. But it had been so long, and she had spent much too long as a shell of a woman.

"Do you want…" He cut off his words with a swallow. "Be sure, Irene. Do you want… me?"

"Yes." She didn't even hesitate. Then when he searched her face, she repeated herself. "Yes, Grant. Please."

His face split into a sudden grin, even as his nostrils flared, and his eyes became dark with hunger. But he didn't move. "I've dreamed of this, you know."

"What?"

"Every night since we danced in that inn, I have thought of you in my bed."

Her lips curved, flattered. A little relieved as well because she had spent a few nights in fantasies of him. "Those aren't exactly dreams," she said.

He released a low rumble. "Oh yes, they were. You tormented my sleep."

She pulled back, not really intending to go anywhere. "Well, if you think it torment."

He tightened his grip on her head, his other hand wending around her back. "I think you owe me another kiss, Irene."

She arched her brow and started to lean down, but this time his tightened fingers held her back. "Not so fast," he said.

"Grant?"

His grin widened. "I get to pick the where of that kiss."

"You do?" she asked.

"I do." And then he slowly—firmly—rolled her down onto the bed.

Ten

GRANT DID NOT LOVE MUSIC. HE DIDN'T HATE IT, OF course, but his soul loved the things he saw. The soaring architecture of a building. The intricate pattern woven into fabric. And the beautiful lines of a woman. He adored the arch of a cheek, echoed in the line of a brow. He worshipped the fullness of a woman's mouth, as puckered and ripe as what glistened between her thighs.

So it was disconcerting when he heard music as he looked at Irene. At first he thought it a new manifestation of his madness, but this song was *her*, and that did not feel insane. It felt beautiful. And if he were going insane, then he did not care. So he focused on her as she lay beneath him, her eyes filled with promise, her mouth red and plump in invitation. He felt her breath—soft, sweet gasps—as he slowly stroked a hand over her breasts. But what he heard was a rapid staccato of a melody, high and tight and much too fast.

To counter that sound, he stroked in long, languid caresses. Her ballgown was soft as it shaped her breasts, but it was not nearly the whisper of her skin. Like one long note, he traced from her neck across her shoulders, and down to circle that ruby of a nipple. Then he remembered he wanted to trace that same path with his lips and tongue. So he leaned down, edging light nips and swirling notes along the melody of her neck and chest. Her breath hitched, adding its own accent to what he did. And he felt her clutch his arms and shift her legs restlessly.

Her heartbeat fluttered against his lips, and her gasps became urgent. But it was too quick—the movements of her pelvis beneath him too urgent. He was mesmerized by the sounds he heard as he looked at her, the song of their exploration. But she was rushing things, and he did not like it. So he pulled back, gentling her with his fingertips along the sweep of her neck.

"Easy, easy."

She looked at him, her expression almost frenzied. "Mr. Grant," she panted, desperation in the sound.

It was that name that shocked him. He had been called Mr. Grant for five years now, but it had been like five years in a prison. There had been no pleasure, no relaxation in that time. Only work, the endless march of numbers and fabric. Sturdy fabric, coarse fabric, and the beautiful designs of his luxury goods. The name Mr. Grant fit with work and textiles.

That this woman with her soft pants and white skin could whisper that name in the midst of her passion was like a ray of sunlight patterned across the mill floor. A reminder of beauty, a whisper of inspiration, and something that he'd learned to cherish as the gift from God that it was.

Except she was more than a ray of light. She was

a whole rainbow of sound and beauty, and it was all given to Mr. Grant. Not just Grant, the spoiled aristocrat who'd once taken women with a careless abandon, but to Mr. Grant, the worker. The gift left him breathless.

At his silence, she began to frown. "Is it your side? Are you in pain?"

Yes. No. How to explain? "No pain," he finally rasped out. "I just... please, this is so new."

She blinked, obviously startled. "But I thought... I mean, I assumed..."

He flashed a rueful smile. "Sex is not new, Irene. It is you. So fresh..." He shook his head. "I have no words."

She touched his cheek. "I am certainly not fresh or new. I am not a virgin, you know. You needn't be careful with me."

That would be like going rough with a perfect rose. He would not do it. It offended him down to his soul. But he didn't know how to say that, especially since his logical side pointed out that he had often enjoyed rough bed sport. Perhaps she was one such woman. But he couldn't do it. Not now. And so he said something else, hoping to satisfy them both.

He trailed his fingers along the edge of her bodice, watching as her skin blossomed pink under his touch. "May I take this off you? Please, may I undress you?"

She frowned down at herself, obviously a little surprised. "Are you sure you are up to it? I don't wish to cause you pain."

He smiled with a slow, hungry expression that he knew she'd understand. "I am very up for it."

She flushed at his double-entendre while he silently cursed himself. That had been a crude joke, the note discordant. Grant had adored such bad witticisms, but not Mr. Grant, who had understood that any bastard could be crude. It was a true man who gave respect by being refined.

"I'm sorry," he said. "That was rude."

She shook her head. "I wasn't offended."

"I was. By myself. And you deserve better."

Her lips curved at that. "I assure you, I have heard much worse almost from the cradle. My father enjoyed throwing house parties, and the conversation was decidedly improper."

Grant grimaced. "You should not have been exposed to that."

She shrugged. "But I was, and I don't mind—"

"I mind," he emphasized as he rolled off her. Then he pulled her up. She went willingly, her lips caught between her teeth in uncertainty. He touched her cheek. "Are you changing your mind? We don't need to—"

"Oh no!" she gasped. Then her face flamed, and her hands flew to her cheeks. She looked away. "You must think me a wanton, but..." Her voice faded away as she looked at the floor.

"But what? Irene, what we are about to do requires plain speaking beforehand."

At his encouragement, she dropped her hands from his face. "It has been years since anyone touched me," she said softly. "Skin on skin—not through gloves or fabric. I hadn't realized how much I'd missed it until we danced in the inn."

He thought back. There had been mounds of fabric between them. Not only clothing, but a bolt of wool wrapped around her.

"Our hands," she whispered. "I'd taken off my gloves, and you weren't wearing any."

So small a thing, and yet she remembered it. He was amazed. So he reached out and stroked again across her bodice. One calloused finger as he meandered a slow pattern on her flesh.

Her mouth opened on a gasp, and she shivered. "It's the most amazing thing," she whispered.

"So let us go slowly. Enjoy every second."

She bit her lip. "It's so overwhelming. I'm afraid I shall go mad."

He smiled, his eyes still watching his finger and the flush to her skin. "One can get used to madness."

She tilted her head. "What?"

He looked at her, replaying his own words in his head. "What? Oh, never mind." He couldn't believe he'd said that aloud. Then he slowly turned her around so he could release the buttons of her gown. "I am addled by you."

He saw the goose bumps on her flesh as he touched the skin above her buttons. On impulse, he leaned forward and pressed a kiss to her there. This time her sigh came to him as a slower note, an oboe of a sound, rich and woody.

"You want to do this, don't you?" he whispered against her skin. "You choose this?"

She nodded. "Yes. I didn't plan this night, but now that it's here?" She twisted enough to look in his eyes. "Yes."

"Yes," he echoed. No triumph in the word. Just pure happiness, because for Grant, this was a miracle.

So he applied himself to her buttons. He kissed down her back, slipping each one free then anointing the revealed skin with his tongue. And as he slipped her gown off her shoulders, there was so much more to adore. Until he came to her stays.

"Stand," he said hoarsely. "Let me release you."

She did without objection, though she smiled. "You make it sound like I've been in prison."

He peeled the gown from her lower body. Years ago, he would have dropped the thing on the floor, but he knew too much of dresses now. He held it so she stepped out of the beautiful thing and then neatly set it aside.

She stood in short corset and shift, and beneath them, stockings and shoes. He stood, barely caring about the pain in his side. He saw her: tall, elegant, with porcelain skin tinted rose.

"What do you see?" she asked. "You are looking so intently."

"I see a song," he answered.

"A what?"

"A song," he said as he stepped up to her. "I cannot explain it, but you make me see music." He touched the fluttering pulse at her throat. "This is a flute's trill." He stepped close to kiss that pulse. "Your shoulders are the strength of the melody—steady notes, perfectly balanced." He quickly undid the knots of her stays. As they released, he heard her inhale deeply, her torso lifting and expanding like the flow of a harp—up and down—a waterfall of sound.

"So poetic," she whispered.

"Never before."

She lifted her arms as he tossed aside the corset. Then before she could think about it, he lifted the shift up and away. She stood before him in nothing but her stockings and shoes. He'd moved behind her, and now his hands circled her narrow waist, slowly drawing her against his naked chest.

Skin to skin, heat to heat. He thought he heard a clash of cymbals the instant they touched. She cried out, and he bent his head—half to hear the sound better, half to nuzzle beneath her ear. Even her scent made sounds. Subtle, earthy sounds. Percussion. He felt the vibrations in his entire soul.

"I don't hear music," he said to himself, still struggling with the incredible sounds she engendered in his mind. "Not like this. Not from touching a woman." He pressed his temple to hers, his hands stroking across her belly, while her abdomen trembled in a waterfall of notes.

She leaned back into him, raising her arms to drape them behind her. She touched his hair, his shoulders. Whatever she could reach. And as she stretched against him, he curled about her. His cock thumped in a steady heartbeat, pulsing for her. His hands strummed her skin—belly, ribs, breasts. Light touches, feathery strokes, and she seemed to hum in response. His head dropped forward, unable to resist tasting her sound, nipping an accent wherever he could touch.

Then he held her breasts, his hands slowly brushing inward to her nipples. She stilled in his arms, her breath suspended, her spine half arched. She was waiting for him to mold her breasts as only a man can. She was of average size, her nipples tight and high. But as he squeezed, she let out a series of sweet gasps. And the more her breath hitched—like the light tap of a triangle—the slower and firmer his stroke.

Until he found her peaks. Hard and tight, her nipples were beads to roll and twist. She cried out as he took them, and her spine rolled against him as he played. Such tiny points, but one touch, and her whole body resonated with sound.

"Oh my!" she cried. "Oh! Oh!"

It was with some shock that he realized she had reached her fulfillment from nipple play alone. Never had he done such a thing to a woman. And never had a woman's cries sounded like the voice of angels. It was ridiculous! She was just a woman, but the sounds in his head as she shivered in his arms were of such glory he could not comprehend it.

"My God," he whispered, as he watched her writhe in the mirror. "My God."

He held her until she sagged against him. Until the crashing booms in his head faded to the soft song of a lute barely played. And then, while she was still boneless in his arms, he reached down and swept her off her feet.

"Grant?" she said in surprise.

He lay her gently down on the bed. Head first, settled lightly on the pillow. Back and hips, then all that long, glorious expanse of legs still encased in her stockings.

"Shh," he said, knowing that awe still infused his voice. "I have not finished undressing you yet."

She blinked, but it did little to dispel the languid

Eleven

IRENE DIDN'T KNOW WHAT TO THINK. OR PERHAPS, more accurately, she had no interest in thinking at all. She'd never believed she would go to a man's bed outside of wedlock, but the night had run away with her. Worse yet, she had wanted it to happen. Ever since that morning when they'd danced in the inn, she had dreamed of this. Except her imagination could not compare to the reality of his touch.

It was the way he went slow with her. Her husband had been an active man: wild and quick everywhere including their bed. She had not dreamed that a man might go slow—that he might relish a simple touch, the gentle build that became a crescendo, to a dizzying, perfect experience.

But Grant did. And as he pulled off her shoes, she felt that patient attention. She closed her eyes, glorying in the sensation of his hands holding her leg high, while the air hit her inner flesh. She felt his hands so large and strong slide up her leg to the top of her silk stocking. She felt his mouth at the line between silk and skin, wet and delicious, as he nuzzled her.

Then slowly, the fastening loosened, and she abruptly looked at him.

"Did you just untie that with your teeth?"

He wiggled his eyebrows at her—grinning—with the white ribbon trailing from his teeth. "Someday I should like to see if I can undress you completely using just my mouth. Quite the challenge, don't you think?"

She stared at him, uncertain what to say. In the end, she giggled. "I think you might have trouble with some of the buttons, especially if they are tight."

"Not if I bite them off."

She blinked. "You mean to destroy the dress?"

"It's one way of getting you naked."

She nodded. "I suppose it is, but hardly that difficult. The real challenge would be to do it without destroying the gown."

He straightened up from her leg, his expression one of mock insult. "You think it's easy to bite a dress off a woman?"

"Of course, it is. If you have the time, I suppose a man could chew off any manner of attire."

"Hmmm," he said, apparently thinking about it. She might have said something, except that his clever fingers had begun to roll the stocking down her leg. He moved smoothly, his fingers spanning her thigh before pushing. Everything before had been soft caresses, but this was a deeper push, harder into her leg. How marvelous the stretch of muscles, the ever so slight kneading of his fingers, all the way down calf, ankle, and foot.

"My God," she breathed. "That's amazing!"

"You are not used to dancing."

She smiled. "I haven't done it for years."

His eyes actually twinkled. "Well, now we're going to do something better than dancing."

"What could that be?" she asked in mock innocence.

He raised her other leg, pulling it high so he could untie the other stocking. Or so she thought. But instead of stroking that thigh, his hand slid up her naked leg. Higher and higher, until he pushed himself inside her. One thick finger—his thumb, she thought—and the invasion was so wonderful she arched off the bed with a gasp.

"Mmmm," he said, the sound almost a purr of delight. His eyes were closed, his head tilted back while inside her, as his thumb circled in the most amazing way. "I knew you would be perfect."

If she hadn't been clenching and releasing around his finger, she might have answered. She might have said that she was simply his instrument. But she couldn't speak, not with her breath catching every time he rolled his thumb.

She felt his fingers slowly stroke her spread thighs. The sensations were overpowering, her body too sensitive, so she tensed. He stilled until her breath eased, then he caressed her again—just a finger on each hand brushing back and forth across her skin. It was as if he couldn't resist touching her, and she smiled at the thought.

"Will you join me now?" she asked, her mind not really engaged in what she said. It was too bold a thing, too intimate to ask. So she didn't think, she just spoke. "There has been an emptiness inside me for so long."

His fingers paused. "You said that before. What does it mean?"

She opened her eyes and caught his gaze. "That I want you to fill me."

He pressed a kiss to her upraised knee. "Nothing would make me happier. But are you sure you're ready?"

She'd been ready for years, but she didn't say that. Sometimes, she thought the loneliness of the last few years would consume her. Suck her away until there was nothing left but an empty shell.

Logically, she knew that having a man between her thighs would not fill the ache. It was not the answer to her pain, but in this moment, on this magical night, she didn't believe in logic. She didn't accept reason or doubts or fear. She simply wanted. So she begged him for more. She asked with her eyes and with her touch. She reached down to help him with his pants, but her fingers were too clumsy, and he stepped quickly out of reach.

She watched as he unbuttoned his attire and pushed it from his hips. Shoes and stockings were long gone, and all that remained was the stark white bandage on his belly, partially hidden by the thick stalk of his arousal.

She reached for his cock, intrigued by the reddish color and the smooth head. She wanted to touch the heat of him and feel the pulse of his desire in her hand. She made to sit up, but he shook his head.

"If you touch it, I will explode."

She bit her lip and nodded. "Another time then." She hadn't meant to suggest they repeat this night. The logistics alone could be difficult. But she was not thinking right now, and so her wants slipped out into the night air without restraint. What she wanted was more of this. More of him.

He flashed her a grin. "Whenever you want," he said. "However often you want."

"Now," she said. "Right now."

He started crawling toward her. She shifted more onto the mattress to give him room. He moved between her legs, stopping long enough to lean down and suckle her right breast. She gasped, loving the brush of his tongue, the pull of his lips, and the way he used his teeth just when she needed more.

Then he let her go. "A symphony," he whispered. "I hear a fully symphony."

She laughed as soon as she caught her breath. "You are so poetic, Mr. Grant. I had no idea."

He quirked his brows. "Neither did I." Then he gently settled his weight upon her.

She released a sigh of delight, feeling his head at her entrance. His aim was unerring, and she flexed her hips enough to push at him, hoping to draw him inside.

"So impatient," he said with a chuckle. "I like that in a woman."

"So thick and strong," she answered. "I like that in a man."

"Are you sure?" He began to push inside her, moving slowly. The first tiny bit was easy. She was slick, and his aim was true. But then she began to feel his full girth. It stretched her in the most wonderful way.

"Yes," she whispered. "I'm sure."

He'd closed his eyes, and now his face took on an ecstatic look. "So tight," he groaned. Then he pushed in another inch. "Am I hurting you?"

"No." She was too breathless to say more. Especially as she shifted her hips, drawing him deeper. He groaned again. Then he opened his eyes, and their gazes caught. His face was in shadow, but there was enough light to see him—nostrils stretched tight, mouth set in a clenched ferocity. But what held her so strongly were his eyes. They seemed to burn with intensity. He was looking straight at her—straight *into* her—and what he saw pleased him.

She stretched up as she tried to meet his lips. But she couldn't, and he was still pushing. So she tilted her head back and arched. Fuller, deeper, harder—she loved every second of his slow penetration.

He paused, and she clenched him, trying to hold him even more tightly. "Don't stop," she cried.

"Couldn't. Not even... if I wanted."

Then he was finally—wonderfully—seated. Deeply embedded inside her, and she felt so full. He was thick and pulsing with life. His weight pressed her down, and she loved that she could feel his heat inside and out. She raised her knees, trying to grip him. She never wanted him to leave.

"Are you all right?" he asked.

She opened her eyes and caught his gaze. She didn't speak, but reached to stroke his forehead and trail her fingers into his hair. His curls brushed the back of her hand—so soft. And yet below, so hard.

"Irene?"

"Don't stop," she whispered. "I want it all."

His smile was almost feral. Then he began to move. Gentle at first. A withdrawal that had her whimpering. The emptiness caved in her belly and pulled at her insides. She tightened her legs along his flanks, and he growled.

"I'm trying to go slow," he said, his voice tight.

"Sweet heaven, why?"

"Because you're worth enjoying." Then he waited, poised at a place nearly out, but not quite. Then he began the return, pushing harder this time. Faster.

"Not slow, Grant." She suddenly arched her hips so that he fell hard against her pelvis. She cried out at the impact, loving the sharp, hard press of it. "Now. Right now."

He looked down, deeply embedded and refusing to move. "I'd like my kiss now, Irene."

"What?" she gasped.

"You promised me two kisses."

"I gave you—"

"One. Just one."

She laughed, and the sensations had them both groaning. "We've been kissing for hours!"

"That was *me* kissing you. I want my second kiss, and I won't move until I get it."

She reached up and grabbed hold of his head. She pulled him down to her and fused their mouths together. The kiss was deep and frenetic. She thrust her tongue into his mouth, and he dueled with her, quickly dominating. Then he pushed into her mouth, moving into her with a speed that left her dizzy.

Almost without her realizing it, he began to thrust. The withdrawal was slow and unsteady, jerking backwards, but not so far as to lose his place. She moved with him, arching first, then gripping his return. And together the pace built.

Out, in.

Faster—

Out, in.

Harder—

Out, in.

He lifted his head. Their eyes met and held.

No breath to speak.

Out, in.

She gripped him without relenting.

He fought her grip.

Drawing out, slamming in.

Hard!

The trigger inside her clicked. Her body clenched and exploded.

Yes!

He bellowed, his whole body jerking against her.

His explosion filled her. Mind and body pounding to his rhythm.

She squeezed him, over and over.

He flooded her with heavy pulses.

Yesyesyes!

A steady beat of joy.

Twelve

IRENE WOKE FEELING BOTH WONDERFUL AND STRANGE. Unfamiliar bed, unfamiliar room, but the scent of lovemaking and the warm body spooned against her brought back all the glorious memories of the night before. Which made everything all the more complicated. She was beyond happy about last night, and yet she couldn't deny that she'd stepped into unfamiliar waters. And she wasn't the least bit comfortable with her decision.

Then again, she thought as her eyes drifted closed, it was wonderful to feel a man, his organ stiffening as she stirred. She could stretch into him—encourage a return to last night's activities. But if they started that again, who knew how long she'd linger here? Her mind was already churning with what she would say to her in-laws. What if they discovered she had not stayed with Wendy last night? What would they say? What would they think?

So she gingerly inched out of bed, feeling the loss of his heat keenly. There was enough light coming from the window to see, and she slipped behind his dressing screen to perform her morning ablutions. But when she was done, she realized she was completely naked, and her clothing lay in a neat pile across the room.

Frowning, she looked around the tiny area behind the dressing screen. For a member of the aristocracy, Grant had precious little attire, and most of it meant for Mr. Grant, rather than Lord Crowle. She lifted up one of his work shirts, feeling the softness of well-worn cotton. It was large, but she slipped it on, loving the scent and feel. She felt surrounded by him, even though she was afraid to step out and face him.

What a contrary creature she was! So taking a deep breath, she steeled her spine and slipped from behind the screen.

He was awake, lying stretched and lazy like a morning cat on the bed. His gaze followed her movements, and a smile curved his sensuous mouth.

"I like the look of you in my shirt."

"I… um… I like the feel. Do you mind?"

He shook his head slowly then peeled back the covers on the bed. "Come let me see if it feels as soft as it looks."

Her eyebrows rose. She knew he was teasing her, but she was not quite ready to return to bed. Not when he played the indolent aristocrat so well. It felt discordant, and so she stayed back. "This is your shirt, Grant," she said quietly. "You know exactly how it feels."

"Not when it's against your skin. Not when…" He bit his lip, slowly straightening on the bed as he looked at her. Then his expression changed into one of chagrin. "I'm sorry. I don't know what I'm saying. You're not the usual flyer, and this must feel awkward."

She blinked, startled by his sudden shift from casual seduction to honest, plain speaking. It was dizzying how quickly he became Mr. Grant—a simple manager of a factory. She swallowed and nodded.

"I've never done this before."

"Of course not." He shifted on the bed, adjusting to face her directly. "I know you probably want to rush home, but if you have the time… I should like to talk with you. For a little bit." He rubbed a hand over his face. "So much happened last night that I'm feeling rather disoriented from it all."

She understood exactly, and so she settled on the edge of the bed. He didn't move to draw her closer, but she saw his nearest hand twitch as if he wanted to touch her. She wanted it too, but she couldn't quite bring herself to reach for him. Not yet.

They sat in silence for a moment, both struggling for something to say. He looked at her, and for a moment she thought there was longing in his eyes. A desperate hunger quickly buried under a tide of uncertainty.

"You're not hurt, are you? I mean from what we did. Or the fight earlier."

"No, no," she said. "I'm fine. A little sore maybe, but it's a nice kind of soreness."

He flashed her a smile.

"And you?" she asked. "We should replace your bandage."

He looked down. Sometime in the night, he'd discarded the cumbersome linen. He lifted his torso enough to expose his wound to the light. "It looks good," he said. Then he gingerly touched around it, pressing until he winced. "Not too painful."

She abruptly grabbed his hand and pulled it away from his wound. "Don't fiddle with it. You don't want to re-open it."

He shot her a wry glance. "If it didn't burst wide open last night, then I doubt poking at it now will have any effect. It wasn't that deep a cut." He grimaced and pulled his foot from beneath the cover. "The real problem is my ankle. That's why I couldn't walk very well. I think I wrenched it during the fight."

She peered at it while he began poking there. It did appear a little swollen. "Just take care of yourself."

He smiled as he looked back at her. Then he gently twisted his hand in her grip until he could entwine his fingers with hers. "I'll be careful," he said. Then he took a breath. "I've been thinking about that attack. There was something wrong about it."

Her eyebrows shot up. "Of course, it was wrong! A man came at us with a knife."

"That's just it. He ran at us with his knife drawn. The normal footpad would stop and demand money. Too risky with just the one against us two."

"I was no help at all in the fight."

"On the contrary, you screamed. You fought."

"Badly and very little. It happened so fast."

"You were a big help, and you got me to the inn." He drew her hand to his mouth and pressed a warm kiss to the back of her hand. It was a courtly gesture, but it was also filled with genuine warmth, and she flushed at his attention. Especially as his fingertips stroked the inside of her palm. It was ridiculous to feel this shy. She wasn't a green girl, and yet everything he did with her, every way he looked at her, felt fresh and new. She peered at him, seeing him watch her with a steady, patient gaze.

Eventually, his thoughts shifted. She knew because his gaze grew less intense, more abstract. "What did the constable say?"

She shrugged. "That next time we should hand over our money. That we were fortunate you got off so lightly."

Grant grimaced. "That's just it. He didn't *ask* for our money. He just attacked."

She thought back and realized he was right. "But why…" Her words trailed away, and a creeping sense of terror stole over her. She bit her lip, refusing to cry out, and her fingers tightened hard on Grant's hand.

"What is it?" he asked, his voice sharp with alarm. "Irene?"

She shook her head. "I thought I was done with feeling afraid. I thought it was over."

He scooted across the bed and gathered her into his arms. She had pulled so tight into herself that she didn't want to move at first. But his touch was gentle even as he steadily tugged her close. A moment later, she crumpled and burrowed into his arms like a terrified kitten.

"I am being silly," she said to herself.

"Maybe not. Tell me what made you so afraid."

She took a deep breath and tried to order her thoughts. It took awhile, but cradled as she was in his arms, she found the strength to talk about her fears. "I started working for Helaine almost a year ago. Before that, I was… floating."

"Floating?"

"Just existing. Living without purpose. Counting the ticks of the clock in my room. Maybe I was lost in grief, but it felt more like I had no direction to any part of my day or night. My every need was taken care of. My in-laws are lovely people, but there was no reason to get up every morning because there was absolutely nothing to do."

He nodded. "I understand."

She shot him a skeptical look. "Grant, you run a mill. And you are an earl. I doubt you have ever been so lost."

He pressed a kiss to her temple. "I've had my share of useless days. None lately, but I know something of having the time hang."

She nodded. "Helaine came and offered me the job as purchaser. Suddenly, I had a reason to rise every morning. With my father-in-law's help, I was able to make deals for fabric and the like. Mama was appalled, but I loved it. And even she could not deny that I was happier because of the work."

"That I understand well, though don't tell Robert that."

"Robert?"

"Lord Redhill, our host last night. He is the one who forced me into managing the mill. Best thing for me, though God knows I cursed it often enough." He squeezed her. "So you see, we are not so different. Each of us working for our bread."

"And enjoying it."

He snorted. "I am not sure I would say that." Then, at her look, he shrugged. "Oh very well, yes, I like my work. Or at least parts of it." His expression turned serious. "Tell me the rest, Irene."

"There's not much more to tell. I started thinking someone was watching me. When I was at the dock or later at the shop. It wasn't anything specific. Just a niggle, like a tickle at the base of my neck."

"Did you ever see anyone?"

"I didn't, but Penny's fiancé did. Mr. Samuel Morrison, the Bow Street Runner. You met him last night. Anyway, he chased the boy, but was knocked on the head."

Grant straightened, his brows drawn together in a fierce scowl. "Someone was following you?"

"Yes. Mr. Morrison said it was a street boy, probably paid to watch my movements. But he was working with a larger man. That's who knocked Mr. Morrison out."

"Did you ever find the man or boy?"

"No. There never was anything other than that one incident. I took precautions, of course. And I was forever looking over my shoulder, but there's been nothing for months. I'd begun to relax again."

"That's very strange, you know. Being followed, then not. You never learned anything about it?"

She shook her head. "And I have talked with Mr. Morrison about it extensively. He seems to think it has something to do with Wendy, and after what she said last night with the gambling debts, I agree there's some concern."

"But why would the Demon follow you?"

She sighed. "That's what Mr. Morrison asked, but I have no idea. It's been months with no incident at all." She tried for a smile, but she doubted she managed a good one. And he didn't seem the least bit inclined to humor.

"I think I should talk to Mr. Morrison."

Her eyebrows raised in surprise. "Grant, surely you have more important things to do than chase down my ghosts."

He looked at her, silent for too long. And she realized with a bit of shock that he seemed to be at a total loss.

"Grant?"

"For five years I have lived with one goal, Irene. I had to make a success of the mill so that I could buy back my land."

She nodded. "And did you?"

"No," he said, the word filled with pain. "No, I didn't. But now, I know that my brother Will managed to get it."

"Well, that's good. You have the land then."

He shifted awkwardly, and she could feel his withdrawal. "It will stay in *his* family, Irene, not with the title. He's the better man to have it. I know that. He's always been the better steward, but now, there is nothing to support the earldom, except a crumbling castle right next to my brother's wealthy home." He dropped his head back until it thunked lightly against the wall. "I had meant to spend the next years working there, rebuilding it as I did the mill."

"And now?"

He looked at her and flashed a mischievous smile. "Now I have nothing but time to spend. On you." He rolled toward her, his expression seductive. She gasped and pulled back, but with a smile on her lips.

"Grant, I thought we were going to talk."

He stopped and flopped back, but with an air of

acceptance. He'd known she'd refuse him. "See?" he said. "If I cannot spend time *with* you, then perhaps I shall spend it *on* you. On talking with this Mr. Morrison about your mysterious followers."

"It was a long while ago."

"It is suspicious, and I want to know more."

He was adamant, jaw thrust forward and expression focused. Irene felt uncomfortable at his sudden intensity. She had barely come to accept that they had spent the night together, and now, he was to investigate her mysterious attack? It seemed like too much, though logically, after their intimacies last night, a few questions with Mr. Morrison were hardly earth-shattering. Still, she tried to distract him.

"You don't have to return to the mill?"

"I thought I'd be headed to Yorkshire now, a victorious landowner again."

"But surely there are other things you could be doing."

He turned to look at her, and his eyes narrowed. "You don't want me asking questions. What haven't you told me?"

"No, no! It's not that. I just… I don't want to impose."

"You're not."

"And you're an earl. Grant, surely this is beneath your notice."

He didn't answer at first. He just looked at her, flashes of emotion shifting in his eyes. They went too fast for her to catch. In the end, he touched her cheek, and with his index finger he stroked across to her lips.

"You're uncomfortable with me now. You don't want to see me anymore."

She shook her head, unable to deny the truth, even as her heart pounded in her throat. "I do," she whispered through dry lips. "I just need a little time."

He nodded slowly. "Perfectly understandable." Then he shifted his hands to cup her face. He held her still as he gently settled his mouth on hers. The kiss was slow and sweet. Unable to resist, she opened to him, softening her back, melting so completely into him that when the kiss changed, she relished it.

What began gentle became more demanding. Soon his tongue was thrusting into her, and he was rolling her onto her back on the bed. He followed her down, his hands opening his shirt with ease.

She gasped as he pulled back, her breath short, her body already on fire. Looking into his eyes, she knew how easily she could lose herself in him. He was so intense, his focus so heady. When had a man looked at her with such hunger? What man had ever touched her like his next breath depended on her accepting him?

"You steal my reason," she whispered.

"Let it go," he answered as he brushed the edges of his shirt aside. She was naked before him, and his hand began to stroke her breast.

She closed her eyes, feeling the strength in his hands, the rough brush of his callouses on her skin, and the pinch and twist he did to her nipples. Her belly trembled, and she went liquid. How easily he aroused her. She ought to be frightened—she was frightened—but not enough to stop him.

"Irene," he said softly. "Irene, look at me."

She opened her eyes. It should have been easy, but

he was still applying himself to her breasts, and every-thing he did made her languid. Then he lifted, shifting his body to settle between her thighs. She didn't fight him. Didn't want to. But as his weight fell onto her, he touched her face.

"It was a near thing last night."

She gasped slightly, her eyes widening, but he quickly shook his head.

"Not the attack. Long before then at the ball. I had just found out about my brother. That Will would get everything."

She nodded, not understanding what he was trying to say. It was especially distracting as he began to push himself inside her. Slowly, but with inevitable pres-sure. She was open and ready, but the push—and the pleasure it engendered—was a potent drag on her thoughts.

"I went straight to the card room, Irene. And I called for a bottle of brandy."

Her arms had wrapped around him, and her grip tightened on his back. "How much did you lose?"

"Nothing," he said. "I didn't play, and I didn't really drink, but it was a near thing. If I'd stayed, I would have."

"But you didn't stay. You didn't gamble." She could tell he had a fear of gambling. She heard it in his voice—an evening of cards or dice would be a very bad thing indeed.

"I only left because I remembered our dance."

"You missed our dance."

He flexed his hips and seated himself fully inside her. "I remembered you."

Her hands gentled on his back, stroking him, feeling his smooth skin and the ripple of his muscles beneath. He was a potent man.

"I know this is too soon for you," he said as he began the slow withdrawal. "I know you need some distance from me. Time to understand what we are about. Space to see that you want to be with me."

He had pulled back all but his tip, and with a sharp look he thrust forward again. Hard and thick, he impaled her, and she gasped in pleasure.

She lifted her knees, slowly drawing her legs up his calves and thighs. Soon she framed his hips and gripped him with her thighs. "I choose where I go and what I do, Grant. You do not frighten me."

It wasn't a lie. She wasn't afraid of *him*. She was afraid of how quickly and deeply she had involved herself with a virtual stranger.

"I am the one afraid," he said. He dropped his head, pressing his forehead to hers. His breath heated the air between them, mingling with her soft pants. "I wasn't a gambler like my father. I wasn't—I'm not—that big a fool. But I could be, Irene. So easily. I could be."

He slid back again, the rhythm slow, but building fast. His words frightened her though. Her father's gambling had been a nightmare without end.

"But you didn't play last night," she said. "It's all right."

"Because I remembered you." He thrust in again. His breath rasped, and his tempo increased. She arched beneath him, increasing the power of his impact, and her breath caught on a soft cry.

He reached down between them, his fingers

burrowing. It was an awkward angle, so he pulled back. He sat between her thighs and then rubbed her so deeply, so perfectly, even while still inside her. He spread her folds and massaged her in a steady circle, while she writhed in pleasure.

"Don't cast me aside, Irene. I know I shouldn't ask this of you, but please let me stay ."

"Stay?" she gasped out.

"In London. Helping you. Talking to your Bow Street Runner."

Her belly tightened, and the blood roared in her ears. Her body arched, and she couldn't catch her breath.

"Say yes, Irene. I need something to keep me focused. Let it be you."

He was relentless with his attentions, his stroke building her passion by leaps. But when she would have soared, he stopped, drawing her knees high as he fell down over her. He braced himself on his arms, his weight well off her. But in this position, he had plenty of room to thrust. Long, hard impacts that sent explosions through her body.

"Say yes, Irene. Say. Yes."

She would say anything at that point. Anything at all, if only he would continue.

"Irene!" he said, stopping his motion, holding himself back.

"Yes! Of course, yes!" she cried.

"Thank God," he breathed. And then he thrust hard. Once. Twice.

Heaven!

She soared, as did he.

An eternity later, he fell not so gently to the side. It

pulled him out of her, and she gasped in reaction. But he cuddled her close, and they lay nestled together. His breath was hot on her face, his body so warm. She felt safe in his arms, and after their discussion, that was no small thing.

But what had she just promised him? That she would let him talk to Mr. Morrison? That she would allow him to investigate into her worries? Surely that shouldn't generate any sense of unease.

But what if he meant to do more? What if his investigation never ended? What if he became intrusive or demanding? And what if he exposed what they had done this night to the world? How would she face her family? She was living with her in-laws, for goodness sake. How would they react to the idea that she had taken a lover?

"Shhh," he said as he pressed a kiss to her temple. "It will be all right," he whispered. "I'll make sure of it."

Of course, he would—unless he turned out to be the problem. Then what would she do?

Thirteen

GRANT FELT A TIGHTNESS AS IRENE WAS LEAVING THE inn room, a vague sense of panic that spurred him to action. "I will ride with you. Just to make sure you make it home safely."

She frowned. "I don't see that's necessary. Truly—"

"We were attacked last night. I won't get out of the hackney, but I won't be at ease unless I see you safely to your front door."

She bit her lip then nodded. He searched her face for more clues as to her mood, but he saw nothing helpful. She was busy dressing, and her eyes kept looking at the clock. It was past eight. The servants had long since been up and about. Fortunately, the time fit with her story that she had spent the night with Miss Drew, the seamstress. She would hardly have risen much earlier if she'd been with her friend. But that didn't solve the problem of her dress and the fact that she would be seen leaving the inn.

"Give me a minute," he said. "I'll see if I can find you a cloak."

It didn't take him long. This inn had seen many

secret assignations, so the innkeeper had a large cloak available for purchase at exorbitant cost. One month before, he never would have paid it. But one month ago, he wouldn't have been in London at all, much less in bed with Irene. And a bare twelve hours ago, he had thought he needed to save his pennies to court Miss Josephine Powel.

As that was no longer the case, he suddenly had money available and nothing to save it for. Might as well spend it on Irene. So he paid the indecent price and whisked it upstairs, while the innkeeper called for a hackney. She was staring out the window at the increasingly busy coach yard.

"I will be seen," she said without turning around.

"You can wear this. It will cover your gown, and no one will see your face. You'll just be a woman leaving the inn."

"With you." She turned and faced him. "They'll know you."

He nodded as his chest tightened. Was she casting him off already? Fighting the fear, he stepped forward and took her hands in his. He tried to be gentle with his words, but in the end, he settled for blunt speaking.

"Forgive me, Irene, but you are a widow. Affairs are common among the upper crust."

"They are not common to me!"

"Of course not," he said, moderating his tone. "But that makes little difference to society." He pulled her cold hands to his lips. "No one will make the tiniest remark upon your actions, even if anyone does recognize you. Which, of course, they won't. You are a widow and can do as you like with your time and your favors."

She sighed and squeezed his fingers. "I know you are right, but I still feel awful."

"Not about what we shared, I hope."

She hesitated a fraction of a second too long, but then she released a sigh. "No, not that. And truthfully, I would do it again."

His mood brightened considerably. Or it did until she hastily amended.

"I mean—I would make the same choice again, given the circumstance last night." She shook her head. "Goodness, I don't know what I'm saying."

He sighed as he drew her into his arms. "You are saying that you don't regret last night, but you also have no intention of repeating it." He tried not to sound disappointed. Worse, he was startled by a sudden surge of anger, especially as she drew back slightly to flash an apologetic smile.

"Yes, I suppose you are right. That is what I'm saying."

"I intend to fight you on that, you know."

She blinked. "Fight me? Grant, you must know that I cannot become your mistress."

"Why not? As I said, you are a widow. I could…" He almost said he could compensate her generously for her time, but two thoughts made the words freeze on his tongue. The first was that she would be horrified by that offer. She was not a paid courtesan, nor would she ever be happy in that role.

The second was that he did not have the money to compensate her generously. Certainly, he no longer needed to do a good showing this season, but that didn't mean he was flush with cash. The mill had just now begun paying off. The only reason he had the blunt to buy back his land was because he'd intended to sell his stake in the mill to Robert. Now that he wasn't doing that, he had enough funds to be comfortable, but certainly not enough to pay a mistress.

Good God, barely two weeks back in the fashionable round, and already he was spending money he didn't have. Had he learned nothing in the last five years?

"See?" she said, her voice gentle. "Even you cannot think of a way to make this work."

He frowned. She had misinterpreted his silence. "I can think of a dozen or more ways to whisk you into my bed without anyone else the wiser. But it is not what I think that matters, is it? It is what you want. And you do not want me anymore."

Never had he thought to voice those words! A woman who did not want to return to his bed? Back when he'd been a profligate young buck about town, the women had flocked to him. He was a good lover, paid well, and was heir to an earldom. He had his choice every night. But, of course, Irene wasn't even remotely the same as those women. Meanwhile, she touched his face, the caress tender, even though it was a definite good-bye.

"Last night was so wonderful, I cannot even express it. But Grant, I have things to do, a life I enjoy."

"I have no intention of interfering with your life," he said. Then, before she could raise more obstacles, he drew her hood up so that it covered most of her face. "Now let me get you home. We can discuss the particulars of when and how we shall meet again—"

"Grant!"

"To discuss what I have discovered," he hastily added. "You were attacked last night, remember?"

"*We* were attacked by a *footpad*." He didn't argue. He simply held out his arm, which she took with a frustrated sigh. "You should be doing other things than chasing after my imaginary pursuer."

"Last night was not imagined, and pray allow me to choose where and how I spend my time."

Her face was in shadow, but he knew she was grimacing in distaste. Damnation, but he would have to fight tooth and nail to remain in her life. He did not pause to consider why it was suddenly so important to remain focused on her. He merely accepted it as fact and set his mind to figuring out ways to do it. But first he had to get her home, so he escorted her quickly to the waiting hackney.

They spoke little in the cab. He tried a few conversational gambits. He asked her what she intended to do this day: she wasn't sure. What parties she might attend in the future: she had no idea. How could he contact her in the future? That question had her grimacing, an expression he could see even in the dim interior. "I don't know," she finally said. "I suppose through the shop. Or through Mr. Morrison. Samuel can get a message to Penny, who will get it to me. But I don't want her involved in something so sordid."

His eyebrows shot up, and he did his best not to feel insulted. "You consider meeting me sordid?"

She huffed out a breath. "Of course not. It's just the passing of messages like that, as if we were in some horrible gothic novel." She rolled her eyes.

"Mama reads them by the dozens, and they are universally silly."

What did he say to that? Aside from the general insult, he had not considered how hard it would be to meet with a woman who worked and did not, as a rule, attend parties. But of course, he was forgetting that he was Lord Crowle. He had an easy way of finding her. It was only because they were used to dealing as Mr. Grant and Mrs. Knopp that he hadn't thought of it earlier.

He waited for his moment. He knew if he gave her time to argue, she would find some sort of excuse to deny him. So at the last second before the hackney stopped, he made his move.

A kiss: swift, sure, and very deep. He nearly missed it. She was pulling her cloak back over her head, and if he'd timed it differently, he would have gotten her elbow in his nose. He took hold of her cheeks, lifting her face. Then he descended, pressing against her mouth, and thrusting into it until she softened. She fought it—a little. Her body longed for him, even if her mind resisted.

"'Ey now!" called the coachman as he rapped on the roof. "Up and at 'em!"

Grant drew back, pleased to see her dazed eyes focus somewhat blearily on him. "I shall call on you day after tomorrow. That should give me enough time for some initial inquiries."

"What? But—"

"Best go now!" he said as he pushed open the door.

He stayed in the shadows. No need for anyone to see him. She made it to the ground, pausing only for a moment to look back. She was gathering her wits and meant to say some objection, he was sure. So he pressed his fingers to his lips and waved good-bye before firmly shutting the carriage door.

Then she had no choice but to huff out a disgusted breath before she rushed to her front door. The cab waited, as he'd instructed it to, until she'd disappeared inside her home. Then with a quick click of the reins, the horse started up again.

Grant stayed right where he was, his gaze on the house as long as possible. He watched it with a longing that pierced him, making his mouth run dry and his hands shake. And the moment it disappeared from sight, he felt a physical pain as sharp and devastating as he'd once felt every time he'd been forced to step away from a gambling table. Or a bet. Any bet.

Five years ago, he wouldn't have thought about that. He wouldn't have worried that he felt the same pang now as he had when his brother had interrupted his fire-blowing mid-wager. But he was alone in a carriage with at least fifteen minutes before arriving at the office of the Bow Street Runners. What choice did he have but to wonder at this ache?

How could a woman get so important to him so fast? That he shook when he left her?

Aw, listen to you, his madness suddenly drawled. *One night of fun, and you have to turn it into an epic tale.*

Grant winced as his madness returned. In Yorkshire, he'd gone whole weeks without a peep from the bastard, but back in London the thing was a buzzing insect that wouldn't go away.

He studiously ignored it, choosing instead to focus

on his hands. He held them in front of him. They were steadier now than yesterday, but he wouldn't trust himself with a sketching pencil right then. The lines would jump all over the page.

He closed his eyes, dropping his head against the hard side of the cab. For five years, he had gone without these symptoms. Without the morning shakes or the physical wretchedness. Years ago, he'd thought them signs of excess drink. Perhaps last night's alcohol was having an adverse effect.

You call a night of tupping an adverse effect? You are an idiot!

But even back then, he'd known it was as lie. In truth, his drinking declined because of the expense. Though there were certainly nights he had overindulged—his sister's wedding being the last obvious example—mostly, he'd drunk from his own flask of "brandy," which was more water than wine. But even then, the wretchedness had not ended. If anything, it had increased.

It's wagering, you bloody fool. You like the wagers.

He grimaced, knowing that his madness was right. For years before his sister's wedding, he'd thought of little else but gambling. Wagers had become his obsession and not because of the money he could win. Certainly, the cash had been important. There were times when his winnings were all that kept his parents from starvation. But his thoughts had been on the game, not the money. And it was leaving the game that had produced such physical wretchedness. In fact, fear of that pain is what kept him playing long after he should quit.

Made you burn down the barn. About time you realized that.

Was that why he'd taken that risk in the barn? He tried to remember that night. He'd told himself it had been about the money, but maybe not. Maybe he simply hadn't wanted to quit the wager.

But there was no wager with Irene. Why now— after five years without a single wager—was he shaking after leaving a woman?

No wager? What was the mill, except for one great, big bet?

He watched his hands curl into fists as he realized his madness was right. Five years ago, he'd been forced to lay everything on the table, so to speak. Sell the land to Lawton on the hope—

The bet.

—that he could make enough to get his land back. Day and night, he'd worked to that end. To earn enough money to buy back his land. Build a business with the payoff being his land and his family's respect.

Buggered that, didn't you?

Yes, he'd failed at that game, and that still rankled. Or it would, if he didn't now have a new game to play. A woman this time—Irene.

Don't be making her into something she's not. She's a woman. Good tits, long legs, and a honeypot sweet enough to make a man forget his cares.

"Stop it!" he spat at his madness. He didn't like that his own thoughts turned Irene into something crude. Thank God that they had finally arrived at their destination, otherwise he might start ranting at himself, and they would lock him away in Bedlam for sure.

So he glared at nothing, silently cursing his own insanity, then stepped out of the carriage. He paid his fare and focused on a surprising moment of satisfaction. He had the funds to pay a cab fare without worrying he'd be short on something else. That was cause for celebration, wasn't it? He hadn't thought that way in… ever. What a glorious pleasure. Though, he thought cautiously, it would be best to walk back to the inn to save his coin.

Then he tucked away his thoughts—madness included—and headed into the magistrate's office at No. 4 Bow Street.

Fourteen

IT TOOK A WHILE TO FIND MR. MORRISON. NOT
because people didn't know him. In truth, every time
he spoke the man's name, someone would shake his
head and say, "Oh, *that* bloke." Sometimes the tone
held anger, sometimes awe, but always there was a
larger measure of suffering. As if Mr. Morrison was
appreciated and hated in equal measure.

It gave Grant some concern, but still he was determined to proceed. Finally, he found the man in a rather
unremarkable room. Someone had said it was reserved
for the runners, but there were no markings on the door
to indicate such. He did see battered desks scattered
about the small room, each with stacks of scribbled
notes upon it. And in the corner stood a lanky man
with curly brown hair. The man was in the process of
shedding his coat, but he stood frozen, his attire half on
and half off, while he frowned at a crack in the wall.

Grant stepped into the room, his gaze shifting to
the crack. He saw nothing remarkable in it, but then
again, he knew little about masonry. Perhaps, if he
went closer. He closed the distance between himself

and the wall, inspecting it in minute detail. He was stretching up on his toes to look higher, when the man's voice cut through his thoughts.

"What the devil are you doing?"

Grant whipped around, his face heating in embarrassment. "I, uh, I was just trying to figure out what was so interesting to you." When the man's frown deepened, Grant gestured rather vaguely toward the wall. "You were staring at the crack."

The man blinked, nodded, and then proceeded to pull on his jacket. "Ah, I see. Sadly, there was an error in your perception. I was not actually *looking* at the wall or the crack, and yes, I have spoken of it to the magistrate. It does need to be repaired, though in my estimation, it will be another year and five months before it actually leaks." He popped on his hat and started heading for the door.

Grant couldn't think of a thing to say to that. Meanwhile, the strange man stopped suddenly at the door, his hand on the knob. "Where was I going?"

"Er, I don't know that you were going. Everyone I spoke with said you'd just arrived." And now, Grant understood every person's reaction to the name "Morrison." This had to be the man, either that, or an escaped Bedlamite.

Meanwhile, the man turned around, blinking. "Arriving. Quite right. Bugger, I'm disorganized today. Most days, actually, but today I'm rather very— most perceptive of you, by the way. I applaud your attempts to understand deeper thought."

"Uh, thank you? But I'm not actually sure that you were arriving. That's just what I was told."

Mr. Morrison paused. "Oh, not about my comings and goings. Can't expect anyone else to understand that. I refer to your attempt to inspect the crack. Most people don't do it, you know, so I applaud your attempt."

"But you weren't looking at the crack."

"True. I just cleared a man of murder. Stupidest thing. Don't know why they didn't see it right away. Poor bastard in goal is left-handed. Killer was right-handed. I realized it the moment I saw that Willy's papers are on the wrong side." He gestured to the desk right below the wall crack. "Must mean he's in the suds again with his wife. Always rearranges his desk when she's angry. Probably their son. Gambler, that boy, and not a good choice for a copper's son. But then, we don't pick our relations, do we?"

Grant stared at him, doing his best to follow what was said. It took him a moment, especially as he had to remember that a "copper" was the common term for a runner because they were usually paid a copper for their efforts. But eventually, he worked it all out. "You were arriving and pulling off your coat just as you noticed the papers on the desk. That led you to thinking about left- and right-handedness, and that made you realize someone was falsely accused of murder. Have I got that right?"

Mr. Morrison's face bloomed into a handsome smile. "Very well done! Well done indeed! Most people just throw up their hands when they meet me. It's a rare person who sorts me out. Especially on a disorganized day."

Grant smiled, deciding he liked this odd man. So he extended his hand and introduced himself. "I'm Grant Benton, Lord Crowle."

The man smiled and extended his hand. "I'm Samuel Morrison, and we met last night at the ball. Though I should like to point out that you're not dressed as a lord. Curious that."

Grant looked down. He was dressed as Mr. Grant today, out of habit, and because he wasn't comfortable when dressed the other way. It wasn't the tailoring. The attire fit like a dream. But it was more the things he thought and did that made him acutely uncomfortable.

Because putting on a shirt makes you pick up the dice. Bugger the clothes. It's your choices that make you an idiot.

Grant winced, forcibly ejecting his madness from his mind. It rarely worked for long, but it would buy him some measure of peace as he talked with the strange Mr. Morrison.

Meanwhile, the man in question shook his hand with a surprisingly strong grip. Then he tugged Grant back into the hallway. "Come on then. You can talk to me as we walk."

"Walk? I thought you were coming here and just forgot."

Mr. Morrison shot him an annoyed look. "Well, of course I was, but I can't leave a man to rot in gaol, now can I? Do try to keep thinking. It will help enormously." Then the man abruptly stopped walking and turned to Grant. "That was rude, wasn't it? Penny says I'm often rude, and I really shouldn't be. She's trying to make me into a better person. Have told her that I'm a lost cause, but she won't hear of it. And perhaps, I'm not, because here I am apologizing. I must be progressing."

Grant felt his lips quirk in a smile. "Actually, you didn't really apologize."

The man blinked. "Oh. Just so. Well, I do. Apologize, that is." Then he took a deep breath and gave Grant a genuine smile, even though his words were slow and stiff. "I am sorry for being rude." Then he blinked and started taking the steps in his long stride. "Now keep with me. You want to speak about Miss Wendy Drew, yes? Can't think of any other reason for you to be here."

Grant rushed to catch up on the steps. "Well, yes. How did you know?"

"Got a good look at your clothing. Excellent cloth, sturdy, but with extra fibers on it." He picked a piece of lint off Grant's lapel. "Alpaca? Oh, you must be from that new factory up in Yorkshire. Ah yes, the one owned by Redhill and Crowle." He frowned a moment. "So is that where you've been for the last five years? Running the mill as Mr. Grant?" The man released an approving grunt. "Must say you've done an excellent job. Even I've heard of your angora wool, and I've been out of the fashionable circle for a bit." He tilted his head. "Can't say I miss it. Real murders are much more exciting fare than who killed whose reputation over cards."

Grant had no words. Sadly, his madness did, and it released a slow whistle of appreciation.

Bugger's brilliant. Quick! Ask him about Irene's attacker before he starts babbling about shoes or figures out you spent the night with Irene.

"Er, you're right, of course," said Grant. "And I'm rather impressed by your deductions."

Mr. Morrison shot him a startled look, but didn't speak. Apparently, people didn't tend to appreciate his unique brand of intelligence. Meanwhile, Grant pushed on before they ended up in the general confusion of the magistrate's main rooms, and the man got completely distracted.

"I'd like to ask about Irene's—er, Mrs. Knopp's pursuers. I understand she was followed."

"Yes, yes. Bothers me still. Street boy paid to follow her, then when I gave chase, I got flattened by a big fellow so high." He gestured to about five-foot-eleven. "Knocked me out, but it brought Penny to tears, so that was lovely."

"It was lovely that Penny cried?"

"What? No, no. Hadn't realized she fancied me at that point. Took getting knocked flat for me to guess that I had a chance with her. She had a rule against crazy nobs, you see."

He nodded, as if any of that made sense.

Focus on Irene.

"Um, why—"

"Have no bloody idea. And that bothers me, I can tell you."

"Uh… what?"

"You want to know why someone would follow Mrs. Knopp. Don't know. Been trailing her on and off myself since the incident, when I can. Though murders and the like have been keeping me busy. You can't imagine how many dead bodies there are in London on a given day. I'm the only one who really handles them, you know. The rest are more coppers and thief-takers. That's what pays best, you know. I do it because I like it. Gratifying to see the guilty men hang and the innocent ones go free." He frowned as they wended their way through the crowd. There were droves of people there, and they banged into one another at every turn. "It's Miss Drew, most likely," he said as he grabbed a boy and snagged something out of the child's fist.

"The seamstress," Grant said, feeling his wits sharpen as he caught the rhythm of Mr. Morrison's speech. "Because of her connection to Demon Damon."

Mr. Morrison stopped then and shot him a strangely intense look. His eyes were narrowed, his brow lowered, and Grant could almost feel the thoughts churning in his head. But a moment later, the man released a huff of disgust.

"Can't see the reason behind it yet," he said in a kind of curse. Then his face split into a grin as he looked over Grant's shoulder. "Constable. Knew you'd be here!"

A tired man in brown with a salt-and-pepper scruff for a beard turned to greet them. His eyes were sharp, but his general demeanor was one of a man too overburdened to enjoy life. No surprise, as he was clearly shepherding prisoners before the magistrate. Still, he paused long enough to give Morrison a raised eyebrow and a hopeful smile.

"Solved another one of my crimes, have you, Samuel? Let's have it. Who do I arrest?"

"Not arrest. Set free. Mr. Hobbs is left-handed."

There was a pause as the man frowned. It took him long enough that Grant ventured into the conversation by way of an explanation.

"I believe Mr. Morrison believes the killer was right-handed."

"Yes, yes," the constable said irritably. "I'd gathered that. But a man can hit with both hands. And the victim could have been restrained by the dominant hand and hit with the non-dominant."

Morrison pursed his lips. "Possible, but rare."

"But possible."

Another long pause and then, almost at random, Mr. Morrison stepped out and grabbed a dirty little girl who had been wending her way through the crowd. The child was just skin and bones, but her eyes flashed fury as Mr. Morrison held her up. He needed both hands to keep the girl far enough away that she didn't kick. "Constable, please. The pouch under her dress."

The constable rolled his eyes, but obediently, managed to pull out the pouch beneath the child's dress. He took a few heavy blows from her feet as he did it, but a moment later, he pulled out a sharp flick knife.

"I believe it was meant for Mr. Wilks," Mr. Morrison said, gesturing at a very large, very angry prisoner. "I believe he intended something nefarious. Likely after he was back in gaol."

The constable released a sigh then gestured at his men, who were suddenly looking alertly at the prisoner in question. Meanwhile, Mr. Morrison handed the girl to one of the constable's men.

"Hold her still. I'm sure you'll want to question her in a moment." Then he turned back to the constable. "I can help you with—"

"No need. I know what's what with Wilks. Tell me again how Mr. Hobbs ain't the bastard I think 'e is."

"Oh, he's a bastard, all right, but not the murderer

in this case. And I don't think he deserves to be hanged for cheating at cards."

"Bloody hell, then who—"

"I should have that name for you in a day's time. Have to check on a few things first. Meanwhile, I believe I need to help Lord Crowle, so I'll bid you good day for now."

"Samuel!" the constable barked. "Don't be harrying off on your own. I'll be free tomorrow morning."

"Of course, of course," Mr. Morrison returned with a wave of his hand. Then he tapped Grant on the shoulder, handed him his purse, which had apparently been lifted—and rescued—at some point in the conversation, before heading toward the door.

Grant scrambled to keep up while—again—his madness released another low whistle of appreciation.

Never play cards with that man. You'd be fleeced before the first hand is played out.

"Come on, man," Mr. Morrison called in good cheer. "Out with it. What's the new clue?"

Grant blinked. "Um, what?"

"Come, come. You wouldn't have searched me out unless something new had happened. Mrs. Knopp told me herself that she believes she must have imagined it. Therefore, if you're here, then something new has come to light."

Grant looked up sharply. "Do you think it was her imagination?"

"I wasn't knocked cold by her imagination. She was followed. So what's the new clue?"

"We were attacked last night."

The man stopped right in the middle of the street,

and once again, Grant was awed by the cold focus of the man's intellect, like a blade cutting to the heart of things. There weren't many men that impressed Grant, but here was one doing it in spades.

"Tell me everything. In detail."

So Grant did. Everything he could remember. And as they walked toward the fashionable center of town, Mr. Morrison listened carefully, asked only a few questions, and—unfortunately—probably made conclusions about last night that had absolutely nothing to do with their attack. Fortunately, he never spoke on that part. Instead, the man slowed his step until they stood outside the Shoemaker shop.

"Have you spoken with your brother?"

Grant gaped, the question hitting him broadside. "What?"

"Your brother. Your heir, right? The one engaged to the newly dowered Miss Josephine Powel?"

"William. Yes, he's my brother. But why would you ask about him?"

"You should talk to him, I think. But in a public place. No reason to take unnecessary chances."

"*What?*"

Mr. Morrison frowned, apparently choosing his words carefully, as if he were trying to be delicate. Apparently, this was not normal for him, and so he was awkward at it.

"Seems to me a younger brother who manages to court and soon marry the lands that were once yours might want something else that is yours."

Grant stared at the man, his mind churning. "You think I was the focus of the attack?"

"You said there was no demand for money, just a quick attack that you foiled."

"Yes, but I thought he was going for Irene."

"Or perhaps, that's what you believed, because you've since learned of her mysterious follower. A good thought and still a possibility. However, I submit that *you* might be the focus of the attack, and who has a better motive for murder than your brother?"

"Will's a prig, not a killer. And he's not in London."

"Easy enough to hire someone," the man answered with implacable logic. "When was the last time you really talked with your brother? Really knew him enough to say what he is or is not capable of? In my experience, every man is capable of murder in the right circumstances."

Grant rubbed a hand over his face, his mind frozen with doubts. Good God, could he really be considering this? Will a murderer? "It can't be."

"It might not be. I simply offer it as a possibility. One that should be explored, if only to prove it is *not* possible."

Grant's chest tightened, and he noted almost absently that his hands had tightened into fists.

Whom do you mean to plug? Will or this bastard?

He didn't mean to plug—er, punch anyone. Except, perhaps himself, for considering that his brother could be coldly plotting his murder. And yet, he couldn't *not* consider it. The idea had taken root in his brain.

"In the meantime," continued Mr. Morrison, as if he hadn't just turned Grant completely inside out, "I shall try to be a little more vigilant in watching Mrs. Knopp. You will tell her to be careful though, won't you? I can't be everywhere, and if your brother is indeed innocent, then the lady could be in grave danger indeed."

"What if this was a common footpad?" Grant asked. *Clutching at straws.*

"Is that what you think?" countered Mr. Morrison.

"No."

"Then why waste time on the question?"

"Because," answered a female who left the shop doorway to stand beside Mr. Morrison. "It's a damned hard thing for a man to think about murder. Makes it even harder when it's in the family."

Mr. Morrison's face lightened suddenly, going from coldly precise to something that some might call soft. Where once there was the impression of only hard angles and cutting intellect, suddenly, the man became almost vague as he stared down adoringly at the woman. Grant recognized her as Penny Shoemaker, fiancée to the odd runner.

"I think of it all the time," Samuel murmured vaguely.

"Well, you're a mad gent, and no mistake about that," she returned with a grin. Then right there on the street, she stretched up to kiss him. Mr. Morrison's hand tightened on her waist, and his head lowered. The kiss was scorching for all that it was public, and Grant felt acutely uncomfortable on any number of levels.

Fortunately, it didn't last long. It was the woman, he thought, who ended the kiss. Pushing Mr. Morrison away, though not hard.

"Stop it, Samuel. It's not proper." Then she turned to give a considering look at Grant. "You're Lord Crowle, aren't you? We spoke last night."

Without thinking, Grant gave her a courtly bow, kissing her rough hand as if she were a queen. "Pleasure to see you again, Miss Shoemaker." He gestured to the shop behind them. "So this is your father's place? Though I never had the pleasure of wearing a pair of his boots, I understand they were divine."

"Thank you, my lord." She dimpled prettily even as she stepped backwards. "But it's my shop now—for ladies—or will be within a few weeks, after I get the insides sorted out. And I make the shoes."

Grant's eyebrows rose, impressed again. It was most unusual to hear of a woman making shoes, much less owning her own shop. Meanwhile, his madness wasn't allowing him to escape into pleasantries.

Forget his girl. Focus on yours!

"Do you think Irene could be in danger?" he asked, his voice coming out a little too abrupt.

"What?" asked Penny, obviously alarmed.

Mr. Morrison patted her arm. "Don't worry. I'll keep an eye on her. Or pay Willy to—."

"No!" exclaimed Grant, though God only knew why he was suddenly so passionate. "I'll do it."

Mr. Morrison's eyes narrowed. "I thought you were going to speak with your brother."

"I am," Grant said, his tone growing colder by the second. "I'm going to do *both*. In fact, I believe I'm going to find Irene right now. And I'll be damned if I let *her* sensibilities deter me!"

There was a moment of dead silence from all three. Then suddenly, Mr. Morrison nodded sharply. "Good man," he pronounced.

That, apparently, was enough for Miss Shoemaker,

and her apprentice Tabitha carried the cloth into the showroom, but with the increase in business and the massive purchase Irene had made from Grant, there just wasn't room. So now, customers came to the back to see their choices.

Irene looked up, knowing that she needed to appear friendly, despite the headache that thrummed behind her eyes. Then her expression froze. Miss Josephine Powel stood in the center of the group, her eyes sparkling and her gestures expansive. Her sister was no less animated as the two argued back and forth, but it was Josephine who drew Irene's cool regard.

The girl was lovely, reddish brown chestnut curls and all. And she had been stunning last night at the ball when Grant had abandoned Irene to rush to that woman's side. Irene had watched—discreetly, of course—as Grant had maneuvered an introduction and had spoken with the woman for a few minutes, then he'd gone white-faced with shock. A moment later, the man had disappeared into the card room.

Irene had no idea what happened, but she had a sudden fierce need to learn all she could about the harpy. So she listened, while pretending not to, and she tried to think of a way to enter the conversation. Then Helaine solved her problem by asking for her help.

"Irene, dear, I wonder if you might help us. This is Lady Lawton and her two daughters Miss Josephine and Miss Megan. Josephine has just gotten engaged and is looking for the right dress for her party."

"Engaged? Best wishes, my dear!" Irene said, her mind working furiously. Was that what Grant had discovered last night? That the girl was engaged?

Of course, it was. Which meant that he went to the card room to cover his disappointment over losing her. And when that wasn't helping, he had sought something else: a woman who *was* available. Irene. Oh damnation, was that all she'd been to him? A way to get past this fiery beauty?

Irene's smile felt brittle, but the others didn't seem to notice. Miss Josephine's eyes were dancing, her cheeks flushed, and it was obvious to everyone that she was ecstatically happy. And the sister was no less thrilled as she discussed the details of the wedding—engagement dress, wedding dress, *her* dress. A trousseau for both girls, it seemed, with all the fashion excitement that entailed.

Irene was pulled into a discussion of silks and buttons, what supplies they had on hand, what could be purchased for the right price. It was dizzying, and it was all for the woman who had broken Grant's heart. The same woman who would look awful in that swath of orange.

Irene was about to point out the silk when she stopped herself. Was she really that spiteful? And to a girl who may not even know what she'd done to Grant? Especially when Irene didn't truly *know* what had happened.

With a grimace of annoyance, she shifted to a silk with a subtle wash of green. That would be divine on the girl. "How about—"

"Irene! There you are!"

Everyone spun around at the loud, male voice that cut through the chatter in the room. It was Grant, his voice half angry, half exasperated as he pushed his way from the front salon into the back workroom, while everyone else fell dead silent and stared.

Helaine was the first to recover. "Sir, this is a place for ladies. I must insist that you wait in the front salon immediately." She glanced pointedly at his attire—which was of a decidedly unfashionable nature—then gestured to the back door. "Or you could always compose yourself outside. I'm sure Lady Irene can discuss her business with you out there."

Grant was about to answer. His eyes had locked onto hers, and he was pushing his way forward as fast as he could without actually shoving the ladies aside. But at Helaine's words, he abruptly stopped and turned to her.

"*Lady* Irene?" he asked.

Oh no! Had she never told him her true title?

Meanwhile, the bride suddenly gasped and clapped her hands. "Lord Crowle! Goodness, I didn't recognize you at first."

At which point, Irene watched everything again, just like what had happened last night. Grant turned, his eyes widening as he saw Miss Powel. His body jolted as he took in not only her, but her sister and mother. And then his face drained of all color. He covered, of course. His skin didn't truly go gray-white. But Irene saw it clear as day, even though he stammered his way through a startled bow.

"Uh… good afternoon. Misses Powel and Lady Lawton. I hadn't realized—I mean, what brings you—well, of course, you're here looking at dresses, aren't you?"

Megan trilled with laughter, the sound too flirty

to be comfortable. But everyone else just smiled at the flustered man. Everyone, that is, but Irene who stepped forward. "Lord Crowle, is there something you wanted?"

He turned, focusing on her. His eyes were piercing sharp at first, but then his expression softened. Then it slid to a slow frown. "*Lady* Irene? I had no idea you were so exalted." Was there an edge to his tone?

"I believe we both understand the reasons for hiding a title sometimes. I apologize if I surprised you."

He blinked and then recovered, while his skin flushed ruddy. "No, it is I who must apologize. It seems I am out of practice with London."

What the devil did that mean? Irene wondered. Meanwhile, the blushing bride pressed forward, her eyes alight with curiosity. "Out of practice? Then you have been traveling. Will has been extremely curious as to your whereabouts."

Grant straightened, and his expression closed down. It was a subtle change, one that Irene wouldn't have noticed if she hadn't been looking right at him.

"Really?" he drawled as he turned to face Miss Josephine. "He has mentioned my whereabouts to you?"

The woman blinked. "Well, only that he has been looking for you all summer. Came down here expressly to find you a couple months ago. I'm so glad that you're here now. We were hoping you would be."

He rocked back on his heels as he considered the girl, and Irene could feel his attention like a sharp point in the air. It was a wonder that the girl didn't bleed.

"Well, I am here now. Is there something he wished to discuss?"

She blinked at his cold tone, obviously startled. "Well, yes, actually. Um, I—we—wanted to be sure you come to our engagement ball. We, uh, we don't have your address, so we didn't know if you—"

"My solicitor handles all my mail. Will knows the address."

She bit her lip, and Irene could see the entire family shuffle their feet in discomfort. Whatever the reason for Grant's chilling tone, these ladies didn't understand it.

He must have seen that as well because he abruptly ran his hand through his hair. "I'm terribly sorry. I've had a rather disturbing day already and am out of sorts."

"Nothing terrible, I hope?" Miss Josephine asked.

His gaze tightened again on her while Irene tried to understand. It had sounded like an innocent question, but obviously, something was bothering the man. "Um, no," he said. "Nothing too disconcerting. Perhaps you could tell me when Will is coming to London. I should very much like to see him."

"Oh!" The woman brightened considerably. "Of course! He will be arriving today! Or perhaps tomorrow. You must come for nuncheon. That way we can all get to know one another better."

Irene saw an expression flit across his face. Wariness. As if he saw demons in every corner, and most especially, in the girl who stood right across from him.

She knew the feeling well—the vague uncertainty that haunted every thought. But for the life of her, she couldn't guess why he would be so suspicious of the Lawton girls. But it was clearly getting the better of him, so Irene judged it time to step in. He might not appreciate her help, but she couldn't bear to see him so at a loss.

"How stupid of me!" she cried as she pulled out a chair. "Lord Crowle, your wound must be paining you. Please, will you not sit down?" She gave him little choice as she all but hauled him backward. Then amid the general chaos of questions, she flashed a smile at everyone. "Lord Crowle was kind enough to escort myself and Wendy home last night. We weren't that far from here when we were attacked by a footpad. Lord Crowle was extremely dashing as he defended us. But he took a knife in the belly for his pains."

If there were expressions of concern before, there was outright horror now. All of sudden, everyone was asking questions and offering Lord Crowle tea. He held up his hands, waving their words off with a horrified look. "Lady Irene exaggerates. It was a mere scratch. I am quite well."

He was not quite well, Irene thought rather loudly in her own mind. But the problem appeared to be in his mind more than his body. Even in the midst of the current chaos, she remembered how he'd come barging in, demanding to see her. Something important had brought him here. Something that had gotten lost amid the awkward discussion with the Lawtons.

Meanwhile, Grant was refusing all offers, his tone pleasant, his expression neutral. And all the while, he kept his gaze on Miss Josephine. Irene couldn't fathom what he was looking for. Whatever it was, he didn't seem to get it. In the end, he grimaced and turned to her.

"Lady Irene, I actually came here to speak to you."

"Yes, I know. Is it urgent?"

"Just some details that we need to make clear. I was with the constable this morning, and there were additional questions."

"Oh… oh, of course." Then she looked at the avid listeners surrounding them. There was a great deal about last night that she had no interest in sharing. "I was planning on walking home. Do you think you are well enough to escort me?"

He straightened immediately. "It would be my honor."

A second later, they were turning to the workroom's back door when Miss Josephine interposed herself between them and their escape. She was adamant, her expression almost fierce.

"My lord, please, I really must insist. Your brother is most anxious to see you. Couldn't you please join us for dinner tomorrow?"

He was caught. She had no idea why he wanted to avoid his brother so desperately, but the bride had been insistent. Now, he had no choice but to accept or be extremely rude to his future sister-in-law. Obviously, he knew that. Especially since he finally dipped his head in acknowledgment.

"Forgive me," he said quietly. "Of course, I should like to see my brother. But your house must be in disarray. You've only just arrived."

"No. We've been here a week so far."

The smile he gave her was clearly strained. "Nevertheless. Do you know of The Crooked Billet inn? I'm having a small gathering there tomorrow night. Quiet thing. A thank you to Robert, Lord

Redhill, for our longstanding friendship." He looked over to Helaine. "Lady Redhill, I came here today to beg you and your husband to attend." There was a silent plea in his gaze as he looked to Helaine. "Say you will be there. Seven o'clock?"

Helaine blinked, a frown on her face. "Why, of course. Robert and I would be most pleased to attend."

Grant sent her a grateful smile before he turned back to Miss Josephine. "Perhaps you and Will could attend as well?"

"Most definitely," the woman said.

"I look forward to it." Then he bowed to the room in general before holding out his arm to Irene. "If you are ready?"

She smiled back, her thoughts spinning with questions. "Thank you, my lord." Then together they stepped outside.

She held her tongue well after the door shut behind them. She kept silent for six steps, ten beats of her heart, or three long, rather frustrated breaths. But at the end of all that, she clenched Grant's arm and spoke quite plainly.

"If you don't tell me immediately what that was about, I swear I shall cause a scene."

He blinked as he turned his troubled gaze to her, then he nodded. It was a slow nod, as if he had the weight of the world on his shoulders. And then he gestured to the side.

"Hyde Park is over there. Fancy a stroll?"

She thought of the time and gasped in horror. "Now? In Hyde Park? I am not dressed for it." She didn't dare mention that what he wore was completely outre. He was dressed as a tradesman and couldn't risk being seen as such. Not by the *haut ton*.

He grimaced. "Oh yes, I'd forgotten."

"Do you know, I believe you have been Mr. Grant for much too long. You have completely forgotten the responsibilities of your title."

He eyes flashed angrily. "Believe me," he ground out. "I am well aware that I am an earl. Today of all days, it weighs most heavy on me."

"But why? Why today of all days? What happened in the few hours since we parted?"

He grimaced then looked away. His feet took them in the opposite direction of Hyde Park. It was toward her home, so she didn't object. Truthfully, she would walk to Bath and back if it meant he explained himself. Fortunately, it didn't require more than a couple steps before he began to speak.

"What do you recall of last night?"

Her face abruptly heated, and worse, her belly quivered. "Um," she began, struggling for words.

He glanced at her, and his eyes suddenly grew languid. "Er, not that. Although—"

"You mean the footpad, don't you?"

His expression shuttered, and eventually, he looked away. "Yes. I spoke with Mr. Morrison about the attack."

She could read the truth in his face. "Mr. Morrison doesn't believe the man was a common footpad. He thinks my mysterious follower is back and…" She couldn't even say the words.

He touched her hand where it lay on his forearm. "Don't be afraid," he said softly. "I have no intention of leaving you alone until we figure out what is happening."

She arched her brows, startled by his vehement statement. It was folderol, of course. He couldn't possibly mean to remain by her side every second of every day and night. Unless, of course, he absolutely *did*.

Her steps slowed, forcing him to stop and look at her. "Irene?"

She didn't know what to say. She didn't even know how to frame her question. Did he truly mean to protect her *all* the time? How?

She could see the worry in his face, the concern that buried his earlier frustration. And at that moment, she realized what he had done. By bringing up the attack, he had neatly distracted her from whatever it was *truly* bothering him.

"I cry foul, my lord!" she said tartly. "We were speaking of you and whatever was happening back at the dress shop."

He grimaced. "I know," he said quietly. "I was getting to that."

She took hold of her temper. It wasn't really temper, more a disquiet of soul. He did that to her, she realized. He made her feel things and think things and worry about... everything again. Just as if she were a... a...

Damnation, she was feeling just as she did when she fell in love with Nate. Oh no, no, no! She bit her lip and roughly pushed the emotion aside. In the midst of everything, that was the last thing she needed to feel. She absolutely refused to fall in love right then. Especially with a lord who made grand pronouncements that he was going to protect her every day of her life. Her father had been one such man with big

statements and wonderful sentiments, until he got
distracted by something else. She'd learned very young
not to trust any man who spoke in such sweeping
ways. So she took a deep breath and glared at Grant.
"The truth," she said. "Now."

He rubbed a hand over his face, but he didn't argue.
"As I said, I went to see Mr. Morrison. He agrees
that was no common footpad, but he offered another
motive behind the attack. A different one from your
mysterious pursuer."

She frowned, suddenly finding it easy to concen-
trate on his words. "But that's excellent! I'm sure what
happened wasn't linked to me."

"Mr. Morrison thinks my brother may be trying to
kill me."

It took some moments for his words to penetrate
her thoughts. And some longer moments for her
rational mind to process that he was serious—enough
to be tormented by the idea.

"Your brother? As in Miss Powel's fiancé?"

"Yes, my brother Will."

"But... but... I don't understand."

Grant shrugged, and as they were about to be
jostled by a pair of rushing ostlers, he started walking
again. "Samuel has a way of pointing out things so that
the logic is painfully clear."

"Yes," she agreed softly. "He does have that rather
unique charm. What exactly did he say?"

"That my brother has done a great deal lately to secure
the wealth of the title in his name. He and Lawton
improved the land so much that I could not buy it back.
Then it all went into Miss Josephine's dowry."

"Will's fiancée. I understand, but it is a rather large step from marrying an heiress to murder."

Grant nodded grimly. "But he has been looking for me. Rather desperately, I hear."

"You are his brother. Did he not have your address?"

He shook his head, his mouth pressed flat.

It took a moment's study, but then she understood. "He does not know you are Mr. Grant, does he? He doesn't know what you've been doing these last five years."

"No one does!" he snapped. "And no one should." Then at her startled look, he shifted awkwardly. "I'm terribly sorry. This has been a trying day."

"Of course, it is," she said softly, reading the anguish in his face. "You are ashamed of it, aren't you?"

He didn't answer, his gaze intent on crossing the street.

"Hard thing to do," she said softly. "Take up a job like a common tradesman. I wanted to do it, but even I struggled with nights of guilt. I don't even feel like Lady Irene anymore. And my sire was as useless an earl as it was possible to be."

"I'll bet my father and grandfather had him beat."

She shook her head. "Let's not get onto the subject of disappointing relatives. We shall never return to the important matter."

He shot her a wry look. "And that would be?"

"Why you believe your brother is trying to… to…"

"Gain the earldom by any means possible?"

She swallowed. "Yes."

"Because he believes me a useless wreck of a man who is destroying not only our family name, but England as a whole."

She pulled back. "Surely you jest. How could you possibly be destroying England?"

"Because I am also a useless earl. As my father before me, and his father before that. As your father was. The days of a responsible gentry, of men who are appropriate stewards to their people—you know, as well as I do, how few of our set live up to that task."

She winced. She did. And she had roundly damned them for years. "But you are not like that."

"I most certainly am. I was not the one sweating during harvest or up in the middle of the night to aid a sow at birthing." He tightened his grip on her arm. "I neither cared for the sheep, nor the homes of our tenants. I stayed in London and enjoyed the fruits of their labors."

"That was before," she said firmly.

"That is all my brother knows of me."

"Then you must tell him differently. You must show him that you have changed. And, if I understand things correctly, you were never that way. It was your father, not you."

He shrugged. "My brother doesn't believe people can change."

"You aren't a useless title. Mr. Grant hasn't wasted his life or his talents!"

He sighed, the sound coming from deep within him. There was an ache in the tone, one that was long-standing.

"You think you're useless, do you?" she whispered, shocked to the core of her soul.

He merely shrugged. "Just because I have spent the last five years locked away in a kind of gaol, doesn't mean that the soul of me has altered whatsoever."

"Perhaps," she said softly. "And perhaps your soul has been good all along."

He snorted, but patted her hand gently. "You know very little of my soul, Irene. And—God willing—you never will."

She pulled back, completely appalled by his dismissal. "Why would you say that? Why would you ask for a distance between us?"

He must have noticed her tone. Certainly, he couldn't miss how she drew back as if wounded. But he held her hand tight, gripping her fingers when she would have withdrawn from his arm. "I am mad, Irene," he said softly. "A stark, raving lunatic. I always have been."

"Ridiculous! You are making up things to give me a disgust of you." She didn't say aloud the inescapable conclusion. After last night, he clearly wanted to be rid of her, and this was the way he chose to do it.

"No, Irene. I am hiding things specifically, so you *won't* have a disgust of me."

She searched his face, startled by what she read there. He was serious. He believed himself mad. Worse, he believed he was as useless as his father.

"I cannot credit that you are so unaware of your own value!"

His eyebrows arched, and his face took on a sad smile. "Will you come tomorrow night?" he asked.

"What?" She had such a hard time following his thoughts sometimes.

"To the party I have just decided to throw."

She nodded, her mind pulling in the details of his event. "You didn't want to dine at the Lawton household." Her eyes abruptly widened. "You think they might try and murder you there? At dinner?"

The shock of the idea made her voice too loud, and he hastily drew her further down the street. She moderated her voice though her mind was reeling.

"Even if your brother has gone mad," she said gently, "surely you don't believe the Lawtons have anything to do with it."

"I don't know what to think," he grumbled. Then at her alarmed look, he shook his head. "No, the Lawtons are probably innocent. And truthfully, I still cannot believe Will would... that he..." His words trailed off.

"But even so, you did not wish to dine at their home."

He shrugged. "It seemed prudent to control the location and food. Harder to poison me that way."

She shuddered, hating that he even thought of these things. Awful to imagine that one's brother might be contemplating murder. Worse to think of all the ways it might be done. A knife in the dark was bad enough, but poison?

"Why invite the Redhills then?"

"Robert is my closest friend. He has a level head and a keen eye. If anyone can see the truth, it will be him."

She nodded. "You will tell him about all this?"

"Yes. I'll see him right after I arrange for the meal." Then he grimaced. "Bother, I cannot leave you alone."

"Of course, you can. I tell you, I am not in any danger."

He whipped her around, so fast that she nearly lost her bonnet. As it was, she stumbled slightly, but he held her safe. "Listen to me Irene. *One* of us is in danger. If it is not me, then it is *you*. And I will not risk you, even while I am investigating my brother."

She swallowed, seeing the intensity in his eyes. It resembled a fever the way his skin flushed and his eyes burned too bright. "I cannot credit either possibility," she whispered. "Why would anyone want to hurt me?" Then she touched his face. "Or you."

He shuddered as she placed her palm on his cheek. A physical tremble that told her he was unused to being touched in this manner. Last night's caresses had been one thing, but this gentle touch on the face in broad daylight? He had not experienced that in a long time.

He turned his face into her fingers, closing his eyes as he held her hand there. Then he kissed her palm, though she could not feel it through her glove.

"So will you come tomorrow night?" he asked.

She hesitated. "You know what it will look like."

He nodded. "That you are my mistress. Or a future wife." He lifted his head to search her face. "Does that bother you?"

Yes. No. Yes. Rather than answer, she gestured to the sign for The Crooked Billet. "Shall we go in? See if they have a private room available for tomorrow night?"

He flashed her a hopeful smile. "A parlor can be private long after dinner guests have departed."

It took her a moment to realize what he was suggesting then she straightened into her most lofty air. "Do you intend bloodshed, my lord? I only stay beyond the evening's entertainment if there is someone in need of nursing."

He laughed, the sound lighter than she had heard

from him all day. "Between my brother and I? Have no fear. Even if he has no intention of murdering me, I can promise that the two of us will always get to squabbling."

"Really? Like two hens over a seed?"

"Like two bloodhounds over a tasty rabbit."

"Ah," she said as they headed inside the inn. "Just so long as you are not the rabbit, I will be quite content to watch the combat. One learns a great deal about a family when witnessing brotherly squabbles."

He nodded slowly. "And you are an extraordinarily perceptive woman. I am quite afraid of what you might find out."

She warmed at his compliment even as she teased back. "Then I say, let the games begin."

They were playing at being silly. The seriousness of what he'd told her was too heavy a thought to bear for long. So they were bantering as if it were the most casual of afternoons. As if he hadn't just asked her to publicly declare herself his mistress. As if his brother couldn't possibly be considering fratricide. But they couldn't maintain the ruse for long, and soon, his expression shifted from playful to deadly serious.

He lifted her hand, pressing his lips to the back. "Thank you," he said, his eyes conveying warmth, gratitude, and perhaps even love.

"I haven't said yes," she said stiffly, her heart lurching in her throat. He could not be looking at her with love, and she could not be considering playing hostess to his party. They did not have such feelings for each other. She knew that because she had been very much in love with her husband. There had been no footpads in her courtship with Nate. No murderous brothers or mysterious followers. There had been flowers and giddy laughter and a warm feeling of security. And nothing like this sick nervousness that shook her down to her toes.

Therefore, she was not in love, and neither was Grant. They were two mature adults thrown together because of a ridiculously frightening footpad. That was all. And so it would continue through tomorrow night when she proved that his brother was not attempting to murder anyone.

She lurched inside, realizing she had just decided she would appear as his mistress in front of his family and her friends. It wasn't such a devastating choice. She would explain matters to Helaine. She doubted any would talk, and of course, the *ton* didn't really care what a nobody widow did with her time. No one would speak of it to her in-laws, and it was more important to help Grant as he faced his brother.

"Irene?" he said when she hadn't moved into the inn.

She looked at him and swallowed her fears. It was such a small thing: playing his hostess for one night. She would be churlish to deny him at such a terrible time. "Of course, I will help you," she said. "And you will see that there is nothing to worry about."

Sixteen

GRANT WONDERED IF THIS WAS HOW MEN FELT BEFORE battle. He was a jumble of contradictory emotions. Calm and jittery, excited and terrified. It had been five years since he'd last seen Will, and their parting had been ugly to say the least. Was the man really angry enough to plot Grant's murder? Of course not, and yet...

"Helaine and Robert are here," said a calm voice to his left. Irene. And thank God for her, or he'd have jumped off the nearest bridge to stop the questions churning in his mind.

"Thank you," he said. Then when she turned away from the window toward the inn room door, he grabbed her hands and brought her around. "I mean that more than I can say. I know what playing hostess makes you appear."

"We have... well, appearing as your hostess only reveals to the world what we are in fact." Her voice was tight, and he knew what that cost her. It was no small thing for her to show anyone, much less her employer and his potentially murderous brother, exactly what they were to each other: lovers. Man and mistress. Lord and *fallen* lady.

It didn't matter that he'd wanted her since they'd first danced together in a different inn. She was giving up a piece of herself merely because he asked it. And, for that alone, he adored her.

She looked away, probably because he was staring so intently. She became nervous whenever he did that, uncomfortable with his feelings, as they were no doubt written boldly across his face. Once he'd been told he had a good face for poker—blank and unreadable. No longer. Not around her.

Meanwhile, she gestured to the small table set for six. It gleamed in perfection there. From the candelabra to the cutlery, all was the best that could be had at an inn. "They've set a fine table here. You made a good choice."

"I was lucky they had the room available."

She nodded then they both heard the warm tones of the innkeeper as he escorted Lord and Lady Redhill to the room.

"You spoke with Lord Redhill?" she whispered before the door opened. "To watch your brother?"

He nodded a quick yes as the door opened, and his best friend entered the room. "Robert," he said with a smile. "And Helaine, you look divine."

They were dressed as was appropriate for wealthy peers. Helaine's gown was one of her own design, and it flowed beautifully about her body. Unable to stop himself, he noted the cut and quality of the fabric in their attire. Robert, he noted with pleasure, wore a waistcoat made from Wakefield Design wool, the pattern on the fabric another of Grant's own.

Grant looked pointedly at the waistcoat. "Amazing what a wife in fashion has done for your wardrobe. Become quite the dapper fellow, haven't you?"

Robert lifted his chin in mock arrogance. "I'll have you know I purchased this long before Helaine came into my life."

"No, you didn't," inserted Helaine from the side, where she'd just finished kissing Irene's cheek. "Gwen gave it to you for Michaelmas last year."

Robert frowned. "Are you sure? You weren't even—"

"Yes, my dear. Gwen and I have discussed your wardrobe often, I'm afraid."

He grimaced at that, and then Grant turned to introduce Irene to his friend. "Robert, you remember Lady Irene." Her title still felt awkward on his tongue, though he didn't know why. He'd known she was a lady from the first moment they'd met.

Irene curtsied, and Robert bowed over her hand. All the proprieties were handled smoothly, and no one looked askance at Irene. At least, not that he could see. Although he did overhear as Helaine whispered to Irene. "You and I are overdue for a long chat."

Irene flushed that adorable shade of pink and nodded quietly. "I would like that very much," she whispered back.

Then there was no more time as everyone heard the other two guests come down the hallway. Robert shot him a worried look, but Grant merely squared his shoulders and faced the doorway as he might a firing squad.

Miss Josephine Powel entered first, and in a way probably typical of her—all flushed good looks and an overly loud greeting. She was nervous, that much was obvious, but her smile seemed genuine enough. Will came behind her, his step slow, his eyes grave. He walked in his typical, unhurried way, and his gestures were reserved. And when he met Grant's gaze, he held it with a long assessing frown. The dour Yorkshire man through and through, Grant thought with a sigh.

There was one difference in his persona though. Something that broke through his brother's reserve and gave Grant hope there was something of the boy still in the man. It was the way his brother treated his fiancée. He stood near her and touched her often. And when Will chanced to look at her, his expression softened, and he occasionally got lost in just the look. As if a part of him couldn't believe the woman was his.

Will was a man in love. And from the looks of her, Miss Powel returned the feeling a thousand fold.

Grant felt a weight roll from his shoulders. He hadn't even recognized his fear that Will was marrying for money until the concern was gone. Of the three Crowle children, he was pleased that one had managed a love match.

Meanwhile, Grant needed to formally welcome his guests. "Thank you for coming. I'm especially pleased that you, Miss Powel, were able to understand my most unusual request to dine here. I know it's odd, but I have yet to find a real house in London. And you were able to come without a chaperone too. I find that especially gratifying."

She smiled prettily. "Oh well, I'm of a rather independent bent, I'm afraid. Papa made a fuss, of course. And there's a maid and a large footman idling away in the hallway. But once I made it clear that Lord and Lady Redhill would be here, Papa was made to see reason." Then she flashed a warm look at her fiancée. "Besides, he trusts Will to keep everything above board."

Robert—newly finished with greeting Will— interjected a rumbling approval. "That's quite a statement of confidence from a girl's father. I'm afraid I don't know much of Lawton. Is he generally of an easygoing sort?"

Both Grant and Miss Powel said, "Not generally," at the exact same moment. That elicited chuckles among the group. Will, naturally, said nothing except to frown at his brother.

Now there's a familiar look, drawled his madness. Grant bit back a curse. The last thing he needed right now was for his madness to interject comments only he could hear. The situation was delicate enough without insanity mucking up the logic.

Meanwhile, he turned to his brother, trying to put a lifetime's worth of feelings into his quiet words. He couldn't, of course. So the words came out polite and probably rather cool. "I'm very glad you could make it too."

His brother nodded back gravely, his gaze taking in Grant from head to toe. "You look... healthy." There was a bit of shock in his brother's words, but nothing compared to the minute of silence that followed.

"Healthy?" Grant finally echoed. "Did you expect me to be on my deathbed?"

From a knife wound perhaps?

Will shook his head slowly. "I didn't know what to expect. I've never known."

There was a wealth of meaning in those few words, but no explanation. Which left the two brothers staring at each other, while everyone else twisted in uncomfortable silence.

"But I told you he looked fine!" inserted Miss Powel with a too high laugh. "I must confess that I was surprised when I first saw you at the Redhill ball, my lord. Between your brother and my father, I half expected horns or bloodshot eyes at the very least, when here you are looking perfectly acceptable." Then, as if suddenly realizing what she'd said, she gasped and pressed her hand to her mouth. "Oh, that is, I didn't meant to suggest that Will or my father—"

"Your father has no love of me, Miss Powel," Grant interposed quietly. "He has not hidden that fact." He naturally left silent the other half of that statement: he had not expected Will to despise him.

"As I said," Will cut in, his voice hard. "You have been missing for five years. I had no idea what to expect, not even if you were dead or alive."

Grant felt his hackles rise. Will had stepped back into his usual pompous self. That he had a legitimate grievance did not change Grant's knee-jerk response. Whenever his brother sought to school him, Grant resorted to a casual insouciance that never failed to irritate the boy. Er, the man.

"Ah well," he said, spreading his arms wide. "As you can see, I'm still well and hale. Lord Crowle in all his glory, so to speak." Then he turned to the well-stocked sideboard. "Something to drink anyone? I am feeling quite parched myself."

He stepped to the sideboard, his hands shaking.

Except for the night of the Redhill ball, Grant hadn't considered a drop of brandy in five years. Now he wanted it with a frightening desperation. Not because he cared for the alcohol, but because he had no wish to face the animosity in his brother's eyes. Did the man really despise him so deeply?

Thankfully, Irene stepped into the breech, asking Miss Powel about her wedding and beginning a discussion of gown fashions. That gave Robert time to take the brandy decanter from Grant and set it aside.

"Steady there. Will was always somewhat dour. That proves nothing."

"Comes from trying to run an estate without a copper to support it." Grant swirled the liquid in his glass, but didn't drink. He was afraid if he started, he'd never stop.

Meanwhile, Robert squeezed his arm. "You had plenty to handle as well. Your father was ten times worse than mine, and considering the comparison, it's a wonder you're not completely mad."

Grant's madness thought that was terribly funny, and it was probably two breaths before Grant could hear anything but the thing's laughter.

Meanwhile, Redhill swallowed his brandy and shot Grant a dark look. "I didn't know you'd kept apart from your family for the last five years. Bloody hell, man, I'd be angry at you too."

"Yes," said a hard voice. Will, of course. Coming up behind them in his quiet way. "What have you been doing?"

Grant turned, the truth on his lips, but he couldn't bring himself to say it. He couldn't confess that he'd been sweating at the mill, working harder than the lowest beast in the field, and starving like a mongrel dog as he did it. He couldn't say that he'd been doing it all—five years of blood and sweat—to buy back their land. Land, incidentally, that Will was going to get simply by marrying the girl he loved. He couldn't say any of it, so other words spilled from his lips. Angry, bitter ones made worse by their almost polite tone.

"I know what *you've* been doing. Putting in a canal, I understand. Improvements to Lawton's land, so it's now a bloody showpiece for the bucolic life."

Will's expression hardened at Grant's cutting tone, and he answered in kind. "Yes, I did," he said coldly. "The minute Lawton signed the papers, I began spending his money. Doing all the things that were five and ten years wanting. Did you think I'd let things remain broken once there were funds to fix them?"

No, of course not. It had been so much easier thinking of everything at home remaining exactly the same. That everyone else would wait while he got the money together to buy the land back.

And what makes you so bloody special that the world would wait on you?

"Nothing. Absolutely nothing," he said to his madness, temporarily forgetting that no one else heard the thoughts in his head. It wasn't until he saw Will's and Robert's gaze sharpen that he realized what he'd done.

Flushing, he shot them a carefree grin, then downed as much of his brandy as he could swallow in one mouthful. It was harsh on his throat and nearly choked him, but he swallowed it with a gentleman's aplomb. Funny how some habits never quite disappeared. He could pour brandy down his throat and not gag. Wondered if he could still blow fire.

And that thought brought him right back to his brother. "You've got it all now, brother dear," he said with false good cheer. "The land you've always wanted, a woman who loves you. All you need is the title, and you'll be the peer England so desperately needs. Landed and lordly as you rule your people like a king."

Will jerked in shock at the statement, his brows lowering into a scowl. "What the devil are you talking about?"

"Nothing, nothing," he said as he threw an arm around his stiff-shouldered brother. "I'm just glad to be with my brother again. I've dreamed of this moment, you know. Course it wasn't at an inn in London, but at home. And we were talking about all the improvements we would do, not about the canal you've already dug that apparently brings in a mint every day."

Will's gaze dropped to Grant's nearly empty glass, his thoughts obvious. Just how much had Grant drunk already? Was he drunk?

"Come, come," Grant said. "Let me pour you something. Ladies? Anything?"

Everyone stared, Irene included. Was this the moment? Was this when he was finally exposed as a madman before the world? If so, then let him do one last sane thing before he disappeared into Bedlam. One last thing sane act because, bloody hell, it was terribly hard to ask one's brother if the man was contemplating fratricide.

"I'll recant the title, Will. I'll give it to you. You needn't go to extremes. You're the better man anyway. We both know that."

"*What?*" That explosion came from Robert, the man nearly apoplectic with shock. Grant only knew that because the man was standing beside Will. Otherwise, he wouldn't have seen it. He was looking at his brother, trying to read his stone-faced sibling. It was especially hard because superimposed over the stiff man was the face of an eight-year-old boy with ruddy checks, scruffy hair, and a look of worship as he followed Grant like a stray puppy.

That was years ago. Decades, even. But Grant couldn't look at the man now without remembering the boy then. How had they come to this place?

Meanwhile, the ladies had come to their feet. Miss Powel moved quickly and silently to Will's side. She didn't touch him, but stood there uncertainly. And, all the while, Will just stared at him. Then finally he spoke, his voice quiet, his expression infinitely sad.

"How long has the madness been back?"

Grant started, then cursed. Of course, his brother would ask about that. No one knew about the voice in his head. Not even Robert. But he had once— many years ago—told his little brother. He tried to answer. His throat worked, but his mouth didn't. And when he tried to make a sound, it only came out as a strangled grunt.

Then Irene stepped in. Irene of the long legs and the soft voice. Irene who didn't understand the truth, but nevertheless, had the answer he needed. She took his arm and gently pulled him back. Not far. Just enough so that she could step up and face his brother. In fact, he belatedly realized, it was in much the same position as Miss Powel had taken beside Will.

"He's not mad, Mr. Benton. He thinks… well, we all think, uh, fear…" She grimaced then took a deep breath. "Grant was attacked two nights ago by a man who meant to do murder."

Miss Powel gasped and pressed her hand to her mouth. She'd known about the attack, but they'd called the perpetrator a "footpad" in the dress shop. Meanwhile, Will's eyes widened, and his gaze jumped to Grant's looking for confirmation.

"It's true," he said quietly. "And so we started asking who would want me dead."

Suddenly, Will's eyes blazed fury. It was less than a heartbeat between Grant's statement and his brother's reaction as the man processed the information and leaped ahead to the correct conclusion.

"Bloody hell!" he spat. His hands clenched into fists, and he looked like he might very well murder someone right then.

Grant took hold of Irene and forcibly pushed her aside. If it came to blows, he wanted her safely out of the way. But that one action infuriated Will all the more.

"You think I'm going to hurt her? You think I'd try to kill you?" The words weren't shouted. It would have been better if they were. Instead they were hoarse and low, as if strangled, as they came out of his mouth. Meanwhile, Miss Powel was stepping forward.

"He'd never do that! How could you even think it?" she cried.

"He doesn't want to," answered Robert quietly. "He doesn't want to believe it."

Meanwhile, Will was looking around at the cozy inn parlor, at the table set for six. "Is that why we're here? Instead of at the Lawton's home? So you could confront me in private?"

Grant nodded, somewhat startled that he could still move in the face of his brother's righteous anger. And yet, even now with his brother ready to deck him, he couldn't stop the questions: was this an act? Was it all to cover his crime?

Will must have seen the doubt in his face. Or maybe the reality of the situation was hitting him—hard and right in the gut. The man curled in on himself, his fists planting on his hips.

"I didn't do it, Grant. Good God, I can't even imagine thinking it!"

Meanwhile, his fiancée would not be deterred. "I don't understand. He got to London today. How could he have attacked you two nights ago?"

Irene touched the girl's arm, pulling her back when she might have stepped between the two brothers. "The attacker was hired by someone."

"But Will wasn't even here."

"I was here," he rasped out. "Weeks ago, looking for him."

"But... but that was weeks ago!"

"And I left messages everywhere, hoping he would contact me. Don't you see, Josephine? He thinks I hired someone to kill him when he finally turned up."

The woman's mouth flattened into an angry line and then she rounded on Grant. "But that's stupid!"

she spat. "In fact, in a world of ridiculously stupid, that is the most obviously, blatantly stupid thing ever!"

It was at that moment Grant finally believed. It made no logical sense. Any man who contemplated murder could easily dupe this innocent woman. But something in her rock solid faith in Will put his mind at ease.

But just in case, he focused on his brother and repeated the offer with calm sincerity. "I will give up the title, Will. I mean that. You're the better man anyway."

"The devil you will!" That came from Will, the words gratifyingly vehement.

Meanwhile, Robert had his own exclamation. "You will not!"

Then before anyone could say more, Will straightened to his full height. He wasn't quite as tall as Grant, but he was solid and strong from hard farmwork. And from building a canal.

"I won't deny I've wished for your title, Grant. Hard enough courting her as a steward. At least with a title, I'd have gotten a second look from her father."

Grant snorted. "Not Lawton, you wouldn't. He's damned all us Crowles—"

"From the beginning. Yes, I'm aware." He paused, his expression tightening into a frown. "But I've never wished you harm, Grant. Far from it. I wanted you to get sober. To think instead of gamble. To—"

"Not burn down the barn?"

Will snorted, an identical sound to his brother's. "Well, yes, I could have done without that. But that only proved that you're the right man for the title."

Grant laughed, the sound tight and cut off, but

it was still a laugh. Not surprisingly, no one else in the room understood the joke. Looking at the others in the room, he explained. "Every Lord Crowle for generations has done one thing in his life that is remembered for generations. One single event that becomes attached to his name forever."

Taking up the tale, Will curled his arm around his fiancé and started talking. "It is known throughout the counties as the Crowle Stupidity. One event followed by something extraordinarily dumb. I," he added with some measure of pride, "have never done a Crowle Stupidity."

Grant raised his empty glass to the room. "I burned down our barn on the day of our sister's wedding."

"You didn't!" Irene cried.

Robert's voice was a low rumble. "He did. I was there and helped douse the ashes so it wouldn't spread to the house."

"And I," continued Will, "kept it from the woods."

"And I," said Grant, "crawled into those same woods and hoped to die from the shame."

Irene smiled, her expression not in the least bit horrified. "However did it happen?"

Grant shook his head. That was not an easy answer. He'd have to explain gypsies and fire-blowing and all the ridiculous choices he'd once thought were a good ideas. But before he could even frame an answer, his brother spoke.

"I never saw him again until tonight. We thought he'd died, but Robert here brought us the news that he'd survived." There was a hard edge to the words, an old anger that apparently hadn't cooled.

Grant acknowledged it with a sad shrug. "You really didn't expect me to volunteer to return, did you?"

Will was quiet a long time, but in the end, he shook his head. "No, I suppose not. I found out the next day that you had sold everything."

"Not me. Father."

"And then, you were gone."

Grant looked away. Yes, he'd disappeared. Off to the mill, and he'd lived there nearly every day since. Will stepped forward, his hand open this time as he touched his brother's shoulder.

"Where did you go, Grant? What have you been doing all this time?"

Grant looked at Irene and Robert. Those two knew the truth. How much harder would it be to tell everyone else? To admit the truth to his own brother?

"I went mad, Will. Stark, raving mad."

Seventeen

WHY IS HE LYING? IRENE LISTENED TO GRANT CHATTER about his last five years. He made it sound like he'd wandered the world in search of sanity. And all of it suffered from a vague lack of detail. For all the specifics he gave, he could have been doing anything from picking olives in Greece to spying for the Crown.

Irene wasn't the only one who noticed his evasion. His brother Will frowned, his lips pursing in disgust. And Robert—who knew the truth—looked like his drink had gone sour. But no one interrupted Grant's cheerful discourse, and then the innkeeper arrived, bringing in a tray filled with succulent dishes. So everything stopped as they settled to eat.

It was a lovely meal. Grant hadn't spared any expense with the inn, and the conversation turned general. They learned more about Miss Powel. That she had lived in India and had learned something about magic potions there. That last was said as a joke, but apparently, she was quite the wizard with a cosmetic facial cream.

Robert and Helaine talked about their honeymoon,

and Irene spoke freely about her position as purchaser for the dress shop. Given her father-in-law's profession as owner of Knopp's Shipping, she was able to mention the current political climate regarding tariffs, especially as it affected prices of the goods she found for the shop. Naturally, that led to a more general discussion of taxes and politics.

She watched Grant closely as she spoke, wondering if he'd have preferred she hide her common labors. He didn't. Or rather, he was such a congenial host that he made sure everyone was comfortable. And that's when she realized he was behaving as an aristocrat. This was a true example of what his table would be like if he fully stepped into the role of his title. Lord Crowle would be a congenial host, able to talk on a variety of subjects, with decided opinions regarding the country's politics without being overbearing.

She glanced to Will, seeing the man's solid strength, but noted that in this he was decidedly outclassed. Will was quiet—almost dour—and though he could speak quite intelligently on farming and Yorkshire, he not nearly so versed on the rest of the world. In this, Will was the perfect counterpoint to the well-traveled, slightly scattered Miss Powel, but he would make a terrible earl.

So as the evening wandered on, Irene discovered two distinct things. The first, it would be a terrible crime if Grant did not pick up the political requirements of his title. And the second, she was indeed falling in love with the man.

She'd first suspected her emotions were tumbling out of control two days ago, so she'd resolutely pushed them aside. That had worked during the daylight only. At night, she was much too aware of how much she longed for him. But now, sitting at his table and listening to his easy conversation, she realized that her heart was truly engaged. It wasn't surprising. Of course, the first man to touch her in years would perforce grab hold of her heart. Inevitable really.

Sadly, she was old enough to know that the relationship could not stand—adoring emotions or not. Perhaps she would be his mistress for a while. Indeed, hadn't she already come to that place? But a man of his standing would need to marry a titled virgin. Eventually, he would say his good-byes and hark off with some nineteen-year-old innocent who would bear him many heirs. The girl in question would grace his table and be a credit to his name, whereas a widowed purchaser at a dress shop could absolutely not fill that role.

And even if Grant could bring himself to decry tradition and look to her for marriage, Irene knew she wouldn't—couldn't—say yes. She had a happy life now, one that she'd struggled hard to attain. She lived in a house with people who loved her. She had work that she adored and friends to share that work with. And most important, she had money she'd earned by herself and that no one could take from her.

Why would she give all that up for the uncertain life of an aristocratic wife? She would have to quit her job, live off her husband's income, and spend her days going to parties, where the smallest nuance of attire or behavior was scrutinized ad nauseam. Certainly, she'd once wanted that life with an aching hunger, but that had been a fantasy built on childish dreams. She now had an adult woman's life, and she had no intention of giving it up. For anyone. Even someone as wonderful as the man she was starting to love.

That thought lent a melancholy note to the evening, but only a little. In general, everyone seemed to have a good time. But then the meal concluded, the after-drinks were shared, and Will pushed to his feet. He was getting ready to leave, and he wasn't the only one realizing the party had come to an end. But as Irene was about to call for coats, Grant's brother said something that brought the entire evening to a silent halt.

"I have made a decision, Grant," he said softly. "I will go to the solicitor and draw up a document that states if you recant the title, I shall do it as well. The earldom will then go to Cousin Cameron, and God help him."

Grant reared back, his expression shocked. "Cam? Why ever would you do that? He's the least worldly nodcock that ever existed."

Will nodded in satisfaction. "Exactly. So I guess you'll just have to keep the title."

"But—"

"It's the only way I can think of to convince you that I'm not trying to kill you. Good Lord, even thinking the thing makes my blood boil. How could you believe I would do that?"

Grant's expression softened. "I haven't for a couple hours now at least."

Will absorbed that with a slow nod. "Are you sure there isn't anyone else? A bitter husband or someone you beat at cards?"

If Will had been offended before, Grant's expression now mirrored the same outrage. "Just what do you think I've been doing? Cuckolding murderous husbands? Fleecing desperate innocents? Will, there's no one else who would want me dead!"

"That's just the point," interrupted Robert, his voice sounding rather tired. "You haven't told him what you *have* been doing for the last five years. Left him to imagine all sorts of nefarious activities."

Grant glowered at Robert, clearly infuriated that he wasn't going to be allowed his evasion. And so the men glared at each other while the tension grew thick.

"Actually, that's not the point," she cut in. "I believe we needed to eliminate Will as a possibility so as to focus on the truth."

They all turned to look at her, but it was Will who spoke. "Which is?"

"That he wasn't the true target."

Helaine gasped, but it was Grant who made it to her side in a few quick steps.

"We needn't discuss this now."

"And how would delaying help? I have been thinking. My father-in-law has a successful business. That would generate any number of enemies. We were attacked on the way to my home. Perhaps the villain was waiting for Papa and chanced upon me."

"But that doesn't explain you being followed weeks ago," Grant inserted gently.

She frowned, her belly tight with worry. This was all so much easier to handle when they'd been the victims of a simple footpad. The idea that someone was looking to harm her was only now beginning to settle into her thoughts. And she hated it.

"Don't worry," said Grant as he possessed her hand. "I shall be by your side constantly. You'll be safe while we sort the situation out."

She shook her head, doing her best to remain quietly logical. "You can't watch me every moment of every day."

"I can, and I have. I've hired a runner to help while Mr. Morrison and I investigate. Between the three of us—"

"Four," added Will.

'Five," said Robert grimly.

"We shall get to the bottom of this quickly. Never you fear, we'll find the culprit soon enough."

Her breath felt tight in her chest. "But you can't do that indefinitely. And besides, we haven't the slightest idea where to look."

Grant didn't answer. Neither did the other two men. They stared at her quietly. It was Helaine who finally said what the men wouldn't.

"Nevertheless, we will take precautions. You're our friend, and we'd suffer terribly if anything happened to you."

Irene tried to laugh, but it came out as a sick snort. "I've only just met two of you, and Lord Redhill—"

"Doesn't matter," he interrupted, his voice almost congenial. "You're a woman in danger. What kind of man would I be if I simply ignored you?"

"But that's just the point. What if it's all a silly mistake? What if—"

"Stop, Irene. Just... stop." That was Grant as he

gently turned her to face him. "Whether you like it or not, I will have you protected. That's all there is to it."

Then Will cleared his throat, his expression awkward. "Uh, about the runner. Even with us helping, he's still going to cost some blunt. Do you... er, I'd be happy to help with that. Got to pay you back anyway for the money you sent us these last years."

Irene felt the impact of those words hit Grant. A recoil, and then a tightening in his whole body. "I have the money, Will."

His brother nodded. "Good. But as I said—"

"And it was my responsibility to see that Mama had food and shelter all these years. If you try to pay me, I'll throw it in your face. And then I'll call you out for the insult." Then, apparently to soften his words, he grunted in a friendly way. "Besides. You paid to replace the barn I burned down."

"No, I didn't. Lawton did."

Grant nodded. "But you did the roof repairs to that blight of a castle. Twice. Plus you got the stillroom fixed and a garden growing."

Suddenly, Will went still, his eyes narrowing. "You know about that?"

Grant nodded.

"*How* do you know about that?"

And there it was, Irene realized. Once again, the five-year silence reared up between the two brothers. Now more than ever, Grant needed to explain where he'd been. What he'd been doing. But the man wouldn't. He simply nodded grimly. "Yes, I came by a couple times. And no, I didn't see you or mother. And

Will…" He looked direct and hard at his brother. "I won't discuss it. Not now. Maybe not ever."

"But why?" cried Miss Powel. The first she'd spoken during all the family discussion. Apparently, the girl had been trying to hold her tongue, but it had gotten too much. She took a step forward, only marginally restrained by her fiancé. "It's been eating him alive for five years! Not knowing if you've been alive or dead. Hoping you were well—fearing that you weren't. He just figured out the money came from you—"

Grant's grumble this time was angrier and carried a full measure of frustration. By which Irene understood that Will wasn't supposed to learn of that at all. But Miss Powel wasn't done, her voice raising in pitch as she continued.

"—and now, you suddenly appear with no explanation. It makes no sense!"

"It makes perfect sense," Will said to his fiancé. "He's never explained himself in his entire life. Why start now?"

And everyone, Irene included, turned to look at Grant. Why indeed did he insist on keeping all this a secret? What was the point?

Meanwhile, Grant shook his head, his eyes downcast. His words—when they came—were almost too quiet to hear. "The things I've done, the sweat and the blood—it is done and I will not think of it again." He lifted his gaze to pin his brother. "Do you understand, Will? I'm sorry you worried. I did what I could to honor my responsibilities, but I'll not account myself to you. *I will not.*"

And there it was. Everyone could see that Grant would not speak of this, and if Will wanted a reconciliation with his brother, he would have to accept that fact. But Irene couldn't help but wonder why. What was he so desperate to hide?

She saw the same question on everyone else's face. But no one dared to push the point. Not even Will, who dipped his chin in acknowledgment. And then, though it clearly cost him to ask, he took it one step further.

"But if you needed my help, you'd ask, wouldn't you? I'm your brother, and I love you. I'm not a worthless child anymore. I can help keep Lady Irene safe, and I can do any number of other things. But you need to tell me, Grant. I can't guess what you need. You have to tell me."

Grant was very still beside her as his brother spoke. And then he simply eased. Or perhaps, it was that the anger drained out of him, leaving him softer, if not exactly at ease.

"You've never been useless, Will. Haven't we both been saying that for years?"

His brother folded his arms. "It's not what's been said that counts. It's what you think."

Grant stood to face his brother square on. Eye to eye they stood, neither backing away or softening. "I *think*," he said loudly, "that you're a better brother than I deserve. And I'm sorry I ever thought any different."

And with that, apparently, Will was content. With a very Yorkshire grunt, he embraced his brother. The hug was done quick and hard, typical among men. But Irene watched Grant's face. He closed his eyes, and his face tightened into twist of grief and relief. As if he had come home after a long time away.

Her heart ached to see it, but she knew that there was healing between the men. Not everything was resolved, but tonight had been a good meeting. And she was beyond touched to have witnessed it.

She met Miss Powel's eyes and saw that she too understood the significance of the moment. Much more open about her feelings, the girl dabbed her eyes with her handkerchief, and Irene was startled to find her own vision watery. Then Will pulled back, his expression dour.

Apparently, dour—she abruptly realized—was the look he had when he was trying to hide strong emotions. That realization completely shifted her idea of the man's general character. Especially as his next words came out almost cold.

"I'll respect your silence, brother, but you're on your own with Mother. If you can keep your secrets from her, then God knows you probably should be working for the Crown."

Everyone laughed, the tension breaking easily and sweetly. It was time for the party to end. Carriages were called, with Helaine offering to play a belated chaperone to Miss Powel. She intended to ride with the engaged couple back to the Lawton home and ease any difficulty with the girl's father. Nothing like having a countess express her gratitude for a father's under-standing to smooth problems at home. Miss Powel was grateful, but Irene caught a flash of disappointment from Will. Clearly, the man had hoped for some privacy with his intended. But he was a good man, and so ceded graciously to the needs of polite society.

A few minutes passed as the men made plans for keeping Irene under protection. She didn't hear what was decided, which was just as well. It would likely make her more fearful about the danger or more embarrassed about the fuss. Both, probably, and in equal measures.

Then it was over. Everyone left but her and Grant, who turned to her with a relieved smile. She touched his face, cherishing his moment of relaxed joy. A difficult evening done. A brother, if not yet reconciled, at least back in communication. She gave him a warm smile, allowing him a long moment to savor the relief. Then she said the words that would shatter his peace.

"I'm so glad that the evening went well. But I will have no secrets between us. You will tell me what happened those missing five years, or I will leave this instant, and you need not bother pursuing me."

Eighteen

HE LOOKED AT HER THEN, HIS EYEBROWS RAISED AND his jaw hard. Irene swallowed, but she would not change her mind.

"There is no secret," he said. "You know what I have been doing the last five years."

"Managing the mill as Mr. Grant?"

He nodded, his eyes narrowed.

"So why would you not tell your brother? First, you cannot hope to keep that a secret. Too many people know. Second…" Her voice faltered as she struggled to find the words. "Second, I cannot understand it. There must be more."

He released a sigh and sagged in apparent exhaustion. She suddenly felt like the most horrible shrew, so she took his hand and led him to a settee by the fire. Did she really need to push for answers now? Every man had his secrets, didn't they? And yet, this bothered her on a deep level.

She stroked her hand through his hair, feeling the silky texture of his curls, liking the way it tickled the back of her hand, even as her fingertips felt the heat of his body. It felt very intimate, and as she focused on that small wonder, she found the words to say.

"You are ashamed, aren't you?" she whispered. "Horribly ashamed of working for your bread."

He nodded, the motion a bare shift of his chin.

She sighed and dropped her head to his shoulder. He turned and pressed a kiss to her forehead. Again, it was a small gesture, but it was something she hadn't felt in years—perhaps ever. Her husband had been about large movements and quick action. His voice had boomed, his laughter had filled her, and even their intimacy had felt like a storm at sea.

But with Grant, it was the little gestures that caught her. The way he tucked her close when they sat together. The press of his lips on her forehead and the stroke of his fingers along her arm. It was a quiet thing, and it felt as if this time together was as much a surprise to him as it was to her.

How horrible to hurt this quiet. There were so many other things they could be doing, but her heart would not let this fester.

"If you are ashamed of making an honest living then what must you think of me? I am a daughter of an earl, as nobly born as you."

"I could never think less of you for that," he said. "I know the strength it takes to work every day, to barter for the best prices, to seek out pieces that will excite your customer. And the exhilaration of a successful deal is something I dream about even now."

He sounded sincere. God knows she felt everything he said. "But it is more than that for me," she said softly. "I used to lie in bed at three in the afternoon and count the ticks of the clock. The sound would echo in my head louder and louder, and I would pray for it to stop. Just... stop."

"Why didn't you remove it from the room?"

"I did. And then it was breaths I counted. Or heartbeats. Or the number of times a branch scraped the window. It was all the same. An endless stream of time with no purpose."

He tightened his hold, tucking her closer into his side. "You were grieving. You'd lost a husband."

She laughed, the sound quiet in the room. "This was long before I met Nate. This was at home or sometimes at school. You cannot know the emptiness of my life then. My father was a gambler, so we were in constant fear of the duns. Even if my mother could stomach the shame of earning money in legitimate work, it hardly mattered. Father spent faster than we could earn. The only hope for the family was if I grew into a beauty."

"Thank God you did."

She snorted. Then she put her hand on his chest, enjoying the steady thump of his heart beneath her hand. "I did not, and you well know it." But she liked that he had sounded sincere. Even better, he pulled back to look at her. He lifted her chin and studied her face.

"Your features are balanced, your skin is clear, and there is power in your eyes that I cannot explain."

She blinked, startled by the honesty in his tone. "You see more than the average man," she said. "And besides, back then my skin wasn't quite as clear, my features were sharp, and my nose was like a hawk's beak."

"Certainly not!"

"Certainly so! The gossip columns reported my first debut as exactly such. 'The hawklike features of Lady Irene will only attract those who want their eyes pecked out.'"

"Good God," he gasped. "However did they get it so wrong?"

She smiled, the pain of that old hurt fading. "They didn't. 'Severe' is perhaps the kindest term for my face."

"But your eyes—"

"Hollow and haunted. Even I could see it. I just couldn't do anything about it."

He touched her face, his fingers a slow caress across her cheek and lips. "You're beautiful, Irene. It's in your face. All those things they decried—your nose and your chin—they are like the facets of brilliant stone. A diamond, or... have you ever seen a pigeon blood ruby? The tone is subtle, but it gives everything around it warmth. That's you."

She blinked, absorbing his words. A ruby? A diamond? No one had ever compared her to such things. Not even her father. It was so ridiculous as to make her speechless. But he was studying her face as if it were true.

"I've sketched you, you know," he said.

She straightened slightly in his arms. "What?"

"A day after I met you. And almost every day since. But I cannot capture your eyes. Or your mouth. Or your... essence. It is too beautiful for my talents."

She did not know what to say. Even Nate had never called her beautiful. He said she was beautiful enough for a rough sailor like him. And, at the time, she had thought him especially sweet. But that was nothing compared to what she felt for Grant at this moment.

So she stretched up just as his lips came down. Their mouths met in the slowest, most gentle of kisses. His tongue stroked her lips, their breaths mingled in a heated tease, and eventually, their tongues touched. A quick stroke, a twist, eventually a thrust. He pressed her backward into the cushions. She absorbed his words and his kisses into her very being.

It was a powerful kiss and one she knew she'd remember for the rest of her life. But before she became too drunk on his kisses, before his compliments stripped her of all reason, she had to explain the rest. She had to let him know why *his* shame hurt *her* so deeply.

"I met Nate at the market while I was staring at a melon I couldn't afford," she said. "We'd long since let our cook go, so I did the shopping with what little coins we had. Mama thought it would be less embarrassing for a daughter to be shopping, rather than a countess."

He sighed quietly, his forehead dropping to meet hers in a gentle press. "You had a hard time of it," he whispered.

"You keep saying that as if it makes me special. As if I deserve praise or sympathy for it."

He pulled back slightly, his eyes impossibly dark. "It does. You do. What you have struggled through takes my breath away. You are so strong—"

"Everyone struggles, Grant. No one has a life of ease. From the lowest bootblack to Prinny in his rich indulgences, we all search for a way to get through."

He swallowed, and she knew he was listening. If only she could express herself more clearly.

"Nate bought me that melon. He was large and handsome, and he had a laugh that boomed through the room. He's much like his father in that," she said. "He made me feel safe, and he had money to spare. I clutched onto him, like I would grasp a rope at sea. Or perhaps, he was a cake before a starving woman."

"You fell in love."

She nodded. "I did. He looked at me as a woman, not a title. He made me laugh, and he bought me presents. Every day, there was something. They weren't even expensive. A ribbon, a bauble, an ugly wooden bird he had tried to carve. He gave these things to me—little things—and he became the whole world to me."

Grant pulled back, his expression open, despite the fact that they were speaking of her first lover.

"When we were together, he filled my days. There were endless stories about the sea. And when his throat grew tired from talking, he would whistle."

"Whistle?"

"Yes, whistle. A tune. Or the call of a bird, though I think he made those up. He had traveled the world, so he could claim it was the call of a yellow songbird from China with a beak like a duck and the wingspan of an eagle. I would never know if it were true or just a story."

"A story, I would think. At least that one."

She smiled in memory. "Yes, that one was. But others, maybe not. It never mattered. He made me laugh, and when I was with him, I was full. Not just my belly, but my whole life."

"And when he was away?"

"I counted the ticks of the clock. Only this time, it was an ormolu clock rather than an old wood clock from my grandmother."

"The waiting must have been interminable."

"Then he died. The news came as I was helping my father-in-law with his accounts. His eyes are failing him, and he needs help from someone he trusts. The messenger came from the boat. He told us they had been attacked by pirates, but Nate had marshaled a defense. They had fought them off, but he had been wounded during the fight. An infection set in, and he was dead soon after."

"I'm so sorry, Irene," Grant breathed, the passion in his eyes shifting to sadness.

She acknowledged his words with a nod, but she couldn't focus on him. Not if she wanted to tell him everything. "Mama screamed and collapsed. Papa shuddered. I remember that. He just shuddered and then sat in his chair. The servants did everything then. They called for the doctor. Papa's secretary handled all the arrangements."

"What did you do?" he asked. She could hear the regret in his voice, as if he didn't want to hear her answer, but knew she needed to say it.

"I took to my bed, Grant. And I stayed there for weeks just counting heartbeats. Or breaths. Or the taps of a branch. There was no reason to get out of bed. At least before my marriage, there had been some things to do. Food to buy, a dress to restitch, and always, the bill collectors to avoid. At school I had a few friends. Helaine, for one. But I'd lost my friends when I married a cit. And since my in-laws are wealthy, they had servants do the cooking and cleaning. They didn't need me for anything."

"My God," he breathed. "What did you do?"

"Nothing at all." She looked at him, trying to explain what was in her heart. "Don't you see? I had everything I ever wanted—people who loved me, good food, beautiful clothes—but there was nothing to fill me. No husband, no children, no... nothing. I prayed for death, you know. Anything to bring an end to the tick of the clock."

"It's a wonder you did not go insane."

"No, it's a wonder that I could be so ridiculously stupid and not realize it."

He started, drawing back at the anger in her tone. "You were grieving."

"I was lazy and self-indulgent. Other women have their base needs taken care of. Other women have missing husbands. They occupy their time with charities or art. They spend hours helping at hospitals or supporting relatives who need an extra pair of hands. Even working at your mill, you gave thought to your mother and to the barn you'd burned down."

"Do not confuse thought with guilt."

She shrugged. "It doesn't matter. I did none of that. I never have. I lay in bed and counted the ticks of the clock. Until the day Helaine came and offered me a job as her purchaser, I did nothing at all."

He shook his head. "It's not the thing for the daughter of an earl to work. Even when charitable, it is for her to supply the goods, not carry the baskets."

She slammed her hands down in her lap, startled

that she had made fists. "But that is exactly my point! I was raised to think that the ultimate life was one of ease—every need provided for, every desire already met. And any woman or gentleman who had those things and chose to work anyway was considered of the lowest mind-set. A woman is seen as less desirable, a man is despised as unfortunate. And neither are accepted in the highest levels of the *ton*."

He nodded, obviously knowing it was true.

"But it is wrong. From the depths of my soul, I say to you, that is wrong thinking. I love setting my mind to a task. I adore finding fabrics that Helaine will fashion into the most beautiful of gowns. I don't even keep the money I earn. I give it to St. Clement Church. The point is that I am working, and nothing has ever filled me so well."

"Then I am pleased that you have found it."

"Are you?" she challenged. "Are you truly? You are ashamed of your work. That tells me that deep in your heart, you despise the very thing that makes you valuable in mine. And the reverse. That you must naturally hate the one occupation in my life that... that *is* my life."

He took a deep breath. She studied his eyes, trying to read his expression or garner some clue to his thoughts. In the end, he looked away. A wood fire had been lit, and it was burning quietly, the logs more a glowing heat than a crackling flame.

"Did you see my brother's face when he spoke about the canal? He has been talking about building it since he was a boy. He has an engineering bent, you know. Always saw how things fit together. Not just mechanically—though he is good enough at that—but in people too. When there was a problem in the village or with a crofter, he knew how to adjust things to make them fit. He said once that discordant things bother him, and he lives to set them right."

She thought back on the evening, focusing specifically on Will. She could see the quiet in him, built on a solid foundation of confidence. She remembered the satisfaction in his voice when he talked about an engineering problem that had been solved or the unrest in the village now at peace. And now, with Miss Powel by his side, Will had a good life ahead.

"He's happy. It's an excellent thing."

Grant nodded without turning his head. "My father had it too. He was a genius with numbers. Got him into trouble sometimes, especially when gambling. But it set the odds in his favor. If any man could make it as a gambler, it would have been him."

Grant's expression lightened. "He used to make this face when he was sorting through the odds. A tight pinch to his brows, like he had a pressure between his eyes. Then he'd snap his fingers." Grant did the same, the sound a loud crack. "It was his idea to buy the mill, you know. He taught me how to calculate the profits and the losses. If he could have stayed with me instead of running back to London, I could have bought our land back two years ago." He sighed and shook his head. "But he left, and I wasn't half the man he was."

"I cannot express how violently I disagree with that statement," she said.

He turned to look at her, a brief smile on his

features. The glow from the fire turned his skin a golden rose. But it did nothing to ease the tightness between his brows or prevent his smile from fading to sadness.

"You have that look too. When you were negotiating with me in the inn. I saw the gleam in your eyes. You adore a bargain. The finding of it, the manipulation to get it, even when dancing with me, you were thinking of how to turn the situation to your advantage."

She felt her face heat. "I assure you, I was thinking of something decidedly more carnal."

"Maybe," he answered. "But you had it just now too. You call it a reason to get up in the morning. You say it is your life."

She nodded. It was. Having now found usefulness, she would never go back to living empty.

"I went to school because that is what future earls do. I was decent at it, but not scholarly. Enjoyed it and my friends. Then the money ran out, and I went to London to try and moderate my father's excesses. That, I was not so decent at, but it was my responsibility, and so I did what I could."

"Moderating a parent is *never* a child's job."

He shrugged. "But it was my task, so I did it. Got distracted into my amusements, but that is inevitable for a young buck about town. I was never as good a gambler as my father. I just didn't have the knack for numbers that he did."

She tilted her head, trying to understand what he was trying to say. She could not. All she could do was listen.

"Then there was Diane's wedding and the celebration to be paid for. It was father who saw the mill, Robert who made me work. I was the one who burned down the barn."

"But that was an accident."

He tilted his head as if listening to something she couldn't hear. "It was a stupidity, and I got exactly what I deserved."

"But you went to work at the mill. You made it into a success. It is one of the best in the country now."

He stiffened, his brow arching. "*One* of the best? I beg to differ."

She smiled. "Very well then. The best wool in all of England. And the very best angora."

His expression softened, moving quickly from humor to reflection to an abiding sadness. "I have never worked so hard in my life, Irene. These last five years have been like gaol, and I was never so happy as when I was finally free of it. I will never go back there willingly. I cannot see how I managed it even now."

"But you did manage it. You did earn the money—"

"Not enough."

She waved that aside. "It doesn't matter. You should be proud of what you've accomplished."

He looked back at the fire. "I am. What I did taught me a great deal."

"So why do you hide it? Why do you despise it so very much?"

"Because it was work, Irene. Hard, backbreaking, mind-numbing work. It wasn't a reason to get up in the morning. It wasn't a talent or a way of making things fit. It was simple, daily work of the kind that makes a man go mad." He exhaled a heavy breath. "And I thank God every day that it is over."

She had no words for that. She still didn't see his message. Then he turned, shifting on the settee until they were face to face.

"Don't you see Irene? I'm not ashamed of the work you do. I'm envious. Of you, of my brother, even of my benighted father. You love every moment of the day, while I…" He shrugged in a sad gesture of hopelessness. "I hate it."

She swallowed, understanding at last the aching sadness she felt in him. The yawning hole that had once been her life was his still. "But that doesn't explain why you keep it all a secret."

"Doesn't it? If I had told my brother the truth of where I'd been, of what I've been doing, what would his reaction be?"

She frowned. "I hope he would be pleased. He seems the kind of man to value hard work."

"Oh he is, most definitely."

"Then—"

"He would expect me to continue, Irene. He would praise me to the skies, then be disappointed when I never went back to that place."

She frowned. "No—"

"Irene, I worked because I had to, not because I wanted to. Frankly, I cannot imagine the desire to work every day and give the money away. I can think of nothing more wonderful than to sit and have my every need catered to." He flashed a wistful grimace. "You and Will and even my father are cut from a different cloth. You enjoy what you do. I, on the other hand…"

"Enjoy nothing?" she asked quietly.

His smile turned lascivious. "There are things I enjoy, Irene. Things I enjoy a great deal."

"But it feels empty in the end, doesn't it?" She touched his face, feeling a pain deep inside. "Even our night together." The night that still had the power to move her. "That was nothing but… a distraction. A way to fill the void."

He looked away, and she could see the truth in every line of his tense body. "I am envious of you, Irene. And that is the shame I will not confess to my brother. He already knows too much of my madness. To tell him that the world is an empty place of toil without joy…" He shook his head. "Don't you think my family has burdens enough?"

"That is why you kept saying you would give up the title. It is yet one more burden—one more expectation—that brings you no joy. Just more obligation. To marry, to bear children, and to maintain a crumbling castle. Give that all to him, and you would be free."

He nodded. "He can support the title much better than I. He is about to marry well, and they will be excellent parents for the next generation. Under his management, the wealth will grow, and the honor of the Crowles will be restored."

"And what will you do when you are free of all this obligation? What will fill your time then?"

He didn't answer. He didn't even look up from the fire. And in the silence, she heard the answer as clear as day. He would do nothing. Just like her in her bed, counting the ticks of a clock to no purpose.

"I nearly died, Grant," she whispered. "If Helaine hadn't found me and given me something to do—something *she* desperately needed—I would have stayed in my bed, eating nothing and doing less. I would have died from doing nothing."

He nodded. A slight motion of his head, and it was in that moment she realized that was his plan all along. He had responsibilities and obligations. But when they were done, he would do as she had. He would simply fade away.

"You cannot do that," she said, horror in her voice. "You are needed in this world."

"The world needs souls who care, Irene. Who work as you do, who love as my brother does. They even need men like my father to see the mathematics in everything. What it absolutely does not need is another useless peer."

And with that, he pushed to his feet and held out his hand. "Do not look so terrified, my dear. I still have a great deal to do, you know. There is your mysterious pursuer. There is my brother's wedding. And I have yet to make peace with my mother."

"And after that?"

He flashed her a smile full of charm and mischief. If she hadn't just listened to him confess his emptiness, she would have been taken in. She would believe him carefree and happy.

"I don't spare much time on thoughts of the future anymore. The last time I did, I worked myself to the bone for five years only to have my brother marry the land that I couldn't buy."

"But—"

"Hush," he said as he pressed his finger to her lips. Then a hard light came into his eyes. Not cruel, just firm. "I am done talking. So we either put your lips to better use, or perhaps it is time to escort you home."

She had no answer for that. For either his emptiness or his mask of carefree insouciance. So she did the only thing she could. She gently pushed his hand away then she stretched to his mouth. Her kiss started out slow, almost tender, but as her mouth met his, anger bubbled up inside—a fury that he could not see possibility in his future. It burned through her blood and set her teeth on edge. What started as gentle became fiery. Tender became dominant, and she all but crushed him to her.

He pulled back, his eyes widening in surprise. But she gave him no more respite than that. Slamming her hands on his shoulders, she shoved him toward the settee. All she did was rock him back on his heels.

She wanted to say something then, but the anger was too hot to rationally form words. So she didn't. She shoved him again, and this time he allowed himself to tumble backward. He landed hard on the settee as a slow smile stretched across his features.

"Irene, you surprise me."

"Really?" she drawled. "Because I've only just begun."

Nineteen

SHE WAS ANGRY. GRANT FELT HIS EYES WIDEN AS IRENE shoved him down on the settee then stood above him like an avenging fury. She was *very* angry, and he couldn't really blame her. After all, he was rather annoyed with himself. He'd never thought of himself as a depressive, but it was clear that recent events had brought out a side he hadn't visited in years.

Aw, shut your gob! You've got a willing woman and a throb in your pants. Pay attention to her!

He listened to his madness. Especially as Irene stood over him with her hands on her hips and her delectable skin flushed rosy.

"Take off your coat," she ordered, her tone as husky.

He nodded meekly, pulling off his coat as humor skated through his thoughts. If she thought he would be intimidated by a beautiful woman ordering him to disrobe, she had a surprise coming.

"Cravat and shirt too. And that waistcoat is lovely, by the way, but I have no interest in looking at it either."

He nodded and continued to strip out of his attire. That necessitated shifting forward on the settee, and she backed up an appropriate distance as he did so. A moment later, he was leaning back, his torso bared for her inspection. Apparently, she enjoyed what she saw because she joined him on the couch, settling onto her knees as she stretched out a hand to his chest. Her lips were parted slightly as she touched him, and he closed his eyes to enjoy the simple pleasure.

"It's so soft."

His eyes opened on a frown. "Did you just call me soft?" he asked, his voice too thick to sound truly insulted.

She smiled. "Your chest hair, silly."

"Oh." He looked down at himself. "Is that... nice?"

"Very nice," she answered. Then her voice abruptly hardened. "And if you think you are going to just sit there, then you are very much mistaken. I am rather cross with you."

He grimaced. "Yes, I had noticed."

"I like you a great deal, and I shall be furious if you just... go away."

He sobered. "I'm not going anywhere. I believe I told you that."

She frowned, obviously frustrated. He knew what she was thinking. He knew what she feared: that he would do the unthinkable.

"I'm not suicidal," he said gently. "I'm just..." His gaze slid away. "I don't know what to do with myself anymore. I shall find our mysterious attacker. I will keep you safe. But beyond that..." He shrugged, having no words.

"Beyond that," she said as she pulled his face to hers. "You will kiss me. Now. Like you mean it."

His expression shifted into a slow grin. "I always mean my kisses."

Then he leaned forward and gently cupped the back of her neck. He felt her breath exhale and could not tell if it came from relief or anticipation. Her breath was sweet—a leftover from the wine—and he felt his entire body surge toward her. But he held himself back, savoring the moment. He loved the hitch in her breath and the pounding of his heart. He loved her heat as it seemed to steam off her body and the silky brush of her hair.

He might have held back longer, but she would have none of it. She closed the distance between them, and to his shock, thrust her tongue into his mouth.

Blood roared in his ears as he opened to her, played with her, and tried not to split her legs wide right there and then. Never had a woman done this to him—with him—and he was stunned by how exciting a demanding woman could be.

She was clumsy in her efforts, pushing at the roof of his mouth, darting and retreating in a frenzied nervousness. Her hands gripped his shoulders, pulling her on top. His free hand was on her waist, steadying her motions, supporting her weight. Her near leg was bent on the settee and as she stabilized in her position, he dropped his hand to slide it up beneath her skirt and trail across her stocking to the top of her thigh.

She murmured her assent as he stroked the few inches of bare flesh. He did not need more encouragement as he slipped his fingers around to the junction of her thighs. A half breath later, he was pushing into the moist heat of her, spreading her folds as he explored in a lazy casualness that he knew would drive her mad.

She pulled back, her breath coming in stuttered pants. She was in the dominant position, her head bowed such that their temples nearly touched. She straddled one of his knees while bracing herself on his shoulders. And yet, for all the power of her position, he was the one who set the pace. Her eyes fluttered closed as he stroked her, pushing into her core before pulling out in a long, hard caress over her hard nub.

Then he abruptly stopped. "I'm sorry," he said with false humility. "You were telling me what to do, I believe. Commanding me, in fact, and I have stepped out of bounds."

She opened her eyes, and it took her a moment to focus on his face. His male pride surged at that. He liked that he could make her dazed. But then, her gaze seemed to spark, her expression tightening into a startling intensity.

"You will finish what you are doing," she ordered. "And it shall not be considered well done until I cry out."

His eyebrows lifted in surprise and a great deal of pleasure. "Until you cry out? As in scream? That is a tall order indeed."

"Not scream," she said. "Cry out. Your name." Then she licked her lips, not in a seductive manner, but unconsciously. And the sight of her pink tongue had his belly contracting.

"My name?" he said, the words and his focus sadly out. Good God, she was winning in this battle of seduction, and that thought nearly sent his organ into spasms of delight.

Then she leaned down to whisper into his ear. Between the heat of her breath and her words, a shudder of hunger wracked his frame. "Grant. But on a cry."

He wanted to say something clever. Repartee was part of the dance. But his words had left him. All he knew was her body pressed against him and the sweetness of her flesh next to his fingers.

As she instructed, he began to stroke her. Thrusting push, long pull. He used his thumb to circle her nub, his fingers to open her wider, and then the push inside. Circle, push. Circle, push.

"Your hair," he gasped. "Let it down."

She took a moment to understand his words. Then she straightened, balancing carefully as she raised her hands to her pins. What a sight she was. She wasn't even naked, but her uplifted breasts seemed to soar before him. Then she pulled out the pins to her hair, and he watched the black silk tumble to curl across her shoulders.

"You should be naked," he whispered. "My God, you are such a beauty."

She flashed him a coy smile, but shook her head. The movement was as much denial as simply shaking out her locks. Either way, he drank in the sight, especially the hard, tight points of her nipples directly in front of his mouth. He wanted to suck on those tips. He wanted to tease them with his tongue and nip them with his teeth. Oh, he wanted so many things, but there wasn't time, as what he did between her thighs overwhelmed her.

Another circle and push. Hard and deep. But it was enough.

She cried out, not his name, but a surprised gasp. Her hands came down quickly to his shoulders, and he steadied her with one hand on her hip. But there was nothing to stop her body's undulations as her pleasure crested and withdrew, peaked then fell. He watched in awe. Then when she finally regained her breath and her equilibrium, he gave her a wolfish smile.

"Irene?" he said.

She blinked, awareness coming slowly into her eyes. "Yes?"

In one motion, he flipped her onto the settee. One second she had been poised above him, the next she was lying flat on her back, as her skirts slid to her waist.

"My turn," he said, his hands leaving her glory to quickly undo his pants.

She smiled, but she held up her hand as if to stop him. "Are you sure?" she challenged. "I don't believe I cried out your name."

He frowned, remembering. "Quite right," he agreed. Then he spread her legs and stepped naked into the breach. "I shall remedy that immediately."

Then to her obvious shock, he dropped to his knees in front of her.

Irene felt her eyes go wide as Grant dropped almost out of sight. Then he kissed his way up her thighs while she squirmed. She was incredibly sensitive, and the slow press of his lips coupled with tiny nips had her gasping as she arched off the settee. But he was relentless, and what he did with his tongue gave her no time to speak. Her belly tightened, and she

cried out, but he stopped immediately—holding off
as she gasped.

"I can't have you too breathless to say my name,
now can I?"

She wanted to say something tart in response, but
she hadn't the breath. She simply lay quivering as he
lifted one of her legs to settle on his shoulder.

"Say my name, sweeting," he said with a wolfish grin.

She shook her head.

"Hmmm," he returned. She thought it was a
comment or one of those thoughtful sounds men
sometimes made. She was wrong. He repeated the
sound—a low hum—as he pressed his lips to her most
sensitive place.

"Sweet heaven!" she cried. Her body arched, the
convulsions nearly pulling her off his broad shoulders.
He held her safe as the peak rolled through her body.
Then whenever the pulses started to subside, he
stroked her again. With his tongue or his thumbs,
it didn't matter. He kept her peaking until she was
fainting from the pleasure.

Then he straightened from his position, standing to
his full height over her. He looked glorious like that,
his skin a rosy gold, his torso sculpted, lean and strong.
But she was looking at his eyes, seeing how he looked
at her hungrily, though she was sprawled before him
in a boneless heap.

"You're beautiful, and I want to make love to you
now. Will you let me?"

She nodded and tried to reach for him. He started
to join her, but then frowned. "I've brought something. A French letter." He stepped for his trousers,

rooting through them before he pulled out a folded envelope. "I know I forgot the other night. I'm sorry, but I remembered this time."

She tilted her head, looking at the item he pulled out. "What is it?" she asked.

His brows shot up, and he grinned. "I love that I can teach you things." Then he turned, putting himself in profile. His organ was thick and proud as it thrust up before him. Then he slowly sheathed himself. "It is to prevent pregnancy. Also, many diseases."

She glanced at his face, alarmed, but he quickly eased her fears.

"I'm very healthy. You needn't fear. But I doubt you want a baby just now."

She felt her face flush as she looked away, the old ache returning. She *did* want a baby, but she understood how it would make her life awkward—his, as well. But the idea of bearing his son made her weepy with want.

Not understanding, he leaned forward to kiss her trembling lips. "Don't worry. It usually takes more than one night to make a child, though, of course, it's possible. But I know many who have waited for years. Besides, we're safe now," he said as he stroked her cheeks.

His fingers came away wet, and he looked down at her in surprise. She blinked, startled by her own grief.

"Irene?" he said.

She shook her head slowly. "You twist me around," she said. "I never know what I will do next with you."

"And does that please you? Or frighten you?"

"A little of both, I suppose." Then she touched his face. "But mostly, I am pleased. Very, very pleased."

"You still have not said my name," he grumbled good-naturedly.

"Grant."

He shook his head. "Doesn't count."

"Then I suppose you will have to do more. Though goodness, I'm not sure I will survive it."

He stroked her cheek. "Do you want me to stop? Are you exhausted?"

"I am empty, Grant. Will you not fill me?"

"With everything I have," he said as he slipped between her thighs.

She was in a rather awkward position, stretched along the couch. But it was a soft piece of furniture, and as he set himself in place, he slipped his hands beneath her bottom to steady her. Then, as he slowly pressed into her slick core, he lifted her, and she let her head drop back. She felt as if she were floating, raised in the air as he entered her.

He was thick, but she was so wet that he slid easily inside. She stretched around him, she gripped him with her thighs, and finally, she felt gloriously filled.

"Oh yes," she said, her eyes drifting shut. "Yes."

"Irene," he said softly. "Look at me."

He was leaning forward over her, now fully seated. She opened her eyes and saw his look. His expression was tight, but his eyes still worshipped her. She saw gratitude, awe, and a hunger that she more than matched.

"I won't last long," he said, his voice throaty. "Say my name."

She was too happy to fight him on their game. Her earlier anger had dissipated beneath a tide of pleasure.

But she still could not give him what he wanted. Not yet. So she mutely shook her head.

Then he withdrew. Fully.

"Grant!" Too late, she arched off the couch, trying to catch him before he left.

"There it is," he said as he thrust into her again. Thick and hard, slamming against her body, such that she seemed to shimmer with the impact—a shower of sparks throughout her body. "You tricked me," she accused.

"All's fair in love and war."

"Really?" she asked, as she tightened her internal muscles, squeezing him as much as she could manage.

He groaned in response, his eyes rolling back in his head. "Irene," he murmured. "Oh God…"

Then he moved in earnest, his body pulling back and slamming in with steadily increasing fervor. There was a possessive power in his movements, a clench to his teeth, and a madness in his eyes. She watched it grow, felt its demand in every thrust. And she gloried in it.

The power in him filled her. It was raw, and it claimed her as surely as a brand, burning deeper and harder with every thrust. She arched, gasping as he built her pleasure again.

Faster. Harder.

Suddenly his body seemed to contract. The pull was intense. The thrust an explosion.

"Irene!"

Twenty

IRENE WAS STILL REELING THE NEXT MORNING—ER, noon, as she got out of bed—her own bed at home. He had escorted her there well before midnight, bowing over her hand as he took his leave. He'd left her in body, but at night, she'd dreamed such images of him. Not only his face as he possessed her, but the way he looked when he was laughing. Then there was that secret smile he sometimes gave her or the way he often appeared to be listening, his head cocked to one side, even though no one was speaking.

It was the way he thought, she supposed. Listening to himself as he worked through a problem. She did much the same, although she usually chewed on a fingernail or her lower lip. In any event, she found the sight endearing. And his presence haunting.

So it was of no surprise that when she descended the stairs for a late breakfast, she found a dozen hothouse roses waiting. She didn't have to look at the card to know they were from Grant. She did anyway, and the words she found there left her smiling.

*I thank you for the taste of your laughter, the sound of
your beauty, and the sweet sight of your sighs. You twist
me backwards and around, but I adore it. Thank you.*

"Is that poetry?" asked her mother-in-law as the
woman peered over her shoulder.

Irene spun around, startled that she'd been so
absorbed in Grant's message that she hadn't even heard
the woman's approach.

"Yes, of a sort, I suppose."

"Odd. Who's it from?" Then before Irene could
answer, Mama gave her a giggly smile. "Is it Lord
Crowle? He's so very handsome, you know. And an
earl! But then you're a daughter of an earl, so I suppose
it's not so fancy for you. But just imagine!"

Irene flushed and looked away. After all, part of her
still felt like a wife to their son, even though Nate had
been gone for years now. "I… um…"

Her mother-in-law squeezed her arm, and when
Irene looked up, she was startled to see tears in the
woman's eyes. "Nate loved you to distraction, you
know, but he's gone. You've grieved him, and I feared
that you would never come out of black. But look at
you now." She gestured to Irene's gentle blue gown.
It was made of thick cotton, fashionable, but service-
able. And it was definitely not black.

"I will always love Nate."

"You are a young woman who should have children at her feet. Papa and I would never want you to
end with him." She dabbed her eyes with a lacy scrap
of a handkerchief. "I should like to dance at another
wedding before I am too old."

Irene smiled, but inside, her heart trembled. Surely the woman understood what society thought of her now. Surely she knew... but of course, she did not. After all, Irene had simply said a dinner party. Not who would attend. Nor that she would appear as hostess, and therefore, declare to anyone who cared that she was Grant's mistress.

That word—mistress—caused a tightening in her gut, but her soul seemed to sing at the idea. So she leaned forward and pressed a kiss to her mother-in-law's cheek. "You are the best mother a girl could have."

"And you the best daughter," the woman returned in her usual blustery good cheer, especially as she drew Irene to the side entry table. "And look what has come today!" She held up five elegant envelopes, all clearly invitations. "We are invited to balls! Can you imagine? These are yours..." She examined three envelopes and handed them to Irene. "And these! They're for me, and a guest! Of course, I shall bring Mrs. Schmitz. It was ever the most exciting time in her life at Lady Redhill's ball. And now, we are invited to two more!"

Irene looked at the invitations, reading them quickly as her mind whirled. She knew these women. All three were friends of Helaine's. Which meant her dear friend had prevailed upon others to bring Irene out of her obscure little corner of London and into the *ton* as she had never been. As the daughter of an earl, she had once expected these invitations as her due. But she'd been an *impoverished* daughter, and so some things had been decidedly lacking. And now...

She shook her head. Clearly, she couldn't decline. Not with Mama looking so excited—the woman was likely to explode. But once in the fashionable throng—even as something so little as a matron who sat on the sidelines with her friend—the woman would eventually hear the truth. She would learn what Irene was to Grant. And then, what would Irene do? How could she face the couple that treated her as their daughter?

"We should go, don't you think?" the lady asked, quivering in her excitement. "It would be good to get out, and I think it would be such a treat for Mrs. Schmitz."

Irene laughed. How could she not? And how could she deny her Mama such fun? "But of course, we should go!" she said. Then she sobered a little. "Provided you understand that not everyone in the *ton* will be pleasant. You know that, right?"

The older woman's eyes softened, and she touched Irene's cheek. "I am a German cit, my dear. Of course, I know. But I will be able to see you there and watch you dance. And maybe that handsome Lord Crowle will ask me onto the floor for something easy. When I was a little girl, I would spin around and around until I fell down. My mother once said…"

The memories went on, one after the other in a lovely parade of words. Irene had heard them all, of course, but not at a time in her life when she had the wisdom to appreciate the repetition. It was good to see Mama so happy, and good too to share in the excitement of preparing for a party. They started talking new clothes and new shoes as they wandered into the dining room, and Irene was served strong tea and a biscuit, as was her custom. Until about ten

minutes later when Papa entered the room accompanied by a jowled, broad-shouldered fellow with kind
brown eyes.

Mama cut off her words immediately, her eyes
growing worried as she looked at the two men, which,
naturally, set Irene on edge. Meanwhile, Papa stepped
forward and bussed her on the cheek. All perfectly
normal, but when he squeezed her extra hard and held
on even longer, Irene's alarm nearly cut off her breath.

Then before she could speak, her father-in-law
stood back and gestured to the man at his side. "Irene,
I think it's time you met the copper who has been
loitering about lately. This is Mr. Tanner. Don't know
as you've seen him—"

She hadn't, although now that she thought about it,
she might have noticed him a couple times smoking a
pipe at a corner somewhere.

"He's been trailing you for the last few days," Papa
continued. "You should have told me that you were
attacked. It's not the sort of thing a man wants to find
out from a Bow Street Runner."

Irene blinked. "It was just a footpad," she said
softly, the lie tasting bitter on her tongue.

Mr. Tanner had his hat in his hand, and he dipped
his head when he spoke. "Begging your pardon, Lady
Irene, but it weren't just a footpad, and so I've been
hired to watch you when the others can't."

She frowned, thinking back as she put the sequence
in order. After all, the men had set up a watch just last
night at the party. But he'd said he'd been watching
her for a couple days now.

"When were you hired?"

"Samuel—Mr. Morrison, that is—put me on a couple days ago. Spoke here with your papa immediately, and we've been keeping an eye out. But miss, I think it's time you understood things a little better. You're in danger, Lady Irene, and I don't like you taking up with strange children nobody knows or going about your day into the docks. It's too hard to watch you."

"Strange children? What are you talking about? And how do you know about my day?"

At which point Mama suddenly gasped, flattening her hand against her mouth in a cry of guilt. Everyone turned, and she immediately dropped her hand. "I'm so sorry. I completely forgot! There's a girl in the kitchen. Scrawny thing, half starved. Very polite, and not that bright. Sent here from St. Clement's. Said Father Michael sent her as your servant."

"Carol!" Irene gasped. She'd forgotten all about the girl she'd hired to be her secretary.

Meanwhile, Mama looked to the copper. "She's done no harm. Just sat in the kitchen. Do you really think that poor little thing is a danger?"

The man shook his head, his jowls quivering enough to make him look like a bulldog. "Easy enough to check her credentials, but it makes my job harder, you see. We all want Lady Irene kept safe."

Irene swallowed, her mind spinning. "This is unreal," she murmured. "It was a footpad."

Which, of course, was a flat out lie. After all, hadn't they just spent the last two days suspecting Grant's brother of murderous intent? But it was only one frightening incident. Or perhaps two. Over a period of months. She had lived for so long convincing herself that her vague fears were a product of her imagination that having her family suddenly take them seriously made her question her own sanity. What if they were making such a huge fuss over nothing?

"It's a frightening thing, to be sure, Lady Irene. But we'll keep you safe. I promise."

"We?" she murmured.

Papa straightened up. "I've brought in a few men—sailors I've known for years—to serve as footmen around the house. Hired them months ago, actually, when you first said someone was following you. Had some nasty business with some sailors then, and I thought it prudent. For all of us."

She blinked. So he *had* taken her concerns seriously? *Months ago?*

"And you're not to go to the docks," continued her father-in-law. "I know you think your job is important—"

"I need to go there! That's where the cargo is! That's where the deals are made."

Papa nodded, his expression grim. "It's too dangerous," he said flatly. "And I should never have let you take that ridiculous job. You're a lady, Irene. The daughter of an earl and my son's wife. Ridiculous to have you gadding about like any tinker's get."

Irene set down her teacup, straightening slowly out of her seat. Still at the table, her mother-in-law released a heavy sigh. "Don't be upset, dear. He's just frightened for you. We all are."

She knew that. She was frightened too. But she couldn't live her life as if someone were about to kill her. Didn't they understand how easy it would be for her to take to her bed again? To crawl under the covers and never come out? She didn't care if there were armed assailants right outside her door. If she allowed herself the smallest bit of fear, then she would collapse.

"And what about the balls?" she asked, her mouth latching onto the least of her concerns. "Am I to be locked inside the house forever?"

Mr. Tanner shifted his feet nervously. "I can't say I like it, but Lord Crowle said he would be with you every second. Then there's the other gents keeping an eye out. He wants you to live yer life—going to parties and the like—"

"And the docks? I have a meeting this afternoon. The *Singing Lady* came in yesterday. I'm to meet with its captain about some silks."

"That can wait—" grumbled her Papa, but Irene was already shaking her head.

"It *cannot* wait as the shop is in desperate need of those silks."

Mr. Tanner dipped his head. "I already knew about the shipment, my lady."

"What?"

"Apologies, but you don't keep your schedule secret. I found out about it from your Papa. I'd guessed you'd want to go no matter what he said—"

"You are correct in that."

"So Lord Crowle and I are going with you. Keep an eye out, fetch and carry, and the like—"

"You can have a few of my men too," interjected Papa.

"But we all thought it prudent that you stop doing business like this. Just until the danger's past."

"But we don't really know that there *is* danger."

Silence met her statement, long and pointed. Not surprising, given that even she'd grown weary of her own denials. But it was the only way she kept the fear from strangling her.

She pushed up from her seat. "For the moment, I will see this child in the kitchen. Then we will go on to *The Singing Lady*."

"And don't forget," inserted Mama. "Lord Crowle is coming to take you driving in Hyde Park this afternoon."

Irene stared at her mother-in-law. "What?"

The woman colored. "Oh, did I forget that too? The messenger said that most specifically when he brought the flowers. Lord Crowle hopes you haven't forgotten your appointment to walk this afternoon in Hyde Park."

Mr. Tanner's heavy sigh echoed through the room. "Just makes me job harder."

Irene blinked. "You can't possibly think someone would attack in the middle of Hyde Park?"

"Probably not," he answered. "But I'll be speaking with Lord Crowle about the details."

He wasn't the only one who would be speaking to Lord Crowle. Meanwhile, she turned to the kitchen. It was time to meet her new urchin assistant. Sadly, she was followed by her in-laws and Mr. Tanner. At least she gestured them to stay in the background as she pushed into the kitchen.

The child was indeed Carol, the girl she'd met so many days ago at St. Clement's Church. She was scrawny with dark plaited hair and large brown eyes. She sat at the main kitchen worktable, her plate empty, and her eyes drowsy from what was probably her first real meal in days. But when Irene caught her attention, the girl abruptly leaped to her feet and performed an awkward curtsey. Then she gripped her hands together and kept her head tilted down. Yet as downcast as her body's attitude was, her eyes were alive and constantly moving, as if she couldn't quite trust her surroundings.

Irene pulled out a chair and sat in front of the girl. "Hello Carol. Is your mother feeling better then?"

"Yes, my lady. Her cough is nearly gone now, and so I were free to come work for you."

Irene glanced at Mr. Tanner. "This is Carol Owen. I met her a few days back at St. Clement's, and I promised her a job." She looked to the girl, who nodded sagely as she passed an envelope to Irene.

"It's from Father Michael," the girl said quietly. "I passed his tests. I know my sums and can read. My memory is excellent, and… and I'm stronger than I look."

Irene smiled as she scanned the contents of Father Michael's letter. It was exactly as Carol said, except for the strong part. The poor thing was much too tiny. She was on the verge of accepting the girl when Mr. Tanner stepped forward.

"If I may, my lady?"

Irene nodded and stepped back as the runner frowned at the girl. He looked rather forbidding, which she supposed was the point. The girl held her ground, her own gaze steady, but Irene couldn't tell if she were brave or terrified into stillness.

"You understand that many a boy could have this

position. You're lucky Lady Irene has such an open mind." His tone indicated that he thought Irene mad, but it wasn't his place to argue.

"Yes, sir," the girl whispered.

"You know that your loyalty is to her and her alone. You do what she asks, when she asks, no questions."

"Y-yes, sir." The girl's stammer didn't indicate fear, but a ready understanding of the question and some of the consequences. After all, the girl didn't really know Irene. What if Irene told her to do something illegal or dangerous? What then? It was a measure of her desperation that made the child agree without argument.

"And if you see something wrong, something that don't sit well, you will report it to me immediately."

The girl frowned, but nodded, her words quiet. "Yes, sir."

Meanwhile, Irene found that she'd had enough. Tapping the runner on the shoulder, she stepped forward. "I believe that's sufficient, Mr. Tanner. I find I like Carol just fine. And as I have a busy day ahead, I suggest we start immediately." Especially since she had slept much too late. "Cook, will you please pack us a small basket? I'm afraid I won't have time to stop for a meal, and I wouldn't want my..." She all but rolled her eyes at the people surrounding her. "My retinue to get hungry."

Mr. Tanner caught her meaning, his mouth flattening into a straight line, but he knew better than to say anything. So with a nod, she dashed upstairs. It was silly really. She rarely worried about her appearance when she left to negotiate with a ship's captain. Her regular practical attire was more than adequate.

But she would be negotiating with Grant beside her, and that called for extra care. She tried to quell the excitement in her breast, the heated flush to her cheeks, and the bubbly feelings that kept trying to burst free in inappropriate giggles. She couldn't, and soon her maid was looking at her with raised eyebrows and a question.

"It's nothing," she said, speaking more to herself than to Anna.

"It's Lord Crowle, isn't it?"

Irene paused, biting her lip as she met her maid's eyes in the mirror. "Do you think it's too soon?" she asked quietly.

"I think it's past time," returned the woman with feeling. "But mind you be looking for a ring, not a just a tumble, my lady."

Irene swallowed. It was too late for that, she realized, her gaze canting down. "I am not the sort of woman Lord Crowle would marry. He has responsibilities to his title, and I do not fit what he needs."

Anna sighed as she touched a dash of rouge to Irene's cheeks. "Then send him packing, my lady, and find a man who has a ring for you."

Irene sighed and nodded. Prudent advice from a smart woman. And yet, couldn't she enjoy herself just a bit longer? Be with a man she adored for a few weeks more?

"Well, I'm stuck with him for the moment," she said softly. And, of all the things that bothered her about the current situation, Grant was the one complication she couldn't regret.

"Don't worry, my lady," Anna said gently. "They'll

find the madman soon enough. Then you'll be free to
find a husband."

Irene nodded. She didn't say what she feared most
was that she'd never be free of Grant. Her heart was
already too entangled. So much so, that when he
finally left to fulfill his obligations to his title, she could
be destroyed. Completely and utterly destroyed. And
no amount of work would bring her back to life again.

Twenty-one

GRANT WAS BARELY OUT OF BED WHEN HE GOT THE message from Mr. Tanner about Irene's plans. Apparently, she didn't have the constitution to lie abed like a bored society matron. He rather liked that about her. If he hadn't been tossing and turning all night—dreaming about her—then he probably would have been up earlier as well. After five years of living by the dictates of the mill, he often found himself awake and alert much too early for any of his London friends. But as he now had no mill doors to open, no ledgers to oversee, and no fabric to inspect, he found himself lingering in bed to no purpose whatsoever.

He'd never known how much he valued being forced to rise until he was back in London with nothing but time on his hands. Thank God he had Irene to occupy his thoughts. Otherwise, he might very well go mad.

He paused a moment, waiting for a wry comment from his madness, but no words filtered through his thoughts. He might have paused to wonder about that, but he had precious little time to get to the docks.

So he rushed through his morning—er, afternoon ablutions—and quickly headed out.

He found them at *The Singing Lady* and was pleasantly surprised by the retinue that followed her. Irene was dressed in one of her hideous black gowns. It was sturdy, practical, but did little to disguise the quality of the fabric or the cut of the fashionable gown. He guessed that everyone on the docks knew her by name. After all, how many fashionable widows frequented the area? So if she could not work in anonymity, at least she had a retinue of two footmen, Mr. Tanner, and a young girl.

They were just boarding the tiny rowboat that would take her to the ship when Grant slipped in beside Mr. Tanner. They managed only the barest conversation before Irene noted his presence.

Her eyes widened, and her mouth opened on a slight gasp of surprise. He was watching her closely, wishing her bonnet didn't shade her face from his gaze. He would have loved to see the sun on her pink cheeks. Still, despite the shadows, he was able to see her face brighten at the sight of him… and then shutter into a grimace of annoyance. As if she'd remembered she was irritated with him.

He raised his eyebrows in surprise, and she pointedly looked at Mr. Tanner then the two footmen. Ah, so she was angry about her protection and obviously blamed him for the necessity. He folded his arms and leaned against the edge of the boat, showing her that he would not feel guilty for ensuring her protection.

The message was understood as she flashed him another grimace. In truth, he half expected her to stick her tongue out, but she didn't. Though in his mind's eye, he saw the flash of her pink tongue, and everything in him hardened at the imagined thought. Ridiculous that he could grow lustful from his own imagination, but then again, after the torment of his dreams, it wasn't much of a surprise. Then an impish thought caught him, and he looked to Irene.

She was still glowering, so it was easy enough to slowly, seductively lick his own lips. Her eyes widened, and her face flamed. Even in the shadow of her bonnet, he could see the red on her cheeks and the way she bit her lower lip. She was too heavily dressed to see if her nipples reacted, but he would bet his last penny that they had. And when she looked back up—peering almost shyly from beneath her bonnet—he knew he'd been right. She'd been tormented as much as he had last night. And that knowledge cheered him immensely.

Then there was no more time for their silent game of tease because they arrived at the boat. They climbed on board, the footmen fanning out quickly, their rolling gait telling Grant these were former sailors. Mr. Tanner kept to a position near and a little to the left of Irene, his gaze taking in everything. Grant took his position behind Irene's right shoulder. It all happened like clockwork, and he was pleased by the result. Even the captain—a grizzled man with a full beard and steady eyes in his weathered face—watched everything before giving a quiet nod of approval.

The only one who seemed discomforted by the group was Irene herself, and perhaps, the little girl at her side.

"Good afternoon, Captain Haverson," she said quietly.

The man gave her a polite bow then nodded at her following. "Good to see, Lady Irene," he said heartily. "Good to see."

For her part, Irene released a huff of annoyance. "I assure you, it is not good in any way at all, but it appears I have little choice in the matter."

"Begging your pardon, my lady," the man said, "but aside from the dangers to any woman on the docks, your father has enemies. It's past time he saw to your protection."

Grant hadn't meant to intrude on Irene's negotiations, but this conversation wasn't about silks or ivory buttons. This was about Irene's safety, and so he took a step forward.

"Excuse me, Captain. My name's Mr. Grant, and I'm keeping an eye on Lady Irene. If you could explain... please? What dangers—specifically—should we be watching for?"

The Captain narrowed his eyes, looking Grant up and down. What he saw must have agreed with him, because in the end, he gave a curt nod. "Mr. Knopp's a fair man and a good employer, but he don't tolerate laze-abouts or lack wits. And he's downright murderous toward thieves."

Grant nodded. "Anyone in particular that you're thinking of?"

He grimaced. "I could give you names of a few I know—sailors who have a temper and a belief that their troubles are laid at Mr. Knopp's door. But I'm only one captain out of a whole fleet. There's bound to be a dozen or more names that I don't know."

"Your list would be a start."

The man pursed his lips as he thought. Ten minutes later, Grant had memorized the five names he'd been given, along with the best way to locate the men. A quick glance at Mr. Tanner showed that he'd done the same. Then it was time for Irene's business.

They went down to the hold—minus two footmen remaining above to guard their way—and Irene began a steady inspection of the merchandise that the captain had reserved for her. It was then that Grant got to enjoy Irene at her most mercenary, and the experience was a memorable one.

He had assumed that their negotiation in the inn was typical for the woman. He thought of their encounter as the first steps in a dance he now labeled: The Seduction of Lady Irene. She had been reserved then, almost shy in her persona of a grieving widow. In truth, it was exactly the best way to play upon his sympathies, and he'd wondered if that had been calculated decision or merely luck.

He now saw exactly how calculated her actions had been. Far from playing the grieving widow here, Irene acted as a critical customer, a woman who bargained with confidence, even as she inspected every purchase for flaws. She always acted the lady—her body and her language portraying elegance—but she was no shrinking violet with Captain Haverson. If anything, they had the feel of a pair of friendly adversaries.

That shouldn't have surprised him, but it did. Never had he seen a woman act so much like... well, like a businessman. She was neither shrewish nor manipulative beyond the usual bargaining tools employed by any tradesman. It was a sight to see, and he was quietly awed by her prowess. So much so that he nearly forgot his task in protecting her.

Fortunately, nothing untoward occurred. In due time, Irene's purchases were transferred to the dock and loaded onto Irene's cart. They were just about to leave for the dress shop when one of the sailors approached him, hat in hand.

"Yes?" Grant asked.

The man—a fresh-faced boy barely into his first beard—wrung his cap between his fingers. Grant recognized him as one who had been on the deck when they'd first arrived. The boy must have over-heard the conversation and was now awkwardly shuffling his feet.

"I 'eard wot you were saying. About men who don't like Mr. Knopp."

Grant schooled his expression into one of open interest without being fearful. "Yes, of course. Do you know of someone?"

He shook his head. "Not exactly. But the angry ones—the ones who hate ever'body—they go to The Dog's Bone. It's a tavern near—"

"I know it," said Mr. Tanner in a low voice. "I'll go round there this evening." Grant hadn't realized the runner was listening closely, but now, he gave the man a nod.

Meanwhile, the boy was dipping his chin. "I don't know of anybody in particular," he repeated. "But I'd hate myself fer sure if something awful was to happen to Lady Irene." He glanced a little too adoringly at the woman in question, and Grant felt his hackles rise.

It was ridiculous. Irene had no interest in this particular boy. She probably wasn't even aware of the man's devotion. But Grant's possessive instincts surged forward. He didn't want anyone looking at his woman that way. Fortunately, he had enough presence to stifle the urge and give the boy a brief—if somewhat cold—nod.

"Thank you for your help," he said. "You can contact Mr. Tanner at Bow Street if you learn of anything else."

"Yes, sir. Thank you, sir," the puppy said before slowly returning back to his ship. And to Grant's true annoyance, the boy kept his gaze trained on Irene nearly the entire time.

"Insolent puppy," Grant muttered under his breath.

Beside him, Mr. Tanner chuckled. "Can't damn the boy because he's got eyes to see and a heart to feel."

"I can," Grant grumbled back. "Isn't fair or rational, but I certainly can."

Mr. Tanner wisely didn't respond. And soon they moved to their respective positions as they headed toward the dress shop to deposit Irene's purchases. On the trip, Grant filled his mind with possible dangerous scenarios as he mentally rifled through the list of potential villains. The list was extremely vague, and therefore, huge. A nameless, disgruntled sailor was at the top of the list, but it could just as easily be an angry footman or a jealous competitor. That didn't add in the possible problems stemming from Miss Drew's activities with Demon Damon. It was enough to put him in a foul mood when they finally arrived at the dress shop.

He was in the midst of unloading bolts of silk when another problem arose in the person of one Miss Penny Shoemaker, fiancée to the runner Samuel Morrison.

"But you must come!" the girl was saying regarding her wedding in three weeks. "Bring them all, if you must." She waved a dismissive hand at Irene's retinue of protective footmen, "but it wouldn't be the same if you weren't there. Irene, you're family. Every one of you are my family—the only ones I have left, except Tommy—and I want you there!"

Grant set down his armful and turned to see Mr. Tanner frowning furiously. When Grant raised an eyebrow in question, the man stepped closer and grumbled. "Awful hard to protect a woman at a wedding. Inside the church is safe enough, but once at the party afterwards? Especially with what she's got planned?" He shook his head, more words unnecessary.

Grant was thinking, trying to sort through polite refusals, when Irene spoke up, her face alight with laughter. "But, of course, I'm coming, Penny! I wouldn't miss it for the world."

❧

Irene rolled her eyes, feeling the pinch of her fashionable clothing, even as she glared at Grant. They had been arguing ever since the dress shop two hours before. Even when they separated long enough to change into their attire for the walk in Hyde Park, their argument lingered. It must have been the same for him because seconds after they met again, the heated discussion resumed, as if there had been no pause.

"I will not have my life restricted on all sides. I will not miss Penny's wedding. And I will not allow you to create a sense of fear in me. I lived too long in that place, and I refuse to go back, no matter what the cost."

"And if it costs you your life?" he asked, his voice a low growl.

She released a slow breath. "Then so be it. It is better than living without being alive."

"That makes no sense at all!" he fumed.

"It makes perfect sense, and if you'd known me a year ago, you would not wish me to return to that pale nothing of a creature ever again."

He grimaced. "I don't want you to retreat, I want you to remain safe!"

"Until you catch our mysterious attacker."

"Yes!"

"And do you have any news on who that man might be?"

"We have some new leads," he said slowly.

"But no proof that any such attack will come again."

He looked away, and she knew she'd caught him.

"Exactly," she said. "You'd have me wrapped in cotton and secreted away for months, if not years, on the fear that something might happen again."

"Your father is worried. He's an eminently reasonable man, and he—"

"He has taken precautions. And I believe *you* are the one who worried him, what with sending around a Bow Street Runner."

"He has enemies."

"Then protect *him*! Goodness, he will not be at the

wedding. Leave me in peace, and go surround him with all your bristling footmen."

Grant released a huff of frustration, only moderately covered as he bowed his head in greeting to a mama and her two new charges—girls in their first come out. The woman was probably some countess. Irene didn't know. She'd never been in the fashionable whirl, and she was rather irritated, suddenly feeling at outs with people who would have been her peers, if her life had gone differently.

Yes, she was the daughter of an earl, but she'd grown up impoverished, clinging to the trappings of a bankrupt title. It was only her marriage to Nate that had brought her any type of wealth, and that at the cost of her social standing. And now, she was a wealthy widow with a job that she loved. She couldn't help but look askance at the need to dress pretty in order to traipse around Hyde Park, so that she could be seen by ladies who thought her nothing more than a fallen bird, all too willing to tromp upon her wings.

But that, of course, was her opinion. Grant, on the other hand, was the Earl of Crowle, and he had a standing to maintain. As a single earl on parade during the fashionable hour, he was also a target for every girl and her mama within the quarter-mile radius.

So they stopped and chatted. The woman was a baroness, apparently, but one with social ambitions. Grant made polite talk with the girls, eliciting true laughter from the children, while Irene felt her teeth clench and her cheeks ache.

Damn them, but they made her feel old. And damn them for being sweet and innocent—exactly the kind of girl Grant would soon be marrying. After all, he had responsibilities to his title, for all that he decried them. Eventually, he would bow to tradition and be forced to set up a nursery with some woman of his set. A virginal woman probably, with blonde curls, blue eyes, and a sweet temperament. A girl who was decidedly *not* Irene.

"Oh look," Irene suddenly interrupted. "Is that your brother over there? With Miss Powel and..." Her voice trailed away.

"And my mother," Grant said, his voice heavy with reluctance.

Irene glanced sharply at her companion. "Is that why we are here today? To meet—"

"My mother? Gads, no."

Then he calmly turned back to the baroness and her charges, able to gracefully detach from the three, only after promising to stop at their ball in two weeks. Then, two minutes later, they were walking toward his family, though his steps were slow.

"I promised Josephine that I would come walking today to meet with her. I thought it would be just her and Will, but..."

"But now, you must face your poor, neglected mama." Irene felt a smile curve her lips. "I am suddenly feeling more chipper about the day."

"Why? You want to see me set down as if I were a small boy?"

Irene laughed. "No, silly. I want to meet the woman who raised such a wonderful man." Then she squeezed his arm. "And yes, I am still a little cross with you and would relish seeing you set down just a tad."

"I knew it."

She laughed. "I have some sympathy for your mother. I cannot imagine why you would remain apart from her for so long. You are her son, and I suggest you start with a most heartfelt apology."

"I know," he said, and there was no reluctance in his tone. Neither did she hear a teasing grumble. He felt guilty, she realized, and now, she felt bad for poking at him.

"She loves you, you know," she said softly. "She will forgive you."

Grant glanced at her. "Somehow that makes it even worse."

Then there was no more discussion because the two parties met up. Will and Josephine were walking together, their eyes barely noticing anyone else, though they smiled and greeted everyone. It was Grant's mother who drew Irene's attention. She was of average height with warm brown eyes, which were now trained hungrily on her eldest son. The signs of age were in her weathered face and wrinkled skin. Beneath her stylish bonnet, her hair was gray and styled in a casually fashionable manner. But the woman often reached to touch her coiffure then pulled her hand away, as if she weren't used to having the pins or the hat.

Meanwhile, Grant stepped forward and greeted his mother, pressing a kiss to her cheek as she grabbed hold of his hands. "Mother," he said, "you look lovely." And when he might have pulled away, she held him still.

"I have you now in my clutches," she said, her

voice unexpectedly strong for a woman obviously aging. "I shall not release you just yet."

Grant dipped his head, his gaze dropping, but quickly returning to the woman's face. He looked at her as closely as she inspected him. Whereas his mother just appeared desperately happy to see her son, Grant's shame was obvious to everyone. Well, at least it was obvious to Irene, in the pink of his cheeks and the hunch to his shoulders.

"I am well, Mama. How are you?"

"Very well now that both my sons are with me. You have lost weight. And there is a hollow look to your cheeks, but not your eyes." Her gaze darted to Irene. "Am I to wish you happy?"

It took a moment for Irene to understand her words. Then she felt her face heat to a bright, hot blush. And burning in her mind were the fresh-faced girls from five minutes before. Maybe one was destined to be the new Lady Crowle. So without even thinking, she shook her head.

"I would not expect such an announcement, my lady," she said. "Though I know how much your son has been anticipating this reunion with you. So I am sure he is happy right now."

"No," said Grant from her side, his expression unexpectedly dark. "No, actually 'happy' is not the word I would choose right now."

If her face was hot before, now her temperature sank to a chilling cold. She bit her lip, horrified by her obvious emotional display. Normally, she was much more under control.

Meanwhile—thankfully—Josephine interrupted the

awkwardness with her own bright words. "We have set a date, by the way. For our wedding and the engagement party. You will come, won't you? Both of you?"

"If you wish it," Irene said, grateful for the shift into easy conversation. "I should be most happy to attend."

"And you?" asked Lady Crowle as she leveled her heavy stare on her eldest son.

Irene looked at the woman's focused expression and realized that was where Grant had learned his intensity—a direct look that seemed to burn straight through a body. No wonder the man fidgeted.

"Of course, I will be there," he said. "Why wouldn't I be?"

"Why would you disappear for five years without a word?" returned his mother.

Grant didn't respond at first, and into the silence, the woman pushed even further.

"Where were you, Grant? What have you been doing?"

And there it was, the question baldly spoken. Everyone turned to look at the man who was swallowing as if his throat had suddenly constricted. Irene waited for that casual wave of his fingers and his bored aristocrat response: oh, this and that, Mama. But apparently, he couldn't get it out. Clearly, he found it hard to lie to his mother.

"Mama, is it really important? Does it matter what I was doing?"

"Apparently so," the woman said tartly. Her eyes narrowed. "You missed your father's funeral. You missed holidays and birthdays."

"I sent what money I could."

"As if I ever cared about that! I wanted my son, Grant. I wanted to know if you were alive."

He looked away, his expression stricken. Then he said the words. They were half whispered, half spoken, and Irene feared that the others wouldn't hear. "I was working, Mama. At a mill."

Irene saw the words hit his brother. Will jerked slightly, and his eyebrows rose in shock. But his mother simply frowned.

"And?" she asked, pointedly.

Grant turned back. "And what?"

Irene leaned forward. "I don't think she heard you."

"I heard him perfectly well," the woman snapped. "Learned to understand his mumbles when he was still in short coats. What I don't understand is why he never visited. Or wrote. Ridiculous to send money and not a letter. Beyond annoying to not even let us know where the money came from."

Grant frowned at his mother. "Mama, I was *working*." He practically spat the last word, for all that it was still uttered in an undertone. "Night and day, aching body, burning eyes. Like a damned ditchdigger."

His mother grimaced. "I heard that. Working. At a mill. Did you also have to work on Christmas day? Were your hands amputated such that you could not pick up a quill?"

Grant ran an obviously not amputated hand through his hair. Fortunately, that gave him an even more dashing appearance. Unfortunately, some of the ladies strolling nearby noticed and looked on with appreciative smiles. And attentive ears.

They were starting to draw attention. And yet, Grant's mother would not let this go—at least not until she'd tortured her son a bit more.

"We have been worried sick," she said softly. "All of us. Why did you not send word?"

Grant swallowed, his expression sick. "Because I was working. At a mill, Mama."

It was clear she did not understand. And it was just as clear that Grant could not express himself any better. So rather than see the two struggle back and forth to no point, Irene decided to do what she could to help. She touched his hand to show her support, but her words were for Lady Crowle.

"I believe he had no wish to shame the family name, my lady," she said softly. "He changed his name to Mr. Grant and functioned solely in that identity for five years. To great success, I might add. The clothing he wears—and my own—were designed and implemented by his hand."

She felt Grant flinch at her words, his arm jerking away, though he didn't separate them. Obviously, he didn't like that she said these things aloud, but really, Irene was rather proud of him. For all that he was ashamed of his labors, she wanted his family to know what he had done. Perhaps they would be proud as well.

Will was proud. She could see that in the way his head tilted. His gaze took in the cloth they wore, and his chin dipped in approval. Lady Crowle, however, barely flicked a glance at their attire. Then her attention riveted right back to Grant's face.

"But what is any of that to the point? It's handsome

stuff, to be sure, but why would you absent yourself for five years? Not a word, Grant! To anyone!"

Which is when she heard Grant take a deep breath. He pulled it in and released it in a huff that everyone heard. And when he spoke, his words were hushed with shock.

"You don't care," he finally breathed, surprise in every word. "You don't care what I was doing. I could have been at a brothel—"

"Grant!" grumbled Will from the side, clearly annoyed at his brother's language.

"In a disreputable den then," Grant quickly amended. "You don't care what I was doing. At all."

"Well, of course, I care," snapped his mother. "Did it work out all right? Did you accomplish what you wanted?"

Grant blinked. "Um, no. Sadly, not."

It took a moment for Irene to remember that he didn't see his work at the mill as successful. After all, he'd meant to buy back the family land. Land that was now in Miss Powel's dowry and would go to his brother. She glanced at Will and saw him look down, his expression shuttered, as he too understood the awkwardness of the moment.

"Well, that's unfortunate," his mother said with a flick of her wrist. "But it is not important."

"Not important?" Grant cried. "It was the whole point!"

"No, my dear," his mother countered. "The whole point was that we might have helped you. We might have been able to comfort you. We might... bloody hell!" she cursed, and everyone gasped. "We might have known you were alive."

Grant blinked. The shock on his face might have been comical, if it weren't so tragic. Did he really think that a mother—his mother—would care what he was doing? Would be ashamed? Apparently so, because he was stunned that her anger was not at *what* he did, but that he'd absented himself.

Will spoke up. "I wish you'd told me," he said softly. "I wish I'd known."

Grant looked over. "That I was a common laborer?"

"There is nothing common about you, brother. Never has been."

At which point, Grant blinked. Then blinked again. His eyes were misty with tears, she realized. A moment later, he was clasping his brother's hand. And then, he turned to hug his mother.

"I'm sorry," he murmured. "I'm so sorry. I was a fool."

It was a touching moment. Finally, Grant had reconciled with his mother and brother. Irene found her own eyes misting with happiness, but she wasn't given the chance. Even before mother and son finished their embrace, they were interrupted.

Another matchmaking mama pushed her way into their group by "accidentally" bumping into Will. Then she apologized profusely before pushing forward her daughter. Introductions were barely finished—and another ball invitation offered and accepted—when a second set of debutantes intruded.

More and more came, one after another. They were, after all, in Hyde Park during the fashionable hour. It was to be expected. But by the time Grant had finished bowing over hands and trading smiles with young innocents, Irene felt as if she'd been kicked in the stomach. Nausea rolled inside her, and she turned away.

"Lady Irene?" Grant said as she stepped back from the group.

"I'm terribly sorry," she said quickly. "I feel as if I've overdone it. Long day and all. I think I shall return home."

"Just a moment," he said as he turned away from a disappointed young girl. "I shall escort you—"

"No, no," she said softly, looking at the vast array of potential girls eyeing him all over the park. "You should be here. I should be home."

"Don't be ridiculous—" he began, but she cut him off as she spotted her Bow Street Runner where he lurked next to a tree.

"Mr. Tanner, would you mind helping me to a hack? Anything would do."

As expected, the man leaped forward to assist. And as she walked away, she counted no less than six unwed girls who smiled in glee at her departure.

Twenty-two

GRANT WAS FURIOUS WITH IRENE. HE TRIED TO MAKE allowances for the strain she was under. He knew better than anyone how difficult it was living with the idea that someone wanted to hurt you. That would be hard on anyone, but add the restrictions to her life now, the constant guard and ceaseless worry—that had to wear on her. In truth, he was surprised she had not taken to her bed and refused to venture out.

But that wasn't Irene. She had fought hard to leave that withdrawn state after the loss of her husband. She would not go back now. That made him admire her. It made him want to learn more.

And yet, he was still furious at her dismissal of their relationship. She did not intend to marry him. That's what she'd said in the park to his mother. And that idea infuriated him. Did she think he trifled with her emotions? Did she think he bedded just any woman and then left her? The very idea had his blood boiling with fury.

As soon as he could escape his family—and all those damned matchmaking mamas in the park—he made haste to Irene's home. She and her in-laws resided in an expensive—if not quite elite—area of London. He arrived quickly and relieved Mr. Tanner for the night. He was taking this shift, hopefully from inside the house. Mr. Knopp's guards would handle the rest.

After a quick discussion with the runner, he crossed to the front door and knocked. A moment later, a rather suspicious-looking butler opened the door. And the man's scowl deepened when Grant gave his name.

"Is there a problem?" Grant asked, his eyes scanning the house, searching for danger.

"No, my lord," came the stiff response. It took a moment, but abruptly, Grant realized that *he* was the problem. The butler took issue with him, probably because the man suspected the nature of his relationship with Irene and did not approve.

Years ago, he wouldn't even have noticed, much less cared, what some butler thought. But after years of working with the lower classes, he knew how important every soul was. He understood the anger that came from being ignored. A butler had no say in the affairs of the mistress, but he still cared, and he still mattered.

"I mean to marry her," he said in an undertone. Where the certainty in that statement came from, he had no clue. He was determined because the idea of separating from her was a physical pain. However, now was not the time to propose. "It's a delicate business," he continued to the man. "And I won't propose while she's in danger. My attention must be on that first."

It was the truth, though he had to admit his

attention was sorely divided whenever he was in her presence. As for the butler, the man paused then executed a respectful bow. When he spoke, his tone was full of approval. "Then I am pleased to welcome you to Knopp house. If you would follow me, I shall announce you."

Grant was escorted to the parlor where the family gathered before dinner. Only the ladies were present, and his gaze went directly to Irene. She was still in her fashionable walking gown, sitting sideways. He noticed the elegance of her neck and profile, the proud way she sat at the couch, and her beauty, despite the tightness in her shoulders. She gasped slightly when he was announced, and she twisted to look at him.

He was watching her closely, so he saw—and took heart from—a softening in her expression, fleeting though it was. Then a split second later, it was shuttered beneath a careful blankness. He tried to contain his irritation. Devil take it! Whatever had he done to make her so guarded in his presence? Meanwhile, Mrs. Knopp leapt to her feet, her exuberant expression and plump figure in direct opposition to Irene's.

"Lord Crowle, what a surprise! You must stay for dinner. I won't hear otherwise."

He kissed her outstretched hand with a warm smile. "It would be my great pleasure to dine with two such lovely creatures."

The woman laughed, the sound hearty and warm. He liked her. Years ago, he might have thought her an encroaching, overly loud cit. But again, the last five years had changed him. He knew how rare that joie de vivre was—especially in a woman who had lost her

only child. So now, he gave her a warm smile before
bowing over Irene's hand.

"I hope I find you well, Lady Irene."

She gestured with her free hand. "As you can see…"

He kissed her hand then held on, refusing to
release her. Meanwhile, he raised his eyebrows. At her
confused look, he prompted her. "I can see what, Lady
Irene? I see that your body is here without apparent
injury, but I know nothing of your state of mind. If
you are afraid or worried or simply annoyed, I cannot
read you. I never have. It is both part of your allure
and a great frustration."

Irene's jaw went slack at his words. She recovered
quickly, but he had done what he'd intended: her
gaze trained on him, and she struggled to give him
an honest answer. "I, uh, I suppose I am embarrassed," she said. "There has been no new attack.
No suggestion—"

"We have been over this," he said gently. "I will
not take the risk—"

"But what if it is all for nothing?"

"Then some good people will get coin for work
well done. And I will have gotten a bit more sleep
at night."

She nodded, her cheeks flushing as she looked
away. "But when will it end?"

He knew that was the main concern. For himself,
as well. No one could remain ever vigilant, especially
in the face of… well, nothing at all. "A little while
longer, please."

"Longer," she echoed. He heard resignation in her
words, and he grimaced.

"You should not feel defeated," he said softly. "I want you to feel cherished."

She looked at him, and her eyes seemed haunted. In the end, she simply frowned. "I am afraid I don't have much experience in that."

He tightened his hold on her hand, forming words that expressed his intention to spend a lifetime teaching her exactly what cherished felt like. But he didn't have the chance as Mrs. Knopp gasped in horror.

He started—as did Irene—both having forgotten she was in the room and listening. Suddenly recalled to their audience, Grant turned, but it was Irene who slammed her hands against her mouth. "Oh no," she rushed to say. "I did not mean what I said. Not like—"

Mrs. Knopp shook her head, her eyes misting as she attempted a watery smile. "No, no, Irene, dear. I understand. Truly, I do. Your father was awful, I know. And Nate was gone so very often. But Papa and I have tried to make you welcome here. To make you feel—"

Irene rushed across the room, dropping to her knees before her mother-in-law. "I am the most churlish woman in the world. Of course, you have made me feel welcome and loved. Cherished, even. I just..." Her voice trailed away as she struggled for words.

"I know," the woman answered, her voice broken. "We are not truly your parents. And if Nate had only stayed home..."

"You cannot think like that," Irene returned. "We cannot live in what-ifs."

Mrs. Knopp nodded, and Grant had the feeling that this was an oft-repeated conversation. At least, the last part. What if Nate had stayed home? What if he had lived? How would her life have gone? Would there be grandchildren by now?

He settled into a seat, doing his best not to intrude, but in the end, a tearful Mrs. Knopp turned his way.

"Look at us, talking about someone long gone when we have... when..." Her voice broke, and she couldn't continue.

"When there is another gentleman here visiting," he finished as gently as he could. "But I would like to hear more, if you feel up to it. I should very much like to learn about your Nate."

Irene looked horrified, but Mrs. Knopp dabbed her eyes. "Would you?" she asked, hope in her voice. "Would you truly?"

"Of course," he answered.

Mrs. Knopp turned to Irene. "You do not mind, do you?"

Irene shook her head, her expression tight. "You know I don't mind."

"But you do," the woman said. "As does Papa. It pains you, I know. But..."

Grant nodded. "But he is your son, and you like remembering him. It is only natural."

"He wouldn't have liked you," she said as she looked at Grant. "You're too handsome, too charming. He would have called you a slick blighter."

Grant almost chuckled. "I have been called worse, I assure you. It would only have made me more determined to show him the truth of my character," he lied. He tended to prove himself to women. To men, he would have taken great pleasure in beating the man in some sort of wager. Unless, of course, he lost at the wager. Then they might possibly have become friends. That is, after all, exactly how Robert and he had first met as schoolboys. "What was he like as a boy?"

"Oh, he was into every sort of mischief. You know how boys are. And with his father sailing most of the time, I had my hands quite full running after him. We wanted more children, you know, but God only gave us him. And he… well, he made me very happy, though he was a terrible son. Always playing tricks, always running off to the docks. He wanted to sail from the first moment he saw the water."

"He took after his father then," he asked. He was simply prompting Mrs. Knopp into memories, urging her to continue, while he kept his gaze on Irene. He wanted to know just how much of her heart still lingered with her lost husband. Was she still buried with her Nate?

Irene's face gave little away. She kept her hands tight, her expression composed. It was damnably frustrating to not have a clue as to her thoughts.

"I understood, you know," continued Mrs. Knopp. "He wanted to be with his father, and a mother is not enough no matter how much she tries."

"He adored you," inserted Irene, her voice quiet.

"I know. And he really wasn't a terrible son. Just an active one. Never still, never content to sit and be quiet. He didn't even sleep above five hours at a time. Always had to be up and around doing something."

"His visits were like intense holidays," Irene said. "I likened him to fireworks once. A burst of light and excitement…"

"And then gone. That was my Nate."

The two women shared a look, identical, wistful expressions.

"How did you meet?" he asked Irene. He'd heard some of the tale, but wanted the rest.

She looked at him, her expression grave. She seemed to be deciding if she would speak, and he held his breath waiting. Then she gave a little shrug. "It was at the market near the docks. I had gone to buy some cheap silk for a dress. I was in my come-out, you see, but we couldn't afford anything. Mama was a fair hand at cutting, able to fashion a dress out mismatched pieces. I did the stitching. So I went in search of a damaged bolt of silk that could be had for a song."

"So you were a purchaser even then," he said.

She nodded, and he saw no shame in it. "That is why Helaine thought of me when she needed someone for her shop. The two of us were raised with almost nothing. We had to make do, finding bargains wherever we could."

Apparently unable to keep quiet, Mrs. Knopp took up the tale. "He saw her at the market. Something about a melon. He knew right away. He came home and told me that he had seen the woman he wanted to marry. Elegant, sophisticated, but could bargain like a fishwife."

Grant's eyebrows rose, but he could detect no shame in Irene's face. In fact, a fond smile played about her lips. "He told me it was my beauty."

"It was that too. But he liked that you weren't…" The woman flashed an apologetic smile at Grant. "… high in the instep, like those other bloody peers. As

I said, I do not think he would have liked you over-much. Nate was quick to judge—for better or ill."

"Do not apologize," he said. "I am not very fond of the peerage myself. Though I begin to think I would have liked your son a great deal." In truth, he was finding he liked the mother. He appreciated her honest assessment of her son when most women claimed the dead as paragons of virtue. "And if he judged Lady Irene as a diamond of the first water, then he had an excellent eye."

"No diamond," Irene said. "Just a poor girl trying too hard to maintain a wealthy façade."

He understood the strain very well. "It must have been hard."

"Nate swept me off my feet. Bought me all manner of gifts: posies and sweets. And though it was improper to buy me anything like silk or thread, such treasures would appear at our door without explanation. I knew who it was from, of course, and Mama was too grateful to speak out against it. Especially when he declared in almost his first breath that he wanted to marry me."

There was such warmth in her voice—part nostalgia, part longing. "You loved him deeply," he said, the words cutting his throat as he spoke.

She nodded, though she glanced at Mrs. Knopp as she did. He wondered what that meant. Of course, she would have to profess deep love in front of her mother-in-law. But the look gave him hope. Perhaps there was room in her heart for him.

Meanwhile, Mrs. Knopp dabbed her eyes. "They were married before the year was out."

"And he was gone not three years later," finished

Irene. The finality in her voice summed up her attitude. Fireworks—spectacular then gone.

He frowned, wondering at what she wasn't telling him. Though he asked many questions, she wouldn't say more. She simply deferred questions to her mother-in-law, who relayed one tale of adventure after another. And that was how they spent the remaining time before her husband appeared.

Once he joined them, however, discussion became general. The talk was of business or politics, of Grant's investigation, and—when the ladies participated—of the balls and party invitations they'd received. By elite standards, it was rough talk, but Grant enjoyed it. He spoke as if he were Mr. Grant, discussing the workers and the lower classes. And to his surprise, Irene listened closely, adding in her own perspective whenever appropriate. It was a lively evening that he enjoyed thoroughly. And he was sad to see it end.

But dinner did end, as did the after-dinner drinks. He remained as long as he could, but eventually, politeness required that he take his leave—without even five minutes to speak privately with her—but there was no help for it. Unless, of course... he thought of the way the house was constructed. He believed he knew where her bedroom was located.

So before he departed, he managed to whisper into her ear. "Open your bedroom window for me." It was half plea, half command, and he prayed he had not struck too bold a tone. Then five minutes later, he was waiting nervously outside her bedroom window, perched awkwardly—and somewhat dangerously—on a tree limb that dipped and swayed beneath his weight.

"Why?" Then she looked at him tensing on the limb to make the leap, and she gripped the windowsill in horror. "No!" she all but screamed. But as she was trying to keep her voice down, it came out more as a hiss. "Absolutely not!"

"I mean to talk to you, Irene. And I will not shout for everyone to hear."

She grimaced, seeing his intent clear as day. Looking around, she judged the jump: about three feet. Not very far, but if he missed, the drop could be lethal. There was only one solution. She leaned out the window and extended her arms.

"Irene!" he gasped, but she was already stretched far.

"Grab hold," she said. "I will pull you inside."

He didn't like it, but she didn't give him a choice. So, with her leaning out and him stretching in, they managed to pull him, such that his belly landed heavily on the windowsill.

"Umph!" he cried, his breath hot on her face. Then there was the awkward struggle and maneuver as he wiggled himself inside. She stepped back, trying to give him room. Fortunately, that also gave her a nice moonlit view of his backside.

"What are you staring at?" he asked somewhat irritably, as he finally pulled his feet inside.

"Hmmm? Just the rip you now have in your trousers." She waved at his left thigh.

He looked down, poked a finger through the tear, and cursed softly under his breath. "I just had this made. The mill won't send more bolts of this for weeks."

She couldn't help but laugh. He lay sprawled on her floor, and all he could do was bemoan his attire.

"I should be very cross with you, Lord Crowle," she said. "But I find it hard to berate a man with a hole in his pants."

He raised his eyebrows. "Truly? I shall remember that and be sure to sport holes often."

"Do you expect to irritate me so very much then?"

He sobered slightly, and his head tilted to one side as he looked steadily at her. "Probably." His eyes smoldered, leaving no doubt whatsoever as to what he was thinking. And even if she failed to understand his meaning, her body responded without her willing it. Her breasts grew heavy; her blood turned hot. And by slow inches, her knees gave way, until she was kneeling directly in front of him.

"Kiss me, Irene," he pleaded softly. "You do not know how much I have ached for you this day."

She shook her head, meaning to pull back. Instead, she found herself moving closer. "You are so different than Nate." After all, her husband would have already claimed her by now. Instead, Grant sat on the floor asking permission, while his eyes burned straight through her heart.

He paused a moment, his body tightening, his breath short. "I am incredibly jealous of a dead man."

"Don't be," she whispered. "You are your own man, and... and I find I like you even better for it."

"Just *like*?" he asked, a note of hurt in his voice.

She swallowed. Did he really wish for her to confess? That sometime between their first dance and his first kiss, she had tumbled desperately in love with him? She hadn't even realized until this afternoon the depths of her feelings.

She loved him, and she hated him for that. She was doomed now to love a man who would give himself to a girl. One husband loved and lost; one lover kissed then allowed to walk away. How ridiculous was her life. And yet, with his breath on her face and his body heating hers, she could not turn away.

So she kissed him with all the wishes in her soul. He returned it a thousand fold, and yet it was just the thrust of his tongue, the tease of his lips, and the tremble in his hands. Then the slow, almost jerky, push to the floor. It was as if he fought himself, trying to hold back, but unable. Meanwhile, she slid her hands around his neck, allowing one to sink into his hair, the other to slide over his broad shoulder to press into his back. How she longed for him to be naked.

"I am annoyed with you," she murmured into his mouth.

"Why?" he asked as he trailed kisses along her jaw and neck.

"Why did you ask about Nate? Why do you stir up something so long gone?"

He paused, and she saw him flinch. "You loved him?"

"Yes," she admitted.

"Do you love him still?"

"Yes." Then at his grimace, she continued, trying to put voice to her thoughts. "He was my world, Grant. I was overcome by him. Always. And when he was gone, it was as if I had ceased to be."

He swallowed, nodding slowly.

"But I am more than I was then. I am not that girl to be lost in a larger-than-life man." She touched his face, drawing his gaze back. "You are different than him. You don't create me. You… match me. And that is so very different."

He studied her face, and then he slowly sunk down to kiss her again. Long and deep. And when he pulled back, his words were a whisper. "That is why I asked. That is what I wanted to know."

She frowned. "But do you understand? Do you understand how I was a girl then but am a woman now?"

"That," he said, as he slid his hands beneath her skirt, "I know very well."

She felt his hands then, strong and sure, as he slowly spread her legs. She opened for him, embarrassed and terribly hungry—for his touch between her legs, deep and penetrating, then swirling in long strokes across her most sensitive flesh.

"I take it back," she gasped as she arched into his caress. "You erase everything but yourself. Oh Grant… fill me. Please."

But he didn't. He continued to pleasure her. "I don't want to erase you, Irene. I want to… match you."

She opened her eyes. "*Fill* me," she said firmly, almost loudly, but she remembered at the last moment to keep her voice low.

He nodded, but he didn't stop what he was doing. He stroked her, he pleasured her, and she writhed beneath his ministrations. It was so maddening. Not the thrust or the swirl, but that he didn't do them fast enough or hard enough. He was casual as he stroked her, his touch too light. And though his eyes burned as they watched her, he still did not take her where she wanted to go.

"Grant!" she cried. "What are you doing?"

"Watching," he answered with a smile. "Will you marry me?"

"What?" she gasped, completely startled. He appeared shocked as well, his hand suddenly stilling as he pressed his thumb against her hard button.

Without conscious thought, she arched onto his hand, pressing his thumb deeply against her. Her body contracted around him. Everything drew tight, compressed into a tiny dot. Then while she was still staring in shock, her body released. Like a flame bursting free, she convulsed, pleasure powering through her. Bright, explosive. A brilliant firework of ecstasy.

He held her gaze the whole time, this man who wasn't a fiery explosion himself, but who gave them to her whenever they touched. And as the light in her body shimmered then slowly faded, he gave her a reverent smile.

"You are so beautiful when you do that."

She sighed, her body growing languid as the warm glow of pleasure lingered. "Grant..."

"I am Lord Crowle and am here on my knees asking you to marry me. Will you, Irene? Will you do me this great honor and become my wife?"

"No."

The word was out—bald and cold—before she could think clearly. And as he recoiled backward, his hand pulling to the inside of her knee, she bit her lip and struggled to gather her wits. Straightening to a sitting position, she faced him with as much clarity as she could muster.

"You are Grant, Lord Crowle, and I am not the

woman who will hostess your dinners, give you an heir, or be your countess."

"The devil you won't!"

"I am a purchaser. The man I love is Mr. Grant, and he will never be an earl. I will never be a countess." She sighed and let her body slump. "I'm sorry, Grant. So damned sorry."

"You're the daughter of an earl. Of course, you can be my countess!"

She opened her eyes. "A countess cannot be a purchaser. She cannot spend her days negotiating with a ship's captain, no matter how many footmen protect her. It is not done, and you know it as well as I do."

"What if I don't care?"

She tightened her body further, pulling in her legs to support her better. His hand slid backward until he only touched her ankle, and she was secretly glad they were still connected. "How long have you been back in London? Not as Mr. Grant, but as Lord Crowle?" She didn't wait for him to answer, but continued relentlessly. "A week? Two? You are only now remembering what it is like to be an earl. It will not take much longer before you realize the truth."

He pulled back, his brow arching to regal heights. The regent himself could not look more aristocratic. "And what truth is that?"

"That I am a purchaser, not a countess. And I will not give up the one to become the other."

She saw her words hit him. In truth, she hadn't even realized how final her opinion was until she spoke it out loud. And when he spoke—his tone almost broken—she felt the horror of what she had said aloud.

"You said you loved me," he whispered. "That you love Grant. That's me."

She nodded. "For a little while longer, yes. But not for long." She touched his face and was relieved when he did not draw away. She felt the roughness of his beard, the heat of his body, but most of all, she felt the vulnerability with his every ragged breath. "Do you recall when you seduced me in the inn?"

"After the attack."

She shook her head. "When you danced with me. We were fully clothed, but you seduced me completely in that one dance. You coaxed me, you tempted me, and you offered everything you had to me."

"I remember," he said.

"That is the man I love. But then you commanded me to join you at the park. You hired a runner to watch me and spoke with Papa without even discussing it with me."

"I am protecting your life!"

"You are taking control as Lord Crowle. And that man will not tolerate a wife who works. Certainly not one who works on the docks." She made the reference crude, suggesting what was obviously not true. She was no doxy, but an earl had no choice but to equate the two. A woman who worked was not fit to be a countess.

"I don't want to change you. I've never wanted that!"

"I won't change. And Lord Crowle won't want who I am. He can't and still maintain his position in the peerage."

His hand tightened on her ankle, his grip not painful, so much as possessive. "You love me!"

She nodded. "And I will let Grant into my bed as often as he wants."

"But I am Grant."

She nodded, her heart breaking. They both knew she was right. Still, she lifted her chin to him. "Then make love to me, Grant. Fill me."

He hesitated. She saw his body urging him forward, even as his mind rebelled. The aristocrat wanted her—body and soul, but she would not give both—only her body. He shuddered, his expression sliding into anguish. "I cannot lose you, Irene."

"I am right here." She reached behind herself and unbuttoned what she could of her dress. It was frustrating and awkward, and after a moment, she gave up the struggle. She looked at him, about to ask him to help, when she realized he was no longer sitting before her.

He'd stood and was even now moving for the door.

"Grant?" she whispered.

"I cannot go out by way of the window. I think I can slip out undetected. The house is silent, and the guards already knew I was here."

She flushed, wondering what the men thought of her now. But that was a small concern compared to the sight of him leaving her bedroom. She didn't want him to go. She had slept before in his arms and longed to do it again. Not to mention the other pleasures they had shared.

"Why are you leaving?"

"You only want half of me, and I am done with being a splintered man."

She opened her mouth to argue, but mostly, to

tempt him back to her side. He never gave her a chance. After a quick nod, he slipped outside her door and closed it quietly. She could have followed. She could have, but how would it have looked to be chasing a man departing her bedroom? And besides, what would she say? She would not change her mind. She would not accept his proposal.

So she let him go. And with that decision came a host of other emotions. Like tiny bits of debris—ashes perhaps—the cold bits left from the fireworks. Fear was part of it. Weariness came next. And the cold desolation of… nothing. It was startling, really, how quickly it all collapsed.

She heard the quiet thud of the front door as he left and with him went nearly all her strength. She used the last of it to climb into her bed fully dressed. Her pillow absorbed her tears, but did nothing to ease the ache in her heart. And in the morning, she did not rise.

It was no matter, she thought, as she turned her back on the sun. After all, she had no appointments. Everything had been scheduled for the day before. As for tomorrow's appointments, there was nothing urgent then either. She could cancel them easily enough.

She left the message for Carol to do just that. At some point later, she began counting ticks of the clock. And so she passed another day.

Twenty-four

GRANT FELT A HOLE IN HIS GUT—AND AN ACHE IN HIS balls—the second he left Irene's presence. He spent much of the painful walk back to the inn silently cursing the woman. She'd thrown him over, and for the most ridiculous of reasons. He'd certainly known of women who would look down on him for his five years as a working man. He'd never expected the reverse snobbery, never thought a woman would refuse him because she didn't want to be a countess. The idea was preposterous, and he mulled over the possibility that something else was at work.

By the time he reached his sparse room, he'd run through a dozen or more explanations for her secret dislike. But it wasn't until he sat on the sagging bed that he chanced to think of something else. His gaze had snagged on the latest report from the mill. It was doing well; all the systems he'd put in place before he'd left were performing just as they ought. And his replacement was exceptional.

Which meant he wouldn't need to return, not as manager, not even as partial owner. It also meant that he had money to spare now. Perhaps he ought to think about getting a more permanent bed. If he wasn't traveling back to York, then he should rent some rooms.

He paused, his breath quieting as he thought. And he waited. At first, he wasn't sure exactly why, but as the silence stretched on, the knowledge came in a blinding flash of panic.

He was waiting for his madness to speak. A wry comment, a snide remark—his madness had always had something to say. From the time he was thirteen, the voice had always been with him. And yet now, his mind was frighteningly quiet.

"What the hell?" he said out loud, just to fill the void. No answer. He heard the noise of the taproom downstairs, the scrape of a branch against the window, even the creek of his bed as he shifted uncomfortably on the sagging mattress. Not a peep from his madness.

He shot to his feet, his gaze roving the bedroom. He hadn't a clue what he thought to find, but he scanned the place three times just in case. Then he closed his eyes and tried to grab his reason.

It was ridiculous to panic because his madness had left. Sanity was *not* something to fear. And yet, he'd had that extra voice in his head for nearly two decades. Why was it gone? What had happened?

He heard a raucous laugh from the taproom, and his hands suddenly itched to hold a pint. He was halfway to the door when he stopped himself. Drink would only fog his thoughts. He wanted clarity— a direction and a purpose. First, to erase the danger that haunted Irene. Second, to find a way to bring her into his arms.

And third... he took a deep breath. Third, to accept that perhaps—just maybe—after nearly two decades of madness, perhaps, he had finally gone sane.

The idea terrified him, but he was a man, damn it. No longer a boy overwhelmed by his father's excesses, frightened by the difficult future ahead, or exhausted by years of hard labor. He was a moneyed man now with a bright future: a title and a woman chosen to be his bride. He would not tremble like a leaf because he was sane.

He would not!

But as he curled up in his bed, his arms ached to hold Irene. His heart hammered in his breast, and he closed his eyes rather than feel then burn.

He didn't think he'd be able to sleep. His body was too tense, his breath too choked. So he focused on Irene instead. First, the longing for her, then her reasons for casting him aside. He reviewed her words, and then finally, saw a pathway. She didn't think she could become a countess. She believed he would not want her once he fully stepped into his role as Lord Crowle.

He would just have to prove her wrong. With balls and musicals and walks in Hyde Park, he would show her that she fit into his aristocratic life as easily as Mr. Grant once fit into her middle class existence.

With a plan in place, Grant was able to relax. His eyes drifted shut, and he dreamed of her.

❧

Irene slept for two days. Well, she slept and cried. Her thoughts centered on Grant... er, Lord Crowle, four words echoing in her thoughts: he had abandoned her.

Worse, she knew it was her own fault. She could have simply put him off after he proposed. Delayed for a time, knowing full well that he would eventually realize she was not the woman to be his countess. If she'd done that, then she could have spent the last two days in his arms.

But she hadn't. She'd been forthright and honest, and now, she lay in bed, crying into her pillow while feeling sick to her stomach. What a sad sack she was, but she was powerless to overcome the lethargy that weighted her limbs. Even when her maid said he waited downstairs to see her, she'd steadfastly refused to rise. What point was there? The end was inevitable, so why belabor it?

So she'd remained in bed, sleeping most of the time, rising only when absolutely necessary, and returning to bed as quickly as possible.

Stalemate. Or limbo. She wasn't sure which as she closed her eyes and drifted back into fitful sleep.

He stormed her bedroom just before noon on the third day. He knocked once—powerfully loud—then simply shoved open the door. She was sitting in bed, looking balefully at her breakfast tray. Nothing looked appealing, though she'd managed some tepid tea. Then suddenly, he was in her room, his hands on his hips as he glared at her.

"You are many things, Irene," he said. Then he raised his fingers and ticked off his descriptions. "Beautiful, maddening, brilliant, but I never thought to call you a coward."

"What?" she snapped, feeling her spirit rise for the first time since he'd left her three nights ago. Damn the traitorous thing.

He gestured angrily. "You're hiding," he said, his disgust plain. "I've spoken with your girl Carol. Says she's been downstairs eating tarts for two days. Says you've cancelled your appointments and lain in bed. Your mama says you're in a decline again and glares at me as if I caused it."

Irene looked over his shoulder to where she saw her maid and Mama hovering anxiously in the hallway. She hadn't thought to see them looking that way ever again. Not since she accepted Helaine's job offer not quite a year ago. And yet, here she was again, hunching into her bed as if it was three years ago when she'd first learned of Nate's death. The very idea made her shrivel in shame.

That was inside. Outside, she folded her arms and glared right back. "Did it ever occur to you that I had a fever? That I might be ill?"

His expression paled, but then he narrowed his eyes. "Has a doctor been summoned? Do you have a cough? A putrid throat? What hurts?"

She looked away. Mama had offered to get a doctor, but Irene had steadfastly refused. "Food tastes strange," she said loudly.

"Then talk to your cook. Later. Right now, you have an appointment."

She lifted her chin. "I do not. I cancelled everything."

"Un-cancel it." Then his voice softened. Not in the way of compassion, but in the way of a man more dangerous when he whispered than when he shouted. "Or not. But I suggest you read this first."

He pulled a letter out of his pocket and tossed it onto her lap. She looked down, seeing Helaine's handwriting.

"It's from Lady Redhill," he said. "She told me what she wrote, so if you aren't going to open it, I shall recite it. It says simply this: the shop needs a purchaser. If you are unable to perform such duties, then she needs to know immediately, so she can set about hiring a replacement."

"She did not!" exclaimed Irene as she tore open the envelope. "She would never say anything so cruel!"

And indeed, reading the missive, she was right. Helaine had written solicitous questions about her health and ability to bear up at this difficult time. She said nothing about sacking her as a purchaser, though she did venture a question. It was simple and elegant, much like the woman herself. "If the current situation is too much of a strain," she wrote, "perhaps we should think of hiring an assistant buyer for the time being."

She had signed it, "With love, Helaine," but Irene heard the message clearly, even if Grant hadn't been underscoring it. Irene needed to perform her duties or release her job to someone else.

It was a logical perspective, but Irene couldn't help but feel abandoned by her oldest friend. Meanwhile, she fussed with the edges of the pristine linen. "Why didn't she come tell me this herself?" she asked the coverlet.

Lord Crowle answered. "I told her not to. She had appointments this morning at the shop, and I said I would deliver the letter. And that you would give her an answer this afternoon at your fitting."

Her head jerked up. "Fitting? What fitting?"

"For the ballgowns you've ordered."

"But I didn't—"

"But you did!" inserted her mother-in-law from the door. Her voice was high and tentative, but the words were clear. "Don't you remember? You said that you would attend the balls with me, but you needed more gowns. Wendy and Helaine know exactly the styles that suit you, and they already had your measurements."

Irene twisted so she could shoot a baleful look at her mother-in-law. "You ordered them for me?"

"You seemed so busy."

She hadn't been busy. She'd been lying in bed. "I have been ill," she said sullenly, speaking to herself. It was a lie, but one she wasn't quite ready to release yet.

Meanwhile, Grant crossed to her bedside. He pulled up a chair quickly, his strong arms easily moving the heavy thing. Then he sat and possessed one of her hands. She didn't want to give it to him, but the moment she felt his warmth stroke her skin, all her resistance melted. She let him hold her hand, and she relished the experience.

"Irene," he said softly. "I have been here every day inquiring after you. I have been told that you were tired, that you were ill, that you were suffering all sorts of ailments."

She blinked. He'd been here that often? Really? She hadn't realized, and how silly was that? To mourn a man who had been here the whole time? She looked away, the pain cutting through her heart like a physical rip. It didn't matter, she reminded herself. He couldn't marry her. She couldn't be a countess, not like he needed. So visit or not, nothing had changed.

Exhaling in frustration—and despondency—she

flopped back against her pillows. "Just go away, Lord Crowle." She made his title a curse. She hadn't meant to, but it came out like that anyway.

He didn't say anything for a time. Then he squeezed her hand. "Throw me over for your precious job if you must," he said softly. "Don't then forgo your job just because you've thrown me aside."

"That's not what I'm doing!" she said, the words all the more heated because it was a lie. "Damn it!" she threw his hand away, the curse at herself and her weakness. One man left her in death, the other because of his titled heritage. Neither was reason to lose herself in a decline, but here she was, undressed and unwashed for three days. "What is the matter with me?"

"Perhaps the same thing that has been the matter with me," he offered quietly. "I cannot walk down the street without thinking of something I wish to say to you. I cannot search for our assailant without worrying if you are well. And I cannot close my eyes that I don't ache for..." His voice trailed away, and she was the hunger in his gaze

She closed her eyes, and without the distraction of tenderness in his expression, she was able to think of the words she needed to say. "I cannot lose another husband. It is too hard. I cannot give my heart and my hand to someone again. Not when society will be allied against us. *Again*. It is too hard."

He exhaled a breath of understanding. "Everyone fought your wedding before. Said you were lowering yourself to marry a cit?"

"They said Papa *sold* me. Nate paid a bride-price.

Did you know that? It was the only way I could get father to agree. He never knew that I was in love. Or, if he did, he didn't care."

Grant muttered a low curse. "Your father sounds like more of a cur than mine. And that's saying something indeed."

She flashed him a wan smile. He understood. He always did. It only took a sentence or two, and he understood everything she was feeling.

Then he suddenly exhaled and tapped the back of her hand with startling good cheer. "Well, you needn't worry about that happening again, my dear. Marrying down to Nate, marrying up to me, it doesn't matter. I have retracted my request. I no longer am offering you marriage."

Gasps of outrage rang out from the doorway where Mama and the maid still hovered. But it was nothing less than the sound that escaped Irene's lips as she stared at Grant's smug face.

"That's right," he said firmly. "If simply asking for your hand has sent you into a decline, I retract it all. Now get up, get dressed, you have an appointment with your employer."

"Two days is *not* a decline!" she snapped. "I felt ill!"

"And how do you feel now?"

She huffed out a breath, trying to decide how exactly she felt. Annoyed. Angry—at herself, as well as at him. And still a little nauseous, but that might be because she'd gone so long eating so little.

She grabbed a piece of toast off the tray and bit into it almost savagely. Then she chewed in sullen anger. She was a child. In truth, she was more childish than she'd ever been when she'd been little. Back then, her mother had been the one to sink into the doldrums—for days on end—leaving Irene to manage the daily tasks, or they would both starve. Just because she had people and money to serve her whims now was no reason to sink into the exact same weakness her mother had exhibited.

"I am stronger than that," she said to the memory of her frail parent. Then she turned to shoot a glare at the man tormenting her. "Get out. I need to wash and dress. You may tell Helaine that I shall see her in an hour."

He pushed to his feet, his expression maddeningly happy. "I shall send the message. Then I will wait downstairs with my watch in hand. We will see if you make your hour's promise, or if I will come back up here to drag you out of your bath." Then he waggled his eyebrows at her in a lascivious gesture. "Your choice."

She shot him another glare in answer, but her belly quivered in delight. It could be fun for him to visit her bath., but that was not an option. Certainly not in her in-laws' home. So she gestured with both hands, shooing him out.

He gave her a polite bow and withdrew, though she would swear his eyes were sparkling with mischief. And as the door closed, she found herself smiling as she mentally lingered over the image. Then she remembered what she'd promised.

An hour? For a bath and a proper dressing? Not to mention the time it would take to travel to the shop. She scrambled out of bed. What had she been thinking? But she'd be damned if she was one minute late if he was downstairs with a watch in his hand!

Twenty-five

IT TURNED OUT THAT IRENE LIKED PARTIES. AND MUSI-
cals, and even walking in Hyde Park at the fashionable
hour. She liked pretty clothes, and she liked having a
very attentive gentleman on her arm. A lot of attentive gentlemen, it turned out, because as the news of
her "wealthy widow" status became known, she found
herself at the center of a great deal of masculine attention.

Against her explicit request, her father-in-law
dowered her with an impressive sum, and the party
invitations started to arrive. She understood his inten-
tions. He told her quite explicitly that he was buying
an entrée to the world for herself and his wife that
had hitherto been denied. A large dowry brought
invitations, but she'd only attend if her mama and Mrs.
Schmitz were invited too.

He also told her that she'd wrapped herself in moth-
balls long enough. They loved her like a daughter, and
it was time for her to get married again, have babies,
and live the life she should have had. It had brought
her to tears and had her swearing that they were the
best parents she'd ever had. She would never ever

cut them from her life. Then they had a great big cry before dressing for the first of what would soon be many outings.

They were always accompanied by someone. Grant was usually in attendance, but occasionally, his brother Will or Lord Redhill made up her entourage. With such delightful company, Irene found herself enjoying life more than ever before. She was popular. She was dressed in gowns that made her feel beautiful. And she had male attention everywhere she turned.

All in all, it made life busy. She was still working. The shop was in desperate need of ivory buttons, and she was on a hunt for the best bargains. Grant didn't stop her from speaking with captains or shopkeepers. He just remained nearby—along with Mr. Tanner and her father's "footmen"—as she went about her search.

No one attacked. And even little Carol was working out splendidly. The girl kept better track of her schedule than Irene ever had.

So why wasn't Irene happy? Why wasn't she bursting at the seams with giggly joy, even as she rushed from one event to another? Why did she take long moments to stare silently at the landscape without saying a word? She just sat. And she longed... for something. Or perhaps, it was someone. Her thoughts—or her gaze—would inevitably find Grant, and she would see exactly what she'd known would happen.

He was becoming Lord Crowle in every sense of the word. While she was enjoying the pleasures of dancing nearly every dance at a ball, he was enjoying masculine discussions with the financial men. Not quite a political, Grant was a man who understood money. Banking, investing, and management were his favorite topics lately. Not much with her at first, but eventually, some of his thoughts bled through. All too soon, they were talking about work and politics in a manner she'd never expected with anyone.

Which would be lovely, if she didn't see the women attached to the financial men. Every one of their wives was a well-born conservative. They'd likely been virgins on their wedding night, and not a one had ever been impoverished. If the *ton* could be critical of her status, she shuddered at what Grant's new friends thought. Bankers, as a rule, were not men who embraced social flexibility.

And though Grant never failed to dance a waltz with her, he began taking virginal girls to the floor as well. Daughters of his new friends, rosy-cheeked and so young it made Irene hurt to look at them. They were courtesy dances, he told her, but she could see the girls blush and smile as he escorted them. He was charming then, and he was Lord Crowle, a newly crowned financial. One day, one of those girls would walk down the aisle to him.

And that thought soured Irene's stomach so much she couldn't find the wherewithal to eat. He was slipping away. She'd known it would happen, but the ache of watching him walk bit by bit closer to some dewy-eyed girl chilled her to the bone. It hurt deep inside—a bitter coldness in places she'd thought already dead. Had she grieved for Nate as deeply? She knew she had, but this pain was fresh, this loss new, because she suffered it again and again every night when he danced attendance on yet another virgin.

Then came the afternoon when Grant stepped into her carriage and asked Mr. Tanner to take Carol home. She had just come from a fruitless negotiation with one of Papa's ship captains. The man hadn't been able to keep any of his cargo for her. Her needs were simply not a large enough purchase. But they had discussed other options and then separated early, which is when Grant had hopped into the carriage.

"What are you doing?" she demanded, her voice short as weariness tugged at her. But even so, she felt warmth in her belly at his presence. No matter what the future was, right now, her body was thrilled. Especially since they would likely be alone in a dark carriage.

"Carol tells me you have nothing planned for this afternoon. So I am rudely commandeering the rest of your day, if that is acceptable. I have need of your feminine advice."

She arched her brows, intending to be curt. He could not just "commandeer" her afternoon. But the words that left her mouth were soft and yielding. Her perpetual state around him, it would seem.

"Well, I am definitely female, and I am told I enjoy giving advice."

"Then I will be eternally grateful if you would share it with me." He rapped on the coach partition. Apparently, he'd already told the driver of their destination. Then he sat across from her, dropping into his seat with a loud exhale of relief. "You keep the most incredible schedule of any woman I have ever known. I don't know why you aren't dropping with fatigue."

"I am rather tired," she admitted. "I would cut back on the parties, but Mama loves them so. She has found some friends now, other matronly hens who love to cluck."

He gave a mock shudder. "That image leaves me terrified."

She laughed, and the feel of such a breezy sound lightened her heart. When was the last time she'd last made that girlish kind of giggle? Years, perhaps—before Nate's death, certainly.

"I like to hear you laugh," he said softly. "You don't do it enough."

"I was just thinking that too," she said as her eyes lingered on the curve of his mouth. "You make me smile, my lord. I don't think I ever thanked you for that."

He blinked, but far from smiling in return, his expression tightened. "That sounds suspiciously like a farewell."

"No, no!" she lied. "Of course not. We still have that mysterious, completely absent villain to apprehend, remember? You cannot be rid of me until you finally declare this ridiculous hunt at an end."

He grimaced, and she could see the way his shoulders stooped. "I know it is hard to be hedged in on every side."

Actually, she'd been surprised at how easy it was to handle. At this point, her protectors functioned as easily as her maid: moving through her environment as if she'd always been protected like the crown jewels.

"The expense must be crippling you," she said softly.

He snorted. "As to that, your fond Papa is bearing the brunt. He is still worried."

"And you?" she asked quietly. "Have you realized that whatever it was—it is now over? There is no threat."

He was silent, as if listening for something. Whatever it was, he didn't hear it. So he leaned forward, his expression troubled as he touched her hands. "I cannot say that, Irene. I... I don't know what to think. At one time, I was sure. Now, I begin to doubt myself."

"No one can remain vigilant forever. Especially without reason to continue."

"A little longer, Irene. Please."

She nodded. What choice did she have? Even if Grant stopped his protection duties, her father-in-law would keep the "footmen" around.

Meanwhile, the coach stopped, and her two extra protectors leapt off the side, presumably to scan the area. A moment later, one opened the carriage door, proclaiming that everything looked "right as rain." Grant stepped out first then extended his hand to help her alight. A second later, he escorted her up the steps of a comfortable home in a neighborhood she recognized.

"Is this close to my home?" she asked as she looked around.

Grant pointed. "Three blocks that way." Then he pulled out a key and unlocked the door before gesturing her inside.

She stepped in, smelling the dust that came with an unused space. In the dim light, she saw the sparse outlines of covered furniture and long-abandoned rugs.

"What is this?"

"A property that I'm considering buying. It's rather large, but the location is excellent. The price is reasonable, and I cannot forever live at an inn."

She wandered through the parlor and to the dining room, then into the kitchen itself. "How many floors?"

"Four. The first has parlor, kitchen, and dining room. Seven bedrooms above—"

"Seven!" she gasped.

"—and more for the staff on the third floor. Storage above that."

"That's a lot of room for a bachelor," she said, her heart sinking. He wasn't thinking of himself as a bachelor. He was thinking of a wife and children. Of nannies and maids, not to mention a cook and butler. He was thinking of setting up his household, and the thought made her heart ache with longing.

"There's more," he said as he gestured up a narrow staircase. It was London, after all, and houses like this tended to be narrow and deep. And tall. This house was very tall.

They wandered the upper floor, viewing the bedrooms. One was larger than the rest—for the master of the house—and she easily imagined his furniture there. Armoire to the left, reading chair by the fire, and a large, handsome bed fit for a king. Or at least an earl.

"It's this last one I want you to see most," he said as he opened the door.

It was the nursery. Painted in light blue, it had a covered cradle in one corner and a small pallet for a nurse.

"Who used to live here?" she whispered, her throat tight. "Please tell me that they lived happy. That they weren't struck by tragedy."

"They did suffer a tragedy," he said softly, a teasing note in his voice. "Poor bastard had the misfortune of striking it rich in mining. Not a problem there, but he'd married a woman who loves fresh country air. He'd held her off, saying he didn't have the money to set up in the country like she wanted. But they have it now, so he lost the battle to stay in London. The woman packed up the whole lot in the spring and moved them out."

She laughed, as she knew he intended. "So they aren't returning to London?"

"Turns out he prefers his wife's company to the dirty city life. Decided to sell this place and stay in the wilds. I heard about the decision from a friend who knew I was looking. He got me the key yesterday, and here we are today."

She took a step forward, unable to resist lifting the cover to look at the cradle. There was nothing special about it. A sturdy piece of furniture without decoration. And yet, looking at it, her heart squeezed tight. It was the most beautiful thing she'd ever seen. And what a ridiculous thought was that?

"So what do you think, Irene?" he asked, his voice a soft whisper. "Do you think this is a good home? A place where a woman could be happy?"

She nodded quietly, unable to trust her voice.

He touched her cheek, turning her to look into his eyes. When he saw her tears, his eyes widened in shock. "Irene! What happened? What's the matter?"

She shook her head, wishing she could explain. "It's nothing. Every childless widow longs for children. Some little one to fill her lonely days."

He caressed her cheek, the soft brush leaving heat in its wake. "You would have beautiful children."

She swallowed, not able to answer. Beautiful or

not, she wanted a babe. Some days she felt so empty. And in a room like this, the lack was like a yawning hole in her life.

He kissed her tenderly, the touch of his mouth and tongue telling her without words that he knew her ache. That perhaps, he shared it too.

"Grant," she whispered into his mouth, wishing he were just plain Mr. Grant again.

"Shh," he answered, as he kissed her neck. "It's me. Mr. Grant. Lord Crowle. We are one and the same."

It wasn't true. The needs of the two men were very different. And yet, at the moment, it didn't matter. She wanted him to touch her. He wanted her as well. And as he undid the buttons down her back, she arched into him. Her dress went slack. And when he was finished with her buttons, she pushed his jacket off his shoulders. As he shrugged out of that, she worked on his waistcoat and shirt.

"Mr. Grant had fewer clothes," she said with a laugh.

"And neither man wears as much as you," he said as he began to work on her corset.

She took a deep breath as her ties were loosened and her shift pulled away. A moment later, his mouth was on her breast, sucking at her nipple until she cried out at the pleasure. Her hands clenched on his shoulders. He was her only support.

He pressed more kisses into her breast, murmuring as he slowly made his way to her other nipple. "I've missed you."

"I've wanted you every night," she said.

He pulled it into his mouth, sucking hard. She cried out, undulating against him. She didn't consciously feel what he was doing, only an overwhelming sense of wonder. He was suckling her, and she never wanted him to stop.

He kept her going for a while, but eventually, he had to stop. He straightened, looking about him. "This isn't the way I meant to—"

"It doesn't matter. I don't care." And she didn't. She didn't care what it would do to her clothing or her hair. She didn't care who might see them or what the footmen outside would think. He was nearly gone from her life. She felt it like she felt the coming of a bleak winter. She would take what harvest she could now.

"Irene," he groaned.

"The cot." Then she pulled back to look him in the eye. "Or the floor. I don't care so long as you fill me."

He paused, searching her face. "I could fill you in truth. We could have children together."

They could, and she nearly wept at the thought. She wanted it so desperately. But that worry she could not simply sweep aside. "Do you have a French letter?"

He nodded, the motion jerky.

"Then..." She bit her lip thinking. She'd learned of something new—sexually speaking. Helaine had whispered it to her, and Irene had been consumed by the thought. "Will you put it on?" she asked.

He nodded, his fingers already fumbling in his pant pocket. As she watched, he shed the rest of his clothing then slid it on. And when he was done, she took a step backward, away from him.

He frowned. "Irene?"

Then she slowly stepped out of her gown, allowing it to pool on the floor. Corset and shift were already tossed aside. She wore only her stockings and her shoes. He watched her closely, his eyes burning, his organ proud as it stretched for her. He was a large man, she realized, but they would fit well enough. They always had.

So she turned around, arching her back as she slowly bent over. She bared her bottom to him as she braced her arms on the sides of the cradle. It wasn't as stable as she'd thought. It was meant to rock, and so she swayed back and forth as she took her position. But one glance behind her told her that it didn't matter.

Grant's face was flushed, his body taut. His eyes burned into her, and he swallowed. "My God," he breathed. "That's the most beautiful thing I've ever seen."

She had been feeling a little inferior lately. In truth, she'd felt old next to all his virgin dance partners. But now, any doubt was swept away. And as she smiled, her bottom high, he grinned and closed the distance between them.

He kissed her back, a delicious sensation, even as she felt his organ thrust between her legs. She was already wet, but the slide of him there made sure everything was ready.

His hands were on her breasts, squeezing her how she liked, but it wasn't what she wanted. So she pressed backward and was rewarded with his groan.

"Fill me," she rasped. "Now."

His hands slid down her sides to her hips. He hadn't even gripped her yet, but his organ was pushing inside. Little thrusts—from him or from her—and he was nudging into her core. She arched her back, wanting more, wanting him.

Then his hands tightened, and he suddenly jerked her back.

Big. Hard. He filled her.

She purred and was surprised by her own sound.

But damn him, he didn't move yet. He was deeply embedded, but he didn't continue the motion.

"I wish this was our home," he said as he pressed a kiss to her spine. "I wish we were here right now making our child."

"I wish that we had met when we were younger," she said. And as she spoke, she squeezed her internal muscles, hugging him tight enough to draw out another of his groans.

"I am done with the past," he said as he slid his hand between her legs. "I want you. I want our future."

He was stroking her in earnest now—clumsy pushes with his finger against that magical spot. She cried out, trying to curl toward his finger and arch back onto him at the same time. In the end, she gave herself up to him. Behind her. Between her. Before her. It was all him.

"Yes," she rasped. "Now!"

Her heart lurched as her body rolled.

Pleasure took control.

She heard him growl, felt his thrust. And then he joined her. He filled her.

Or rather, he filled the condom, keeping that magical future out of reach.

She pretended it didn't matter. She reveled in the pleasure still coursing through her body. Eventually, they both pitched forward. They went slowly, with him doing his best to support her as her knees bent, and she collapsed across the cradle. He pulled out then, and she mewed in distress, but she had no strength to prevent it.

Then they lay there, her head on her arms, and his body surrounding hers. He pressed kisses into her shoulder, even as he tightened his arm around her belly.

"Am I too heavy?" he asked.

"No. Don't move. Stay with me, just like this."

She felt the rumble of his chuckle. "I'm not sure I could do anything else."

She smiled, and she closed her eyes. She let her mind drift and her body relax. Then when her resistance was at its lowest, she forced herself to say the words she had held back for so long.

"I am afraid to love you," she said. "I am afraid I already do."

She felt him still against her, a sudden tension, and then a hard squeeze as he pulled her tight. Then he rolled his face into her back and held still.

It lasted a long time, while her heart hammered and her mind rebelled at what she had revealed. Then she felt him relax his hold. He kissed her again. Tiny kisses at the back of her neck. And then, he slowly pulled back.

She felt a tension in him long before he spoke—anxiety that transmitted without words from his body into hers. He was anxious, and that made her stiffen in fear. Then he spoke, his voice laced with regret.

"There is something you have to know," he said. "Something I have to tell you."

Twenty-six

HE DIDN'T WANT TO LET HER GO. HE DIDN'T WANT TO tell her the things she needed to know about him. And yet, he didn't want to share it with anyone else. And he feared if he didn't talk about it to someone, he would go mad.

Or more mad. Or less sane.

Bloody hell. He pressed his face one last time into her skin. He smelled her musky scent, tasted the salt on her skin, and he waited a moment more.

One moment more.

She was the first to move. She stroked her fingers across the back of his hands. "Whatever it is, you can tell me."

He rolled away, feeling exposed, and not just because he was naked. He didn't stop touching her. Just sat on the floor and held her hand. She looked at him, her hair tousled, her cheeks flushed, and her breasts hanging free. "You're so beautiful," he breathed.

"And you're avoiding the topic." She sat beside him, curling into his arms. "What is it?"

He took a deep breath then forced himself to speak.

"Do you recall when my brother asked me if the madness had returned?"

She frowned. He felt the shift in her expression where she was pressed against his chest. But then, she nodded. "At the inn. You told him what we suspected, and I remember he looked very sad. And then he said your madness had returned. I meant to ask you about that, but forgot."

"When I was thirteen years old, I had a tutor named Claymonte. He was pompous and very French. He was also very smart. He had this way of telling me exactly what would happen if I did something. He never stopped me, but he would point out the stupidity of my ways."

She shifted, lifting her chin to flash him a smile. "And that only pushed you into greater excesses."

He shrugged, his lips curving a bit in memory. "Yes. As I said, he was very French."

"I doubt all Frenchmen are pompous, but go on. He must have tormented you mercilessly."

Grant shrugged. In truth, he didn't remember much of the real Claymonte. "Then that summer," he continued, "I had an illness. A brain fever. I was sick for a month. My mother said I hallucinated things when the fever was at its worst."

"Things?"

He shrugged. "I don't remember it." He paused, shifting his hold so that she wouldn't look at him. He didn't want to see her face when he told her the next part. "What I remember most is that I heard Master Claymonte's voice in my head. Always before I was about to do something stupid. Or later, when the work at the mill got too hard. Always, I heard his voice telling me to do something different."

She shifted, trying to pull back, probably so she could look at his face. He fought her at first, but in the end, surrendered to the inevitability. She wouldn't understand any other way. So he released her, and she sat up to look at him. They still touched. He made sure of it. Knee to knee, fingers intertwined. He distracted himself by holding onto these sensations, as well as the sight of her lush black hair curling about her shoulder and over one breast.

"What do you mean, you heard his voice? While you were sick?"

"No," he whispered. "At least, not that I remember. Afterward. After the brain fever passed, after Master Claymonte had long since gone on to teach others. I could still hear his voice."

"Like a reminder? Don't forget to milk the cows. Don't forget to write a letter to Aunt Someone."

He shook his head slowly. "Like a voice. In my head. Usually, calling me a damn fool."

She was silent, looking at him with her brows drawn together in confusion.

"It's a madness, Irene," he said softly. "It doesn't make sense. At first, I thought my dog had talked to me. Or that the tutor was hiding to trick me. But over time, it became clear that the voice was only in my head. No one else could hear it."

"A voice. Calling you a fool?"

"Sometimes it was more specific. Often it told me—just like Master Claymonte used to—what would happen if I continued. It warned me that blowing fire in the barn would burn it down."

"You blew fire inside a barn?"

He waved that away. "I had a reason," he said. "Not a very good one, I'll admit, but that's not important."

"But the… the voice told you to burn down the barn."

"No!" he huffed out a breath. "The voice warned me if I blew fire there, the place would burn down. And it was right."

She nodded. "I would think that was obvious."

He shrugged. "As I said, I had a reason. Mostly having to do with a bet that I would win. And I would use the winnings to pay for my sister's wedding."

She nodded slowly. "So you bet on whether you could blow fire in a barn."

"I… yes. The point is that the voice told me not to."

She bit her lip, thinking hard about that. "So it's like the voice of your conscience. Your smarter self, maybe?"

He frowned, trying to remember. "I suppose. But you have to understand, Irene, it's a voice. Words, tone—a sound only I can hear. Or at least, it was."

She straightened slightly. "Was?"

He nodded. "I can't hear it anymore." He couldn't believe that his belly quivered when he said that. At least he thought his hands had remained still, but that was only because he was gripping her so tightly.

"But that is all to the good, is it not?"

He nodded slowly. "I suppose." Then he caught himself, damning how tentative he sounded. "No, of course, it's good," he said firmly. "It's just that I have been hearing that voice for so long. There were times when it was my only companion."

"You… you got used to it."

"Yes."

"But it's gone now?"

He nodded, closing his eyes against a wave of misery. "I haven't heard it for a month now." Then he frowned, counting backward and lining up the time in his thoughts. "It stopped soon after we met."

She nodded. "Perhaps it's because you don't need a childish tutor telling you what to do anymore."

"I haven't needed that for more than a decade," he said dryly.

"Then perhaps it's because you have friends now. A family again, now that you're reunited with Will and your mother."

He thought about that, feeling a whirl of confusion and self-doubt. Then she squeezed his hand, leaning forward to press a light kiss on his lips.

"Or perhaps, it has merely taken this long for the brain fever to pass. But the voice is gone now. You don't hear it anymore." She only stumbled a bit over the word *voice*—a short hesitation that could be anything. Except that he knew it was fear. She was not nearly as sanguine about it as she appeared.

"It is madness," he said quietly. "And I have had it for most of my life."

"But it is gone now," she said firmly. "And I would think you would celebrate."

He nodded and tried to flash a smile, but it was weak. "Of course, I'm happy," he lied. Mostly, he was confused and at a loss. "But you see, it's like losing a friend. A pompous, sarcastic, always right friend. I... I'd come to rely upon it."

She swallowed. "For advice?"

He nodded.

"I thought you always ignored what the voice said."

He grimaced. "Most of the time. But sometimes I listened." He released one of her hands to gesture vaguely. "And sometimes it was wrong. Sometimes I won the bets, or sometimes I needed to work longer hours at the mill. Sometimes I knew what I was doing without benefit of an imaginary tutor."

"So it was your imagination?" she said, obviously latching onto the sanest option.

He sighed. "It was a voice that spoke to me, clear as day. And now, it is gone, and I feel…" He swallowed and forced himself to continue. "I feel alone."

Then her expression did soften. All the worry and anxiety slipped from her face as she touched his cheek and stroked a finger over his mouth. "But you are not alone. I am here. Lord Redhill and your brother are here. You have friends now. Confidantes and brothers-in-arms."

"Brothers-in-arms?" he asked, a little startled.

"What would you call men who take shifts watching me without pay? Tell me that Will or Lord Redhill or even Mr. Morrison have asked for coin in return for their services."

He shook his head. "Of course not. They are doing it out of fear for you."

"And love for you."

He flinched slightly, uncomfortable with the term when applied to his friends. Except, even as he recoiled from the word, warmth entered him. Those men were his friends. And Will was his brother.

"Comrades-in-arms," he said softly. "I like that."

Then he looked at her, grabbing onto a different topic because this one had become too painful. "Did I tell you that Robert has a new investment he wishes me to look over? I shall need more funds if I am to restore Crowle Castle to anything habitable."

She smiled, obviously more at ease. "No, you hadn't. What is it?"

He expounded on what Robert had in mind. They chatted easily then, dressing slowly, exchanging lingering kisses. It was a normal conversation, or at least, as normal as it ever was with Irene. After all, he couldn't think of any other woman who would understand business the way she did.

But the topic of his madness lingered like a pall over it all. Was she afraid of him now? Did she think less of him? Would she leave him? That thought struck a lance of pain through him, such that before they left this tiny nursery, he had to know what she thought.

"Irene," he called when they were fully dressed and heading for the door. "You said before that you loved me." He swallowed, dreading to ask the question, but needing to know. "Do you still?"

She hesitated. She was across the room, and he watched her tuck her hands together. "I said I very much feared I was in love with you."

He nodded. After what he had just told her, she had reason to fear. Any woman would. "And now?"

She grimaced, looking to the floor. "Why did you bring me to this house? Why did you choose now to tell me about... about..."

"About my madness? This is the home that I want to buy. This is the home where I want to have a wife and children. I have never thought about that before. Not seriously. But I am now, and any woman who…"

He stopped speaking. He didn't want to say this from across the room, so he crossed to stand before her. He wanted to take her hands, but she had them gripped tightly together. He touched her arms instead, stroking them lightly up and down.

"Any woman who talks about love should see this home. See this room." He took a deep breath. "And she should know that my madness might pass on to our children."

She gasped at that, her hands going to her belly. He had a moment's panic then. Was she pregnant? But no, she couldn't be. They had been using prevention. Except, of course, for that first time. But surely she would know by now if she were pregnant. Surely, she would have told him.

Eventually, he realized that she'd made an instinctive gesture. Every woman did that, even great grandmothers. When anyone spoke of babies, they touched their own bellies. The gesture meant nothing.

"Your madness came from a fever," she said.

"Yes." Then honesty forced him tell all. "I spoke with a doctor once. He said the fever could have triggered something—a weakness of some kind. The same could happen to any child of mine."

She swallowed and looked at him. "Did he recommend a treatment?"

Grant snorted. "He wanted to lock me up and experiment with any number of medicines. He had an asylum with plenty of patients, he said, who were just like me."

"Just like you?"

"They heard voices, spoke to unseen people. They had delusions about who and what they were. One claimed to be Jesus. Another claimed to be a woman trapped in the body of a man. They were all lunatics," he said softly. "Or so the doctor said."

"And he said you were one of them?" She pressed her hand against her mouth.

"He did. He said I would grow worse. The madness would take root, and I would soon become just like them. Raving." He swallowed. "Violent."

"But..." She closed her eyes, took a deep breath, and then opened them to search his face. "But the voice is gone now."

He nodded. "And I never became violent," he said. "I never did anything but hear a voice—sometimes— telling me I was a damned fool."

"But this doctor said you would get worse."

"If I wasn't treated... if I didn't take his medicines."

"And did you?"

He shook his head. "I ran as fast and as far as I could. Ended up in a gypsy camp learning how to blow fire."

"Oh," she whispered. "I suppose burning down a barn makes a little more sense then."

He smiled, though the gesture was hard. "No, it doesn't," he corrected softly. "It was foolish and stupid, but it was the only way I could win enough money to pay for the wedding. And from there, I ended up at the mill."

She frowned, obviously thinking hard. "Most of your life then," she whispered.

He had told her that already, but this was not something a person absorbed quickly. So he nodded and remained silent. He wanted to tell her he loved her. He wanted to imprint it upon her skin and her body so that she would never leave him. And he wanted her to say it back with all the strength and conviction that he felt.

But that was too much to ask, so soon after telling her all this. He could not add the burden of his love now. Not yet. So he said nothing. And, in the end, she changed the topic. She gestured toward the late afternoon sun.

"We need to leave soon. Mama will wonder where I am."

He nodded, lifting his arm to escort her out. He was terrified that she wouldn't take it. That she would be too afraid to touch him even through his coat and her gloves. But there was no hesitation as she set her fingertips lightly on his arm. They walked out of the nursery and down the steps to the front. He was in the process of opening the door when she squeezed his arm to stop him.

"Grant," she whispered.

"Yes?"

"It's a beautiful house. Any woman would be happy to live here."

It was on the tip of his tongue to ask if she meant herself. Would *she* be happy to live here? But again, that was too much to ask. And so, he simply dipped his head in a nod.

"Thank you," he said.

"Thank you for asking," she returned.

They walked in silence to the carriage. Ten minutes later, he escorted her to her front door. He did not stay for tea. He had no interest in doing the pretty with her Mama just then. Besides, he had to finalize the purchase of the house. So he simply touched her hand, holding it for as long as he dared.

"Shall I come by in the morning? Escort you to Penny's wedding?"

She bit her lip then shook her head. "It will be early, and I have my other protectors." She gestured at the footmen who had melted seamlessly into their positions about the house, while the butler remained alert beside her in the hallway. "I shall meet you there."

He had no choice but to accept her decree, though it felt like he had cut off his arm. Or perhaps, more like she had cut out his heart. Either way, there was nothing to do but nod and bow deeply over her hand.

Then he walked away.

Twenty-seven

IRENE WOKE LATE ON THE MORNING OF PENNY'S wedding. She'd spent the night suffering nightmares of Grant turning into a violent lunatic, and she felt shaken and horrified by her own dreams. He was not mad—at least he wasn't at the moment—and she was being ridiculous.

Yet there was no controlling her fear or her dreams. It didn't help that her stomach was still tetchy. It always had been, truth be told, whenever she was anxious. But today was Penny's day, and Irene refused to darken the celebration with her own anxieties.

She bathed as quickly as possible, dressing in a brand new gown made specifically for this day. And as a special treat, Penny had made matching shoes for all the ladies of the shop. Irene admired the perfect stitching in the light pink slippers. They weren't practical, of course. Imagine walking about London in pink slippers! But they were beautiful, and Penny had written Irene's name and the date on the sole. That made them just like real wedding slippers, except there was no groom's name.

As Irene held the beautiful items, she imagined Grant's name there. She pretend wrote his name with her finger. She put it right below hers, along with his full title. How wonderful that would be, she thought sadly, her heart clenching in longing.

How silly she was! How could she want something so desperately when her mind was busy listing the reasons it could never happen, and her emotions were chock full of fears regarding his sanity? He had responsibilities to his title and position. She had no desire to risk an insane husband, or worse, a damaged child. Not when her life was so perfectly ordered now.

And yet, she wanted it. Yearned for it, in fact. And all the logical reasons that it could not be didn't seem to matter. She loved him. She wanted to take those risks. And yet, her fears made her hands tremble, especially with the nightmares so fresh in her mind. So with a sigh, she slipped on the beautiful shoes and tried to be happy wearing wedding slippers with only one name on the soles.

She arrived at the small church early for the ceremony, but late for the gathering of the bride's friends. She felt ridiculous entering with two footmen—one walking in front, the other behind—and for the thousandth time, she cursed the paranoia that had created this situation. Fortunately, her friends understood as she knocked on the door that led to where the bride waited.

Penny bid them enter, and Irene waited in irritation as her footman scanned the interior and nodded, stepping back to allow her to finally greet her friends. Penny was radiant, her gown specially designed by Helaine to show off the girl's curvy body without restricting her sometimes forceful movements. Penny was a powerful woman, in body and mind, as she was the sole support for herself and her toddler brother. And now, she had a man who loved her desperately and had an income, since Samuel was a runner. He was the perfect man, and Irene already knew the two would be radiantly happy.

She greeted Penny, handing over her gift in the form of a small box. Behind her, the other women—Helaine, Wendy, and Francine—all craned to see.

"What is it?" Penny asked.

"Open it and see."

With a giggle, the girl pulled off the ribbon and looked inside. Her gasp of awe wiped away the last of the tension in Irene's body. This was what life was about: good friends with happy faces, celebrating the wonder of life. Meanwhile, Penny pulled out a couple of the two-dozen pearl buttons that lay inside.

Irene smiled as everyone admired them. "They are the last that I could find in all of London. And they are for you, Penny, not some other lady's shoes."

"But what need do I have for such pretty things?" the girl whispered. "I'm just a cobbler's daughter."

"You are an artist who designs beautiful shoes. And you should wear these in your new shop. Make all the ladies envious as you walk around in slippers so amazing that everyone must have a pair."

"Except," inserted Francine with a giggle, "they won't be able to get the pearls. They are just for you!"

"Oh, I shall be able to get more," inserted Irene casually. "But not ones nearly so fine and not for another month at least."

Ever the businesswoman, Penny looked up with a frown. "What if I charged an extra premium for more buttons just as beautiful as these? Would you be able to get them then?"

Irene grinned. "For you, my dear, of course!"

Then they hugged again, and everyone began talking weddings. Francine's was coming up soon. She was marrying their bookkeeper Anthony. Helaine mentioned Will and Josephine. The girl had purchased a whole trousseau, and Helaine was busy designing dresses for the wedding. Irene laughed as joyfully as the others. Or she did until she caught Wendy's eyes. The seamstress looked sad. As far as Irene knew, the woman had no suitor and was too busy to find one. And the problem with Demon Damon was apparently still unresolved. No man would want to court a woman trapped in the Demon's clutches, and so the girl was single—and apparently, wistful about the lack. Irene understood, having her own full measure of turbulent emotions regarding weddings.

The time flew by, and soon the ladies were making their way to the pews. Irene was surrounded by her footmen, but they took up discreet positions in the shadows. Irene was seated next to Helaine, who was reminiscing about her own unusual wedding day. Then suddenly, Irene felt a warm body press a little too closely.

Grant.

Her whole body welcomed him, even before she turned to greet him. Her spine softened, her belly warmed, and a smile curled her lips. And that was all before she actually saw him dressed in the finest fabric his mill made. It was a somber black, but the waistcoat sported a red and gold design that... she blinked. That perfectly matched the color of her gown. Yes, she was wearing the soft angora he had wrapped around her that day so long ago at the inn. Wendy had been able to repair the cut from the knife attack so long ago.

"Did you know I was going to wear this?"

He nodded, smiling. "I asked Carol. She told me."

Irene grimaced. "That girl knows more about what I am doing than I do."

"Which promises her a bright future as a secretary."

Irene nodded as her gaze flowed over him. He appeared relaxed. Actually, he looked stunningly handsome, but what she felt took her in the opposite direction. He seemed tense. His eyes constantly roved the church then abruptly returned to scan her. His hands were set calmly to either side of his legs, but they twitched restlessly. He was not so calm as he pretended, and she supposed she understood why.

His confession yesterday lingered in their thoughts. It would take some time before he understood that she had no intention of shunning him because of his previous madness. But he wanted more than simple friendship, and as her body ached for him, her mind kept her apart. In the end, she did the best she could. She touched his hands, quietly intertwining their fingers.

"I am glad you are here," she whispered.

He clutched her hand tight and flashed her a grateful smile. "I would be no where else."

Then the ceremony began. Samuel waited in resplendent attire at the front of the church. His brother served as attendant, looking supremely happy, even as he muttered something to the groom.

"I'm not fidgeting," Samuel responded, loud enough for everyone to hear. "I have simply worked out who stole that silly tiara and wanted to make a note—" His voice cut off, his thoughts obviously lost as his bride walked in.

As Penny's father was gone, Lord Redhill walked her down the aisle. Beside Irene, Helaine released a soft sigh of delight. Penny carried hothouse roses, brought by Helaine, but even those rich blooms paled at the happiness in Penny's face. She was stunning, her eyes so filled with happiness that Irene's chest ached. The woman's step never faltered, her gaze never wavered. And when the two met at the altar, it was as if two halves of a perfect whole snapped together. They touched, they smiled, and when it came time for vows, their voices were strong and clear.

Wedded. And with no doubts whatsoever, Irene realized. "Amazing," she murmured. Even as in love as she'd been with Nate, her voice had trembled over her vows. She'd had fears, especially as none of her family had come to the wedding to wish her happiness.

But Penny and Samuel had all their friends and family around them. And the strength of their bond rang louder than their words, stronger than their rings. It was there in every gesture, every grin, and in their sparkling eyes.

"Oh, to love like that," she whispered.

"So sure," Grant murmured.

"So strong."

He looked at her then, and she met his gaze. He

knew. She read the understanding in his face just as clearly as he read the doubts in her own.

"Grant…" she whispered, but he cut her off.

"Don't fret. I don't blame you for a moment."

But she blamed herself. He was a good man. And he was *not* mad. How did one simply forget fear? How could she simply close her mind to such concerns? He squeezed her hand and looked away. She saw heartbreak in the way he held himself stiffly beside her. His profile was remote, but he still held her hand. She took solace in that.

To cover the moment, she grabbed for a question— anything to ease the awkwardness. "Are you coming to the wedding breakfast?"

"Yes, of course."

Meanwhile, the couple turned to the congregation, and people were rising to congratulate them. Like everyone else, he pushed to his feet, but she could hear his words clearly.

"The breakfast and the shop unveiling after that."

"The what?"

He laughed. "Carol really does know your schedule better than you do. After the breakfast, Penny is going to open her newly designed shoe shop for us to see."

"Oh, how wonderful!" she gasped. "She's been working hard on that for months."

He didn't answer. They made it to the top of the line and were busy congratulating Samuel and giving best wishes to Penny. It was rushed with all the people, but the wishes were enthusiastic, and Irene found herself grinning. It was impossible to dwell on her worries in the face of such joy. So she embraced happiness as she kissed Penny's cheek.

Then they moved aside, and Grant joined her in the carriage that would take them to the wedding breakfast, generously hosted by Lord and Lady Redhill. Even more, it would include special cakes made by Francine herself.

All of that flitted through her thoughts, a brief moment of knowledge soon lost as she looked at Grant. He loved her, she realized. Though he had never said it aloud, the knowledge was a quiet assurance that still managed to crackle and pop in her mind—like a fire roaring to life.

He loved her.

She loved him.

And yet, they held apart from each other. Fear. Duty. Madness. Only words, but they were like bricks set between them as impenetrable as any wall.

"I understand, Irene. It's a hard thing to wed a lunatic."

She spit out a very unladylike curse. "You move from one extreme to another, my lord. And it makes me want to scratch your eyes out!"

He recoiled, obviously startled. "And you accuse me of being extreme?" he said blandly. He was retreating into his charming persona, but she would not let him do it.

"Do you not see? You cannot just win a bet. You have to learn how to blow fire and burn down a barn to do it. You cannot just work at a mill. You change your name and separate yourself from your family for years. You cannot just hear the voice of your conscience. You are a violent lunatic, whom—I might point out—is neither violent, nor hearing things anymore. And yet you put me in fear for our children." She huffed out an angry breath. "It is not hard to love a lunatic, my lord. It is hard to wed a man who cannot simply be... simple."

He arched his brows. "Simple?"

She huffed. "Not simple stupid. Simple, as in not complicated." She twisted on the seat to look at him directly. "Grant, do you not see that you are fighting me? I think you are Mr. Grant, and then I find out you are Lord Crowle. We are attacked by a footpad, and you turn it into a murder attempt. I tell you I love you. You tell me you are insane. It's not a voice in your head that makes you mad, Grant. It's the way you cannot simply be a man in love. A man who wants to marry a woman."

He looked at her a long moment, but in the end, he shook his head. When he spoke, his voice was soft, with such aching sadness that it broke her heart. "I cannot be a young boy for you just as you cannot be a naïve girl for me. I am thirty-two years old, Irene. I have lived a strange life, and as much as I try to make it easy, it isn't. Not now, and probably not ever."

"I'm not asking for an easy life."

"Aren't you? You're asking me to simply be a man in love with a woman. I am. I love you, Irene. I want to marry you."

Oh, to finally hear those words now, when her thoughts and her heart were at war. They warmed her. They frightened her. And most of all, they had her pressing her hands to her eyes to hold back the tears. "But what of your title? You need a virgin wife who doesn't work. What if our children are mad? What if—"

"Irene," he said softly, the quietness of his words stopping hers. "Those are not my objections, but yours." Then he gently pulled her hands from her face. And while she was trying desperately to steady her breathing, he slid off the seat of the carriage and onto one knee. "I had not meant to do it now, but I can see that you will make me do this over and over until we come to the right answer. Lady Irene, I love you. Will you do me the greatest honor and become my wife?"

Twenty-eight

SOME PART OF GRANT'S CONSCIOUS MIND REALIZED that the carriage had stopped moving. Some part of him heard the bellows of the coachman and the shift in weight as the footmen jumped off the carriage to deal with whatever problem was clogging the often difficult London streets. Some part of him was aware, but most of him was focused on Irene.

He watched as myriad emotions shifted through her expression. He thought he caught hope and delight… or was it horror? His own mind was filled with thoughts—fears—that he couldn't be sure of anything.

And in this most difficult moment, the bizarre occurred. The carriage door flew open, and there silhouetted in the doorway was the footpad. He looked worse than he had before, his eyes wide and his mouth set, firm and angry. There was a long, sharp knife in his right hand. Grant saw it distinctly as the sunlight flashed on the blade. Then he saw the man search the interior, focus on Irene, and lunge for her— knife outstretched.

If Grant hadn't been on the carriage floor, he

wouldn't have been in a position to react. He certainly wouldn't have had his bent leg lodged with the foot against the opposite door in the tight confines of the carriage. He was on the floor, and he was in a near perfect position from which to spring toward their attacker.

But he wasn't quite fast enough. The assault caught him by surprise. The bastard had his hand on Irene's dress and was hauling her bodily out of the carriage before Grant could gather his strength. What he'd missed in speed, he made up for in sheer fury.

He launched himself at the attacker, his focus completely on the knife. While Grant tackled the man, throwing him backward, he grabbed hold of the wrist that held the knife, making sure to shove it in the opposite direction from Irene.

Irene screamed, and he heard a thump as she banged against the side of the carriage. Meanwhile, the footpad twisted beneath him, bellowing his fury. He was trying to keep hold of Irene, but he hadn't the strength. Not with all of Grant's body slamming him back into the street.

The man fell, Grant on top, and they hit the cobblestones. Grant felt the jerk of impact then heard a loud thudding splat. He barely noticed, so focused was he on the knife. He slammed that hand down, doing his best to break the man's wrist on the stones. Thankfully, the knife skittered away.

Then Grant straightened, readying his fist to deliver a punishing blow to the man's face. But the bastard didn't move. In fact, the footpad wasn't moving at all, and it took him a moment to realize why.

The scent of blood filled his nostrils, and he saw a pool form beneath the footpad's greasy hair. Grant was still breathing hard, his heart beating loud in his ears, and his mind simply could not comprehend what he saw.

The thief was dead. Grant had launched himself forward, toppling the man backwards. One hard slam on the cobblestones, and his skull had broken. Only now did Grant remember hearing a choking gurgle, a dazed blink, and then...

Dead.

Men ran forward. Irene screamed his name. But he just crouched there looking at the bastard, while his fury warred with confusion.

The man was dead?

"Grant! Grant, are you all right?"

Irene was scrambling out of the carriage, even as one of the footmen was trying to keep her inside. Grant turned to her, absurdly panicked at the idea of her seeing a dead man in the street.

"Stay back!" he bellowed. "Don't come out. Not until we're sure it's safe."

She froze half out of the carriage, her gaze burning over his body as she checked him for wounds. He did no less as he stared at her. Her gown was ripped and her hair mussed, but there was no blood. No wound that he could see.

"Grant," she whispered.

"I'm fine. Just get in the carriage."

She nodded then shrank back inside. Meanwhile, the other footman was squatting down beside their assailant. "That's Hank Bagley," he said with a grunt.

Grant frowned. Did he know that name? The man answered without being asked.

"He's one of the men we noted at The Dog's Bone. Got tossed off his ship for drunkenness and theft. Couldn't get a job, then his daughter gets sick and dies. Blames Knopp for everything."

"Knopp? Why?"

"It was Mr. Knopp himself who caught the man thieving. Fired him on the spot then made sure everyone knew what the bastard had done."

Grant straightened, his mind slowly piecing bits together. "So he couldn't get another job."

"And when his daughter died—"

"The anger becomes a murderous rage." Grant frowned. "But why attack Irene?"

"Here's why," said a calm voice. Samuel Morrison, still in his wedding attire, squatted beside the body. As Grant looked over, the man revealed a dark tattoo on Bagley's inner arm. It said *Exodus 21:24*. "An eye for an eye," Samuel said. "He lost a daughter, therefore Captain Knopp should as well."

"Oh no," Irene murmured from her position inside the carriage. "Oh… no."

It was her thready moan that snapped Grant into motion. They couldn't just stand there staring at the body. And Irene shouldn't sit in a carriage in the middle of London. Not with a body right beside her.

"Let's get you out of the street," he said as he looked about. They weren't far from Redhill's home.

"I'll stay here and make sure everything is settled," offered Samuel, but another man interrupted.

"The devil you will," said Mr. Tanner. He'd been

a guest at the wedding, but had chosen to walk to the Redhill home rather than use a carriage. "You've got a bride to see to, man." Tanner clapped Samuel on the back. "Right fine ceremony, Samuel. Now go on. See to your woman." He jerked his head back to where Penny was stepping out of their carriage.

Samuel's expression flashed to alarm, and he smoothly moved to block Penny's view of the body. "Get back inside, my dear. I'll be there in a moment."

"Go on," said Mr. Turner. "I'll talk to the watch. You two…" he said, pointing to the footmen, "… help them get the carriages moving." Then he made shooing noises to everyone else: Samuel, Grant, and the half-dozen people gawking nearby. "I'll come to Redhill's house after it's all sorted. Explain it then."

Grant nodded, and he turned to climb into the carriage. Irene shifted to give him room, and he studied her face as entered. She looked pale but composed. He settled onto the seat beside her then turned and gently touched her arm. It was all that was needed.

A moment later, she was curled against him, her body shuddering in his arms.

❧

Helaine and her husband were waiting by the door to their home, having been the first to depart for the wedding breakfast. They had no idea what had delayed everyone, and as Irene and Grant rushed quickly up the walkway, their faces shifted into alarm.

Irene tried to speak, but no sound came out. She just couldn't get anything past the thickness in her throat. She looked to Grant, who summarized what had happened in quick, short sentences. Lord Redhill's expression went grim, but it was Helaine who took charge.

"Let me get you some tea to steady your nerves," she said as she reached a hand for Irene.

Irene was still wrapped in Grant's arms and loathe to leave him, but that was ridiculous. The danger was past. The man was dead. God. "It's over?" she asked as she looked at Grant.

He gave her a slow, reassuring nod. "I believe so," he said, but he didn't release his hold.

"It's safe," she said softly.

He nodded, and their gazes caught and held. Everything was over. Life could return to normal. She had no need to cling to Grant as if he were her bulwark in an uncertain world. She watched him swallow, his eyes haunted, but in the end, he nodded.

Slowly, he released his grip. She was trying to tell her own fingers to open when a scent hit her nostrils. *Kippers.* That's what she smelled. Strong. Nauseating. Her stomach roiled, and she clapped a hand over her mouth.

"Oh!" she gasped.

Helaine grabbed her hand. "Upstairs. Now." Together they sprinted for her bedroom. They burst into the beautiful chamber where, almost front and center, was a chamber pot set out as if for this purpose alone. Irene dropped to her knees and retched. Her stomach cramped, her body rebelled, and what little she'd eaten in the last twelve hours came back up.

Fortunately, there wasn't much. Just agonizing cramps that eventually eased. And when she was done, she sat back on her heels, while a maid she hadn't even noticed passed her a damp cloth to wet her face and neck. Almost immediately, she was handed a dry piece of toast to nibble.

Irene took it gratefully, only now having the breath to look at her best friend. Helaine had her eyes closed and a hand clamped to her mouth. She was breathing shallowly through her nose, and her whole body was tense.

The maid glanced at her mistress nervously. Then she looked over as a footman knocked quietly at the door. He was holding another chamber pot at the ready. Quick as a wink, the used one was replaced with a new one, and everyone waited in tense silence while Helaine just stood there. A second later, Helaine held a hand out to her maid, who pressed another piece of toast into her hand. Helaine nibbled it without even opening her eyes. Meanwhile, the girl passed a glass of water to Irene.

Eventually, Irene's stomach eased. Helaine's too, apparently, as her breath deepened.

"Well," murmured Helaine finally. "I believe that's over for the moment." She smiled warmly. "Thank you, Ruth. I think the danger has passed for now."

Irene, too, managed a weak smile. "I feel much better. Thank you."

At that, the girl bobbed a curtsy and withdrew, shutting the door quietly. Meanwhile, Irene was able to focus on her friend. "Congratulations," she said. "I take it you're increasing?"

Helaine flashed a wan smile. "I was over the moon when I realized. But I have to say, it's terrible being tired all the time. And the nausea." She sighed and gave a wry gesture. "As you can see, the whole house has had to adjust for my difficulties." Then she frowned as she looked at her friend. "How about you? How are you feeling now?"

"I... I'm all right now, I guess. I've been feeling so... so..." She swallowed. She'd been about to say tired and nauseous. The same symptoms that Helaine had claimed. Except Helaine was pregnant. Helaine was *married* and pregnant, which was wonderful. Whereas Irene was *not* married, and she couldn't possibly be pregnant now, because that would be a disaster of epic proportions.

It would be, except that the very idea filled her with giddy warmth. Was it possible? Well, of course, it was possible. But was it true? Was she was pregnant with Grant's child?

She took a moment to take stock. She tried to still her racing heart, but she couldn't. She wanted a baby. She desperately wanted Grant's child. A babe with the man she loved.

Was it true?

Yes.

She was pregnant. She knew it on an instinctive level. And honestly, she felt a fool for not realizing it earlier.

"Oh," she breathed, having no more words than that as she looked at her belly. Was there a bulge? A tiny bump? She didn't think so, and yet her imagination had no trouble bringing forth the idea of a little baby growing right here.

It took Helaine perhaps ten seconds to realize

what had just happened. She slowly settled onto her bed, and the women exchanged looks. "Oh my," the woman murmured.

Irene smiled, slowly at first, but with growing strength. "Oh my, is right! Oh my my!"

Helaine picked up the smile then soon began to giggle, which Irene echoed. Within moments, they were laughing together as they hadn't done since they were schoolchildren: with joy and hope and no fear whatsoever.

It couldn't last. As wonderful as it was, the adult fears settled in. The realization that she was unwed and pregnant. That it was a child who might carry madness. What would her in-laws think? What did she think?

"I take it the child is Lord Crowle's?" Helaine asked quietly.

Irene nodded. "He was proposing in the carriage," she said quietly. "Just before..." She closed her eyes as images flashed through her thoughts. The attack, the dead man, the look on Grant's face when he'd realized he'd just killed a man.

"Oh my," she said, that last thought taking root in her mind. She pushed to her feet. She had to go to him. She had to make sure he was all right. There was nothing wrong with what he'd done. He'd been protecting her. She might have died without his immediate interference. And yet, she'd seen his face. She still shuddered at the enormity of it all. He'd killed a man. He should not be alone at a time like this.

Helaine rose as well. "Does he know?"

"Does he—oh!" She blinked, her mind whirling.

"Everything is happening so fast. I don't know what to do!"

"First," Helaine said, taking hold of her hands, "you must take a breath. Settle your thoughts. You love him, yes?"

Irene's eyes watered. "Yes. But Helaine, I... I..."

"You're afraid. Of course, you are." She smiled, her expression so warm and sympathetic, Irene nearly collapsed into tears. "You are afraid that if you marry him, he will die like Nate did. You know that's not going to happen. He's not a sailor for one."

"That's not the point," Irene said, her voice becoming tight.

"Of course not. Fears never are."

"What?" Irene frowned, trying to follow her friend's words.

Helaine gently pulled her back to the bed, and together they sat hand in hand. "Do you know that I am terrified? I'm elated about this child, but there are so many things that could go wrong. So many women die in childbirth."

Irene winced. She hadn't even thought of that.

Helaine tightened her grip on their joined hands. "I'm not helping am I?"

"No." Irene's word was thick with misery.

"And then Robert could die too, just like your Nate—an infection. Thrown off a horse. The house could catch fire too. Sometimes the cook overboils something, or maybe a poison seeps into the air."

"What?"

"There's disease, famine, the four horses of the apocalypse."

"Helaine!"

"And I haven't even started on the fears my mother spouts. She was afraid that if I went walking, I would fall."

"Fall?"

"And break my neck before she got a grandchild out of me."

Irene started to smile. "I'm sure she was more worried about you falling than the lack of a grandchild."

Helaine gave her a wry look. "I'm not so sure. The point is, my dear," continued Helaine, "that the minute one starts enumerating fears, there is no end. They mount up until one never gets out of bed." Then she snapped her fingers. "Bed! That's another list of fears. Do you know that it's possible to be killed by one's own sheets? If you're a particularly twisting sort of sleeper, you can strangle yourself. And I heard of someone who just spontaneously burst into fire. Just started burning from the inside. Died horribly within minutes."

"That's not true!"

"I absolutely did hear it. Came directly from my maid, who got it from someone in France."

Irene laughed. "Now you are bamming me."

"I am not!" Then Helaine sobered. "You need to face your fears, Irene. Otherwise…"

"I will lock myself in my room and wish myself dead?"

Helaine didn't answer. She didn't need to. They were both thinking of the state she'd been in when Helaine had first offered her the purchasing job.

"Do you love him? Does he ease your fears?"

"There is madness in his family," she suddenly blurted.

Helaine laughed. "My dear, look hard enough, and there is madness in everyone's family."

"But this madness... he says... he fears..."

"Ah, so you are magnifying both your fears, aren't you?" She shook her head. "But he does not seem a particularly fearful sort of man. Quite the opposite, actually."

Irene smiled, her thoughts on Grant. "He saved my life today. And..." She took a deep breath. "And when I am with him, I feel...."

"Excited? Lustful? Girlishly tittery?"

Irene laughed. "Yes, all those things! But I was going to say *safe*. He makes me feel safe. Except when he is purposely trying to frighten me."

Helaine's eyebrows shot up. "Does he do that often?"

Irene shook her head, honesty forcing her to tell the truth. "He wants me to know him. And sometimes, what he says frightens me."

"What? The madness?"

Irene pressed her hands to her cheeks and closed her eyes. "I don't know what to think."

"Well, there's your problem right there! Stop thinking. What do you feel? Afraid?"

"Yes."

"Happy?"

Irene nodded, the thought of a child too new for anything but excited joy.

"In love?"

"Yes," Irene whispered. "I have loved him for a while now."

"And you said he was proposing to you? So he must love you, yes?"

Irene's eyes opened. "I believe he loves me too. He has said so."

"Ah, then it is simply fear that is keeping you apart."

Was it so simple? Boiled down to the basics… that was it, she supposed. But fear was not simply cast aside. One did not just wish it away. "I don't think I'm a brave person."

"Ah well, then, I have the solution. First off, Lord Crowle appears to be a rather brave man. After all, he took on an armed assailant to save you. Twice!"

"Yes, but—"

"No, buts. There is something else you haven't thought of. Something vastly important that I believe will sway your decision."

Irene lifted her head anxious to hear anything that would make everything clear. "Yes?"

"When one sleeps in the same bed with a husband, it is impossible to strangle oneself with the sheets. You can't twist too much without rolling smack dab into your husband. Therefore, life is much better and much safer with a man in your bed. A man such as Lord Crowle who has twice defended your life."

"Helaine!" she scolded, though she was laughing as she spoke. "You are deliberately being ridiculous."

"And you are being a coward," the woman shot back, her voice softening, even though her words were hard. "Do you recall when I first approached you about your job? How you said that you wished for a child—"

"But perhaps it was for the best that there hadn't been one. Because I was so ill."

"You weren't ill. You were grieving. And I told you—"

"That I would have been strong for the child."

"Yes," Helaine said, her face softening into a coaxing smile. "You are strong, Irene. And you have been happier with Lord Crowle than I have ever seen you."

"And I love him." She pressed a hand to her belly. "I already love this child."

"Of course, you do."

"But what about the madness?" she wondered out loud.

"What about being strangled by your bedsheets?"

Irene smiled, but the expression didn't last. "You must think me the weakest of creatures."

"I think," Helaine said slowly, "that you are one of the strongest women I know. You have lost a husband, my dear. You continued to work while a madman stalked you."

"I didn't really believe—"

"Yes, you did. You just didn't want to believe it. But you have found love, my dear. Do not become frightened now. Not when the worst is over. Besides," she said, leaning forward in a conspiratorial whisper, "many women lose a husband. How many lose *two*?"

Irene blinked. "What?"

"Think on it. You have already had terribly bad luck. It is your turn to be happy now."

She hadn't really thought of herself as unlucky. Just that for some reason, whenever something good happened, the bad was only a step behind. She was the daughter of an earl, but he was a gambler and a fool, so they were perpetually on the edge of ruin. She'd fallen in love and married into wealth, but her husband had died soon afterwards. She'd found a job she adored, but a madman had tried to kill her. And finally, she'd fallen in love again, but the man who loved her thought he was insane.

Put like that, she had the worst luck in the world, and she should… well, she should take to her bed, where she would likely be strangled by her own bedsheets.

"Or," she whispered, "I can take what happiness I have now and deal with the consequences when they happen."

Helaine squeezed her hands. "You have found your courage then?"

Irene shrugged. "I'm not sure. But I suspect he is downstairs anxiously awaiting my return."

"It will be all right," her friend said as they hugged. "You will see."

Irene closed her eyes, trying to take the words into her soul. "Well," she finally said, "at least I won't strangle myself in my sleep."

They separated on a laugh, and then Irene went downstairs to tell Grant the news.

Twenty-nine

GRANT WAS WAITING AT THE BASE OF THE STAIRS, HIS
whole body twitching to run up and see if she was all
right. The only thing that kept him in place was the
knowledge that Helaine might be better suited to help
Irene than he was. That bitter thought burned in his
gut, but if Irene needed her best friend, then the least
he could do was stay away.

Even though he might go mad—again—with the
waiting. Then a large hand settled on his shoulder.
Robert. Trying to be comforting.

"Come sit down. Have something to eat. They'll
be down in a minute."

Grant had to restrain a snarl in response. Instead, he
bit out two words. "I'll wait."

Robert's hand slipped away, but the man didn't
move. Eventually, he spoke, his voice low and
soothing, as if he were calming a dangerous animal.
Perhaps he was.

"You know you're in love with her, right? I've
never seen you so... complete as when you're with
her. You ought to marry her."

Grant turned slowly, and his glare would have intimidated anyone but Robert. "I was on one knee in the carriage. Had just proposed when the bastard—when——" When he had killed a man.

Robert's eyebrows shot almost to his hairline. "Oh. Well. What wretched bad luck."

"And now, she's upstairs. Probably ill. Probably horrified by what… by…"

"You saved her life, Grant."

"I killed him. In front of her." God, he couldn't believe he'd said that aloud. He couldn't believe he'd done it. He rubbed a hand over his face. "I'm not a soldier. Never have been. Never thought I'd…" *Kill a man.*

Robert's hand returned to his shoulder, squeezing in sympathy. "You didn't mean to. It was self-defense. You're not in trouble anywhere on this."

"Except in her eyes." And maybe, in his own. But there hadn't been any other way. And truthfully, it had been an accident. He'd just wanted the man away from Irene.

"You don't know what she thinks."

"I don't know bloody *anything*!"

"Then how about we go upstairs and…" His voice trailed away as Helaine and Irene appeared at the top of the staircase.

Grant's breath released a huff of relief. Irene looked well. Her clothing and hair had been set to rights, her body appeared whole, and her movements were assured. And when he looked into her eyes, fear rising again, she smiled.

She smiled at him.

"Irene?" he whispered.

Beside him, Robert chuckled. "Lady Irene, you look much better. If you would allow it, I think my friend here would like to speak privately with you. My library is just this way. No one will bother you." Then he held out his hand for his wife. "Helaine, are you all right?"

"Perfectly fine, my love," she said with a warm smile. "Have all the guests arrived?"

"Yes, they're all here, all seated. Samuel's figured out the entire crime between the street and here."

"Of course, he has."

Robert glanced at Irene. "He'll share his theories whenever you're ready."

"I know them," grumbled Grant. "I'll tell her."

Robert's grin widened. The prat. "Of course, you will. Just this way, Lady Irene."

Helaine abruptly reached between them—delaying him for yet another moment—and kissed Irene on the cheek. "I'll go in to the guests. Take your time, my dear. Speak from your heart."

Grant twitched, his gaze hopping between the women's faces. What did she mean by that? What did Irene have to say from her heart? Bloody hell, he was a babbling fool. He needed to gather his wits. But there was no more time as Robert escorted them to the library. Irene glided forward then settled into one of the chairs by a low fire. Grant followed, wondering if he should go back down on one knee. But, of course, he couldn't. That could be incredibly bad form if her mind was on what had happened. So he stood there, awkwardly searching her face while Robert left, shutting the door.

They were alone. And suddenly, what he wanted to say was right there, his body and his mouth moving without conscious thought. He dropped to both knees before her.

"Irene, I'm so sorry. I'm sorry about what happened, but not sorry it's over. You needn't be afraid anymore."

Irene took a deep breath. "He was a madman angry at Papa?"

"Yes."

"And now—"

"And now, he will never bother you again." He swallowed. "I'm just sorry you had to see—"

His words cut off as she touched his face. "How are you doing? It must be hard on you."

He closed his eyes, feeling her warmth all the way to his soul. "I know I had to do it. And I honestly didn't mean to."

"You were protecting me. It is one of the reasons I love you. You act from your heart without thinking so hard of the consequences." Her lips quirked in a rueful smile. "It is something I want to learn from you. I'm afraid I think too hard and too much about all the things that could go wrong. It freezes me." Then she leaned forward enough that their foreheads touched. "You bring me to life."

His hands went first to her shoulders, then wrapped tighter around her back. Hers mirrored his, and soon they were wrapped in each other's arms.

"Are you sure you're all right?" he asked.

"Are you sure you're fine?" she asked at the same moment.

Then they pulled back, looked into each other's eyes, and spoke again at the same second. "I'm fine."

Her smile widened. "Grant, I have something to ask you."

"Anything."

"Do you still—"

"Love you? With every breath in my body. I know all your objections, all your terrible thoughts, but I tell you, it's all poppycock. I love you. You love me. We should be wed. Immediately." Then he searched her face, reassured, as her smile seemed to grow warmer. Hotter.

He licked his lips, wishing he could kiss her right then. Wishing he could do a whole lot more. A man had tried to kill her today, and he wanted nothing more than to drag her back to his room, lock her inside, and then spend the rest of his life pleasuring her.

Meanwhile, her gaze had grown misty soft. "I love you too. With all my heart. And I think, with your help, I shall not be so afraid anymore."

"Don't be afraid, Irene. I will keep you safe." He pulled her hands to his lips, pressing kisses into her palms. "Please say you will marry me. I know it is not the time to ask, but I cannot hold the words back. I love you. I want you as my wife."

She frowned for a moment, lifting her hand to his face so that he was forced to look at her. "I want to keep working," she said. "As long as I can, whenever I can. In truth, it's only the lifting and carrying that is strenuous. I've already spoken to Helaine. She said we'll work out the details."

He frowned, not following her words. "Irene," he finally said. "I would never stop you from working. I understand the strength one can find from doing a job well."

She smiled. "I know you do."

"But… but what do you mean about the details? About Helaine?" And damn it, was she going to marry him or not?

"Lord Crowle," she said, her tone light despite the formal phrasing. "It would be my greatest delight to marry you."

He surged forward, kissing her deeply. Yes. She was saying *yes*! But then she was pulling back, holding him away while she moved his hands. She pressed them down. Much further down, until his palm lay flat on her belly.

"And I hope you will love your child too."

He blinked. His mind blanked completely, as if he'd been hit with a white-hot stroke of lightning so beautiful, so all-consuming, that it blanked out everything else. And all the while, he was staring at his hand against her belly, imagining a child there.

"A baby?" he whispered. "You're increasing?"

She nodded. "I realized it upstairs. I'm with child, Grant. We're going to have a baby."

He searched her eyes, seeing the happiness shimmering, and suddenly, everything in his world settled into place. As firmly as a machine part dropping into its slot. As clearly as the last stroke on a fabric design. As perfectly as the way he fit into her, and she around him.

His world was right. She was right. And they were going to be happy together.

He was old enough to know that the feeling wouldn't last. The world didn't stop with a single perfect moment, but that didn't lessen the impact of her looking at him with her heart in her eyes.

She loved him. He loved her. And they were going to be a family.

"I love you," he whispered. "I cannot even find the words to say how much."

"And I love you."

He kissed her then. Softly. Tenderly. So carefully that he thought he would break from the sweetness. Then abruptly, he pulled back.

"I have to go. I'll get a special license. We can be married in an hour."

"An hour!" she cried, laughing. "No! This is Penny and Samuel's day."

"Tomorrow then."

She smiled. "Tomorrow then."

Then he surged to his feet, picking her up as he swung her around in his joy.

Epilogue

IRENE TOOK A DEEP BREATH, THEN IMMEDIATELY regretted it, as the foul odors of the East End assaulted her senses. Then she nodded at Grant. He stepped forward and rapped sharply on the door of the second-story flat where little Carol's family lived.

There was noise inside, and then a small boy pulled open the door. Carol's little brother. A moment later, Carol's exhausted mother appeared. Her eyes widened when she saw them, her mouth going slack before she stepped back.

"My lady!" She bobbed a curtsey even as she spun around. "Carol! Lady Irene is here. And…" She glanced back.

"Lord Crowle, ma'am," Grant said a little coldly.

The woman nodded, bobbing another curtsey. Then Carol came stumbling out from a back corner.

The room was nothing more than that—a square room with a fireplace. One corner had what appeared to be bedding. Table, cooking pot, chamber pot. That was about all this little family owned. Carol stumbled forward from the bedroll, her eyes wide and rimmed in red.

"Carol," Irene said softly, her heart sinking into her belly for what she was about to do. "Carol, I've a couple questions."

The girl swallowed but straightened, rubbing her hands awkwardly on her skirt. Meanwhile, her mother stepped back and gestured them inside.

"Thank you," Grant said, his tone hard. "We won't take up much of your time."

Irene took a breath, hating what she was about to do. Samuel had worked out that somehow, Hank Bagley had gotten Irene's schedule. How else would he have known to attack along that route?

In the last three weeks, only two items on Irene's schedule had been for sure: the date and time of Penny's wedding and the wedding breakfast afterward. Somehow Bagley had learned of that. Somehow he had worked out that the one place Irene would surely be is on the route between wedding and breakfast. And the most likely suspect for sharing Irene's schedule was little Carol.

Irene stepped forward, crouching to look the girl in the eye. "Did someone ask you for my schedule, Carol? Did you give it to someone?"

The girl visibly flinched, and her lip began to tremble. Irene could see that she was about to cry, even as the girl glanced to her mother and brother. Irene didn't need to look. She knew the family was desperate. She even guessed what had happened.

"Someone came to you—a man, probably. He offered you money if you told him when and where I'd be in the last few weeks. Is that true?"

The girl nodded, misery in every line of her body.

To the side, her mother gasped and sunk onto her knees, pulling her son close. She reached for her daughter, but the girl was too far away. And Grant was blocking her anyway.

"How often?" Grant asked. "What did you tell him?"

It took three tries until Carol got the words out. And when she finally did, the sound was nearly inaudible. "Every week. Sunday after mass. He asks what your plans are for the week and…"

"And you told him," Grant finished for the girl.

"I didn't know it was wrong!" Carol cried. "I swear, I didn't know—"

"That's a lie," Irene snapped. "You are the smartest girl I've ever met. And you've lived all your life here." She gestured vaguely at the crime-ridden East End. "You knew no one would pay for my schedule, unless they meant some sort of harm."

Tears were flowing hard now, and the child sniffed. But she didn't lie anymore. She simply nodded miserably.

"You had to know it was wrong, Carol," Irene continued. "Dangerous to me, and wrong for you. I can't employ someone I can't trust."

The girl didn't answer, but to the side, her mother cried out. "Oh no, my lady. Please. She's a good girl—"

The woman was silenced by a hard glare from Grant. Meanwhile, Irene held the girl's gaze, trying to gauge if she could trust the child at all. "How much money did he give you?"

"Two coppers, each week."

Two coppers. Her life had been sold for two coppers a week. And yet, looking around this hovel, Irene knew that even so small a sum would be a vast help.

"I won't do it again, my lady! Please! I swear!"

Irene grimaced and looked at Grant. She'd already made the decision long before coming here, and nothing she'd seen had dissuaded her from her course. So with a nod, she straightened, leaving it to Grant, the harder and scarier one, to make the next bargain.

"I told Lady Irene she should sack you without a reference. Immediately."

"Oh no!" cried her mother. Little Carol said nothing, though the tears were flowing steadily. Meanwhile, Grant continued, his voice cold and hard.

"She convinced me to make a new bargain." That was a lie. It had all been Grant's idea. "If anyone approaches you again, you're to tell them *maybe*. Do you understand? You say maybe, and then you come immediately to me."

The girl gulped, her eyes widening in fear.

"Yes, to *me*," he said, his voice cold. "You tell me everything. I will pay you double whatever the bribe is. Double, do you hear me? Only if you come directly to me. Do you understand?"

"Y-yes," the girl stammered.

"She does!" cried the girl's mother. "She's a good girl, my lord. She just didn't know before."

Grant nodded absently to the mother, his hard gaze never wavering from the girl. Carol needed to understand, and she needed to be frightened.

Eventually, he relented, straightening as he looked at Irene. "I think we're done here." Then he glanced at the girl, almost as an afterthought. "Mr. Bagley is dead. He'll not be coming to you ever again."

The girl frowned, and Irene felt a cold chill run

down her spine as the child spoke. "Mr. Bagley? I don't know 'im."

"What?" Grant said. "Wasn't that the man who paid you for Lady Irene's schedule?"

"N-no, my lord."

Irene reached out, her fingers going instinctively to Grant's. "Then who paid you?"

"Demon Damon."

❧

Wendy clutched the small satchel to her stomach. She held it tight as Freddie pulled open the heavy office door. Then he gestured her inside, a smirk on his thick, flat face.

Wendy ignored it. She'd been coming to this gambling hell for months. Or was it more than a year now? It didn't matter. Her time here was done, and she felt a surge of mixed feelings.

Part of her would miss the excitement of the gambling hell. The thick air, the turn of a card, and the rattle of dice had their own allure. Money, desperation, lust—all those intense emotions—had played out a nightly drama before her, enticing enough that she'd been tempted to play as well.

She never did. She was there to work and to pay back her idiot brother's debts. But now, she had the money in hand.

She and Bernard were finally free of Demon Damon. Or, at least, they would be the moment she handed over her satchel of coins. So, with a surge of relief, she stepped into the luxurious office. Damon was there, his hair dark, his body languid, and his smile like a temptation from the devil himself.

Wendy wasted no time. "I've got it all, Demon," she said clearly. "I'm here to pay back everything Bernard owes."

If anything, the man's smile widened, though there was something horribly feral about the look. "Really?" he drawled, and Wendy felt a shiver of excited fear skate down her spine.

"Yes. Right here." She showed him the small stack of coins.

"Then by all means, my Wendy, come closer. Show me exactly what you have, and I shall tell you if it is enough."

About the Author

USA Today bestselling author Jade Lee has been scripting love stories since she first picked up a set of paper dolls. Ball gowns and rakish lords caught her attention early (thank you, Georgette Heyer), and her fascination with the Regency began. An author of more than thirty romance novels and winner of dozens of industry awards, she finally gets to play in the best girl-heaven place of all: a bridal salon! In her new series, four women find love as they dress the most beautiful brides in England. Lee lives in Champaign, Illinois.